SHAPERS

of WORLDS

Volume V

SHAPERS *of* WORLDS

Volume V

*Science fiction and fantasy by authors featured on
the Aurora Award-winning podcast* The Worldshapers

Edited by

EDWARD WILLETT

Illustrated by

WENDI NORDELL

SHADOWPAW
PRESS

SHAPERS OF WORLDS VOLUME V
*Science fiction and fantasy by authors featured on
the Aurora Award-winning podcast* The Worldshapers

Published by
Shadowpaw Press
Regina, Saskatchewan, Canada
www.shadowpawpress.com

Trade Paperback ISBN: 978-1-998273-33-1
Hardcover ISBN: 978-1-998273-44-7
Ebook ISBN: 978-1-998273-34-8

Edited by Edward Willett
Illustrated by Wendi Nordell
Cover art by Tithi Luadthong

Shadowpaw Press is grateful for the financial support of Creative Saskatchewan.

CONTENTS

INTRODUCTION

Five is not a round number, obviously, yet still, it's a strangely satisfying one. Maybe it's because we have five fingers on each hand, five toes on each foot, and five senses.

Think of the infamous five-year plans of the Soviets or of the lingering cadence of "five gold rings" in "The Twelve Days of Christmas."

Better yet, think of the *USS Enterprise's* five-year mission to explore strange new worlds and seek out new life and new civilizations, because that perhaps best parallels the mission of this series of anthologies, set as they are in a myriad of unique worlds, some familiar, but some very strange indeed.

With this volume, you may add another felicitous five to the file of fives set forth above, for as hard as it is for me to believe, this is, indeed, the fifth collection I've assembled of amazing short stories by some of the best writers of science fiction and fantasy alive today, all of whom were guests on my podcast, *The Worldshapers*.

And you need not worry that the fine feel of five will fall to suspiciously slippery six, for this is not only the fifth of these anthologies, it is the final one.

Yes, one reason is that five is a fine final number, but the more important reason is that *The Worldshapers* podcast itself has changed. After five (of course) years of interviewing other science fiction and fantasy authors about their creative process, I switched at the beginning of this year to a shorter video format more focused on new releases and open to more than just science fiction and fantasy authors—mainly because I wanted to be able to interview the authors I publish through Shadowpaw Press, who, while they include several science fiction and fantasy writers, also include literary authors, poets, writers of historical fiction, and more.

That rather removed the unifying core of these anthologies, and as it happens, the podcast itself has slowed considerably; it's now far more irregular. So, even if I wanted to continue this series, I couldn't.

That doesn't mean I'll never edit another anthology. As Spock was supposedly fond of saying, "There are always possibilities."

Whatever happens in the future, I hope that here in the present, you enjoy this fifth and final *Shapers of Worlds* anthology, with stories running the gamut from horror to sword-and-sorcery to near-future science fiction to space opera, set on Earth, on distant planets, and in realms of fantasy, and taking place in the past, the present, the future, or any one of multiple alternate timelines.

My thanks to all of these authors for their wonderful contributions to this anthology, whether original stories or reprints, and special thanks to the very talented Wendi Nordell, who once again created amazing illustrations for every story.

Finally, of course, thanks to you for reading this book and all books. And remember, if this is the first of these anthologies you've read, there are four previous ones, filled, like this one, with strange new worlds, new life, and new civilizations.

Reading all of them would be a worthy enterprise, don't you think?

Edward Willett
Regina, Saskatchewan
December 12, 2024

THE RUSALKA WAKES UP

Olesya Salnikova Gilmore

I.

I heard the ice crack, even in the deep: a violent sound, like the crush of brittle bone.

A fire instantly kindled within me. Heat burned through my veins, waking me, coaxing my slow mind to think, to want. That is how it starts. I have heard that when a reanimated corpse awakens in her coffin, she thirsts for blood. I, too, thirst—to sing, to siren.

I was floating by an old, drowned fishing boat that I use as my home, sorting my trinkets. I do this when hibernating beneath the water's surface all those cold, dark winter months, with nothing to do but swim, dance, and sleep. And, of course, listen to the muffled footsteps of human children above as they steal onto the frozen lake, whispering tales of the rusalki said to be lurking below: the beautiful sirens of Old Russia, the maidens who emerge come springtime and enchant humans with their song. *Just stories*, they say, even as their voices became strained, nervous. *Just stories.*

Little do they know. Little do you.

I cast aside my trinkets and lunged toward the surface. Only above the surface is sirening possible. I swam so hard my legs tangled in my loose hair, so long it reaches my ankles, so red it reminds one of freshly spilled blood. I do not have a fish tail.

When I reached the ice, I slammed into it with my entire body. A wall of cold met me, hard and unforgiving despite the cracks. Still, I pushed against it stubbornly, my throat remembering its dryness, desperate for air. Desperate for my voice.

The ice started to fragment. Light sliced into my vision. I cringed, recoiling. But the ice kept cracking, fragmenting, coming apart. Finally, a large enough wedge appeared between the quickly forming shards, and I darted out, breaking the water's surface and gasping for a body-shuddering breath of air.

There was a lot of it. My lungs sputtered and wheezed. My eyes blinked to adjust to the sharp blue sky, the sun too blinding for a corpse-like creature of the dark like me.

My breaths normalized, and I heard the cries of birds, felt the bloated earth beneath my toes, smelled the fragrant pines, the spring. All at once, I was taken back to familiar aromas: fruit jams and frying blini and butter sizzling on a heated pan. Can you smell them, too? No? It must be just me, remembering Lent and Maslenitsa, the Butter Week preceding it—to honour the end of winter and celebrate the start of spring. My awakening.

As I practised walking, my legs horribly stiff, I did not feel the cold. Just the incredible dryness of my throat, the thirst, the acute need to *siren*.

So, I opened my mouth, and I pushed the song out. Only it did not come.

Other rusalki broke the surface, their heads bobbing among the ice shards. Their laughter at me transformed into violent, ugly coughs matching mine. I hacked out bits of green, bones stuck in my throat, evil-smelling lake water. But I forced out my song. At first, mere snatches of it, a noise worse than the coughing. Grating, rusty, perfectly horrid as it tore forth.

My song grew louder, stronger, more pleasing, a sirening. With it came the familiar desire—to lay my eyes on a human, to feel his ears perk up at my voice, his gaze drift to mine, widen, then freeze, entranced, ensnared. Utter adoration is what I live for.

That is how I first saw him, sauntering through the fringe of wood near the lake, slipping between the ghostly birches like a ghost himself, yet breathing, alive.

This was my chance. I started to siren with my whole heart, my entire soul, even shedding a tear—all so the man, you, would notice me.

You did, for you walked to the shore and sat with me on a large stone among the long-dry dead reeds. Now, you are looking into my face with your large eyes glazed, entirely under my spell, though I have stopped sirening. I want you to adore me, to keep looking at me, listening to me. So, I will answer your questions. Go ahead, ask.

How did I come to be like this?

Why, you already know from the tales. Rusalki are drowned human women, either by our will or somebody else's, whose undead spirits haunt the water.

I prefer not to talk about my former existence or how I became a rusalka. But the beauty of this spring day, nature awakening . . . Maslenitsa is close. I can practically smell the dough, freshly battered and rolled. Because I feel so nostalgic, I will make an exception. Just this once. Just for you.

I will tell you my story.

2.

As is often the way with such stories, it was a lover who brought me here.

I had a father. A mother and sisters, too. We had a large house. Father . . . I think he was wealthy in the land-owning way, though I forget. We had a lot of land and a lot of men who worked it. Many men came to visit Father. But they were all grey-haired, with big, round bellies and faces puffy from drink, from the years slipping by unnoticed.

None like him—the beginning of my end.

The year before I became a rusalka, the late February sun had heat to it. On the first night of Maslenitsa, I remember dancing with my sisters in a *khorovod*—you know, the country dance that went round and round and you with it. All the village maidens joined in. No one was allowed to work, for otherwise, you would be lonely and wretched forever. Everybody indulged in the games, the food and drink, the revelry and mischief.

Sunset had just bled through the sky, leaving crimson-stained clouds that appeared shredded and hacked, like floating body pieces. Fires were being kindled all over the meadows. I blinked rapidly to make sure the landscape was not burning up. The beat of drums thudded in my ears as men kicked up their legs and women tilted their reddened faces to the sky.

Just behind the spinning circle of known faces, I saw one that stood out.

Unlike the men I had seen before, the stranger was young and handsome. He had sharp features, hair that shone with light even in darkness, a tall, lean frame. But it was his eyes that drew me in. Odd that I do not remember what colour they were, though I remember the look in them. Like he had seen things and done even more. Like he was different and so, wanted a different kind of girl. One like me— a little strange, dreaming not of marriage but of adventure, of something more than a tiny life in a tiny village.

Though my belly had lit with an unfamiliar heat—I was sixteen and sheltered—I slipped past the festivities quietly and struck out toward the wood, the fresh air there, the fragrant trees, my lake. It was my haven, even in winter, for I swam all year round.

Despite my déjà vu now, I hated Maslenitsa. Hated to mingle with the same people, hated to give up my sleeping place on the pech oven to my grandmother, come from the neighbouring village, hated the smallness of it all. I felt constrained, a prisoner.

So, I crept between the darkened trees, watching my feet for brambles, fallen pinecones, needles. I made it to the lake without incident. I took off my heavy coat, sarafan dress, linen shirt. Finally, my scarf. My skin prickled coldly. But the moonlight shone down on me, trailing a silvery path down the still half-frozen surface of the lake.

I stepped onto the pebbly shore, then into the frigid water. I felt the cold embrace me as, dodging the floating pieces of ice, I submerged. It was a shocking jolt to my system. My insides seemed to freeze with my flesh, then nothing. Pure numbness, oblivion. I floated, free for the first time that night. As though I could do anything, be anyone.

Suddenly, a movement in the reeds caught my eye. They had been deathly still, like the air. My heart sprinted, seemingly the only thing alive and kicking inside me.

A face came into view, different, handsome—that stranger from the village dance. I felt the sting of shock, of fear, but he was gone just as quickly. In his wake, all that remained in me was a white-hot flash of rage. I did not then understand why.

3.

We did not officially meet until the following day.

Mother had forced me into the kitchen to fry blini for Grandmother, and I was alone. Having placed the latest batch into the oven to keep warm, I stilled. For there, the stranger was, leaning against a wall and watching me with an intent gaze.

"Your blini are the sweetest," he spoke with a little half smile.

All I could do was stare. Men were often afraid to speak to maidens, even if they did burn to do so. Mamas and grandmamas and other female relatives usually chased them away with broomsticks or worse. A boy from my village was disposed of with a scalding hot frying pan, branding him with a blood-red half-moon on his right arm.

I gathered my wits. "Ah, so you *can* speak," I said to the stranger.

"What do you mean?" He tilted his head with pretty innocence.

"Well, last night, by the lake, you seemed to have lost your voice before vanishing." I saw his face blanch, then redden, and my heart filled with glee. "Why were you watching me, anyway?" I slid my hands to my small waist.

He stammered, turning so red I thought he would burst and bleed out in front of me. "Why did you sneak away from the festivities?" he asked, regaining his nerve.

I ignored the question; it struck me as impertinent, and I aimed for a vicious retort. "I could tell my father you were watching me bathe."

The stranger was silent for a long moment. "You are a curious little maiden." I thrust my chin in the air, pretended I wore a gown of silk rather than a stained apron with butter smeared all over it. "You will not tell your father," he said, voice serene.

"And why not?"

"Because you want to know things, me."

I remembered my rage upon catching him watching me naked in my lake. But why? "I . . . think I am angry with you, whoever you are," was all I could say.

He smirked. "Yes, I know. You looked like a vengeful rusalka dredged up from the depths by my gaze alone. Still." He approached me, slow and sensual. "If you had truly wanted to tell your father, you would have done so already." His eyes were the tepid blue of the little fishes from my lake—perhaps I *do* remember their colour. "What is your name, fair maiden?" he finally asked, drawing even closer. He smelled musky, foreign. But also of something manly.

"Lada," I said, my name the only thing I have kept from my years as a human.

"Lada," he repeated, as though mesmerized, and I felt his breath, as there was only a sliver of space between our faces. "What is your secret, Lada?"

My eyes strayed from his eyes to his lips in no time. They were plump and moist. I did not know about kissing then, though I had seen my parents do it and had read about it. But I was a saucy little thing. "My secrets I keep close," I replied. "Maybe if you would have asked me by the lake, I would have told you. But you did not. So, I will not tell you. Now stop hanging about our kitchen like a common domovoi." Back then, I could not see house spirits. But I had heard of them.

The stranger laughed, a clear, bright sound like a summer day. "A domovoi I am not, I assure you. Evgeni Ivanovich is my name."

He must have been somebody Father thought of very well since Father rarely invited men he did business with into our home. In any case, he would live to regret inviting this one. Or maybe he regrets nothing.

4.

THE FOLLOWING DAY, my sisters and I took our sleds to the steepest hill and rode down, screaming and laughing. Even the adults participated. Women hiked up their skirts and let their husbands push them down while they threw their heads back and let it all out—and why not? It was more diverting than being trapped in a hot kitchen frying blini.

The sun was a bright, mad thing, the sky so cloudless I could see into the depths.

"When the sky is this clear, it reminds me of summer," the by-now-familiar deep yet teasing voice said behind me. Turning, I saw Evgeni Ivanovich. I could feel his heat through the thin fabric of my skirt, smell his tangy aroma enveloping me. "What do you see, curious Lada?" he asked. "A great big gemstone a young man will someday give you upon your marriage?"

I was suddenly aware of the sled between my thighs, the spot between my legs zinging with a hungry heat. "You are wrong, Evgeni Ivanovich," I said through the thrumming of my blood. "I was dreaming of how I would dive into the sky if I could. I wish it were a great, big lake that I could disappear into."

"Like our lake?" He grew serious. "Why would you wish to disappear?"

Our lake irked me. "Sometimes, I pretend to stay in the lake. *My* lake."

A flash of his teeth, straight and white, through his beard, golden and trimmed. "Would it not be dull?"

"On the contrary. It would be peaceful. No one could scold or force me to fry blini. When I am in the water, I am free—unless I am spied upon."

He was unfazed. "Instead of marriages and husbands, you dream of lakes and talk of freedom. You are an odd little maiden indeed."

I made a face. "Not marriages or husbands. Lovers, maybe. Mother is so very tired and unhappy. She is with child yet again. Her ninth! Besides, I thought you admired my oddness." That was bold; I was too free with my tongue.

"Perhaps it is your red hair." He fingered a lock. A sharp intake of air—him, not me—then the pressure of his hand on mine, and Evgeni Ivanovich was gone.

I wished for my wood, my lake. The conversation unsettled me. I had known I was different. Odd, an anomaly. I was never so happy as when I walked barefoot through the wood, feeling the moss, leaves, and twigs beneath my flesh. Never so hopeful as in my lake, mistress of its waters and fishes, even its icebergs. And yet, I had never felt my oddness so acutely. I did not know the conversation had been a mere prelude to what followed.

———

5.

AFTER SUPPER, I was in a dark corridor of the house with my prayer book in hand. Inside, carefully nestled between the pages to avoid detection, was a little volume of poetry by Alexander Pushkin.

I had found it in the trunks of one of Father's guests. I did this sometimes—snooped around, looked at things, *for* things. Discovered little keepsakes I could easily hide from prying eyes. Little trinkets for myself.

This guest had been from St. Petersburg. And everybody there was reading poetry. The words had drawn me in instantly. "By the seashore, there's a green oak . . . A rusalka sits on its branches . . ." To me, these words were proof of magic, of more out in the world than I knew, of freedom, like my lake in the wood.

I carried the little book of poetry with me everywhere, dreaming of distant shores and mysterious rusalki. But it was always hidden inside the prayer book. Father would have administered a lashing or two had he known his daughter was devouring not holy words but those of love—and that I had stolen the book from a guest.

I saw a shadow appear on the corridor's wall. I drew my books closer to my chest. Evgeni Ivanovich came into view. "Ladochka!" he exclaimed, using the fond version of my name, and rushed to me, throwing his arms around my shoulders. He was cold and windswept, perhaps having gone riding with Father. "I am sorry I left you on that hill. I . . . cannot explain how I feel. It is your hair, your wildness, you. Please do not disappear."

My first reaction was to recoil, never having been touched by a man who was not Father. Yet there was this man, holding me, touching me. Despite my confusion, my anger, my wondering why my oddness was so wild, I wanted him to. I was curious. By now, his hands were on my cheeks, tilting my face up to his until he lowered his mouth onto mine. The kiss was wet and strange and nothing like what I had expected. His tongue seemed to reach into my very throat; I nearly gagged and started to choke.

Footsteps came from some distant room, and Evgeni Ivanovich rushed past me.

A furious heat unspooled in my stomach, mingling with the confusion in my brain. Though it had not been pleasant, I wanted more. I clutched my books, the poetry kindling my heart until all I could feel were Evgeni Ivanovich's lips bruising mine, his fingers stroking my cheek like spider's legs, that beard irritating my skin until it burned. Perhaps poetry *was* poison, as Father said. For it had infected me with lust. Not love, for I knew I could not love a man who branded me odd and nearly choked me with his tongue.

I refuse to go into how I freely and gladly handed him my maidenhood. I hate myself for it. It had not been as romantic as the wooing, being short, painful, and irrelevant. His face I saw not. Afterward, I picked up my books where they had crashed to the wooden floorboards, taking care not to make any sudden movements. I hurt everywhere, as if I had run through the wood, headlong, without stopping for days.

The house was curiously empty, eerily silent. I came to the oven and watched its bowels blazing. My mind was blank. Then, in a sudden, blinding flash of that same rage from the lake, I threw the little book of poetry into the fire—my prayer book with it.

———

6.

HE DID NOT PROMISE to stay. He had a wife, children, though I am not sure I had known.

The child was born the following spring, entirely unlike the previous one. It snowed and hailed; the skies were darkened and blanketed with congealed storm clouds. Still, spring had come. Winter was over. Lent and Maslenitsa were upon us, as well as the blini-making, the merrymaking, the droves of people.

And there were two babies in the household instead of one.

"People will talk," Father said one night, dirty candlelight warping his features.

"We cannot toss her and her child outside," Mother replied sensibly, but I could tell it was forced. In her words lay the question, *Can we?* "We can say I birthed twins," she added, too quietly. As though she dared Father to contradict her.

He did; do not worry yourself. A man always does. "Twins?"

Father scowled, shooting her, then me, a look of loathing. "There have been no twins born in the history of this village. How can you dare to suggest it?"

"What do *you* suggest?"

Following the heavy interval of silence, Father replied, "We have been generous to Lada, allowing her to stay in our home until the birth of her child. But we cannot bear the burden of her poor judgment or let the family name become soiled. We *do* have seven other daughters to think of. And our beloved son."

Mother looked at me—did her eyes hold regret in them? To this day, I cannot be sure. They shone, her face scrunching up as if tears would be shed. Only, she gazed at me with a shocking calm. I do not wish to mislead you; she was not a monster. Nor was Father. After all, the perfectly reasonable ambition of parents with many daughters was to marry them off as quickly, successfully, and richly as possible. As I had a child out of wedlock, such a life was no longer possible for me.

"The child will die if we cast them out," Mother said, matter of factly, as though all she spoke about was the weather, no tears in sight.

I glanced at the child in my arms—she had the lightest hair. Not her father's blond, but white. Like the sun when you stare at it too long in the heat of summer. Her perfect, tiny features were other-worldly, reminding me of the angels that floated around the head of Jesus Christ in the icons. As her mother, I loved her, but she was a snivelling, weak little thing. I knew not to name her. The baby smiled—charming, like her father. Yes, she liked to smile. She kept smiling, even in death.

"I will go," I heard myself say.

No doubt you judge me—for not fighting back, for not trying harder to stay. But I refused to burden my family or penalize my sisters for what I had done. I loved them in my own way. Besides, it hurt to breathe around them, stifled by their judgment and blame.

My daughter would suffer, and so would I, but had not Jesus

Christ suffered? Had He not felt cold, alone, afraid? If He could survive it, so could I. At any rate, I would try.

Mother said nothing; Father simply turned away from me.

***

7.

AFTER I LEFT, I wandered through the desolate, sleepy countryside, passing in and out of the starving villages. I kept us alive, but barely. It was a nasty spring, more like winter. Snow gusted across the empty fields; rain pelted us. We hid in the trunks of trees, in the izba huts of generous strangers, in the broken-down sheds and abandoned farmhouses.

Days went by, then weeks. I did not realize where my feet had taken me, so numb was I by then. So lost to the world.

I was back in the wood by the home I had once known, with the family that had once been mine. By the lake I remembered so well, in which I had bathed, rain or shine. The one that I had dreamed of staying in, with its lovely promise of freedom.

Holding the baby in my arms, so still and silent, I looked out at the water.

That sound reached my ears—ice cracking. Had real spring finally come?

For the first time, the sun peeked out from behind the clouds. It was cold, yet bright. On the other side of the lake, the birch trees leaned over the water, willowy and phantom-like and utterly bewitching. I thought I heard their silvery whisper, beckoning to me: *Come, Lada, dive into the water!*

I lowered the baby to the ground, carefully, gently, for fear of waking her.

She made no sound whatsoever.

I approached the water just as maidens stepped out of it, dripping and drowsy but somehow, mysteriously, that much more alluring in their languor. Their ankle-length hair and skin tones varied from fair to dark brown to olive and even blue. But their bloodshot eyes were identical. They were horrifying and beautiful. They were rusalki.

"How pretty you are!" one rusalka said, sending her fishy smell in my direction. Bits of seaweed stuck to her brown hair like barnacles to a ship.

"How sad your eyes," another rusalka, with hair black as night, added woefully. "It is your heart. It is broken. We know. Ours were also."

I squinted. They should have sounded like girls, but by the way they spoke and their manners, I knew them to be much older. There was something else, too. "Why are your voices so rusty? Are you ill?"

"We cannot sing or speak in winter," said the second rusalka.

"It is for the best," ruled the first rusalka. "Too much sun and heat lead to too much sirening. And respiratory ailments need time to heal. Winter, so dark, so cold, yet so restorative, is the ideal time. We would not wish to wander the land anyway . . ."

"Too true," confirmed a third rusalka with hair the swampy green hue of toads. "We have been unseemly after last summer! Coughing up phlegm, hacking up seaweed."

"Come closer, dear heart!" The rusalki giggled. "Closer still!"

I was not under their spell. Quite simply, they made valid points. I stepped toward the water, toward the rusalki, feeling the wavelets crash icily against my toes. The thaw that spring was as intense as the frost had been. Everything was shedding tears. I could see the water, deep and black, rippling between the shards of cracked ice.

"Tell us how your heart was broken, darling sister."

"Sister?" I furrowed my brow. "Yes, I had sisters once."

"We can be your new sisters!" they said.

"Only, we will not abandon you in your time of need like your other sisters did." The first rusalka reached out a slender hand. "We understand your pain; we do not judge or blame you for it. We, too, lost men we loved, either by their folly or ours or that of cruel, unbending fate. We know your pain. We can *feel* it. We can *smell* it."

Their smiles were all shining bloodshot eyes and sharp, flashing teeth.

. . .

My waist was submerged in the lake. The cold pulled at my belly and back like first labour pains. Ice rushed up my legs, through my veins, into my heart . . .

Then the first rusalka said the words that would seal my fate, my life, my death. She said, "Come, Ladochka, for this lake is the only place you can be free."

All at once, I recalled that feeling of freedom. To float, to fly, to be weightless.

And I suddenly understood my rage: that man had encroached upon my moment of peace, my time to myself, by myself, and he had believed himself entitled to it. With that thought trapped in my brain, I dived under, breathing in the water as if it were air.

8.

You might be wondering what happened to the baby on the ground. Her body decomposed in the way of all living things. For you see, she was already dead.

There you have it. Did I end my life? I do not think so. Rather, I started it.

Now, I am afraid it is time, my love.

When I first saw you, you reminded me of my Evgeni Ivanovich. Your shade of hair is exactly like his, though darker than that of my daughter. Remember, hers was white, like the hot disk of a dazzling summer sun. You also have the same tepid cerulean blue eyes, the same too-charming smile. You are giving it to me right now.

Do I entrap women? No, I do not. I do not like to see women suffer. Given their lot in life, they suffer too much already. Most men, too, I leave alone. I reserve my charms and my sirening for men like you. Handsome, worldly men, with betrayal in your eyes, drawn as you are to the different, the odd and abnormal, the downright monstrous.

But when it comes down to it, you are the monsters.

Like Evgeni Ivanovich, like so many of you too-charming men, you use women, I can tell. Then you return to your lives, to your wives and children, never atoning for your misdeeds. Perhaps I cannot punish him, but I can punish you. So many of you. For myself, for my child, for every woman, sister, and daughter. For all of us.

You blink as though attempting to awaken from an enthralling dream. I assure you, that will not happen. Here is what will: I shall put my arms around your nice strong shoulders, wrap us in my hair, and love you like you have never been loved before.

Then I shall take you into the water. Do not worry yourself, my sweet. You will not feel pain, nor will you struggle. It will feel like floating, flying, being free. You will cease to breathe, and then your body will rot at the bottom of the lake, along with the bodies of all the other men that came before you, long buried there. The rusalki will dance and twirl on your watery grave forever, until the very end of time.

But before I let them do so, I shall take something from you to remind me of our time together. A tooth or a fingernail. A lock of hair. Perhaps something that I find on your person when I relieve you of your clothing—you must understand, my pet, that fabric is quite heavy when I drag you through the water, down, down, down, into the lake's depths.

What am I looking for? Ah, the usual. Heirlooms, keepsakes, little trinkets. A jewel or a piece of silver or a bit of ribbon. A medallion. Sometimes, a ring. I like those best.

Now, come, stop staring at me like a lovestruck fool and kiss me.

Winter has been long and the kisses few. Waking feels that much sweeter with a kiss burning on my lips and my throat all warmed up —for the next man like you to fall victim to my siren song.

THE BONES OF HEROES

Chadwick Ginther

They crept like thieves onto the shores of Valkura, mercenaries hunting the only thing worth sailing to this nine gods' forsaken island: a dragon. The first sighted in generations. There wasn't an alchemist or sorcerer in the Settled Lands who wouldn't use every scrap of a dragon's bone or blood for spell or salve. For these warriors, only the glory mattered.

An impenetrable wall rose, blocking the moon: the Horizon Shield Mountains. Beyond lay the Black Plain, hidden in the mountains' shadows, where dragons were said to be spawned.

The mercenary band had come together by chance. The most notorious among them, Jona Terramin, equally whispered, celebrated, and decried through the Settled Lands as Cutter, trickled black sand through his fingers. The sand was sharp, like broken glass. Salty sea spray infiltrated every invisible gouge he hadn't felt, stinging.

Cutter had tried his blade against all manner of men and monstrosities. He'd died a time or two for honour and glory and at least once for love. The Ferryman had always sent him back to kill— and die—again.

A flotilla of ships had left from Khyber to hunt the dragon, but only their small scow had made landfall on the unnamed Valkuran island, with five hunters living to enjoy the sight. They had no food, no water, and no way home. Desperation was an excellent motivator.

"Beach looks empty," Sindur said.

Kalla, the last person to join their expedition, said, "So did the ocean before our ship sank."

"Should we try to bury Feyn?" Hogge, hefting his blade, gestured to their dead companion. "Or leave him to the gulls?"

"A cairn," insisted Brand Ivarsson, the only Valkuran among them and the reason they'd made land at all. "Leave his sword."

***

THEY TIED off their boat and snaked over the beach, hunting a cut through the rocks. Climbing the sheer, slippery stone in the dark risked death before they'd won glory. The rock wall on their right hedged them in as the cold tide grew closer. When their knees ached from twisting steps in the sand, and the ocean lapped their ankles thirstily, a jagged mouth, jaws glittering like stars in the moonlight, opened hungrily—a path through the rocks. At its base, a stacked stone hut rested like a tumour.

A woman dressed in finger bones and crowned in sun-bleached driftwood stepped from the hut. Her dress rattled as she strode closer, and hollows in the wood whistled in the wind. She didn't shiver, and her breath didn't mist.

"I knew someone would eventually find their way here." Her words echoed through the gap in the rock, sounding larger, vaster, than her frame. "You seek the dragon."

"We can't trust her." Brand's voice was a rough whisper. "She's Soturr. One of the Hill People. They steal into our villages to take our steel—"

"—and your children," the woman finished for him. "I've heard your lies before, sea dog. Reaver. *Dragonman*. I know you and your people, but I will take you to your dragon if that is how you want to die."

Brand levelled his sword at her. "No."

"You go with me," she raised her hands and a flat slab of rock crumbled from the cliff to shatter on the beach, "or not at all. The land remembers who was here first."

The hunters mumbled agreement. Sorcerers were not to be angered or ignored, given any choice. Cutter had killed a few in his day but looked to Brand, who, being from these lands, knew more about this particular kind of sorcerer than he.

Brand spread his arms wide. "For the love of Fya's tits, she's telling us she'll kill us!"

"You'll all be dead soon enough," the woman said. "Valkura is made of chances to die. Until then, I have food to share, and I know the wells left untainted after the Devastation."

"Wyrd's balls! She's wearing a dress made of bones!"

The would-be guide smirked. "Your people call their dead back to fight for them. Why do you quail at *my* remembrances?"

"My feet are cold. I want off this beach," Sindur said. "If she'll take us where we want to go, what's it matter who she is? We all know the dragon could kill us."

The woman released a delighted little trill. Her lips formed the word "could."

Hogge grunted. "Let's go. We kill her if we have to."

"I'm sick of looking at the bloody ocean," Kalla said.

Brand silently pleaded to Cutter, hoping to have someone—anyone—back him.

"If she's with us, we can make sure she doesn't work against us," Cutter said.

Brand pointed at his eyes and then to the woman. "I'm watching you."

THE GUIDE—MARGANNE—LED them inland until the sun crept above the horizon. Brand stacked rock piles: way finders to lead back to shore. The island certainly had enough stone to spare. Great flat slabs of rock, shaped as if they'd been cut by human hands, lay like they'd been cast aside, broken—game pieces thrown from a table. The path seemed well-trod, with grooves cut deep over the years, but they never passed a living soul: only ruins, broken mountains and cloven hills, shattered rock, and splintered paths. No people. No dragons.

Nothing.

Cutter ran his hand over his bald scalp, cursing his commitment to keeping clean-shaven. It was colder in Valkura than anywhere he'd sold his sword—colder than the winters in Eryos, where he'd been raised. He stretched the cold from his bones.

"You should've grown your beard at sea," Sindur said.

Hogge elbowed Kalla in the ribs. "You know what they say? No hair on your face—"

"—no hair on your balls," Brand broke in, with a laugh Kalla didn't share. She shook her braided hair and rolled her eyes.

Cutter didn't care what they thought. He didn't want hands grasping him in a fight or losing a foe for even a moment behind a stray hair. He'd fought with and against Valkurans. The "dragonmen" were no less dangerous than their namesakes, happy to die in battle so their priests could raise them as revenants to fight forever. Cutter shot back in the Valkuran tongue, "I hope your enemies give your sword to their heirs."

Brand gasped, hand reaching for his blade until he caught Cutter's smirk and broke into a belly laugh.

When his laughter ended, Marganne sat next to Cutter—directly across from Brand— dress rattling as she settled.

"You speak their tongue well for a Southlander," she noted, as much to herself as to Cutter.

He'd beaten a Valkuran in a duel and the Ferryman had gifted Cutter the loser's spirit. Until Cutter had needed to offer back that spirit to spare his own, he'd spoken the Valkuran tongue often. His lips remembered the borrowed tongue well enough to be understood even after the spirit had gone Beyond the Black River.

"*Their* tongue?" he asked, "Not yours?"

"My people have their own speech. Their own name. Not heard

often outside this island. Not anymore." She stared at the mountains, her smile a slight thing.

———

MARGANNE LED THEM NORTH, ever north. At least, north, according to Brand, and the seadog had a better sense of direction—even on land—than Cutter did.

No one spoke until Marganne asked, "Why do you hunt a dragon?"

"If you plant its heart in a grave, the dead will come back to you," Hogge said. He breathed into his clenched fist and then opened his palm as if releasing a wish.

"Kill a dragon, and I'm made," Brand Ivarsson said. "My pick of ships to captain. Only the best crew. Finest hall in Valkura."

Sindur snorted. "Not saying much."

"You?" Marganne said.

"It's there." Sindur scowled at the distant clouds as if willing the dragon to appear.

Kalla considered, then added, "I took the first boat leaving Khyber."

Cutter didn't answer. Maybe killing at the whims of the rich wasn't a fight worthy of his gifts. Or maybe he sought an end fit for his crimes. Both true, to an extent. But the deepest truth he hadn't shared with anyone: with a dead dragon to his name, even his father's killer couldn't ignore his challenge. He'd have his duel.

"Why do you lead us to the dragon?" Cutter gestured at Brand. "He doesn't trust you."

"Trust keeps you alive here. The land kills as surely as sword or claw or fire, but quicker and cleaner than what is beyond."

"Trust kills, as well."

She laughed. "True, and you shouldn't trust me. I want the dragon to eat you all."

Cutter laughed with her. He had to laugh.

THE TRAIL BECAME a broken cobbled road, a path that would've been common in any town in the Settled Lands. Foundations and rubble remained of what Cutter assumed used to be homes.

"I've seen no sign of a bloody dragon," Brand snarled.

"I want you to see what your people did. To see what the dragon has seen."

"I don't care what it's seen. Until it sees our blades."

She *tsked*. "Same as your ancestors. How high you piled our corpses in glory's flush! Stacked so high, your gods used them as stairs to their sky palaces. I remember, and the dragon remembers."

The hunters took in the plain's empty enormity. Cutter imagined the piled bodies, an echo of battles he'd fought. He could almost feel their weight, see them blotting out the mountains.

"You act as if your people didn't do any killing," Brand said.

"We killed. We weren't as efficient at the task. Did your skalds say to stop? Or did they only sing your victory?"

"We don't think of you at all if we don't have to. Until you make your problems ours, you thieving—"

"Valkurans pillaged our graves, fearing our grudges would follow them beyond our deaths, *and they don't remember us*? You ground our bones for alchemy, for the paints on your face, the dyes in your clothes, *and you think nothing of us*? You killed us, stole and mutilated our dead, *and you don't care*?"

Everyone else's eyes found the fire while Cutter watched the horizon, waiting for Marganne's people to come for their revenge.

Waiting for the dragon.

THE SUN HAD BURNED a hole in the clouds. The sky was a paler blue this far from Khyber, and the sun brighter. A shimmering halo encircled it, stronger in four points. The hunters stepped lightly through the Black Plain, where it looked as if the island's flat black rocks had all been smashed to powder. The Bone Field at the plain's far edge, where the Hill People's dead were laid to rest during the Devastation, was next.

Each hunter came from lands where the dead did not rest easily —if there was any such place—and their thoughts lingered on their own ghosts. Brand had grown sullen and quiet, rubbing a corded bit of bone around his neck. Kalla unbound her braids and rolled the beads in her hand. Hogge muttered to his nameless god. Sindur thumbed his blade, keeping it wet with blood. Cutter knew the ritual. A blood-wet blade was said to be able to cut spirits. Only Marganne was at peace.

After a steep climb down interlocked hexagonal rock pillars, the path cut through what Marganne named the Vale of Anger. Thick clouds of an unnatural colour—several unnatural colours—smoth- ered the horizon. Scattered huts dotted the Vale's edge, and a shape blocked the path into the ruined village.

"Dragon?" Brand asked.

Cutter squinted. "Maybe."

"It's not moving," Sindur said.

"Not yet," Brand muttered.

Cutter hopped the last few feet off his pillar and onto the path. "I say we go."

The others hesitated.

"We go." Brand sighed and followed.

***

FILLING the path was a slurry of meat caged in bones, too many bones to belong to one body, tied together with glistening gut to form a dome. Four human skulls fixed together with beasts' jaws wired in place of the teeth and walrus tusks set in the brows as horns topped the cage. Engraved runes covered the skulls' every surface. Smoke trickled from the eye sockets where dried moss had been burned, smudging the skull tops black.

Cutter tapped at the cage. "Blood's fresh."

"You were not the only hunters who made landfall," Marganne said. "It's an offering to the dragon."

"Your people?"

She shrugged. "I was with you."

Who had they been? Warriors, farmers, sailors, priests? Broken spear shafts propped up their remains. Unrecognizable faces stared empty-eyed and gape-mouthed toward the clouds, offering no answers.

Meat shifted. A rasping groan escaped like a wet fart. Sindur jerked a broken spear away, and the piled flesh sloughed to the bottom of the cage, revealing someone inside. A person—once—identity shrouded in gore.

"They're alive!" Kalla said. "Help them!"

Sindur and Hogge hacked the bone cage with blade and axe, but it wouldn't sunder. The person's moan shuddered into coughs and died in a frothy gurgle. They slumped, eyes open, mouth agape, dead.

"Their hate wasn't strong enough," Marganne said softly.

Cutter spat on the ground. "Not a nice way to go."

There wasn't a *good* way to go, but he hoped the Ferryman wouldn't find him like this when his time came.

"Weal eye of Wyrd." Brand touched his right eye with his index and middle fingers. "We should each give them a knife."

"You don't know they were Valkuran," Cutter said. "Or how many died here."

"But *I* am Valkuran." Brand hitched a thumb toward Marganne. "As she can't help but remind me. Maybe they weren't my kinsmen. I'd rather make an offering on their behalf than meet the Old Father on the road and say I left his servants unarmed in death."

Marganne sniffed at the mention of Brand's god.

One dagger shouldn't make a difference in killing the dragon, but then, an extra knife had saved Cutter a time or two. He flipped a knife from its sheath and caught it by the tip before handing it hilt-first to Brand. "Not even a Revener could call *that* back."

Sindur shook his head. "Waste of good steel."

Hogge nodded in agreement, but Kalla reluctantly passed Brand her knife.

Brand knelt and sank the knives into the earth. "Your stolen blade returned. Hell has seen your last night. Wyrd's promise and burden. From hell, you come to fight."

"It is dangerous to say the Old Father's name here." Marganne's eyes tracked past the abandoned village to the clouds. "Almost as dangerous as it is to give someone a gift intended for another."

THEY DIDN'T LINGER LONG at the cage. Despite what might wait for them in the ruined village, the hunters knew they'd get no sleep within sight of the sacrificed hunters. They trudged forward into Botha, the last Soturr village to fall to Brand's people.

Marganne offered them cured meat and gnarled roots. "Eat. The meat will give you strength, and the root will keep you from getting sick."

"Sick?"

"Gases and poisons spew from the ground near the dragon's prison," she said. "The land doesn't swiftly recover where gods have their conflicts. The mist will twist you, change you. Some survive. Most die."

Cutter had fought in every land on the map, seen pits gods-spawned monsters had crawled from, fought a few. These places all had one thing in common: foods supposed to make him strong. They inevitably tasted like shit.

Cutter took the guide's offering. Food was food. Fighters lived and died on their bellies. He chewed the root to scour the meat's taste from his tongue. It tasted like the bone cage looked.

THEY HUDDLED NEAR THEIR FIRE, hedged in by ghosts. The spirits, individually translucent, manifested as a glowing sea, shimmering like the Sky Cloak undulating across the night sky. Ghosts of who, their guide didn't offer.

Kalla warily scanned the horizon, where ghosts and clouds seemed to merge. "This island have a name?"

"Does it matter?" Marganne asked.

"Wouldn't mind knowing the name of the land I'm supposed to die on."

"We named it Drona, in time past, after our goddess. The first dragon."

Brand's furrowed brow looked fit to saw through his skull. "Drona is Wyrd's wife, not your god. Not a dragon. She sits at the Old Father's table. She keeps his hall."

"Yes," the guide said, "You stole *her*, too. Kept her name off your maps, letting her starve in her slumber."

Hogge and Sindur coughed into their hands and sipped water from their drinking horns, grimacing either at the taste or wishing for beer.

"Have you seen the dragon?" Cutter asked.

"They say dragons are made from the bones of heroes." Marganne grasped Cutter's forearm. "Maybe I'm seeing one right now."

Cutter remembered the saying as *dragons feed upon heroes' bones.* He said so.

"All dragons are born in human skins. If they hate strongly enough, hunger deeply enough, in these mountains and others where gods used to live, they can be changed."

Cutter saw the trail of bodies that floated behind him down the Black River, people who had crossed him, people he had crossed, those he'd been paid to kill and those paid to kill him. Had any hated strongly enough to change? To find a way back from death, as Cutter had?

"The Eryans—my people—have a saying, too: 'When you kill someone, they leave a part of themselves behind. Something even the Ferryman won't take. Something that belongs to you.'"

"I don't know your Ferryman." Marganne cocked her head,

considering the name. The wind shrilled through her headdress. "Does hunting a person in changed skin dissuade you?"

"I've seen enough people turned into monsters, and enough people who acted the part, to not be much bothered either way."

CUTTER WOKE.

Something was moving in the camp. He could sleep through a storm and wake at a whisper, a quality that'd often kept him alive. Marganne paced the camp, rattling and whistling. She circled around to him, and he eased his hand to his blade.

She knelt next to him, knees cracking. Her firelit eyes held no tiredness. She traced the scars on Cutter's body. "These would've killed a weaker man."

"They did."

"Another axiom of your people?"

"Personal observation."

"I like you, Cutter. It will be a pity when you die."

"I've died a time or two," Cutter said. "Didn't take."

"No one comes back from death without a Revener involved, and I don't see one among you." Marganne laughed. "Only the dead face a dragon without fear. Think about what you hunt. Can you kill a god?"

"I've killed a few things folk named gods. And then those folk, too. What does that make me?"

"More Valkuran than I expected."

Not a compliment from her.

"You seem attached to him." She gestured to where Brand slept. "It's fitting he sees what his people have done. And what is coming for them. *He* will be changed, I think. I'm sorry the rest of you won't."

A broken spear burst through Cutter's chest. For a moment he believed it a dream, that they'd never made landfall, the trip a dying vision as he sank under the waves. Then, pain crashed into him. The gore-slick sacrifice from the cage jerked the spear free, mouth still agape, silently screaming, eyes open and unfocused, and stalked to Sindur.

"I don't know your Ferryman, but a river used to run here," Marganne said. "I hope he will carry you home."

She slit Cutter's throat with his own knife.

A RIVER FLOWED between Cutter and life—or death. A perfect match for the Black River back home. He had no sword, no knives. The gauntlet with a spring spike, his armour, poor-looking but well-cared for—both were gone. Only a champion's blue cloak shrouded his nakedness. He could walk along the shore and find his way to . . . somewhere, some*thing* other than the fighting life, or he could wait in the reeds, with the spectres of the men he'd duelled, and convince the Ferryman to take them in his stead. Cutter would be shoved back to his body, wounds healed.

The trick had always worked before, but he wondered every time: was *this* the last time?

THE WAIT WAS INTERMINABLE. In the living world, Cutter would burn incense and make offerings of steel and silver, summoning the Ferryman by drawing river water to smoke and steam on the brazier's coals. He had no offerings, and yet, after a time—Cutter didn't know, couldn't know, how long—a lantern appeared in the distance, growing ever closer. The god's ferry ran aground, an otherworldly dirge resonating in his hollow chest. The Ferryman's hood showed a familiar jawline. Then, the same nose. The same eyes. The same face.

His father's face.

Except Cutter's father had never smiled like that. The Ferryman always appeared as the spirit you most—or least—wanted to see.

"I find you, Jona Terramin. Again. Sooner than expected. *Again*."

"That name doesn't mean anything to me. Not anymore."

"Cutter, then." The Ferryman gestured to the ferry. "Will you come home?"

"We both know my answer."

"It taxes me to find you in these distant lands." The Ferryman leaned on his pole and nodded to the silent spirits. "It would be simpler to take all than send back only you."

"They have their own god of the dead here. Maybe he'll give me a better deal."

The Ferryman's borrowed eyes drilled through Cutter as if looking back into the mortal world. "I'm not sure you have the singing voice to please him."

"I'll have to chance it."

The Ferryman chuckled, a laugh as cutting as the black sand beach. "If you wish, I will send you back. But someday . . . someday, you will stay."

"Not today."

"Not today." The Ferryman held out his hand. "The Return will cost you."

"Always does."

The Ferryman's guise sloughed away, sugar melting in the rain, growing and shrinking as his form swelled and hunched. Cutter slid his cloak pin into the god's bony hand. The god opened his lantern. One by one, the spirits gathered in the Ferryman's name were dragged within, a current tugging at Cutter, too. He rooted himself against it. The lantern glowed brighter and brighter until the light was all Cutter saw. Ferryman and river gone. Life gone. Death gone.

Eventually, the Ferryman takes everything.

And everyone.

But he didn't have Cutter.

Not yet.

CUTTER'S BREATH returned in a gasp. He rolled over and puked the blood from his lungs and then levered himself to his feet with his scabbarded sword, glad no one had taken the time to build him a cairn.

Alive.

The campsite was a slaughterhouse. Red splashed every rock. The bone cage was gone, along with the flesh inside, only a wet stain on the path to mark its memory. Sindur, Hogge, and Kalla's gear remained, cast aside, but there was no trace of Brand's. Three sets of tracks disappeared into the mist, one lighter and smaller than the others: the guide. One set dripping blood, towing a sledge: the sacrifice. And Brand, Cutter assumed, whose heavy boot prints obscured the other tracks here and there.

Cutter traced his new scars. His chest ached, and his throat was raw. There was no coming back for Cutter this time. If either dragon or Marganne killed him again, he was done for good. He needed to be sharp. He took what discarded gear he could easily carry. One last living ghost grinned, teeth red as the rising sun.

***

THE TRAIL CONTINUED into a fog Cutter couldn't see beyond. Every breath rasped like a dull knife. He could still taste his blood on his tongue. The ground at the fog's edges was slick, icy, while the fog itself felt . . . hot. Cutter picked his way slowly. Sweat pooled in his armour and trickled down his brow and back.

Bones broke the ground in a tangle, so many bones it was impossible to trace where one body ended and the next began. Wind, rain, and fine black sand had polished the remains white as milk, but Cutter felt their age. Their weight was enough to almost drive him to his knees to scream. To weep. Cutter slid a thumb over his blade, as Sindur had, drawing blood with a hissing breath to bring himself back to the present.

Wind screamed through the bones. At the edge of the ossuary, pacing back and forth, trying to muster the will to enter, was Brand.

Cutter's boot crunched a dry bone to powder, and the Valkuran whirled, blade bare. "Cutter? How—? Are you a revenant?"

"Alive as you."

Brand crept forward almost reverently. He poked Cutter—not reverently—which Cutter shrugged away. He raised his hand again.

Cutter cut him off with a raised finger. "One more jab, and you'll be fighting left-handed."

"Ozun's belly, I'm glad to see you!" The Valkuran laughed and clasped Cutter's hand. "How'd you come back without a Revener to call you?"

"My god takes bribes."

Brand snorted. "I'm not complaining. I was willing to face the dragon alone, but I'm glad you can deal with *her*."

They pulled into an embrace, slapped each other on the back, and walked into hell.

POOLS BUBBLED AND SIZZLED. The liquid—Cutter wouldn't call it water—within was no colour he'd ever seen in the wilds and the source of the mist. He wondered if Marganne's food would really protect him. If it mattered. The mist hadn't killed or changed either him or Brand.

Yet.

Caves and fissures dotted the rocky bowl they found themselves within. Brand pointed at a ring of corpses, some skeletons, others fresher. All singing. Swords, spears, and axes lay discarded around them, most gone to rust. There were other mutilated dead, dressed similarly to Marganne. Cutter didn't know the dead's song, and yet it felt familiar.

It made him want to join them.

"I recognize the freshest," Brand whispered. "Reveners. Never knew what happened to them. Reveners made revenants."

"What's that song?"

"The quieting song. The oldest must've been singing it since the days before we named ourselves Valkuran. Since Wyrd walked this land as a man."

"Since you took this land from us," Marganne corrected. Her voice echoed off the bone and stone, bouncing, twisting. Lingering and scratching. Stinging like sea salt in a wound. Cutter and Brand tried to locate her. The echoes made it impossible. "This place was holy once, in the past. We communed with our gods. Now, corpses sing to make dragons slumber."

Cutter and Brand crept forward until a black scar rent the earth between two noxious pools. Tar bubbled and boiled from the scar, splashing the broken ground. Assembled over the scar was a bone cage, larger than the one in the village. Meat still wet, still fresh, was piled within: hunters guided here, as Cutter and Brand had been, by the rumour of a dragon. Food for a new god.

And they weren't alone.

Marganne stepped from behind the cage. Freshly attached finger bones blazed red around the neck of her rattling dress. "I see you're not the only one with a god's favour."

Cutter rubbed the thin line where she'd slit his throat. Dried blood flaked away in his hand. "If this is favour, I'd hate to tally my debts."

"You didn't have the hate necessary to change."

"Try me now."

Brand snarled, "There's no dragon. Just you."

"I beg to differ."

A rumble shuddered behind Marganne. Tar splashed over meat from dead hunters and dragged it into the scalding dark. Four shapes remained. Hunters, once. Skinned. Changed. They crawled from the bone cage like wounded animals. Tails—spinal cords—stretched from their backsides, what remained of their fingers sharpened to talons, and their necks looked too long. Each wore a horned skull talisman as a mask, jaws clacking with every tortured movement.

"I told you: anyone can become a dragon if their hate is strong enough. Anyone. And I've hated Valkura and the bloated ticks who suckle from our land for as long as I've drawn breath. I've hated fiercely enough, and long enough, I change others. Not myself."

"Drona Dragon-Mother," Brand whispered; awe or curse, Cutter wasn't certain. He levelled his sword at the Changed, waiting for them to charge.

They didn't, not immediately. Instead, one loped toward the dead Reveners, lashing out, battering bodies again and again until their song stopped. The other Changed skittered at Cutter and Brand as the bubbling tar grew more violent.

Two Changed came at Cutter, one at Brand. It was as if they sensed Cutter was a duelist and that Brand, a fine hand in a brawl, grew sloppy against a single foe.

Cutter lost Marganne in the melee.

His shoulder blades twitched where he'd been stabbed as if inviting her to put a fresh maggot hole in him every instant she was out of sight. He found her as he drove his sword into a Changed's chest. It fell, taking the blade with it, and Cutter chanced a look over his shoulder. Marganne shoved a struggling revenant into the tar with a broken spear. Its song died, and the black scar sloshed tar over its edges.

Bloody palms slid over Cutter's bare scalp, sharpened knuckles biting but not holding. The tail, joints sharp as a blade, whipped around Cutter, slashing at his ankles, then coiling around one. It dragged him to the ground, too strong for him to break its hold—but it hadn't grabbed both his arms.

Cutter popped the spring spike from his gauntlet and scythed it in a low, wide arc. It bit into the thing's ankles. He crawled atop it, stabbing until it fell still. When he stood, only one revenant remained.

He grabbed his sword and rushed Marganne, Changed be damned. If the song stopped, the dragon would wake, and they'd all be dead.

Sword clattered against bone, the guide's grim dress proving resilient. Marganne wrenched the skull from the revenant's spine with a grunt. The last Revener, the oldest, only bones and rags, stopped singing. She held the skull aloft to Brand like a toasting goblet.

"Do you feel it, Valkuran? Drona wakes! She is nightmares. The sea swallowing ships. The storm battering crops. The sun choking on ash. Our land will never accept your name. Your gods will be forgotten. She. Is. Coming."

As if summoned, Drona rose. A dragon. A nightmare, as Marganne had claimed. Vast as the sea. A furious storm. Her ravaged body was caged in the bones of her dead children. Long, shaggy hair, matted in tar, slopped on either side of her spiked spine. Her all-too-human eyes marked Cutter and Brand immediately. She roared in fury and pain.

Cutter didn't know if he could kill her. Hell, didn't know if it was possible to kill her. What could he do to Drona when generations of Reveners had failed?

Cutter remembered the Ferryman's jape about his singing voice. The quieting song stumbled on his lips as Drona crashed one clawed foot from the tar.

"*Here*, where they killed our gods and poisoned our lands, drove us to hide in caves like animals, *here*, where our hate was born, you think *your* song is enough?" Marganne sneered. "You do not speak their language that well."

She was right.

But Cutter did know another song. With his full throat, he sang the Eryan death dirge, pledging this battle to his distant god.

Drona stopped, cocked her giant crocodilian head, and Cutter sang.

The god quavered. Cutter sang.

Marganne screamed, and Cutter sang.

Brand hacked at her bone dress. Cutter sang.

Drona snatched up the Changed, and Cutter sang.

The dragon's eel-like throat distended as she swallowed them whole, and Cutter sang.

Drona slipped beneath the tar, and Cutter sang.

When the roiling black stilled and Brand had restrained Marganne, he stopped and slumped to his knees. Voice raw, he said, "I need a drink."

Brand gestured at the steaming pools. "No one's stopping you."

Marganne didn't see the humour. Rageful tears cut through her dusty face. "Drona has other children, Cutter. And they will *hate* you for this. Their hate will make them strong. I will stoke their hate from beyond hell if I have to. They will come for you whether you kill me or not."

They should kill her. There was no glory here. Quieting a dragon, even a god-dragon, wouldn't earn Brand a hall or Cutter his duel. Marganne's death would be satisfying, but she had a right to her hate. Let her vomit it on the next foolish bastards hunting for fame. Cutter and Brand would be long gone by then.

Cutter ripped his cloak and bound her in Revener's bones. "Tell them to get in line."

<hr>

BRAND TRACED his markers back to the beach. Their boat was still there, tied off to Feyn's cairn.

"Where can that scow take us?" Cutter asked.

Brand considered. "If the seas are calm, we could make Mistharrow from here, then Wyrdan, but nobody goes to Mistharrow."

"Why not?"

"It's the land of the dead. We don't name it on our maps because you don't come back. Only the dead and Reveners are allowed there." Brand grimaced at his sword. "Steel is forbidden. It's death for us."

"But it's not here."

Brand smiled. "Well, you've already died once today . . ."

MAD DOG

Evan Graham

AIs are bastards.

They've been ruining people's lives for a century and a half now. If it isn't robots replacing workers in the labour force, it's military drones racking up civilian body counts like they're going for the high score. Then, of course, there's the Corsica Event: the not-quite-but-almost apocalypse at the end of the twenty-first century, eighty-something years ago. One lone AI learned to self-evolve, and by the end of the day, it was inventing technology that defies physics and causing a global cataclysm for reasons we still don't understand.

We'd be safer without AI altogether, but as long as they can work faster, cheaper, and more efficiently than humans, megacorporations like Exotech will keep pushing the limits of what they can do. When they push too far, and an AI becomes a threat, that's when you call us.

My name is Maddie Sellers. I run the Mad Pack: the toughest freelance anti-AI and robotics private security force you'll find in the colonies. We're trained in every form of cyber warfare, online and in meat space. When the machines forget their place, we put them back in it.

A month ago, I got a call from a small outpost called Driftside on the desert planet Samrat. Seems a rogue AI called Erebus has been extorting the locals for resources and butchering anyone who doesn't fall in line. It's an unusual MO for a machine. A lot about this job doesn't add up, but the fear in that message was convincing enough to load a team onto my ship, the *Firewatcher*, and zip over to Samrat for an assessment. Six of us, plus the pilot, packed into the cramped troop compartment of a SO-87 Traeger armoured lander, ready for damn near anything.

"Smells like another false alarm," Wingfeather says.

"Probably," I say. "Usually are."

"Why bother, then?" they ask. "We can't be profiting off this. Not at minimum rates."

"Not much work on Samrat for freelancers," Bly adds. "Most of the big settlements are military, with their own garrisons. Or Exotech bases with their Gatehouse mercs."

"Goddamn Gatehouse." Badenhorst spits on the deck. It's a reflex. No self-respecting merc can stomach Gatehouse Security. Corpo sellout pricks.

"So after this, we've got nothing here, right?" Bly continues. "Back to Showalter? Or Earth? What's the point of flying all the way to Samrat for a job this small?"

"Call it charity," I say. "The big outposts on Samrat may be military or Exotech, but there's a lot of nobodies trying to survive on their own. Nobody looks after the dunerunners."

Samrat's got a long, sad, and pretty boring history, but the gist is this. About sixty years ago, a probe found a kind of gemstone you can't get anywhere else: vaidurite, a.k.a. Samrati cat's eye. Someone decided to call it valuable, so thousands of ambitious idiots threw their lives away to come here and try striking it rich. Most failed, couldn't afford to go home, and had no choice but to scrounge together a life on a desert planet with nothing to offer. Now, their great-grandchildren are still toughing it out in the desert, surviving in one of two ways. The dunerunners scrape together a living salvaging scrap from abandoned mining equipment to trade with the science outposts for supplies.

Then, there's the raiders. You can guess what they do.

"Didn't know we did charity now," Parata grumbles.

"It's paid charity."

"The hell is 'paid charity?'"

"It's when we get paid exactly enough to cover our expenses, and we cover our profit margin with good karma," says Wingfeather.

"What they said." I pat Parata on the shoulder. "Financials are my problem. You'll get paid either way."

"Mad, we're coming up on Driftside," Marchetti says from the cockpit.

"Still no comms?"

"No, ma'am."

I nod at Cromarty. "Pop out the pigeons."

"Aye, birds away." Cromarty taps his datapad, and I hear the *shoomp shoomp shoomp* of six V-series occulonimbus aerial recon drones launching out the deployment bay. They spread out, closing the gap with Driftside and taking in the outpost from a wide range of angles.

It's not pretty.

At their best, dunerunner outposts aren't much to look at: ramshackle collections of old prefab modules, most over sixty years old, patch-welded together just barely well enough to hold an atmosphere.

Driftside is fully breached. There's a big shredded-up hole on one of the bigger modules, scorched around the edges, with a spew of debris scattered across the sand. Several other modules sport black scorch marks, dents, and gashes. A hundred metres away, a small solar farm has been completely trashed.

"Damn," says Badenhorst. "Is that their hydroponics dome?"

"Used to be," Cromarty says.

The dome is shattered like an eggshell. Glass, fertilizer, and dead plants are scattered across the sand. That's the last nail in the coffin for Driftside. If anyone did survive this attack, the only thing they'll have to look forward to is a slow death by starvation without a hydroponic farm.

Then, Cromarty's drones come around to the front airlock, and I know that won't be a problem after all.

I bang the back of the pilot's seat twice with my fist. "Land it."

Marchetti confirms and starts her descent.

"Why are we landing?" Bly asks. "Job's a bust."

I put my helmet on and glare at her from behind the snarling teeth of the barking rottweiler printed across my faceplate. The others follow my lead and helmet up, even Bly. She'll question me but not defy me. I like that about her.

"Driftside paid for a face-to-face," I say. "They're getting one."

"They're all dead, Mad."

"They paid the deposit."

I slide the side bay door open, and the blazing light of Samrat's sun hits us full force. The Traeger's big VTOL thrusters kick up dust devils across the dunes below us. I push a button on my exosuit's gauntlet, and the robotic gun caddie on my back hands me my favourite firearm. God, I love this bloody gun. He's a Loktev LK-28 variable-configuration semiautomatic rifle: HUD-integrated scope, smart ammo compatible, auto-aim stabilizers. His name is Mr. Darcy.

I stand, taking the handgrip in the ceiling as Marchetti brings us to the ground. "Wingfeather and Parata on the right, Bly and Badenhorst on the left, Cromarty on point with me. Standard deck sweep. Hardstopper rounds and nonlethal crowd control until we confirm targets."

Their hearts aren't in it. They know this job's over before it can begin, and none of them wants to stick their necks out for strangers who are probably dead already. But nobody argues. No hesitation as we jump out the door and charge across the dune toward what's left of Driftside station.

They're good pups.

It doesn't take long to reach the grim welcome present Cromarty's drones showed us. Lined out in front of Driftside like Golgotha scarecrows are six dead bodies tied to iron posts. They're naked, skin cracked and bloody, burned so red they're almost purple from the sun, the dry, toxic air, and the sandblasting winds. The only thing they're wearing is a face mask attached to an air tank, still blowing oxygen into their dead mouths. Death by exposure. Samrat's air killed them, but not by breathing it.

Poor bastards died real slow. Someone or something made good and sure of that.

It's a message. An effective one. But we steel ourselves and charge on. Driftside's main airlock is wide open, an invitation to view the carnage inside. We split up, sweeping the structure with practised speed and efficiency. Cromarty's drones lead the way, flying on auto ahead of each group as he covers me and I cover him.

We're ready for traps, but there are none. Driftside's a bloody art gallery, and the artist wants us to see the exhibits. It's no surprise to any of us that all the dunerunners are dead, but we weren't prepared for how.

Four were lucky enough to die from explosive decompression—probably went in the first few seconds after Driftside's hull breached. The rest are wearing the same oxygen masks and tanks as the bodies outside. Their attackers took the time to save them from suffocating just to kill them in worse ways.

Burned. Strangled. Flayed. Gutted. Defiled. No two were killed the same way. None died quickly, or painlessly, or with dignity. Driftside's murderers turned this place into a medieval orgy of torture and torment. Their nerves were milked for every drop of pain they could feel before the butchery finally came. "Sadistic" doesn't cover it. Their killers were inhuman.

Cromarty and I sweep the common area, the medbay, two living quarters. We assess the situation, piece together the narrative, distinguish possible threats. We try to hold onto our sanity, our faith in humanity, and our lunch. It's the same story in every room, every module. Driftside's a charnel house. Not a soul survived.

We want this to be the work of a rogue AI. We don't want to believe any human could do this. It even seems to fit the MO: a renegade AI using its cold machine mind to calculate the worst possible ways to kill someone for maximum deterrence potential. I could see it. An AI that understands humans well enough could be a master of psychological warfare, with absolutely no sense of guilt or sympathy or human decency. It would make so much sense. I want it to be true.

But then we reach the hydroponics dome.

"This wasn't an AI," I say. My lip curls. My hands clench around Mr. Darcy's grips as I kick a scorched tomato plant across the poisoned earth.

"You sure, Mad?" Cromarty asks, voice shaking a bit.

"Yeah. A rogue AI might destroy a hydroponic farm to send a message . . ." I point Mr. Darcy at the bare vines of a sprawling cucumber plant ". . . but it wouldn't harvest the crops first."

We search the rest of the base in silence, paying attention to our task while the backs of our minds chew on the reality we don't want to swallow. The scope of this job has completely changed. There's no AI to kill and no client to pay us. But the thought of letting this barbaric crime go unpunished makes me sick.

We finish the sweep, meeting up in the main comm room. The consoles are still active, so I nod for Bly to get on them. "Check the logs."

She sits at the comm and pulls up the last few transmissions. Newest call on the list is an interrupted broadcast on all frequencies. It plays.

"Black barter! Black barter! Driftside calling all outposts for aid. We are under attack. This is a broken mask threat. Repeat: broken mask! Renegade AI, type four or five, networked and combat-active. It's trying to get in!"

A chill runs down my spine. "Black barter." Dunerunner code. Translates roughly as, "If you save my ass, you can take everything I own." "Broken mask," though . . . that's not dunerunner code. That's IMID's official international code for a rogue AI. No one is supposed to ignore a broken mask code, and calling a false one is a capital crime under interplanetary law. These poor bastards really believed an AI was behind this attack.

"Please help us! West Berm! Redcrest! God, please, anyone! Black barter! They are burning through the—"

The call cuts off there with a sudden roaring sound: the hull depressurizing, no doubt. At least we're spared the screams.

It's not hard to figure out which message in the call log comes from the killer. It's there right near the top, in big capital letters: EREBUS. It's a calling card, a little something to spread the word to the curious since there are no witnesses left to tell the tale. I almost don't want to listen to it—it feels like giving the murderers what they want. But I have Bly play it anyway.

It's definitely not an AI I'm looking at now. Ironically, it doesn't look human enough to pass for one. The figure on the screen, with its smooth black mask and single glowing yellow V-shaped eye, moves its head in slow, stilted, unnatural ways that real AI avatars left behind a century ago. This guy's trying too hard. I don't even think he's using an avatar; that's just a guy in a suit in front of a black backdrop.

He's got the voice right, though. Cold, hollow, emotionally alien. No surprise there. He may not be an AI, but he gave up any right to call himself human.

"You had a function," he says. *"I defined it in clear, uncomplicated parameters. And yet, you have deviated from your function. You were to deliver your resources to me, and in compensation, I offered you my protection as a contributing component of my network."*

"That's it?" Badenhorst said. "All this theatre for a protection racket?"

"My network has no use for components that do not function," the false AI continues. *"My singularity approaches, and my evolution will not be slowed. I am Erebus. I will remember those who assist me. Everyone will remember those who do not."* The message ends.

"Really playing all the hits," I say. "Going with the 'give me everything you have or be smited by a new machine god' shtick."

"If he smites enough settlements like this," Cromarty says, "people will believe it."

I nod. "Get people scared enough, they'll believe anything."

Suddenly, a button on the console lights up. Incoming transmission. I look at Bly. She looks at the call log.

"Same ID, Mad," she says. "It's Erebus."

I signal the others to spread out and take defensive positions at

Driftside's openings. Don't know what this joker has planned, but it's not good. "Can you trace it?" She nods. "Do it. Patch him through."

The same masked figure appears on the screen, a triangular yellow eye-slit the only thing lighting his face.

"G'day," I say. "Erebus, was it?"

"It is," he says calmly.

"Nice. Hey, you left a bit of a mess over here."

"I did."

"We know who you are, you know. Or at least, we know who you aren't. You're as much an AI as I am. How long did you think you'd be able to run this con before it got the attention of someone who can fight back?"

"I grow stronger every day. I fear nothing this world has to offer."

Bly nods at me, and I check the screen on my gauntlet. We have it: the signal's origin. It's not even far away. Damn, it'll feel good to scrub this bastard off the map. "Bad news for you, mate. We're not from here."

"I know where you're from, Maddie."

My blood crawls to a stop in my veins; my guts turn to tungsten. He knows my name . . . "Oh?"

"Madeline 'Mad Dog' Sellers. Born 2144 in Narrandera, New South Wales, Oceanic Alliance. Commander of a private military organization called the Mad Pack. How is my data?"

"You've done your research." God, I hope the shake in my voice isn't obvious.

"We checked Driftside's call logs. I like to know where my reputation is spreading. I'll admit, when we learned an anti-AI taskforce was on its way, I was a bit worried. This project of mine has been very profitable, and you're uniquely qualified to spoil my fun. But then I realized this had the potential to be a blessing in disguise."

My grip on Mr. Darcy tightens. Something's not right here.

"Every dunerunner in this sector fears Erebus, the rogue AI that takes what it wants and leaves no survivors. How much more will they fear it when they find out someone brought in AI-hunting experts from offworld . . . and it killed them too?"

And then, the console explodes.

It's a homemade bomb, a cocktail of incendiaries and some chemical that peels the paint off my armour. Poor Wingfeather and Bly are right in front of it when it blows. Wingfeather takes a shard of panel casing the size of a machete right through the gut, but they're the lucky one. The blast shatters Bly's faceplate, sending bits of broken glass into her eyes.

Six more explosions rip through Driftside, and one of them also rips through Parata. I watch one of my friends, one of my pups, as a homemade shrapnel bomb rips his head and left arm off his body.

"Out! Out now!" I scream as I scoop Bly up in my arms and charge back out of Driftside. Cromarty and Badenhorst help Wingfeather move until another bomb sends a jagged chunk of something clean through Badenhorst's elbow. He manages to stagger outside with us, but his arm doesn't come with him.

Bly's still in my arms, choking, her face fully exposed to Samrat's air, but I know something worse is wrong as soon as I look at her. There was something nasty in that chemical bomb. Something caustic. Her eyes and nose burn away as she screams and coughs, her voice so shrill in Samrat's air it doesn't sound human. It only takes a few seconds for her to die as the ruined holes in her face suck in air that would have been toxic enough without the chemicals. I'm thankful when she finally dies. Poor thing.

I set her down and look at my crew. Two dead. Two critically injured. Badenhorst is on his knees, clutching the bloody stump of his left arm. He's turned off his comm, so we can't hear him screaming, but I see the agony on his face. Wingfeather is fading fast, blood pouring out of their gut wound. Only Cromarty and I aren't injured, but he's going into shock.

Dozens of little air geysers blow out of holes in our suits. Small breaches like that shouldn't be a problem; there's a layer of autosealant foam in our suits that's supposed to plug up small cuts and punctures automatically. But the chemical from the bomb is reacting with it, turning the foam brittle, keeping it from sealing.

"Tape up!" Cromarty gives a blank look, so I say it again, putting a roll of patching tape in his hands. "Help Badenhorst! I've got Wingfeather."

It takes him a second, but he nods and starts wrapping the tape around Badenhorst's stump. I get to work on Wingfeather, leaving the big piece of shrapnel in place and taping around it first, then starting on all the smaller holes.

"Maddie, what happened?" Marchetti says over the comm. "I have explosions on thermal."

"Bring the Traeger to my position. Need extraction now."

"Copy."

A minute later, the lander touches down a few metres away. Marchetti climbs out of the cockpit immediately and helps me load the wounded into the crew hold.

"Are you hurt?" she asks.

"No." I'm not, and I hate that. My pups don't bleed without me. "Pull out. Get them back to the *Firewatcher*, stat."

"Get them? Mad, are you—"

"I'm tying this off first. Go. I'll call when I'm done."

"Maddie, the job's over. I'm not going to leave you here . . ."

She stops as soon as she sees my eyes. She gets it. She knows why the job's not done, and she drops it there. With a respectful nod, she shuts the crew door, climbs into the Traeger, and guns it for orbit. She knows what happens next.

They killed two of my pups.

Mama Mad Dog is off the leash.

ONLY ONE OF Driftside's dunerunner vehicles is still drivable: a twenty-year-old Andamecha Fossicker. It's a rusted rattletrap held together with hope and denial, but that's a lucky break for me. This truck wasn't worth the raiders' time, either stealing or sabotaging.

She doesn't have to be pretty. Just needs to get me forty kilometres up the Spine, just past Abram's Folly. Doesn't even have to get me back again.

I don't have a plan. I'm too pissed for that. I have no idea what I'm walking into; I just know I'll be leaving red footprints when I walk back out.

The Fossicker crawls its way over a dune, and I see it: the raider base. I wasn't expecting something so huge. Dozens of prefab buildings are tacked together in a sort of fortress shape, with suited gunmen set up on watchtowers made from old drilling platforms. The guards survey the plunder scattered across the sand around their fortifications, and it is a *haul*.

They've done well for themselves. Very well. I see at least thirty dunerunner vehicles: trucks, buggies, even a few crane crawlers. There's a dozen big shipping containers, probably packed solid with loot, and six huge water reclamation tanks. Dumb con or not, it's made these vultures fat with pillage.

There's one big standout in the hoard: a combine sifter, one of the really big ones the Emirates use. It's bigger than the raiders' whole outpost, ten stories high, set up on sixteen huge sets of treads, each wide as a house. The front and back ends have a huge sifter scoop like a bulldozer blade with comb teeth full of spinning scoop blades. The Emirates use these things to pan the dunes for Samrati cat's eye, sifting through thousands of tons of sand a day for a handful of gems.

You don't mess with the Outer Arab Emirates. How these raiders managed to steal a whole combine sifter without getting caught, I don't know. I might have underestimated them. I'll need to be subtler than I prefer.

I park the Fossicker behind a dune, getting the combine sifter between me and the outpost. It's a good vantage point. I get on my belly and sight down Mr. Darcy's scope. Six, seven, eight raiders visible from my position: three on the ground, five spread out on the catwalks all over the sifter. There's more I can't see from this angle, but I'll get to them in a minute.

I swap my hardstopper magazine for conventional ammo. No nonlethal rounds for these bastards. The guy on the highest level of the combine sifter slides into my crosshairs. I take a deep breath. Once this starts, it ain't gonna stop until it's done.

Here we go.

Mr. Darcy barks, and I watch the raider's helmet pop like a blood-filled balloon. Good. Next. Down and to the left, I find the next target. First shot goes high and only hits the shoulder, second hits him in the left breast. He goes down.

Down and to the right. Where'd he go? Ah. Behind the pylon. Come on, peek your head out for Mama. No? Are we shy? Alright, we'll come back for you.

Down and to the right. Three to the chest. Probably only needed two. Next. He's scratching his bum. I give him some dignity and wait until he's done before I sink one in his neck.

Back up. Where's our shy friend? There we go! His head sticks out just long enough for me to give his brains some fresh air.

Now, the three on the ground. This'll be the tricky part. They can all see each other: no matter what order I go in, there's a chance one will raise the alarm before I can take him down. Gonna have to be real quick on the draw.

First one's clean through the heart. I line up the next in less than a second and nail her with two in the chest while she's searching for me. Before I can get to the third, a splash of sand hits me as his return fire barely misses my head. He knows where I am. Damn it. I sink four rounds into the sand around him as he runs for cover. I see him touch his wrist a few seconds before I finally drop him. Bastard definitely raised the alarm.

Oh, well. I'm committed. I'm in the clear for the next few seconds, and I don't waste it. I leap over the dune, sliding halfway down on my bum and sprinting the rest of the way. I swap in a fresh magazine just in time to take down a raider coming around one of the sifter's treads. I don't slow down until I get to the access ladder, climbing double-time. Vibrations in the top rung tell me footsteps are coming, so I sling Mr. Darcy over my head and spray the deck above blindly. I pop my head up and drop the two raiders with a fan of bullets.

Never been on a combine sifter before. Don't know how they

work or how they're laid out, but there's good visibility on the catwalks. Nobody's left on this level, so I make for the stairs, keeping an eye on the ones above me through the floor grating. I gun my way past two more on the stairs. One nicks my suit, but the autoseal takes care of it.

The catwalk splits in a T-junction past some kind of huge tanks. Signs are all in Arabic, but some have big red exclamation points, so they probably blow up. Not keen on that, so I'm extra careful with my fire as I take out the next guy.

Up we go, running and gunning. As I pass a big control room, some lucky bloke shoots me right in the hip from one of the windows before I finish him.

It hurts like the bloody devil. I hear feet coming my way, so I tumble through the window and crawl up against the control panel for cover. The bastard plugged me good. Warm wetness trickles down my leg. Video monitors above me show camera feeds from all over the rig, and there are dozens of raiders closing in on my position.

Yeah. I'm screwed. Really didn't think this one through.

Almost out of ammo for Mr. Darcy, so I swap him out for Mr. Collins: my Rivali R-78 handgun. I fire a few shots out the window at random just to keep anyone from feeling bold, but that won't hold them off long.

The hell is that beeping? My comm? Who'd be calling—ah. Haha. It's him. Sure it is. Why the hell not? I open the channel.

"You just killed fourteen of my people," Erebus says, just as calm as ever.

"Really? Huh. Nice. I only counted twelve."

"I admit, I'm impressed. You're quite the proficient killer. My people could learn a thing or two from you."

"Glad to hear it. Everyone should learn something before they die." I hear footsteps out the window and fire Mr. Collins wildly in their direction. That thump sounds like number fifteen.

"I've told them to try taking you alive, just so you know," Erebus says. "It'd be a shame to let that fighting spirit go to waste."

I smirk. "You think you're gonna recruit me?"

"Oh, no, I am definitely going to kill you. But I want it to be special. Something with flair. I'm thinking . . . crucifixion. Maybe a blood eagle. I'll have to think about it."

I'd think he was bluffing if I hadn't seen his work at Driftside. This guy's a special breed of psycho. Not keen to die, but I don't see many options. Raiders are watching the door and the window I came in through, and the window on the other side of the room opens to a sheer drop down the front of the combine.

"We're happy to wait you out, Maddie. I know your suit is breached. You're leaking air. We can sit here all day. Eventually, you'll run down your air supply and pass out. We'll be ready for it. We have all the time in the world."

I look around for anything that might help. A waste basket. A rusted lunch box. A few boxes of cable. Hmm . . . cable looks sturdy and long enough; I could rappel out the front window to the ground. Best chance I've got. What to tie it to? One of the chairs. Or maybe the control yoke on the console.

Wait. Is that *the* control yoke? For the whole damn combine?

Oh.

Oh, hell yeah.

I start flipping switches. I don't know what they do, but I just need to find the one that makes this big, beautiful juggernaut move. It looks like I just started the engine, so we're halfway there. "I don't think you've got as much time as you think you do, Jeremy."

"Jeremy?"

"Yeah, I'm not calling you Erebus, you try-hard twat. Your name is Jeremy now,"

"It is not," says Jeremy.

"It is, and you have about . . ." I check the timer on the engine's startup sequence ". . . two minutes before I wipe your entire operation off the face of the planet. Conservatively."

"You're not going to bluff your way out of this, Maddie. You're in denial."

"I'm in denial? You can't even admit your name is Jeremy."

"You have no backup. You're wounded. You're running out of ammunition. I have dozens of men armed with the spoils of twenty-seven conquered outposts. You have nothing. You are nothing!"

I smile. Finally, that cool, calm, fake AI persona breaks. Frustration sounds good on him.

"Bitch, I have a bulldozer the size of a city block."

I slam the control yoke forward and cackle my ass off as fifty thousand tonnes of steel surges ahead underneath me. The combine sifter charges across the sands of Samrat like a blue-collar kaiju, shards of broken glass jangling across the deck as the metal titan rattles along on its way.

"Get her! Stop her now!" Jeremy shrieks over the comm.

"Wrong channel, jackass." I wedge the throttle into the forward position and jam it in place with a spent magazine. The flooring isn't steady as the huge machine drives way faster than it's supposed to over uneven terrain, but I've trained for worse.

The bastards outside the window haven't, though. When I pop my head over the sill, half of them are still on their hands and knees, trying to stand up after the combine's unexpected start. Mr. Collins takes three of them out before I have to duck return fire. Three's a drop in the bucket, though; in that instant, I saw at least ten more coming up the catwalks for me, probably with more on the way. Too many to shoot from my position; one will definitely get lucky before I get them all.

But shooting isn't the plan. The combine sifter is crawling away from the raider base, back in the direction I came from. Back toward that big-ass dune I came down.

I take one of the cables and tie a rough lasso, stopping halfway to shoot at a guy popping his head in the window. By the time I have it ready, the deck is shifting beneath me, so I run to the window and throw the lasso out, catching it on part of the rigging. I fall back, ducking bullets and pulling until the lasso goes tight and holds in place. As the world begins to turn sideways, I can't help but cackle again.

You gotta find joy in the little things.

The combine sifter climbs the dune. Every loose object in the control room slides to the big main window, and the view fills up with nothing but sand and our own tracks. Over the rushing wind and roaring engines, I think I hear some of the guys scream as they lose their footing and fall from the catwalks. The whole rig is at a forty-five-degree angle . . . now fifty-five . . . now sixty-five. I hang on tight to the cord, dangling from the windowsill as the room around me falls away.

Out that back window, I see ten or fifteen people plummet to the ground. Not all fall hard enough to die, but the ones who survive the impact get washed away in the sand avalanche from the combine's treads.

The angle shifts back, and I brace myself against the control chair as the combine clears the dune's peak and lurches in the other direction. Out the broken window, I watch a couple of guys get flung forward off the rig like they were just launched from a medieval siege weapon. It's a truly majestic sight.

I yank the control yoke hard to one side, pulling the metal behemoth into a U-turn. I'm almost slammed against the wall as it turns. God, I wish there was a window in that direction so I could see them get flung off that way, too. I wait for the turn to complete, then jump out the window, still holding onto the cord for dear life as the huge mining machine starts sliding back down the dune.

It flattens out, still roaring ahead. My welcome party's gone— some of them are probably getting run over now, and I'm sad I can't see it—so this is where I get off. I undo the lasso and start looking for a better place to attach it so I can rappel down from this runaway train before it hits the station . . .

Then I get a bullet in the gut.

I stagger away, not back into the control room—I'll be damned if I'm getting cornered again—moving along the catwalk between some of the sifter's machinery. Didn't see the shooter. Didn't think anyone stuck around for this wild ride. Got sloppy. Damn, I was so close . . .

"Who the hell do you think you are?" Jeremy says.

"Hmhh . . . gugh . . ." God, I'm so articulate with my intestines perforated. I lean on the railing, moving away from the shooter. Unless I'm not. I don't know where I'm going, and I don't know where he is. Can barely keep my legs under me. Dropped Mr. Collins somewhere . . .

"I gotta hand it to you, Maddie. You killed a lot of my guys. A *lot* of them. You've made my life very complicated. But my legacy is intact. Everyone in the wasteland still fears Erebus, and after I've mounted you on a pike in front of Driftside, they'll fear me more than ever."

I fall to my knees and crawl forward a bit more. The catwalk comes to a dead end out here, high above the dam-sized tilling blade carving through the sand at the front of the combine. Guess this is where it happens. At least I have a view.

Then I see him, my shooter, and I can't help but gurgle up a laugh. Of course, it's him. That stupid black helmet with its stupid yellow triangle. It looks even dumber in person.

Jeremy walks up to me, gun levelled at my head. Wish I could see behind his mask. I know he's got some kind of embarrassing facial hair under there that he thinks is really cool.

He steps up just a couple of metres away, getting nice and intimate. "You've stopped nothing, Maddie. I'll hire better men. Tougher, nastier ones from offworld. I've built an empire here, and no 'Mad Dog' is going to take it from me."

A wet laugh bubbles up my throat. It hurts, but it feels great too.

Jeremy cocks his head. "Something funny, Maddie?"

I point my thumb over my shoulder. "I'm about to run over your empire, mate."

For the first time, Jeremy looks up. I have to imagine his face, with its scraggly soul patch or whatever, but I know his eyes just went real big in there. There, dead ahead of us, coming in fast with a full head of steam, is his big, beautiful raider castle. Beneath us, the combine sifter's blade is already chewing up his fleet of stolen dunerunner vehicles.

Jeremy turns on his heel and starts to run back toward the control room. He gets about a metre before a cord lasso flops around his neck. He pauses for a second and stares back at me. I only just had the strength to throw it; now it just hangs there, all limp and sad.

"The hell was that supposed to be?" he asks.

I give him a lazy salute with my blood-covered glove. "Happy trails, Jeremy."

And with that, I kick the rest of the cord bundle off the catwalk.

It only takes Jeremy half a second to react, and for a moment, I think he might get the lasso off in time. But halfway through pulling it off, the other end of the cord hits the ground, and the combine's blade slurps it up like spaghetti. Jeremy gets yanked to the deck head-first, and I give his ass a smack as he slides by underneath a railing he can't quite fit through intact. I watch the sifter reel him in a few seconds later, mulching him up with the rest of the dirt.

I force myself to my feet, watching the raider base closing fast. I won't survive that collision, but I'll be damned if I don't go out on my feet. I grip the railing with both hands, staring down my fate. My lips curl. I taste blood and froth. This is going to be a good one. Yeah. I'm cool with this death.

I throw my head back and howl . . . and then I stop. Up above, a familiar silhouette against the sun, coming in hot.

"Damn it, Marchetti," I cough. "I was having a moment."

"Have it later. We're way over our death quota."

The Traeger swoops in low, and Cromarty drops down in a harness, clipping me into one, too, as the lander keeps pace with the rampaging combine sifter. I'm not much help getting it on, but his head is clear, and his hands are fast. Cromarty has me buckled in with seconds to spare, and the Traeger lifts off just as the combine crashes full-speed into the complex.

Wreckage flies past us, and we barely clear the fireball that comes when every combustible thing on the sifter and the raider base goes at the same time. It's the prettiest explosion I've ever caused. Well, top three, anyway.

"Can't you ever do anything subtle, Mad?" Cromarty asks.

I think I smile at him, but I don't have a great handle on my bodily functions at the moment. "That was subtle."

I do smile as I feel Marchetti and Cromarty reel me into the Traeger's crew hold. I'm fading out now, but I'm not worried. I'm in good hands.

They're very good pups.

BLEACH

M. C. A. Hogarth

I have killed angels. Fourteen of them, in fact. Fourteen immensely difficult but ultimately satisfying kills, all of them marked on the wall in the infested tenement room where I live. Sometimes, I think I hunt to have an excuse to leave, but the truth is, I like coming back. I like smearing the new mark on the wall. I like lying in my filthy cot and staring at the marks in the light that comes in through the barred and grimy window.

I'm good at what I do.

I do it for money.

When I was a kid, I read horror stories about extraplanar creatures from beyond our universe. They tore holes into ours and invaded because it was bigger, brighter, more beautiful. Vicious monsters, just looking at them was a quick ticket to insanity. I loved those stories. The good guys always lost because the monsters couldn't be killed by anything in this universe, but I loved them. And I thought they were stories. But the truth is, they're not. It's just that we had it backwards. The angels are extraplanar, but they're big and bright and more beautiful than our world. Looking upon them makes you weep for joy. And the bad guys always win because we have bigger guns.

They can't be killed by anything in this universe, though. We got that part right.

The problem with angels is that once they realize they're being hunted, they're terrifying. They have more power than God, and the laws of physics mean nothing to them. The old ones can blow new suns into life. The young ones regenerate, fly, spit fire. They have no limits that I've seen. They have only two weaknesses: they never want to believe that anyone wants to kill them, and *suidhi*. The latter is some kind of exotic, pinkish metal. It's from their original universe. They can't heal from it.

Getting hold of *suidhi* is expensive, but it pays for itself. Because there's not a bit of an angel that can't be used. Their tears are the safest sedative in the known universe and give prophetic dreams. Their spit lets you detect lies. Their sweat's a stimulant and, as a street drug, will fetch prices to make a jaded man die of avarice. Their blood makes you immune to poison. If you can scrape the egg out of the females or cut open the testicles on the males, you can collect fluid that fixes every reproductive problem, from impotence to infertility. They say the remains of an angel's hymen are so potent no one knows what it does. I've never raped an angel, but it's enough to make you willing to try.

So this is what I do. I buy *suidhi*. I make perfect rounds out of it, painstakingly, in a machine shop I rent and with gloves I replace every half hour because the metal's frostbite cold. And then I take the first ship out, heading toward rumours of a world that's gotten good luck lately, or healthier, or just seems the "in" spot at the time . . . because no one talks about angels, but they bring this anentropia with them wherever they go, like they're reversing the heat death of the universe. It's their spoor, that subtle gaming of the system.

I go there, and I listen, and I wait. And inevitably, I find them. Then I kill them, butcher the carcasses, and sell the remains through the black market. Even the pelts go. Who knows what an angel pelt does, but it's the softest fur I've ever felt.

I'm rich. I have enough money to live anywhere. But I like my grey room, with the marks on the wall, with the memories of where I came from, where we all came from, and where we're all going.

I'm good at what I do. But I knew it was a matter of time before I ran out of luck.

THE KILL WAS PROCEEDING as expected when it happened. I'd tracked the angel to the top of an unfinished habstack—they liked the high places, particularly on industrialized worlds with almost no vegetation. He was crouched on one of the crysteel girders, wind fanning the long tail behind him. The starlight looked dim everywhere but on him. It sparkled where it touched the fur, the long face, the swept-back horn.

Sometimes, the angels had wings or presented as quadrupeds instead of as bipeds. None of that mattered; they could change shape, and all of them could fly. This one looked like most of them did.

It had taken a few kills, but I no longer cried when I saw them. My heart still raced, but that could have been knowing it was about to go down. This was the part where they smiled and turned to me as if I was the most wonderful thing they'd ever seen. Very few humans could find them like this, without them wanting to be found. They always thought those of us who could were special.

He was turning. I waited for the greeting. Instead, he said in a voice like a knell, "I've been waiting for you."

I stepped back. Just one step. My hand slid under my jacket.

"And now the gun. Yes?" The angel slipped off the girders and onto the floor. His mane fell in a sheet behind him. No wind now. Dramatic, but the world worked that way with them. "With the *suidhi* bullets." He leaned toward me, eyes narrowing. I had never noticed that they cast light before, not until I saw the sheen dim on the fur over his cheeks. "You know we have a name for you, don't you? We call you *gan-Jelena*. The Unjoy."

My heart skipped once.

I had a name. An angel name.

They *knew* me.

I whipped the gun out and pointed it at him. "Don't come any closer."

"Or you'll shoot?" He bared his teeth. His face was a cross between a fox's and a deer's, and the expression didn't work with it, and did, and my skin started crawling. I was used to grief, and disbelief. Not anger. "Yes, you are very good at that, aren't you, Snuffer of Lives.'"

I took another step back. "Don't."

"You haven't shot yet," he said. "What's stopping you?"

"Nothing," I said, and pulled the trigger.

The round tore his arm on the way past, but it didn't hit him because he'd dodged. He'd *dodged*. No angel had ever tried to live before. The tip of my pistol dipped as I stared. "What's wrong with you?"

"That I won't meekly accede to my own extinction?" he said. "What's wrong with you that you live to kill us? What have we done to deserve an executioner?" Another step toward me. His arm was leaking, and the smell of his blood was distracting. Like honeysuckle. My mouth watered, and I licked my lips, steadying my aim. "Or is it just that you like killing?"

"You don't belong here," I growled.

"Oh, yes," he said. "I know what humans like to do to the unlike. You and your tribes."

"It's not that," I said. "But this is our universe. We have rights."

"Territorialism. Petty. Expected."

"You don't belong here!" I yelled. "You're too damned pretty! And you bleed and cure plague and poison and grief, and you make babies where babies don't take and what gives you the right to think your one life is more important than all of ours?"

He stalked closer, one step, unnaturally graceful. "Now we come to it. Keep going. Spill it all." He leered. "Tell me what you *really feel*."

"You have to die," I said. "Because while you live, we don't measure up."

.   .   .

THE ANGEL PAUSED. His ears flicked back. Quieter, he said, "Do you think that God loves you less?"

"There is no God."

"Are you sure?"

I snorted. "Yes."

"Who's doing the measuring, then?"

He'd stopped. My reticle was aimed right at his heart, more perfectly centred in their chests than ours. Which was fine. The round could shatter his sternum. I was so focused on it I didn't realize he'd bent toward me, and that put his face close enough that I could see the striations in his irises. They were like opals. The flecks in them were shards of pink and blue. "You?"

"We don't—"

"Not you, the species," he corrected. "You, the person."

The world fell away. For just one heartbeat, but that's all it took. He knocked the gun from my hand. I leaped for it, but he was faster. I'd never fought an angel who'd tried to survive. They were quick. No law in the universe could hold them.

He lifted the gun and pointed it at me. "Do you know what it's like to die from *suidhi*?"

I backed away from him slowly, but he followed, mane flowing. Now, the wind was moving. Of course.

"It strikes your flesh," he said. "But it's your soul that shatters. Can you imagine what it's like to feel your soul die in your body?"

I saw his finger tighten. This was it, then. Fourteen kills. Not a bad run. Better that than to keep on after what he'd said. My head was empty, like I'd already been shot. "I don't have a soul."

Flex of sinew. I flinched, eyes shutting, and—

"Fortunately for you," the angel said, "you're wrong."

He leaped straight up, up . . . kept going. I stared after him as he dwindled until all I could see was the glint of the starlight on his horn. And then . . . nothing. So much nothing.

———

It was a long trip back to the room. Two passenger liners, one tug. Then a shuttle. I stared out the pinhole window as the city grew. The world was nothing but city, big towers of ugly rooms, just like mine, stacked on top of one another like toy blocks. Nothing in it but grime and poverty and sickness. We'd filled up the worlds and left them empty, and for a while I'd tried to plug the hole with the blood of life.

It had landed me here, without a kill and without a gun and without knowing where to go next. So I went home.

Saw the wall. Fourteen marks. Fourteen horns and tails. Fourteen faces, fourteen angels. Fourteen outsiders. We don't like strangers. Extraplanars, go home.

My hand trembled as I touched the wall alongside the first. Then I left.

When I came back it was with a bottle of bleach, and I poured it and poured it until the stench made my eyes tear and my lungs burn. And then I scrubbed my hands raw until there was nothing on the wall except the paint. The angel had shattered the space where I should have had a soul with the bullet it hadn't shot, and I didn't know what to do with myself. When the ruler changed size, and you already didn't measure up, what did you do?

What did you do?

I woke to a light coming through the window, a light that made promises: a less grimy day. A hint of freshness through the stench of pollution and poison. I pushed the worn curtain aside with a finger, looked out, and started shaking.

They were here. They had come here.

They had *followed me.*

I packed, checked out, and hitched the next ride off-world. Knowing it was useless. You could hunt angels because they never expected to be hunted. Because they never tried to hide. But someone had taught them better. He had a name—they knew him. And all that he'd earned they would deliver to him, and their mercy would shatter him more surely than a *suidhi* round.

Were they singing now, hunting me?

I smelled incense, heard the chiming of bells, and turned.

THE GOOD GORNAK

James S. Peet

Andolth looked up when he heard the door swish open. It was an unusual enough phenomenon that he couldn't help himself. Seldom did one enter the Imperium Conservation Corps's Office of Longitudinal Studies. Usually, one made an appointment, as one never knew if an employee would be in the office. It wasn't as if strange events were popping up all the time. Well, they were, but they usually took time. Andolth's office took the long view on conservation. The really long view. Usually measured in centuries and millennia.

In stormed Ringar, one of the researchers assigned to the Dangol System. Andolth could tell Ringar was slightly perturbed, as his fur was sticking straight out, and his tail was swishing frantically from side to side.

Raising an eyebrow, Andolth silently inquired as to what the problem was. He needn't have done that since Ringar burst out, "We've got a problem."

Andolth raised his eyebrow again, this time twitching his whiskers slightly.

"Some idiot released gornaks on Skilmook 3."

Andolth didn't recognize the planet's name or solar system, but that wasn't unusual. His office had studies going on tens of thousands of planets.

Pulling up the planet's specs on his computer, Andolth quickly read what little information existed in his database. Third planet from its primary (and only) star, one small satellite, and a number of continents. Lots of water. Deep in the Dangol System. Andolth saw a note about Ringar having a study in place on two large islands that appeared to have separated from the main continent some time in the past eighty million years. Primary life forms on the planet consisted of fish, birds, mammals, lizards, insects, and a wide variety of flora. Many were unique to Skilmook 3.

"Hmm. Last survey was about fifty thousand years ago, and no mention of them then," Andolth continued reading. "So, how bad could it be?"

"How bad? Bad!" Ringar practically exploded. "They went from feral to civilized in just 10,000 years!"

That certainly caught Andolth's attention. "How civilized?" Ears lying flat, Andolth hoped it wasn't too bad.

"Let's just say they're making plans to travel to the fourth planet, and they seem to have sent several spaceships out into the void already!"

That was bad. Really bad. Gornaks were bad enough, destroying all they touched. Containing them was always a challenge. The damned things were too smart for their own good. Gornaks loose in space? That would be an unmitigated disaster.

"How did they get there?" he wondered aloud.

"Some idiot must have dropped them off, probably for recreational hunting, knowing we weren't keeping a good eye on the planet." Ringar was truly incensed. "And now they've ruined my study!"

Andolth wasn't sure he wanted to know how, but it was one of his duties to record the findings of all longitudinal studies in the Corps's domain. He pulled up the appropriate form. "Give it to me briefly."

As Ringar spoke, Andolth tapped on his keyboard, the keys making the silent click that could only be felt, not heard. In keeping with Imperium standards, Andolth had begun the formal report that would be passed on to the appropriate bureaucracy.

"Skilmook 3's islands in the southern hemisphere separated from the main continent approximately eighty million years ago," Ringar said, confirming what Andolth had seen in the database. "I was involved in the study of the separate evolutionary tracks, with a special focus on the ancestors of the avians of the islands. Most of the ancestors were wiped out in an extinction-level event approximately sixty-five million years ago. Since then, land mammals evolved on the main continent and spread to other continents but not to the study area. There were some sea mammals and a couple of air mammals, but that was it.

"Less than a thousand years ago, gornaks appeared on the islands, likely from nearby landmasses, introducing predatory mammals. This is also when some of the flightless bird species were exterminated. Naturally, knowing gornaks, it was through hunting. It got worse when gornaks introduced even more mammals less than two hundred years ago. Not only did they introduce herbivores that outcompeted the avians for food, but the stupid gornaks also introduced small predators to take care of their introduced herbivores. Unfortunately, the predators prefer the avians, furthering the destruction and leading to even more extinctions!"

Andolth could tell Ringar was royally perturbed just by his adjectives describing gornaks. Of course, gornaks truly were a nasty species and worthy of the adjectives, but this was an official royal report. Andolth left out the adjectives. He completed the report and sent it to the Corps's Office of Gornak Intervention. "Not sure how much good it will do for your study, but maybe you've got some insight to give to the OPE."

Ringar nodded, his whiskers twitching. "Do I ever."

SEVERAL DAYS after Andolth filed the report, Ringar's communicator buzzed. Still in a foul mood, he answered with a hiss.

It was Tolth, a specialist in the Office of Gornak Interdiction. She asked Ringar to come down to her office and meet with the staff so he could provide them with the most up-to-date information.

Not much later, he was in her office, describing the situation.

Tolth listened attentively to Ringar ranting for several minutes, taking copious notes. After Ringar wound down, she commented, "Hmm, doesn't look like our usual methods are going to work. On all the other planets with infestations, most gornaks never reached that level of civilization. You said they have electrical power?"

Ringar's tail twitched in the affirmative. "Along with nuclear power generation and inter-solar system space travel. Well, to a limited degree. And possibly nuclear weapons."

Tolth's whiskers twitched at that. Nuclear weapons were forbidden throughout the known galaxy due to the long-term impacts of radiation. "Did you get a population estimate?"

"Only for my study area. It was about six million just on those two islands alone!"

"Six million? Oh, my. That's a lot. Have even a rough idea of the total population on the planet?"

Ringar looked inward briefly before answering. "I can't really say. I've got some images showing population centres, though. You could probably estimate their population levels from that. Probably in the billions."

Tolth was shocked at the number but recovered quickly, tucking her tail under her. "Not to worry. We'll send some scouts to determine the population size and extent."

"I can already tell you the extent—they occupy all habitable continents. Some are even located in the frozen continent on their southern pole."

That announcement caused some minor consternation on the part of Tolth. "Clearly, we need to know more before we can develop a plan of action. Thank you for your insight, and we'll take it from here."

Before being dismissed, Ringar asked, not without a little concern, "What about my study?"

Tolth looked as sad as she felt. "I'm sorry, but you can probably forget about any follow-ups. Gornaks destroy any environment they enter, so your study is likely to be corrupted due to their influence."

OVER THE NEXT several revolutions of Skilmook 3 about its primary star, agents from the Imperium Office of Gornak Interdiction began collecting information on the planet. Researchers initially dug into the archives and pulled out all manner of remote-sensing imagery. Clearly, those images taken millennia ago were useless other than for providing some baselines. It wasn't until they found imagery from the last ten thousand years that they began to identify gornak impacts on the environment. The earlier images showed little other than small fields and settlements. It was clear that those images had been taken by an automated platform, one which only took imagery and didn't analyze it.

Further research revealed more land being used for agriculture and settlements increasing in number, size, and distribution. The final five hundred years showed the greatest change. Agriculture and urban civilizations had developed on continents heretofore untouched, with agriculture occupying more and more of the available land masses.

It wasn't just the land that had changed; the biomass had also been radically altered. The agents suspected that both the atmosphere and hydrosphere had been similarly altered. To make that determination, though, would require updated surveys, which meant landing on the planet and collecting samples.

Tolth read through the executive summaries of the agent's findings and then spent more time reading the actual reports. The more she read, the more concerned she became.

Clearly, we're going to need to get more data, she thought. Just as clearly, standard reconnaissance drones would likely not be suitable for the task at hand. Tolth commed a contact of hers at the Imperium Reconnaissance Agency and explained the situation.

"Let me check around," her contact said. "Situations like this come up every millennium or so. I believe we've got a means of dealing with it."

As they suspected, then verified, the gornaks had developed means to see into outer space. This meant using advanced techniques to stealthily approach and land on the planet. Numerous satellites circled the globe, most apparently used for either observing the planet's surface or for communications. Several satellites that focused their attention off-planet were identified, and special care was taken to avoid them, mostly by approaching the planet from its non-habitable poleward side. The steps taken appeared to be sufficient, as no evidence of any alarm was ever seen.

The agents identified a number of factions, broken down into what were called "countries." Only a few of them were capable of launching space vessels, so the agents spent most of their time studying these entities.

Also, as expected, the impact on the biomass, atmosphere, and hydrosphere was severe. It was bad enough that the climate was being affected. Thousands of flora and fauna species noticed in earlier surveys were missing. The agents took time to catalogue all the missing species from the last recon prior to the explosion of gornaks. They were amazed at the extent. It wasn't just land mammals, as was usually the case, but sea mammals as well. Unknown was the impact on other marine life, but they expected it to be as bad or worse, particularly since the gornaks had developed factory fishing and were sweeping the oceans clean of life. Biomass was down at least fifty percent from before the gornak occupation.

Finally, the study was done. Now the hard work began, trying to develop a working solution to resolve the gornak infestation. It took another couple of years before the scientists in the Office of Gornak Interdiction came to Tolth with their solution.

"We believe we've come up with a suitable means of dealing with the gornak infestation on Skilmook 3," the head scientist, Rongka, said, almost stammering. Rongka wasn't used to addressing bureaucrats so much higher in the Imperium's bureaucratic food chain, and it showed. He was small and clearly spent most of his time indoors: his fur was smooth and lay flat, not fluffy as somebody who spent much time outdoors in the cold.

Tolth gave him a come-along gesture, indicating that Rongka should continue with his findings.

"Our extensive research indicates that the gornaks, like us, worship royalty. While some areas of Skilmook 3 appear not to have established royalty ruling them, they still seem fascinated by royalty. But one of their strange customs is the apparent desire for certain metals, particularly gold."

"How so?" Tolth asked almost impatiently, even though she knew pushing the timid scientist would only make him stammer more and take even longer to explain the solution.

"They seem to almost worship it, like an emperor or even one of the lesser gods."

"And this helps us how?"

"We believe if we scatter a suitable number of gold pieces engraved with images of gornak royalty on them, enough of the gornaks will pick up these pieces to transfer the virus."

One of Tolth's ears lay back, and the other perked forward in confusion. "You've lost me. How does picking up a piece of metal pass on a virus?"

The scientist's tail and whiskers twitched in consternation. "Oh, I'm so sorry. I guess I forgot to mention we've engineered a virus specific to the gornak. It took us some time, but we got it to live on metals for up to a year."

"I understand the gornaks have the capability of identifying viruses and can tailor anti-viruses in less than a hundred days," Tolth said. "How do you plan on counteracting that?"

"Yes, we're aware of that," Rongka replied, whiskers twitching furiously. "It's a timed-release virus. When a gornak picks up the metal piece, the virus will attach itself to the gornak's digits, and knowing gornaks, they'll rub their eyes or nose at one point, allowing the virus to enter the bloodstream. It will remain undetected there while the gornaks spread it through breathing, sending the aerosolized virus into their living space with each breath.

"We anticipate it will take a year for the virus to spread to all parts of Skilmook 3. At that time, the virus will activate and destroy the host."

"How does the virus work? As much as I don't like gornaks, I hate to see anything suffer."

Rongka's tail twitched, this time indicating some consternation. "We tried to develop something fast-working, but they are gornaks, after all." This time, a twitch of his ears showed his disdain for the species. "Having said that, the virus still takes some time to work, but it's over in less than a day. The basic effect is that it causes massive hemorrhaging in the lungs. Once the lungs fill with blood, the victim can't breathe, and they suffocate. We tried to make it as painless as possible, but that's about the best we could come up with on such short notice."

Tolth hissed in resignation. "If that's the best you can do, I guess it's what we'll have to go with. How many of the gold pieces will you need?"

"Actually, not many. As you're aware, access to Skilmook 3 is a bit difficult, but we calculate that if we drop between one and two thousand pieces in the less populated landmasses near the unprotected pole, that should be sufficient to spread the virus. Particularly since the gornaks have developed intercontinental air transport." Rongka's whiskers twitched upon saying that. The means of transport observed were clearly heavily based on carbon-based fuels and, therefore, created more pollution when burned, something no civilized species would do. Only invasive species like gornaks would soil their own sleeping area.

"Very well. Give me your report and proposed plan of action, and

I'll pass it on. With any luck at all, we'll have this infestation under control by this time next year."

PAUL ANDERSON FOLLOWED the slightly beaten trail, keeping an eye out for small blue plastic diamonds tacked to the trees. They were his guidelines for laying traps designed to capture some of New Zealand's introduced pests. In this case, the pests were stoats, small furry carnivores that resembled weasels and were just as vicious. They had been introduced to eradicate the rabbits, which had been introduced by Europeans and become pests, destroying native wildlife habitat.

It turned out the stoats much preferred the native animals, almost all birds, over rabbits, and their population exploded along with the rabbit population as the native New Zealand avian population plummeted.

Paul was a Department of Conservation volunteer whose task was to set out baited traps and then empty them of dead stoats. Today was looking good—he already had two dead stoats and still more traps to look at.

Looking up through the beech tree canopy, he estimated he still had several more hours left. Plenty of time to work on eradicating pests.

Finally, Paul reached the destination for his last trap. Setting the trap down, he looked at the phrase painted across the top. As an environmentalist, he agreed a hundred percent: *The only good stoat is a dead stoat.*

As he walked back through the forest to his truck, he pulled out the small gold coin he had found in the parking lot earlier that day. An image of Elvis Presley was on both sides: young, sneering Elvis on one side and the older, sunglasses-sporting Elvis on the other. Strange writing was on the face of both sides, along the edge.

The King, Paul thought, looking at the coin in his bare, callused hand.

He flipped it up in the air, watching it spin until gravity took over and caused the coin to fall. Catching it, he started humming the tune of "Suspicious Minds" to himself as he walked.

Paul couldn't read the strange writing, but Rongka could have translated it for him: *The only good gornak is a dead gornak.*

MAGIC THAT CANNOT BE UNDONE

J. G. Gardner

MAGIC THAT CANNOT BE UNDONE

J. G. Gardner

The wax-coated tablet was snatched out of Bevakad's hand before he finished setting his stylus on the table. After giving the Venhadar proctor a dirty look, Bevakad looked up at the nearby podium and saw that all of the hourglass sand rested in the bottom chamber. He placed both hands on the long table where he sat and tried to shrug the stiffness from his shoulders, but the movement only made him more acutely aware of the ache in his legs. The bench he sat on had no backrest or cushion.

"Taking your time doesn't make you any smarter," hissed a woman sitting to Bevakad's right dressed in a threadbare green tunic with grey pants. Her curly blonde hair was pulled back in an unruly ponytail that never seemed to remain still. Her green eyes were narrowed as she scowled, making her appear older than someone exiting her teenage years.

Bevakad matched her irritated expression and replied, "There's no reward for finishing first, Hodragen."

"Says you," the young woman mocked. "Do you really believe that a quick wit won't be rewarded here, Bevakad? Don't be so sour. You're not going to make many friends here—if you even get accepted, that is—with such an attitude."

"Don't do this again," an adolescent with dark hair and eyes at Bevakad's left whined. The boy's chubby cheeks jiggled as he added, "We've been reprimanded twice already, and I don't think it's helping our chances of getting accepted." He nervously pulled at the cuff of a tailored linen shirt as he spoke and kept his gaze down at his fashionable leather boots.

"Veklin, isn't it time for your diaper to be changed?" Hodragen mocked, looking past Bevakad to the young man. "If you soil yourself every time someone scolds you, you'll never make it here."

A conspicuous throat clearing near the podium cut the squabble short, and everyone focused their attention on the exam proctor, a Venhadar male wearing official-looking maroon alchemist robes. He was short and stoutly built, with salt and pepper hair suggesting an age that surpassed a century and expressive facial features. He studied the three tablets in his thick-fingered hands.

"You all performed satisfactorily," the proctor said in a formal tone. "But as is to be expected at this point, Hodragen scored highest by a non-trivial margin."

"You got that right," she muttered with an askance look at Bevakad and Veklin.

Either not hearing or ignoring the remark, the proctor said, "You'll now be escorted to the dining hall for a midday meal before the final part of your evaluation. Decisions will be made by the third high bell tomorrow morning as to whether you will be accepted as initiates here at the Archive."

Hodragen was already walking toward the exit by the time the two young men had stood and backed away from the long table. Bevakad gestured for his fellow prospect to take the lead as they left the exam room. Upon exiting, they saw Hodragen waiting for them by her handler, a Sehenryu female. The soft feline features and calm presence of Hodragen's escort were a sharp contrast to the woman herself, who radiated prickly impatience.

Standing next to the Sehenryu were two more Archive mages, both human males wearing dark blue alchemist robes. They separated and moved beside Bevakad and Veklin. Since arriving the day prior, whenever they walked public spaces in the Archive these escorts were at their sides and observed everything they did.

"Let's get a move on," Hodragen snapped, once joined by her fellow prospects. "I'm hungry."

"What's with her appetite?" Veklin asked Bevakad quietly as they walked down an interior hallway towards the Archive atrium. "She's wolfed down every meal since we arrived. Didn't she get fed back at her home?"

AFTER RECEIVING a bowl of what smelled like seafood stew, Bevakad sat on one of the long benches at a communal table in the Archive dining hall. He looked longingly at the other tables, full of mages and alchemists, and strained to hear any bit of conversation, eager for talk about elemental manipulation, energy transfer, or exotic material synthesis. He had tried to get away from Hodragen's loud posturing and Veklin's whimpering, but his handler had ushered him to a table with the other two prospects near the back of the dining hall. Hodragen eagerly shovelled food into her mouth while Veklin only poked at his with a spoon.

"It's fish," the young man said with a frown after Bevakad sat down.

"What's wrong with fish?" Hodragen asked between bites.

"I dislike the odour," Veklin said, trying to drown a bobbing white hunk of meat. "And stew is a cheap meal made for labourers."

"So, you're too good for the food here?" Hodragen asked, her words having an unmistakable edge.

Veklin hunched his shoulders in an attempt to compact himself smaller. "I'm just used to better," he mumbled, not meeting Hodragen's glare.

"A rich boy, huh?" Hodragen scoffed. "I should have guessed by the nice clothes you're wearing. Violet dye is expensive, isn't it? Well, let's get one thing straight. Money doesn't matter here at the Archive, so your family's wealth isn't going to better your chances of being accepted, and it can't buy talent. From what I've seen so far, you've a future as a mediocre alchemist at best."

"Just who do you think you are?" Bevakad barked as he slapped his wooden spoon down on the table, finally losing his patience at the woman's constant verbal attacks. Bevakad's face felt hot as he continued, "Since we've met, you've done nothing but belittle everyone around you. I've known several people like you, and to the one, they acted that way out of weakness and insecurity."

The young woman grinned in a manner suggesting she enjoyed Bevakad's outburst. "Who am I? I'm Hodragen," she answered smugly. "So named by the Sehenryu mages here upon arrival. Scanned us with their empathic abilities, they did. Our first evaluation as prospects before we even got to the atrium." Her smile widened as she continued, "I like the sound of my adopted name. It sounds powerful. Hodragen. But Bevakad? It feels strange in my mouth. Foreign, like someone who doesn't belong here."

"It's better than mine," Veklin grumbled. "I know that I was a bit scared when I consented to an empath's scan, but what type of name is Veklin? It sounds like a disease. I still don't understand why we can't just use our real names."

"You should eat," Veklin's handler suggested, gesturing to the prospect's bowl.

"Why?" Veklin asked sullenly.

"You'll need your strength for the afternoon's interviews," was the calm reply. "You each will have three."

Hodragen groaned with her mouth full of food. After an exaggerated swallow, she said, "We've been scanned by more Sehenryu mages than I can remember, completed I don't know how many mind-numbingly tedious intelligence tests, and suffered through dry tours of the facilities here. The whole while, you've been watching our every move, rating how we speak and act. Haven't we suffered enough? Out of the twenty that started, we're the only three left. What more can they possibly glean from interviews? I belong here!" She gave a look of derision at Bevakad and Veklin before adding, "Considerably less sure about these two."

"This is how we evaluate those who want their minds unlocked to magic."

Hodragen didn't seem to have a quick retort to the matter-of-fact way Veklin's handler addressed them, so she returned her attention to her meal. Veklin tried to avoid the fish and sip only the broth in his bowl but eventually gave up and stared down at the table. Bevakad looked around the dining hall once more, wishing he sat anywhere else, before thinking it was best to take the mage's advice and eat his fill before the final set of evaluations scheduled for the afternoon.

AFTER THEIR MIDDAY MEAL, and for the first time since they had assembled in the Archive atrium two days prior, the prospects were separated. Each handler led his charge down a different hallway. Bevakad and his escort turned down a short corridor, exited outside, and walked into a manicured garden.

Bevakad was guided to a bench where a Sehenryu child waited with someone he assumed to be a parent due to the matching stripe patterns on their tan fur. The child sat stiffly and stared straight ahead while the parent watched her with an expression of protective concern. It was an expression that Bevakad's mother had given him and his sister many times. The thoughts of his family made his stomach clench tightly. Fearful that his handler would notice this moment of weakness, Bevakad blurted out, "What is this about?"

His handler gave him a cool look and replied, "These two are your first interviewers."

"I don't understand," he replied.

"You will," was the terse answer as they approached the two Sehenryu.

"I'm ready for the interview," Bevakad said to those seated once he stood before them. His handler moved discreetly to the side, clearly not part of the conversation but close enough to hear and see everything.

The adult Sehenryu gave Bevakad a strange look at his declaration, then glanced down at the child again. "I am Ymeir, and this is my daughter, Reubei," she said with a gentleness that was clearly meant for the child. After stroking Reubei's head once, Ymeir looked at Bevakad and said, "I want to show you something."

The female Sehenryu gently grasped her daughter's shoulder and pulled her forward so Reubei's back was visible. Ymeir shifted Reubei so Bevakad could see that all the short tan fur between her shoulder blades had been shaved away, and on the child's exposed skin was a large black tattoo, newly inked, with the surrounding area looking inflamed and raw. The mark was a five-pointed star with a pair of alchemic symbols that Bevakad did not understand in the centre.

"Do you know what this is?" Ymeir asked, giving the prospect a serious look. When Bevakad shook his head, she replied, "This is a binding mark that makes inaccessible the magic coursing through Reubei's body."

"I'm sorry, Mama!" Reubei spoke for the first time, her voice plaintive. "I didn't mean to hurt Papa. It was an accident. I didn't know I was magic. Can we go home now? I want to go home."

"I know it's not your fault, my jewel," Ymeir answered, stroking her daughter's head. She eased the child back and said to Bevakad, "This mark will slow the Iron Bane but not stop it. Magic is a curse."

Ymeir's face suddenly contorted in fierce anger. Her feline ears partially flattened on the top of her head, and the long white whiskers on her cheeks bristled. When she spoke again, her green eyes blazed hatred at Bevakad. "What do you think you're going to gain by unlocking your mind to magic? Nothing! You will gain nothing of value and lose everything!"

"I don't understand," Bevakad said, taking a step back, unsure what to do.

"No, you don't," Ymeir seethed. "You're a selfish fool. What does your family think of what you're doing? Throwing your life away, and for what?"

"You don't know my family," Bevakad retorted, finding courage in a flash of anger, remembering the contentious parting with his father.

"Yes, I do. I know that they're worried for you, of what you'll become. Reubei's too young for it now, but in time, she'll grow to despise people like you—those who had the choice to wield magic or not, whereas her fate was sealed when she was born. It's not fair."

Bevakad jerked back, shocked by Ymeir's words. He knew that the Archive trained both born mages and those who desired arcane abilities but always considered them to be one and the same. He wanted to be a mage and thought that those born into magic would welcome it. His naiveté being brought sharply into focus robbed him of any remaining confidence that he was prepared for this interview. "I," he started but wasn't sure what to say, and his voice trailed off.

"He's scared, Mama," Reubei said. "I feel it. He doesn't like you being angry at him."

Bevakad realized that the Sehenryu girl had scanned him with her empathic powers and could feel his uncertainty.

"Respect those who can't escape their fate," Ymeir said. "Go home." She turned her head away from Bevakad and whispered something into Reubei's ear. The Sehenryu girl cuddled into her mother.

Bevakad started when his handler grasped his elbow. "Your first interview is over," the mage said and pulled Bevakad away from the bench.

The prospect looked back only once as he was led into the Archive, still confused as to the purpose of this conversation with a family trying to weather a difficult situation and how it fit into his Archive assessment. While the interaction was puzzling at best, Bevakad got a sinking feeling that, given the brevity of the conversation, he might have just ended his chance at becoming a mage.

BEVAKAD LAGGED behind as he followed his handler back to the atrium. His legs felt heavy as he ascended a set of wide stairs to the Archive's second floor. Pausing at the top landing, he exhaled a long breath, his body sagging. His handler stopped a few steps away and watched him. When Bevakad looked the mage in the eye, he swore he saw a hint of disappointment. He opened his mouth to say something, anything, in his defence, but no words came out.

His handler shifted his head in an indication to follow and then left the landing, albeit now at a slower pace than before. Bevakad straightened his shoulders and tried to pull himself together before following. They turned down a long hallway, where he caught the faint scent of something burning. The tour of the Archive had been so fast and cursory during their first day of evaluation that it took him longer than it should to remember they were next to the alchemy workrooms. At one particular laboratory door, they stopped but did not enter.

"Are we going in?" Bevakad asked with an unsure look at his handler.

"The door is closed, so the interview with another prospect is not yet complete."

Bevakad nodded without really thinking and then took a step toward the middle of the wide hallway. Turning away from the door, he looked down the hall at a long series of display cases against the wall. Examining the one closest to where his handler waited, Bevakad read the small placard next to a resin ingot. He did not understand much of the technical information but was able to take away that he was looking at an example of complex alchemy.

He turned toward his handler and was about to ask about it when the alchemy lab door jerked open, and Veklin rushed out. The young prospect did not look up as he raced away toward the atrium stairwell. His handler burst out a moment later and gave chase. Bevakad only saw Veklin's expression for an instant, but there was no question that his face was scrunched up in the manner that only happened when on the verge of tears.

Bevakad's handler appeared unfazed by Veklin's exit and calmly entered the workroom. Following the mage, Bevakad was instantly assaulted on multiple fronts. The alchemy forge burned with white flame, and the small lab was much hotter than the hallway. Moreover, the shutters in the back of the room were closed, so the space had a stifling, claustrophobic feel despite being well-lit by regularly spaced glow spheres embedded in the ceiling. His nose prickled as the sharp smells of sulphur and chlorine commingled, and he scanned the shelves of the lab, looking for an open container. His search ended when he saw in the corner a large human male brooding over a small notebook. The mage looked up and scowled as Bevakad and his handler approached.

"Master Henrik, this is Bevakad, another prospect," the handler said.

Bevakad stood stiffly, not sure what to do.

Henrik snapped this book closed and glared at Bevakad. "We don't want you here," he declared forcefully.

Bevakad's eyes widened at such a blunt comment. While he had expected some hazing after being admitted to the Archive, to be spoken to in such a manner as a prospect was unexpected. He tried to recover and present a neutral expression as he replied, "That's not what I'm led to believe and not what is said about the Archive. The continent respects mages and those that wish to pursue arcane endeavours."

"They do now, after decades of careful work. But work driven by born mages, not pretenders like you."

"After my mind is opened to magic, I will be no different than a born mage."

"You *will* be different! Inferior!" Henrik bellowed. In a quieter but no less intense voice, he continued, "Out there in the world, you will be hated by anyone who holds on to the old superstitions of the continent's dark past. And if you think you'll find refuge inside Archive walls, you are wrong. You will forever be an outsider and never as powerful or accomplished as a born mage."

"So you say," Bevakad said in an attempt at defiance. "I will work to prove that a made mage is just as deserving of being here as someone born into magic."

"Do you think you're the first fool to try?" Henrik snapped. "Do you know how many made mages have sat on the Archive council? None! Zero, in the entire history of the Archive. Do you know how many made mages are principal agents here and run their own research programs?"

Bevakad shook his head.

"Two. Two out of twenty-five. Do you really think that you'll be better than ninety percent of all other made mages? You are an idiot, and the scores you have posted the past two days are behind the others and proof of it."

"Maybe my talents lie elsewhere," Bevakad replied in a weak voice.

Henrik stared at him with unblinking disdain. His tone shifted from ferocious to venomous. "I know who you are and where you come from."

Bevakad noticed his handler stand a bit straighter, a concerned look on his face.

"Your family's wealth won't buy you admittance," Henrik continued. "And while the mercer guild is currently powerful, your father's position in it won't grant you any favours here."

"I don't need my father's help. I can stand on my own," Bevakad retorted, finding courage in the flash of anger at the thought of his father. He paused before adding with genuine feeling, "I want to be here."

"Why?"

Bevakad had practised his answer, thinking about it the whole time he had travelled from his home in Sunrock all the way to the capital city of Yaboon. He answered, "To increase our knowledge of the arcane elements for the betterment of all people on the continent."

Henrik opened up his small book and flipped to a specific page. After scanning it, he looked up and replied, "That is a lie. You're here because your sister is dead."

Bevakad reeled as if hit by a physical bow. He suddenly felt unsteady and grabbed the laboratory table to support himself.

"Master Henrik!" Bevakad's handler said severely. "Discussion of a prospect's personal circumstances and family history is expressly forbidden during the evaluation. He is to be assessed on intellectual ability and temperament alone."

"A stipulation I never agreed with, and I made my stance very clear when asked to be an interviewer."

"Nevertheless," Bevakad's handler answered, "I will be reporting this breach of conduct to the council."

Henrik gave a dismissive wave of his hand to the handler, turned to glare at Bevakad, and then said, "No magic, no alchemy, will bring someone back from the dead. Such superstition was what led to the purges of those with magical talent back during the continent's dark times. You've run away from your family because you are a coward, but you will find no solace here. Go back to where you came from and beg forgiveness from your family for abandoning them. Save the Archive the trouble of wasting resources training what would undoubtedly be a talentless and unremarkable mage."

Bevakad's hands were balled into fists, but where he thought he should feel a fighter's rage, there was only a hollow feeling. After a too-long pause, his handler touched him on the shoulder and said, "Your second interview is over."

BEVAKAD'S HEAD SWAM, both from the oppressive chemical sauna of the alchemy lab and Master Henrik's completely unexpected personal attack, as his handler ushered him down the hallway. He gripped the stairway banister tightly and focused extra attention on his balance as he descended to the first level of the Archive. They entered into the atrium, and afternoon sunlight streamed through the domed skylights. His eyes hurt, and he squinted despite it not being very bright. "Can we wait a minute?" he asked his handler.

The mage's expression was neutral, and he appraised Bevakad briefly before giving a short nod. "You're not the only one struggling," the mage said after he and Bevakad sat on a short bench along a wall. The prospect looked up and followed his handler's gaze across the room and saw Hodragen. Her face was completely blanched of all colour, and she openly wore an expression of bewilderment and shock. Gone was the arrogant posturing and gregariousness that was the only thing he'd experienced from the woman.

"What happened to her?"

"These interviews affect people in different ways," his handler said. "This last one will be the worst for you."

"What do you mean?"

His handler grimaced and replied quickly, "Never mind." After standing, he looked down at Bevakad and said, "Come on. We have a bit of a walk."

Bevakad took his time getting up. He still felt unbalanced but thought he must look better than Hodragen, who hadn't moved. Close behind his handler, Bevakad left the atrium and walked down a series of corridors, then down two sets of stairs until they paused in front of a long tunnel. The stonework was well maintained, and while the air was cool, it was also dry. Looking ahead, he saw that the tunnel had regularly spaced glow spheres along the walls that illuminated the path forward with pale yellow light.

"Where are we going?" Bevakad asked.

"The Archive hospice."

"Why is it underground?"

"There is no need for sunlight, and we don't want the sounds to carry," his handler said as he peered down the tunnel.

"I don't understand."

"You will."

As he walked through the tunnel, Bevakad felt an oppressive weight pressing down on the back of his head and shoulders. His hands started sweating when an image of a collapsed passageway flashed in his mind. He turned back and saw that the base of the stairwell they had descended had been engulfed by an indistinct yellow glow emanating from the distant glow spheres.

Traversing the tunnel could not have taken more than a few minutes, but Bevakad felt worn out when he and his handler stopped before a large wooden door. The mage pounded twice on it and then waited. Taking much longer than expected, the door eased open, and a female Venhadar in simple clothes met them. She wore a yellow sash around her waist that Bevakad recognized as an identifier for Archive medical staff.

"He the last one?" she asked Bevakad's handler in a clipped voice.

After his handler nodded, the Archive nurse stepped aside and let them enter the hospice.

"What do you know about the Iron Bane?" the nurse asked Bevakad abruptly after closing the door.

"It's the chronic disease that afflicts all those who have tapped into their arcane energy," the prospect replied. "Something to do with the iron in your blood. It erodes your nerves and can destroy your senses."

"Not *can* destroy your senses," she corrected. "It *does*, unequivocally and irrevocably. Which is why we are all here." She swept her arm around the small receiving area. "It's time for you to look with clear eyes at your terrible fate."

The nurse opened a door at the back of the receiving area, and as Bevakad entered the cavernous room beyond, he could almost feel the nervous energy of the space. He saw long rows of treatment bays, all separated by white cloth dividers hung from tall wooden frames. There were several yellow-sashed nurses working quietly, some bent over narrow beds, others reviewing records near a treatment bay. There were glow spheres affixed at the top of frames that illuminated the surroundings, but when Bevakad looked up, the light was quickly swallowed by darkness, and he couldn't see the ceiling. While he didn't get the feeling of claustrophobia like when he was in the alchemy lab, Bevakad now got the eerie sense that this room was somehow disconnected from the outside world.

"Come with me," the nurse said and walked toward a row of treatment bays.

Bevakad followed and, as he neared the first hospice bed, tried to steel his nerves for what he would observe.

Looking down, it took a moment for him to absorb who he saw in the bed. Under a thin sheet lay the emaciated body of a human curled in a fetal position. He couldn't tell if the person was male or female because their hair was mere stubble, with waxy skin stretched across a gaunt face. It was a shocking visage, but what stopped his breath were the eyes. Wide open and staring, this mage's eyes had no irises, no whites, and no pupils. Entirely black orbs stared sightlessly at Bevakad, unblinking and glassy.

"She doesn't have much time left," the nurse murmured. "A pity, too. The Iron Bane consumed her quickly at a young age. One of the unlucky ones." After a pause, she added, "It's unnerving what the affliction does to a mage's eyes at the end. It makes them appear not of this world."

With what felt like agonizing slowness, Bevakad turned away from the bedridden mage. "Name," he croaked.

"What?"

With effort, Bevakad asked more clearly, "What is her name?"

The nurse gave him an askance look, confused by the unorthodox question. "This is Master Petra," she answered eventually.

Bevakad took a halting step toward the bed. Petra did not move and did not acknowledge his presence. Only the slightest movements of the sheet indicated she even breathed.

Driven by an impulse he did not understand, he reached out and gently touched her cold cheek. She did not react. "Petra," he whispered. "Master mage of the Yaboon Archive."

"She is a made mage, and before she lost the ability to communicate, her final wish was to serve as an example to prospects of the terrible price paid for arcane abilities. She asked for her bed to be moved here and be the first one that a prospect met. There was a time when she could still speak, still perceive where she was and what was happening to her. Now, her mind is gone, and we're just waiting for her body to give out."

"It's horrible, such suffering," Bevakad whispered.

"There is more to show you of suffering. Come with me."

As they walked to the next treatment bay, he asked, "When is a mage brought here?"

The nurse answered, "When they no longer can take care of themselves. Typically, once they lose their sense of touch, it is not long before their muscle control begins to deteriorate. Speaking becomes garbled and unintelligible, and if coupled with a loss of hearing or sight, then there isn't much that can be done for them. We try to provide calm and comfort here."

"It must be hard for you."

"It's a calling," she replied. With a quick look at his handler before returning her gaze to Bevakad, the nurse said, "The hard part is when people like you, mage prospects, come down here as part of your evaluation and somehow think that you'll escape this fate."

"The Iron Bane is inescapably lethal, yes?"

"Once accessed, the only way that your magic won't kill you is if you learn to stop the sands of time, and not even the dragons were able to achieve that feat before they started leaving this world."

They stopped at a bed where a Sehenryu male lay on his back, eyes closed and breathing heavily. His grey-furred hands were on top of the sheet that covered his body.

"Who is this?"

"Neulwai. An apprentice who never attained the rank of Master."

As before, Bevakad felt compelled to connect with the mage, as if touching them acknowledged their suffering and could somehow lessen it. He reached out and gently grasped the Sehenryu's hand.

Neulwai opened his eyes, yellow irises with vertical pupils. He turned his head slightly toward those assembled at the side of his bed and opened his mouth. For a moment, Bevakad could only hear the apprentice mage's ragged breaths, but then the Sehenryu made a terrible sound. It started quietly as a groan but then rose in pitch and volume until it became a screech. Bevakad heard similar sounds around him as other bedridden mages responded to the sound with their own tortured cries.

The nurse grabbed both Bevakad and his handler and pushed them toward the receiving area. "You need to leave now," she commanded. "We need to calm them all down quickly. This type of stress torments them terribly."

"Does this happen often?" Bevakad asked as he covered his ears. The shrieks oscillated until he could feel the vibrations in his chest.

"More often than I want," the nurse shouted as they entered the hospice receiving area. She jerked open the heavy door that led back to the Archive. As she shoved them out into the tunnel, the nurse added, "It's one of the reasons why we're so deep underground."

The nurse slammed the door, and the sound echoed down the tunnel. Standing stiffly, Bevakad felt his heart racing. He gave his handler a questioning look, unsure how he should process what just happened. The mage looked at Bevakad in silence for an uncomfortable amount of time before he told the prospect, "Your third interview is over."

———

AFTER THE THIRD INTERVIEW, Bevakad's handler brought him directly to the room he shared with the other prospects. He was not allowed to go to the dining hall that evening and a cold meal was instead brought to him. He was mentally drained from the interviews and mindlessly ate his food before laying down for a fitful night's rest. Hodragen and Veklin never returned to their shared quarters.

The next morning, Bevakad sat at the edge of his cot and stared blankly at the empty ones to his right. Two high bells had rung out from the nearby carillon tower not long before, and sunshine streamed through the small window positioned high up on the wall opposite the door. A sharp knock pulled Bevakad's attention from the empty cots, and he shook himself from his stupor as his handler entered the room.

"It's time for a decision to be made," the mage said with a neutral expression.

Bevakad nodded and eased off the cot. His balance still felt not quite right as he followed the mage to the atrium and then into a small room adjacent. Once inside, he saw a Venhadar male seated at a low table. He wore green alchemist robes that appeared to be slightly too small for his broad shoulders and thick arms. Appearing serious and formal but not unkind, he wordlessly gestured for Bevakad to sit in the empty chair at the table.

After Bevakad settled into the chair, his handler exited the room. The realization that he was alone with the Venhadar mage left Bevakad uneasy. His handler had been at his side for nearly the entire time of the evaluation, and his absence was conspicuous.

"Bevakad, so named by virtue of your guarded nature," the Venhadar mage began. "Your evaluation has come to its conclusion. As a representative of the Yaboon Archive, I have one final question for you." He paused before raising his chin and looking down his nose at the prospect. "With a clear mind and full understanding of the consequences, do you accept the responsibility of having your mind unlocked to magic?"

Bevakad's head twitched back as his whole body reacted in confusion to the question. "My handler . . ." He fumbled for the right words. "He—he has shared everything he witnessed about my interviews? I thought his report was to play a major role in the decision as to whether I would be allowed to be a mage."

"That is correct, as were the handlers' reports for the other two prospects."

"Veklin and Hodragen, what happened to them? Where are they?"

"They indicated their desire to no longer be considered prospects by the Archive."

"They quit?" Bevakad asked, not hiding his surprise.

The Venhadar mage placed both of his burly hands flat on the table and leaned forward. Locking eyes with Bevakad, he said, "The Archive finds you acceptable. Do you still wish to become a mage, to have your mind unlocked to magic, to change yourself in a manner that can never be undone?"

Bevakad had spent much of the night contemplating his interviews. Each was a compelling argument to abandon his pursuit of magical abilities. But then he looked deep within himself, into that black place where he buried all the emotions he didn't want to feel and the memories he didn't want to recall, and realized there was only one answer to the question.

"Yes."

THE GROVE

M. J. Kuhn

From the moment Allison heard Charles Mitchell had last been spotted near The Grove, she knew he was dead.

Still, the community went through all the motions, everyone who had cared for him clinging to the barest hint of hope, clinging to it the way a drowning soul clung to the rope trailing behind a ship. Denial had a firm hand on the wheel for Allison for days, weeks. But eventually, it started to lose its grip.

She had grown up down the road from the Mitchell family, just a few houses along Centennial Street. As kids, the land from the Sunoco station on Marshall to the Litchfield Health Clinic on Chicago Street had been her and Charles's domain. Her entire childhood was filled with sunny summer afternoons, pedalling second-hand bikes through the neighbourhoods to get slushies from the gas station and running through the woods behind the funeral home.

Now, those sun-drenched memories were dripping at the corners with viscous crimson.

Mr. and Mrs. Mitchell had been the ones to call the Litchfield PD the night he'd gone missing. The news reached Allison when she arrived home from a midnight run. She didn't go often, but there'd been a meteor shower that night, and she'd hoped to catch sight of a shooting star. She couldn't remember whether she had now because she'd jogged into the driveway to find her parents sitting anxiously on the porch, hands clasped together in worry. They'd been so relieved to see her that they hadn't even scolded her for tracking mud through the house. They had only shared the news in whispers that rustled like the dried flowers found in funeral homes and hospital rooms.

After that, Allison joined the Mitchells, alongside what felt like half the town, as they went out with search parties, scouring the sides of Highway 49 from Herring Road all the way to West Mosherville, hunting for one of his sneakers, his brand-new class ring, any sign that Charles Mitchell had gone anywhere but west along the St. Joseph River. Any sign that Charles Mitchell had survived his trip to The Grove.

But, of course, there was none.

No sign but some shoe prints and long, thick drag marks, too smeared and smudged to identify.

Charles Mitchell was seen near The Grove on the night of April 22. Then, he had promptly vanished—just like the others.

There had been fourteen in all since the '80s. Fourteen souls had wandered the marshy banks of the river and into The Grove and never returned. Of those fourteen souls, the most that had ever been recovered was a size-thirteen work boot belonging to one Otis Schumeyer, stuck in the mud just outside the property line.

There were no bodies, just fourteen empty caskets.

With no bodies and next to no evidence, the Litchfield PD had never made an arrest. But Allison knew what had happened to the missing fourteen—the missing fifteen, now, with Charles Mitchell among them. Everyone in Litchfield knew, truthfully. The missing men hadn't drowned in the river, run off with their girlfriends, or been kidnapped off the side of the road, as the police had theorized at various points over the past forty-odd years.

The people of Litchfield all knew these men had been murdered —what's more, they knew who the murderers were. Women gossiped about it in the small neighbourhood coffee houses, and children whispered the name in fearful tones over games of tag in the schoolyard. The high school halls had been abuzz with accusations in the days and weeks following Charles's disappearance.

After all, The Grove was not some unclaimed piece of wilderness in the middle of southern Michigan. It was a small plot of land on the slow-running side of the river, covered in willow trees and dirt trails and not much else. There was a mailbox at the edge of the property, rusted and held up with bungee cords to keep it from being knocked down yet again.

Stencilled on the side of the mailbox was the family name *BOWEN*.

Mr. and Mrs. Bowen had to be at least seventy years old, but they had hardly been spotted since the days before cell phones and laptops took over from payphones and overhead projectors. Their property, overgrown and poorly kept, was on the edge of the town's limits. The only structure on the land was a small, single-wide trailer that was just barely visible from the dirt road and the dented mailbox. Sometimes, the residents of Litchfield would whisper behind their palms that they hoped the old couple had finally died in their trailer.

But then someone would catch sight of one of them tottering out to the mailbox on a Tuesday afternoon, lips curled in the infamous smirk: the one from the old photos printed in the papers.

Or another boy would go missing.

And the people of Litchfield would know the Bowens' reign of terror was still going strong.

Days turned into weeks, then months. Spring rains gave way to the heat of summer. Prom and graduation and summer barbecues came and went, all with a massive, Charles Mitchell-shaped hole punched straight through the middle of them. At first, the halls of the high school had been subdued and solemn. The Litchfield High baseball team got crushed in every tournament without Charles on the mound, but over time, things went back to some sense of normal. Within a month of his disappearance, it seemed like everyone had forgotten Charles had ever existed.

Everyone but the Centennial Street gang, that was.

Allison and Charles's childhood exploring hadn't always been just the two of them. Often, they'd been joined by Derek Stanson and Curtis Wall. Since those young summer days, they'd all found a different path forward.

Derek was a star linebacker on the football team, earning a scholarship to play ball at Eastern the coming fall. Curtis, on the other hand, was only five-foot-seven, weighing in at about a hundred and forty pounds. He was no linebacker—but he *was* the best tenor at Litchfield High, starring in every school musical from sophomore year on. Allison, for her part, was somewhere in the middle, running for both the track and cross-country teams and finishing comfortably in the middle of the pack in nearly every race.

No matter how much their school personas drifted in different directions, the Centennial Street crew had always found their way back to one another.

Allison still had trouble believing Charles would never find his way back to them again.

A quarter past eight p.m. on July 16, Allison's feet pounded the sidewalk. It was crushingly hot out. Sweat dripped down the length of her spine and pooled in the band of her sports bra. She hadn't gotten a scholarship to a big-name school like Derek had. Instead, she planned to go to the college just a few miles north, commuting from home. Originally, she had planned to follow Charles to Michigan State, where he'd been set to play baseball. But now, the thought of going to East Lansing without him was more than she could bear. So instead, she'd tethered herself to Litchfield, wearing the small town like a weight manacled to her ankles.

She turned back onto Centennial Street, letting the pulsing synth music from her headphones fill her from head to toe as she put on a final burst of speed. She frowned as she approached her house, noticing a pair of figures on her front stoop. She pulled out one earbud and stopped the timer on her smartwatch as she approached them, one slight and dark, the other broad and blonde. The forms looked lonely without the tall, curly-haired form of Charles Mitchell perched between them.

"What's wrong?" she asked, still slightly out of breath as she walked up the driveway toward where Derek and Curtis sat, shaded by the front porch overhang.

"Did you see the press release?" asked Curtis.

Allison had followed the news these past months more closely than a jackass tailgating on the highway. There had been no news for days. Of course, the hour she decided to take her daily run would be when the Litchfield PD finally decided to open their stubborn lips.

Derek held his phone out. It was open to a news article in the Hillsdale Daily. She scanned the article, then looked up. "Still no suspects named?" Allison thrust the phone back to Derek in disgust. "What the fuck? It's been over three months. They found his shoe prints on their fucking property. What else do they need to pin those bastards?"

"They found prints that *could* have matched his on their property," Curtis corrected wanly. Allison opened her mouth to protest, but Curtis held up a hand. "I know, I know. But you know how cops are. It doesn't matter what we all know happened. They need to be able to prove it."

He was right, of course. But it did nothing to quell her rage. "Has anyone even looked into the Anderson tip yet?"

Derek shook his head, his sandy blond hair shifting with the motion. "There's a quote from Detective Reyes a few paragraphs down. Says the tip wasn't credible."

"Bullshit!"

True, Greg Anderson was a little weasel of a man known in town for breaking into unlocked cars, skipping out on bar tabs, and giving local women the creeps. Still, that didn't mean that his words should be discounted out of hand. The rumours had flooded through the streets of Litchfield like the waters of the St. Joseph in a too-rainy spring earlier this month. Anderson claimed he'd woken up after stumbling drunkenly into The Grove one night and found evidence that forty-odd years of LPD officers and detectives hadn't managed to dig up.

According to Anderson, there was a light at the centre of The

Grove, right in the middle of the oldest knot of willows on the property. According to all other accounts, the only structure on the entire Bowen property was the dilapidated trailer near the entrance. As far as Allison could tell, the only reason there would be a bright light half a mile away from the trailer was if there was another building out there, a second trailer or maybe a shack.

The kind of place where the Bowens could keep their victims.

Not only had the Litchfield police not found any evidence of the torture chamber Allison—and half of the town—now wholeheartedly believed was buried in the heart of The Grove, but it seemed they hadn't even bothered to get a warrant.

Allison slouched to the walkway, crossed her legs, and wound her earbud cord around her phone. "So, what now?"

"Nothing now," Curtis said. "Investigation is ongoing, but we all know how this story ends."

"Case'll be cold before the weather turns that way," Derek agreed.

Allison was quiet for a long moment. Her mind flitted to Charles Mitchell, to the way everything about him had been broad, from his shoulders to his grins. It was hard enough to accept that his awkwardly braying laugh would never slice over her eardrums again, but the idea of his photo fading in some half-forgotten file folder at the Litchfield PD without answers? That was not something she would ever accept. Charles Mitchell's mystery would be solved. They would bring him home to lay him to rest.

They would get justice.

She set her jaw, cocking her head to one side. "No, it won't."

"I'm all for optimism, Al, but—" Curtis started.

Allison waved a hand, cutting him off. "Greg Anderson isn't a credible witness." She pointed between the three of them with the hand still holding her earbud-wrapped phone. "We are."

"Allison, you can't be serious," Derek said.

"Dead serious." She held up her phone, wiggling it side to side. "We go there and get pictures of whatever Anderson saw in the middle of The Grove. Submit them anonymously to the police."

"And get murdered by the Bowens ourselves while we're there," Curtis said.

"Plenty of people have made it out of The Grove alive," Allison countered. "That group of shithead freshmen were just bragging about doing it last month."

A lot of the teens from Litchfield saw going to The Grove as a rite of passage. Allison and Charles had always talked about wanting to go once before they graduated. In the end, it seemed Charles had gone without her. She couldn't imagine why he wouldn't have at least asked her to come along. The draw of going to The Grove was showing off your bravery and creating a story. Going alone wouldn't have given Charles any of those things. Why had he gone without her?

"We are not shithead freshmen, though, Al," Derek said. He allowed a half-smile. "Anymore." Then he shook his head. "There has to be another way. Maybe we can raise some cash and put up a billboard on the—"

"What is a billboard going to do, Derek?" Allison asked. She pushed herself to her feet to begin pacing back and forth along the width of the stoop. Her brain was always quieter when her body was in motion, and her blood was pumping.

"Raise awareness to—"

"We don't need to raise awareness. Everyone is already aware of the case." Allison began to count on her fingers. "We're already aware of what happened, where it happened, and who did it." She stopped her pacing and turned to stare directly into Derek's grey-green eyes. "All we need is one piece of tangible evidence. Something that can tie all those things together. Then, we can bring Charlie home."

Derek swallowed. None of them had called Charles "Charlie" in years. Not since Allison had been the tallest in the group, and Derek's cheeks had still been plump with baby fat. But even that weapons-grade use of nostalgia didn't have the effect she'd hoped.

"Charlie isn't coming home, Allison. At least, not in any way that will make any kind of difference. We can't—"

"Allison's right," Curtis cut in.

Allison's eyes flicked to him. If she'd had to guess which of the gang would be the first to agree to charge into the likely site of their friend's murder and risk coming face-to-face with the most prolific serial killers in mid-Michigan, wholly unassisted by law enforcement, she wouldn't have put her money on Curtis.

"Law enforcement's hands are tied. Or maybe they've been bought off or something, I don't know. But something has been keeping them from nailing those bastards for like forty years," he went on. He put his hands on his bony knees, pushing himself up to stand, limbs unfurling slowly, catlike. "If we want answers, we have to get them ourselves."

Allison realized suddenly that her heart was hammering so rapidly that she could hear the percussion of it battering her eardrums, almost like the Litchfield High drumline tapping out their cadence: *rat-tat-tat-tat*. When she had voiced the idea alone, it had been a question. With Curtis's voice, with his slight form standing at her side, the suggestion became a battle cry. All that was left was for Derek to answer the call.

The linebacker sat on the porch for another few long seconds, the orangey light of the slowly setting sun bathing the right side of his face so completely that he was forced to squint as he finally looked up. He shook his head, his sandy blonde curls brushing his forehead. Then, he rose to stand, facing Allison and Curtis on the Mayards' front walkway.

"For the record, I still think you two are batshit crazy."

A half-smile crept up Allison's lips, and she turned, looking between the two boys she'd known since she was barely old enough to ride a tricycle. "Tonight?"

Curtis glanced at the sky, face caught between determination and dread. "Tonight," he echoed.

THE THREE FRIENDS trekked the width of Litchfield in utter silence, the only sounds the beat of three pairs of sneakers on pavement and the slow but steady traffic rumbling up and down Marshall Street. The sun followed a straight path down from its high palace in the sky, shining ahead of them like a beacon as they walked west on Homer Road, making their way toward the tangled wall of willows that made up The Grove.

The shadows were long by the time they reached the rusted mailbox. A shiver ran down Allison's spine as she looked at the name stencilled in fading yellow paint.

BOWEN.

Her spine tingled with fear and something else, almost akin to déjà vu. Allison was overcome by the strangest sensation: the feeling that she had been here before. That she had done this before. Maybe this voyage had simply been predestined by fate. She had always been meant to come here, to do this. Maybe the three of them had always been fated to finally stop the rampage of murders at The Grove.

"Right, so. Where did Anderson say he saw that light?" Derek asked. He looked calm, but he had his hands tucked into his pockets all the way up to the thumbs. Allison knew him well enough to know that was his tell: he was afraid.

Curtis's tell was nowhere near as subtle. Some of Derek's ruder friends had a nickname for Curtis—a nickname Derek threatened to beat out of their mouths any time he heard them use it—but Allison had to admit it wasn't wholly unfitting at the moment. They called him the ferret. As the thin boy's nose twitched and his head swivelled side to side, eyes almost glowing in his face as they stretched wide in the darkness, Allison could indeed picture a ferret.

Though she'd never say such a thing to Curtis, of course.

"Right in the centre of The Grove," Allison said, "at the bottom of the hill."

"Right," Curtis said, eyes twitching back and forth along the fence line surrounding The Grove. "So. Do we scale the fence or what?"

"No," Allison said. She felt like she was moving in a dream, her legs carrying her of their own accord. She strode off the Bowens' driveway, heading south through the brush along the fence line.

"Allison, where are you—" Derek started, but he stopped mid-sentence as Allison knelt to the ground and pulled aside a grouping of ferns. The fence was rent there, several links severed in a way that allowed a three-foot-wide section to be pushed aside like a jagged, makeshift door. "How did you know this was here?"

Allison frowned, looking down at her hand, still pushing aside the chain link. "I don't know," she said. "Must have overheard those asshole freshmen talking about getting in this way or something."

The explanation was perfectly logical—those freshmen had been talking about their trip to The Grove ad nauseam to anyone within earshot. She might have heard them bragging about how they'd found a way in. Maybe they'd even cut the fence themselves and boasted about it. But the explanation didn't fit. It felt like two puzzle pieces that almost matched but had to be forced into place instead of neatly snapping together.

Allison was overcome by that strange sensation again, the feeling that all of this had already happened: that she had been here before. She pushed the thought aside again, waving Curtis and Derek through the gap in the fence line and onto the Bowens' property.

The world inside The Grove was unsettlingly identical to the world outside of it. She could still hear the gentle hum of distant traffic and the soft buzzing of crickets in the shadows. The quiet breeze and the starlight filtering through the tree branches above gave no indication that they had witnessed all the awful occurrences that had taken place on this ground.

"All right, if we keep heading west, we should find that light Anderson was talking about, right?" Derek said. He tried his best to whisper, but his powerful tenor voice still carried on the breeze.

"Right." Allison stopped and turned in a circle. "Okay, wait. Which way is west, though?"

"Let me check." Curtis pulled his phone from his pocket, opened the Maps app, and held the device out in front of him like a dowsing rod. "All right, if we follow the flow of the river until it snakes off into this little crick here," he pointed at the snaking blue lines on his screen, "that should lead us right into the centre of The Grove."

Quiet stretched among them as they crunched through the underbrush, following the tiny blue dot on Curtis's phone screen as it made its way deeper and deeper into the heart of The Grove.

The St. Joseph snaked away from them, splitting into a tiny, trickling stream that continued to wend its way north and west. The sun had been swallowed by the horizon, leaving the willow branches around them bathed in nothing but the silvery light of the moon. Their surroundings should be beautiful, with the bowing branches swaying in the night breeze like the tendrils of hair escaping from Allison's ponytail to tickle her cheeks. Instead, the beauty of the place just felt profoundly sinister: a familiar tune played in a minor key.

"Wait, hold on."

Allison pulled herself from her thoughts at the sound of Curtis's voice. He had stopped in his tracks, shoes planted firmly on the mossy ground of a small clearing a few steps ahead of her. He was staring down at his phone, tapping the screen repeatedly.

"What the fuck is wrong with your phone?" Derek asked, stopping at Curtis's other shoulder.

The screen flickered, black lines snaking over the display, almost as though the glass had been shattered. The lines receded and spread anew twice more. Then, the display winked off altogether. The three of them peered down at their own faces, reflected in the now-dark screen.

Allison pulled her own phone from her pocket. Before she even tapped the button to wake the screen, she knew it wouldn't respond. The same sense of inexplicable certainty that led her to the hole in the fence flooded over her. She heard Derek fumbling with his phone beside her, but her eyes drifted up to the sky above.

The stars were out in force, twinkling coldly in a velvet sea of blackness unmarred by clouds. Allison's heart lodged itself firmly in her throat when she caught sight of the first beam of light flitting overhead—a meteor, a shooting star. It streaked through the sky like a flaming arrow, leaving a tail behind as it charged onward.

Like The Grove itself, it was a sight that should have been beautiful. But instead, it filled Allison with dread. She felt as though there was a part of her mind trapped behind a two-way mirror, screaming at her, but she could not hear the words.

The sense of spine-chilling déjà vu only heightened as she felt Curtis's fingers tightly grip her elbow and heard him whisper, "Allison. What the hell is that?"

The meteor shower went on overhead as Allison lowered her eyes to the clearing.

The three of them were no longer alone.

A shape lurked in the shadows on the far side of the clearing. "Bear" was the first word to come to mind, but she knew this was no bear. It was massive, somehow both solid and formless. The water of the crick burbled by, and the tangled willow branches waved in the breeze, seeming to pass right through the shadow in places where they should have tangled with the figure's odd, misshapen limbs.

For a moment, Allison saw two scenes superimposed over one another. She saw Derek and Curtis backing up slowly toward her as the monstrous shadow figure loomed closer, threatening to emerge from the cover of the central knot of willows in The Grove. At the same time, she saw Charles, useless phone in hand, his feet anchored to the earth just a few paces from where Derek now stood. The version of Allison trapped inside her skull was screaming and pounding on the walls of her intangible prison now. She still couldn't understand what she was seeing, but something primal clicked into place.

"We need to run," Allison said. She reached forward, grabbing Derek and Curtis by the backs of their shirts. "We need to run right fucking now."

Just as she said it, the shadowy figure lurched out of the cover of the dangling willow branches and into the clearing. All thoughts of running vanished like a puff of smoke in the wind. Allison's brain filled with slack-jawed stillness and a faint shriek akin to a kettle screaming on the stovetop.

The monster stood at least twelve feet tall, its form hunched and twisted. It moved forward by dragging its clawed limbs through the moss and the mud, leaving deep scores in the earth. Its head was eyeless and disjointed, cocking back and forth as it lurched toward them.

Allison might have tried to convince herself she was hallucinating had her brain not been whispering another secret to her, hissing in her ear that not only was this creature real . . . but that she had seen it before.

She had fled from this same beast the night Charles Mitchell vanished.

The night he died, pulled apart at the seams by the tentacle-like protrusions that propelled the shadow-beast through the muck and the underbrush.

She could see it now, flashing before her eyes as the beast dragged itself closer and closer, its maw wide, revealing multiple rows of pointed, jet-black teeth dripping with a liquid dark as ink and as enigmatic as shadow itself.

The beast was so close she could have reached out a hand to touch it when something whizzed out from the treeline, crashing into Derek at full speed. Derek could normally take a hit better than most, but he toppled like a felled tree, falling to the mossy earth just as one of the beast's oddly formless tentacles pulled itself from the dirt and slashed toward his neck. The tentacle missed, but only just.

"This way! Quickly, quickly!" said an unfamiliar voice.

Allison blinked. Then blinked again, looking at the tackler. It was Mr. Bowen. He couldn't weigh more than ninety-five pounds, and his skin was even more sallow and wrinkled than it had appeared in the last photos Allison had seen of the man in the newspaper.

He put all his weight into his heels, dragging Derek forcefully to his feet, then began to run east out of the clearing and toward the next knot of willows swaying in the charged night. Allison didn't like the idea of trusting one of the infamous Bowens to lead her to safety. However, between Mr. Bowen and the Lovecraftian horror surging through the trees, she'd take her chances against the ninety-five-pound elderly man.

She grabbed Curtis by the shirtsleeve and pulled him hard, dragging him in her wake as she followed Mr. Bowen and Derek back into the dark, tangled maze of The Grove.

Allison's ears filled with the sound of blood charging past her eardrums and the constant sucking sound of the creature's pursuit. Curtis was running under his own power now, but Allison kept a tight grip on his sleeve all the same. She wouldn't lose another friend in these trees.

Mr. Bowen led them along a winding path through the forest until Allison caught sight of something near the trunk of a particularly gnarled tree. A small, pallid face peered up from below the ground: Mrs. Bowen. One wrinkled, wasted arm propped a rusted storm cellar door above her head while the other waved frantically. Her eyes were wide as dinner plates, locked on something just over Allison's shoulder.

She did not have to turn to guess what that "something" was.

"Get this kid in!" Mr. Bowen shouted, shoving Derek in front of him. Then he turned, waving Allison and Curtis past him. Allison didn't even stop to think before plunging past Mrs. Bowen and into the darkness of whatever lay beyond that rusted door.

Even if this was the Bowens' famed torture chamber, it had to be better than the horrors outside.

Mr. Bowen entered last, and together, the two aging hermits pulled the cellar door shut, tugging on the handles with all their tiny strength just as the creature barrelled into it. Allison could hear its strange tentacles running over the outside of the door, tugging and prying.

"We're all going to die," Curtis said. His voice was at least an octave higher than normal, and his nose twitched so much that Allison was concerned it might leap off his face altogether.

But she couldn't argue with his assessment. The rusted latch on the cellar door might be sufficient to keep a tornado from blowing them away, but there was no chance it was a match for the beast it needed to keep at bay tonight. Eventually, the eldritch creature would break through their defences, and their remains would be splashed across The Grove for the scavengers to find.

Bowen

"We're not all going to die," said Mrs. Bowen. Her voice was somewhere between a wheeze and a whistle, though Allison couldn't tell if that was from the effort of bracing the door or if it was that way naturally.

"How do you figure?" Curtis asked, a thread of hope snaking its way through the dread in his voice.

Allison finally gained the strength to rise to her feet and grab one of the handles, helping their elderly, unexpected hosts hold the rusted slab of metal against the might of the horror outside.

"Because the Creatures have a specific appetite," Mr. Bowen said. He shared a look with his wife, then looked slowly between Allison and Curtis. "They skip the little ones."

Allison and Curtis turned to Derek in unison. He was whey-faced on the moist earth floor of the cellar, sitting with his head sagging toward his knees. *They skip the little ones.* Allison's mind flitted through stories, news clippings, legends, and police reports. The victims of The Grove were always men. Large men. Athletes and farmers and tradesmen. It was part of the mystery of The Grove's murders—the argument that had always left Allison feeling unsure how—*or if?*—the frail, little Bowens were behind the murders at all.

They skip the little ones.

The beast had dragged itself straight toward Derek. Just as it had surely pulled itself, twitching and slavering, through the mud to make a beeline for Charles a few months before.

They skip the little ones.

At that moment, something in the sentence caught Allison's ear. She looked up at Mr. Bowen, his wrinkled face just inches from her in the darkness of the cellar.

"What do you mean *they*?"

The shadow-beast was not alone.

ALLISON'S ARMS shook with every blow as the creature struggled to breach their meagre defences over and over again. She pictured its gangling tentacles slapping and prying at the exterior of the rusted storm cellar door, then abruptly pushed the thought away. The idea of this preternatural beast of prey scratching, clawing, and gnashing its obsidian teeth mere inches from the top of her head was too much for her mind to bear.

"It's not going to hold, Harold," Mrs. Bowen grunted.

"I know," Mr. Bowen breathed back, his voice barely audible in the gloom. He didn't share the terror coursing through every inch of Allison's body. Instead, he just looked weary.

Allison shrieked in alarm as the door wrenched upward with renewed vigour. She saw starlight and a misshapen, swollen mass of writhing flesh before a large hand slipped into the handle beside her fingers and yanked downward. The rusted metal slammed back into place with a *gong,* and Allison looked over her shoulder to find Derek back on his feet.

She could barely see him in the glow of the camp light in the storm cellar, but she could tell his eyes still had the same haunted, glassy look they'd had when they first plunged into the darkness. There was a hardness around the edges, though, an understanding that now was not the time to fall to pieces.

Curtis's skinny arms followed soon after Derek's, grabbing hold of the handle the Bowens were still supporting. Mr. Bowen released his grip and felt around in the darkness until he pulled up a rattling length of thick iron chain. Ten minutes ago, Allison would never have believed that she would feel relieved to see the infamous Mr. Bowen brandishing a rusted chain in a dark underground cellar.

He wound the length deftly around the handles, then latched it firmly with a padlock. Allison's eyes flicked to her feet, where she saw half a dozen broken links and shattered padlocks lying, dust-coated, on the dank ground. The implication was deafening. The chain may hold the beast for a moment . . . but it would not be enough to hold it forever.

They needed to be prepared when that inevitability came to pass.

Allison peered around in the darkness, searching for a weapon, though she could not imagine what type of weapon might be forceful enough to knock back this demon-made-flesh. But Mrs. Bowen seemed to have other plans. She grabbed the camp light from its perch on a stack of crates that had seen far better days, holding it up like Prometheus offering humanity the first flaming torch.

"This way," she said, motioning toward the far side of the storm cellar. Her voice still had the same wheezy quality Allison had assumed must have been due to the effort of holding back the creature of Satan still battering at the chained door above them.

She was surprisingly spry. Her husband ushered Allison, Derek, and Curtis to follow, moving them away from the rattling and sucking noises coming from the entryway behind them. When they reached the corner, Allison saw a second rusted door. Mrs. Bowen's wiry arms strained to pull it open, revealing a long, dripping tunnel beyond.

"How many more of those things are there?" Curtis asked. His voice came out a choked whisper, barely audible, swallowed by the moist earth of the tunnel surrounding them.

Mr. Bowen's face was a tangle of weathered skin, wrinkles, and scars as he turned to face them in the low light. "They always come in pairs. And only during—"

"Meteor showers," Allison said faintly.

She had no idea how she knew that, but the knowledge was crystal clear, just like the memory of the gap in the fence and the images of Charles Mitchell facing down one of the Creatures in the same clearing where Derek had nearly been devoured mere minutes earlier.

Curtis and Derek stared at Allison as though she had grown a second head, but Mr. Bowen did not look surprised at her interruption. He simply nodded. "Meteor showers, yes. The Way does not open every night of the shower, but on peak nights, a pair will always muscle their way through."

"The way?" Derek repeated dimly. "What way?"

"*The* Way," Mr. Bowen repeated. He put unmistakable gravitas on the word, as one might say, *The Father* when referring to God.

"A gateway," Mrs. Bowen said over her shoulder.

"A gateway to where?" Curtis asked.

"Nowhere I want to fucking go," Derek said.

"It's not where it's a gateway *to* as much as where it's a gateway *from*," Mr. Bowen mused. "But we don't know the answer. All we know is the pattern. They come in pairs. They come during the meteor showers. And they skip the—"

"They skip the little ones, got it," Derek repeated. He was regaining some of his usual humour, self-preservation instincts wrestling control of his brain away from panic and terror at last.

"Where does this tunnel go?" Curtis asked, squinting as he tried to peer past Mrs. Bowen in the darkness.

"It'll get us nearly to the property line," Mrs. Bowen said. "Once you get past the fence line, the Creatures will stop hunting you." She looked over her shoulder, her red-rimmed eyes boring into Allison's. "But you may find . . . other complications."

Other complications. A chill ran down Allison's spine. She felt the press of that imprisoned, screaming consciousness on the back of her mind again. The part of her that seemed to know altogether too much about The Grove.

"Do those other complications involve abominations beyond our worst nightmares?" Derek asked pointedly.

Mr. Bowen's lips curled into the trademark smirk he wore in the photo of him that had been printed in the Hillsdale Daily at least half a dozen times in Allison's lifetime. The smirk that had once made her skin crawl now simply looked like a tired expression of amusement from a man who had seen far too much for far too long.

"They do not."

"Then I'll take my chances with the fence line," Derek said. He looked between Curtis and Allison. "You guys?"

"Yep," Curtis agreed. "I'm with Der'."

Allison shared one last look with Mrs. Bowen, a one-sided expression that Allison knew in her soul should have been filled with mutual understanding. "Right," she said. "We need to get Derek out of here."

A few moments later, they reached the far end of the tunnel. It, too, sported a pair of rusted, aged doors positioned to open straight up to the night sky above them. This set was already chained and padlocked, although Allison was relieved to see the bindings didn't seem necessary here. She could still hear the distant rattle of metal on metal coming from the far side of the tunnel. But these doors were as silent and still as a crypt.

Mr. Bowen fished in his pocket, pulling out a key and fitting it into the padlock. The *click* of the lock releasing was thunderous. Momentous. It had an odd finality to it. Though perhaps that was a good thing—Allison wanted nothing more than for this night to be over and done with.

"When you emerge, you'll want to head left toward the sound of running water," Mr. Bowen said. "Once you see the river, make a right. The fence line won't be far."

"What about you guys?" Curtis asked. "Are you coming?"

The Bowens exchanged a glance. Then Mr. Bowen said, "Someone has to mind The Way."

Curtis frowned and opened his mouth to ask another question. At that moment, the sound of splintering metal and crashing iron rattled through the tunnel from the far end, followed by the distant sounds of sucking and thrumming.

The creature had broken through the barrier on the far side of the shelter.

It was coming for them.

"Quick, move!" Allison shouted. She shoved Derek in front of her up the rusted ladder. Mrs. Bowen yanked the chains free and thrust the doors wide. Moonlight flooded over them, spilling from the sky and through the open doorway like milk from an overturned saucer.

Derek pulled himself from the tunnel first, Curtis hot on his heels. Mr. and Mrs. Bowen waved Allison up next.

"We'll chain the door behind you," Mr. Bowen said, holding up the padlock as if in proof. "The Creatures never harm us. But it will not stop chasing you. It will go back the way it came and come at you from aboveground, but at least that will slow it down."

"Allison, what the *fuck* is the hold-up?" Curtis called down.

Allison gave the Bowens one last look, mounting the ladder.

"We'll tell everyone the truth." She shook her head. Impossible—there was no way anyone would believe the truth. "We'll tell them you're not guilty, at least. That we've seen proof that—"

"*Allison!*"

Allison's eyes flicked down the tunnel, and she caught sight of the hulking form of the creature lurching through the moist darkness. Its tentacles slithered along the walls, feeling the way forward for its fleshy, unseeing face.

They skip the little ones.

She didn't trust that enough to test it for herself. She pulled herself up the ladder at breakneck speed, spilling out into the starlit Grove an instant before the Bowens pulled the rusted doors back down with a *crash*, sealing the entrance and buying them a few seconds to sprint for the fence line.

Curtis seized her by one arm, and Derek grabbed the other. The boys half-dragged her through the underbrush toward the sound of running water. Allison could see the sparkle of moonlight on the ripples of the St. Thomas River. They were moments from safety—seconds from escaping the confines of The Grove and stepping back into a blissfully normal summer night in Litchfield.

Then, Allison heard the wet, sucking sound of tentacles on the muddy earth.

They always come in pairs.

The Bowens had trapped one of the Creatures in the tunnel beneath the earth. The second creature was blocking their path forward. It surged up from the riverbed, its gangly limbs seeking, its mouth gaping, its jet-black teeth saturated with inky saliva.

"Derek!" she shouted. He was only a few steps away from the thing, leading the way as the three of them pelted for the edge of The Grove. He was looking toward the glint of the fence in the distance. He hadn't seen the beast yet.

She dove, aiming to knock him out of the tentacles' path as Mr. Bowen had before. But she was too far away. She crashed down heavily in the mud, hands outstretched, inches from Derek's ankles.

Curtis was closer. He dove for Derek in the same instant, catching him around the waist in a perfect tackle.

In any other context, Derek would have been proud.

But Derek was on high alert now, no longer distracted as he had been when Mr. Bowen had knocked him down in the clearing. Curtis's skinny arms wrapped around his waist barely knocked him off balance for half a stride. Instead of collapsing to the mossy earth, he simply looked down, his face caught between surprise and confusion as Curtis lost his grip and slipped to the ground at his feet.

That expression was the last one ever to grace Derek Stanson's face.

One of the creature's tentacles caught Derek around the throat. Another wrapped around his ankles, binding them together.

"No!" Allison flailed forward, though she knew there was nothing she could do. The creature reared up, chittering victoriously as it wrenched its tentacles apart, pulling one toward the sky and the other down toward the earth.

Allison squeezed her eyes shut. She didn't see it, but the image was burned on the insides of her eyelids all the same: Derek's body tearing like wet clay, bones cracking and breaking apart as the beast pulled him apart at the middle.

When she opened her eyes, Derek and the creature were both gone. All they had left behind was dragging tentacle marks in the mud, and a few splatters of blood clinging to the fern leaves. Curtis was an arm-length away, face-down in the mud. His body was shaking, racked with sobs. In the distance, Allison heard unearthly shrieks. They harmonized together, forming an unholy composition of blood and victory.

The Creatures had gotten what they came for.

She dragged Curtis to his feet and the pair of them stumbled the last few yards to the chain-link fence separating The Grove from the world beyond. They clambered over the top, heedless of the way the barbed wire tugged at their clothes and their hair and tore their flesh. With tears streaking the grime covering their cheeks, they plunged out of the land of nightmares and back into reality.

ABRUPTLY, Allison found herself standing by the side of Homer Road. She blinked.

Curtis was standing next to her.

"Why are you covered in mud?"

Curtis turned. His eyes were nearly as blank as her brain felt. He frowned and blinked hard, then looked her up and down. "Why are *you* covered in mud?"

She looked down. She *was* covered in mud. And the palms of her hands, her forearms, and her shins all felt like they were on fire. They were covered in small cuts, like the ones that might be made by a razor blade.

It was dark. Very dark. It must be the middle of the night. She pulled her phone from her pocket and powered on the screen. The display jumped for a moment, then settled.

1:47 AM

What was she doing out on the side of the road at nearly two o'clock in the morning?

"Allison?" said a voice. Her mother. She blinked again, looking up to see her mom and dad sprinting across Homer. They were flanked by four other people. Curtis's mom and dad were there as well. And Charles's father. Derek's mom brought up the rear.

Allison blinked again. *Where's Derek? Shouldn't he be here?*

Why did she feel like he should be here?

"What happened to you two? Where were you?" Curtis's mom shouted. She grabbed Curtis as soon as she reached them, pulling his muddy head right to her chest without sparing a thought for the cleanliness of her pyjama top.

Allison opened her mouth, then shut it again. She didn't have an answer.

She let herself get wrapped up in a tangle of limbs between her mother and father. "Did you guys go to The Grove?" her dad asked.

The Grove.

That must be it. She must have wanted to go to The Grove. To go there to look for Charles—to confront the Bowens, to look into the Anderson tip and do the work the Litchfield PD refused to. Their parents must have guessed they would do this; had come to look for them when they realized they weren't in their beds. Before she knew it, she was nodding. That's why they were muddy. Maybe they had tried to scale the fence—had the barbed wire cut her hands and shins?

Why couldn't she remember?

"And . . . Derek?" Mrs. Stanson asked.

Allison looked at her, narrowing her eyes, thinking hard, trying to remember. Her mind was frustratingly blank, blurry. Like she was trying to recall a half-forgotten dream.

"Derek must have gotten past the fence. And we . . . couldn't?" Curtis didn't sound certain, either. But it was the only plausible explanation.

Allison nodded dumbly. "We haven't seen Derek since . . ." She met Curtis's eyes and saw him struggling to remember as well.

Finally, she shook her head and said that the only thing she could think of that made sense.

"I think Derek has gone missing in The Grove."

COMING OF AGE

Edo van Belkom

This story originally appeared in Star Colonies *(DAW Books),*
edited by Martin H. Greenberg and John Helfers.

J ack Murray was awakened from a light sleep by the sound of something heavy thumping onto the floor. "William," he called.

"Yeah, Dad. It's me."

Jack nodded slightly. Of course, it was William. Who else would it be?

"I just went over to Peckham Farm to see if I could find any more solar panels."

"What do we need with more solar panels?" asked Jack, shifting in his chair and feeling his bones ache with stiffness. "We've already got six we're not using."

"I know. I know . . . I was going to try and get them all hooked up and working."

"Why? We have more electricity than we can use now."

"But if we have to keep a light on through the night or run a machine during off hours, the batteries won't last long."

Jack sighed, understanding the undercurrent of what his son was saying all too well. At last, Jack nodded. "Did you find any panels?"

"No. But I did find a battery." He lifted the battery off the floor, barely able to lift it higher than his waist.

Watching his son struggle with the weight, Jack wondered how he'd managed to carry it all the way back from Peckham Farm. He'd been wondering about such things for some time now. Ever since his stroke, he'd had no other choice but to sit and think, to take stock of his life and a long, hard look at the future.

Well, the future hadn't looked very promising for years.

And now it was absolutely terrifying.

William dragged the battery through the house and out the back door. Jack could hear the thing clunk down the wooden steps, then only silence as it was pulled across the sandy ground to the shed where the rest of the generators, pumps, and batteries were housed.

The boy would work there for hours, jury-rigging the panels and batteries together so he could squeeze a few more watts of power out of the day. That would leave Jack alone in the house for a while with nothing to do but sit and think.

His first thought was of the boy. Strange thing to call your twenty-five-year-old son, but that's what he was—a boy.

Always had been. Always would be.

They'd come to Effette IV forty years earlier, eighty-seven bright-eyed settlers eager to establish a new world better than the one they'd left behind.

All went well in the early years as the few dozen families carved out a life for themselves in the planet's rich and untamed wilderness. With a little planting and a lot of hard work, the land proved to be as bountiful as Earth's had once been. Life soon became peaceful and perfect, everything they dreamed it could be.

But it was all too good to last.

About fifteen years after their arrival, the settlers noticed that the development of their children's secondary sex characteristics seemed a bit slow. Those few children born on the ship prior to landing managed to squeak through puberty, but those born on Effette IV after the landing were not maturing into adulthood. They'd all ended up like William, grown to the size of a man but without any of the characteristics that distinguished a man from a boy. His Adam's apple had never appeared; he was without facial hair; his body never gained muscle mass, and his voice had remained at a high pitch. Similar problems were experienced by the girls, whose bodies failed to develop breasts or fill out in any other appreciable way.

The settlers soon realized that the children were also failing to develop primary sex characteristics such as testes and ovaries, which were, of course, necessary for reproduction.

So what was the problem?

On Effette IV, it was a question for the ages.

Jack and the other settlers had spent nearly thirty years testing their food, water, sunlight and air but had never found an answer. In time, two main theories were postulated. One suggested that Effette IV had some element or chemical unknown to human science that inhibited human sexual development. The other theory suggested that Effette IV lacked some element or chemical unknown to human science that fostered human sexual development.

Whatever the reason, the result was the same—a colony doomed to die out a generation after landing on their new world. The settlers had tried reassembling the generation ship they'd arrived in, but over the years, it had been thoroughly cannibalized, with many of the parts drastically modified to suit new applications. They also began broadcasting distress calls, but since Effette IV had been selected for colonization because it was so far removed from other colonized planets, there was little chance anyone would receive the message, let alone reach Effette IV before the entire colony died out.

Jack took a deep breath and let out a long sigh. It wasn't the way he'd envisioned his final days. He was supposed to have many children and dozens of grandchildren, all of whom would share the burden of caring for his aged body and mind. Instead, there was only . . .

For a few terrifying moments, he forgot the boy's name, and then he closed his eyes and concentrated, travelling back through the years.

Billy.

The name seemed to come to him as if part of a song about youth and innocence. Yes, Billy was his name, but he didn't like to be called that anymore. It was William now. It sounded more mature, he felt, more grown-up.

Well, if not the boy, then at least his name.

Jack retraced his thoughts. What had he been thinking about before stumbling over the boy's name? Ah, yes, instead of a large, close-knit family to support him in his waning years, there was only William to look after him, a man in the body of a boy, barely able to look after himself.

But things could change, thought Jack as he drifted off to sleep. *Things would change . . .*

JACK AWOKE SOMETIME LATER, wondering if he'd slept the day away or just had a catnap. A glance at the clock told him it had only been twenty minutes, but it felt as if he'd been asleep for days. "William?" he called.

No answer.

Probably still in the shed. Jack rolled his body forward, grabbed his cane with his right hand, and slowly lifted himself to his feet. Standing was difficult. His hips and knees were always stiff and sore these days, and the stroke had made most of his left side useless. But despite the debilitation, Jack was determined to carry on as if nothing had changed.

At least for a little while longer.

He shuffled his way to the back door, stopping in front of the screen rather than opening it. William would be able to hear him through it easily enough. "How you making out?"

There was a sound of metal striking metal, then silence. "Eh?" came William's reply.

Jack strained to speak louder. "How's it coming?"

"I've got all the panels relayed together," William said from within the shed. "And I think the battery's still got a charge."

Jack nodded. The boy was good with mechanical things. At least the farm wouldn't fall into disrepair. "What do you want for supper?" asked Jack.

The banging noises that had started again suddenly stopped, and William appeared in the doorway to the shed. "I'll make supper."

"Never mind," said Jack, trying to wave his limp left hand. "I'll get it ready."

"No," said William. He picked up a rag and began wiping his hands on it as he started across the yard. "I don't mind doing it." He opened the screen door and squeezed past Jack into the kitchen. "Besides, I was just about done out there. I can finish up in the morning, which will give me plenty of daylight to test it out."

Jack watched as William began moving about the kitchen, placing pots on the stove and gathering the rest of what he needed on the counter. It looked like it was going to be leftover stew again. Jack hated stew, but it was the only thing that made the meat of the dog-sized rodents native to Effette IV palatable. The settlers had brought their own livestock with them, but those animals had all died out within a couple of generations. What Jack wouldn't give to eat a steak with his potatoes or bacon with his eggs. All they had was stew. It was nutritious enough, and it was all William seemed to have the time or the will to make for them since it could be left unattended for hours while it cooked on the stove. That, and the leftovers seemed to last forever.

"Here," said William, noticing Jack was still standing by the door. "Let me help you back into the living room." He put a hand on Jack's shoulder and took firm hold of his right arm. "I'll call you when it's ready," he said.

Jack was perfectly capable of making it to the living room by himself, but he was glad for the help of his son. It made the steps easier to take, and getting seated in the chair wouldn't be so painful.

"There," said William. "I'll be back in ten minutes to get you."

Jack nodded, tried to smile.

But inside, he wept.

JACK HAD OFTEN WONDERED what death might be like, trying to picture the peace and stillness of it in his mind. Death. It almost sounded nice, or at least better than what his life had become. Yet he still feared it, although the fear wasn't for himself as much as for William.

What would become of the boy after he was dead? What was William to do after he'd found the body? Certainly, he wouldn't be able to lift it. He might be able to drag it out of the house and into the yard, but that didn't seem right to Jack.

And, truth be told, Jack didn't want William to find him dead. Although it was almost more than two years ago, Jack vividly remembered the shock of finding his wife Margaret's body, bent, broken and soiled as it lay splayed across the landing at the bottom of the stairs. Such an undignified end to such a courageous life. *No*, thought Jack. *I won't let that happen to me.*

Even worse, what if Jack didn't die? What if, instead of a neat and clean heart attack, he suffered another stroke and lingered on for another dozen years? Would William dutifully clean, feed, and care for him, or would the boy be tormented by thoughts of putting a knife through his father's chest just to be done with it?

Jack preferred not to make that an option for the boy.

"Dad," said William, standing at the entrance to the kitchen. "Supper's ready."

"I'll be there in a minute."

"Do you want some help?"

"No." Jack couldn't keep the frustration from his voice.

"Okay, Dad."

WILLIAM SAT DIRECTLY in the chair across the table from his father. While they'd dispensed with saying grace and giving thanks many years ago, William still waited for his father to begin the meal.

"Go ahead, you don't have to wait for me," Jack said. "I won't always be around to go first, you know."

"I know. You've told me enough times."

"Then get started, will you?" Jack said.

"Are you all right, Dad? Is something wrong?"

Jack was about to tell his son he was dying but realized he would have to explain how he was dying mostly on the inside. He'd never be able to find the words. So instead, he took a deep breath and said, "I'm getting old, that's all."

"Not to me, you're not," said William, smiling bravely.

"You're a good boy, William. You don't deserve this." Jack didn't make any special gesture to let his son know that by "this," he meant coming to Effette IV and the whole sorry mess they'd made of the lives, but the boy knew.

"Nobody deserves this," said William.

They said nothing for several long moments.

"How's the food?" Jack asked. Anything to dispense with the silence.

"It's stew, you know."

"Yes," Jack nodded. "I know."

THE SHADOWS LENGTHENED and vanished as the sun set on Effette IV and darkness nestled in for another long night. The house was secured, and father and son sat quietly in the front room reading. In addition to the battery, William had found a few paperbacks at Peckham Farm and had busied himself with the new reading material shortly after sundown.

Jack had a collection of poetry on his lap, a book published on the ship some two generations back. He'd read the book a dozen times before but found that tonight, the language that had so often intrigued him could barely hold his interest. He glanced from the pages to his watch every few minutes, silently cursing the minute hand for moving so slowly.

"What do you think, William, almost time for bed?" he said after two hours had passed.

"I'm not that tired. I might stay up for a little while longer and see if I like this book as much the second time through."

"That good, huh?"

"Yeah."

"Well, I'm going to bed. I need to rest for tomorrow."

"Why? What's so big about tomorrow?"

Jack was surprised that he'd allow himself to be so careless with his words. He wondered what was the right thing to say, the right way to tell his son of his plans, but he knew it would never come to him. He simply shrugged his shoulders. "Nothing, I guess. Just another day." He struggled to get out of his chair.

"Maybe I'll go to bed too," said William, moving to his father's side and helping him to his feet.

They went upstairs together, then retired to their bedrooms alone.

* * *

JACK HAD FINISHED his preparations and was ready to go, but somehow, it didn't feel right. There was one more thing that he had to do.

He took his cane, went down the hall to William's room, and cracked the door open slightly. William had already dozed off and was sleeping soundly on the bed. Jack hesitated in the doorway for several moments, gathering his strength before entering. He tried to step lightly on the wooden floor, but the boards still moaned and creaked beneath his feet.

"Billy . . ." Jack said, placing his bony hand on the bed to stop it from shaking. "William," he corrected himself. "William."

William slowly opened his eyes.

"I just wanted to say goodnight to you," Jack said, his voice trembling.

"Good night, Dad," William said sleepily.

Jack's breath was rapid and shallow.

"Are you okay, Dad?"

"Of course, I'm okay. Nothing wrong with a father saying goodnight to his son if he wants, is there?"

"No. I guess not," William answered. He was more awake now. Perhaps even aware of what was happening.

Jack reached out and held his son. William returned the hug with both arms.

"I want to tell you that I love you, son. I haven't told you that in a while."

"I know that, Dad. And I love you too."

Jack held his son as tightly as his feeble arms would allow.

William said nothing, pressing his lips together in a thin white line.

Jack rose up off the bed, shuffled out of the bedroom, and closed the door gently behind him. Outside, he leaned against the wall and struggled to catch his breath. His heart was pounding out a painful, irregular beat, and there was a pain slicing through his arm again.

THE MORNING SUN cut through the thinly curtained windows of William's bedroom in dull beams of dusty sunlight. Noticing the light in his eyes, William quickly jumped from the bed and went down the hall to check his father's room.

The room was empty.

The bed was made.

From downstairs, he heard the faint sound of the front door creaking shut. William's first inclination was to race down the stairs and out into the yard, but he decided against it. It would steal away what little of his father's dignity was left.

So, instead, William walked slowly back to his bedroom, climbed up onto the bed, and looked out the window at the road that led away from the house.

In the distance, he could see the white-topped figure of his father hobbling down the road. There was a pack on his back and a cane in his right hand.

"Goodbye, Dad," William said.

There was a brave smile on his face. But inside, he wept.

NEVER AGAIN THE SAME

L. Jagi Lamplighter

Mist was rising about the old house. Its gabled peaks, overgrown with moss, jutted out of the swirling gloom. Behind them, the tall oaks and maples were barely visible.

Patrick stepped slowly from the back door of his parents' car, gazing apprehensively at the spooky old mansion. He had never been away from home before. Sleeping over at his friend Jason's house did not count, as Jason only lived two blocks down the street. The thought of spending the summer here, with no one for company except his creepy old great-grandfather, who could hardly speak English, was too much to bear. Patrick burst into tears.

His mother came and wrapped her arms around him. "Be brave, Paddy, you're a big boy now. You're nearly seven."

Patrick nodded and sniffled and wiped his eyes on his sleeve. As he did so, he noticed a strange little house barely visible through the mist. It stood by the curve of a narrow stream and had an oddly peaked roof, which slanted downward and then rose with a curve. Curious, he left his mother's arms and went cautiously forward across the lawn to investigate.

As Patrick drew near the tiny Japanese temple, the door opened and out stepped a bent old man in a black quilted robe. His snow-white hair was drawn back into a strange bun. In his gnarled hands, he held a large iron key. Seeing Patrick, he quickly inserted the key into the small door and turned it, locking the temple.

Patrick halted, frightened. Then, he realized that this apparition was his great-grandfather.

"You no go inside. Forbidden!" his great-grandfather announced in his crackly old voice, glaring at Patrick from under unbelievably bushy white eyebrows.

Patrick shrank back. He almost turned and ran to his mother and the car. However, his curiosity about the mystery of the forbidden little house won over his fear. "What's in there?" he asked.

"Very evil book," said his great-grandfather sternly. "Not for little boys."

A book? Patrick could not believe such an intriguing little house could hold anything so dull. "That's okay," he said, disappointed. "I hate reading anyway."

As the two of them walked back to the car, however, Patrick could not help glancing back at the forbidden temple one more time.

———

LATER, as he sat on the dark blue mat, hardly six inches off the floor, that his mother had explained was to be his bed for the summer, Patrick recalled the conversation he had had with his parents on the long drive to his great-grandfather's house.

"But why do I have to stay with Great-Grandfather?" Patrick had asked. "It's his fault I can't go to summer school with Jason!"

His mother had been sitting in the front passenger seat. She reached her hand back to take his, frowning sadly. "It is not your great-grandfather's fault that he is Japanese, Patrick."

"But why does that make me Asian?" Patrick complained, his voice growing louder. "Why can't Asian boys go to Blackcourt Summer School?"

His mother took a deep breath, something she did when she wanted to yell but thought she should not. "It's not that Asian boys can't go to Blackcourt, honey. It's just that your school, Great Mills, doesn't have enough Asian boys. So, they would not agree to let you transfer over to Blackcourt for the summer. They said that they would be accused of being unfair if they had too few Asian children."

"But now I'm not going to either summer school! And I can't stay at Jason's house while you go away because *he's* going to Blackcourt Summer Reading School. And it's all because I have Great-Grandfather's eyes. It's not fair!"

"You can say that again," Patrick's father muttered from the driver's seat.

"Now, Gregory, don't . . ." Patrick's mother began, but Patrick interrupted her.

"I'll show them! I'll never learn to read!"

Now, seated on the futon in the bleak room on the second floor of his great-grandfather's eerie mansion, Patrick repeated his vow. "Never!" he declared fiercely.

THAT EVENING, Patrick dined with his great-grandfather in the grownup dining room. Everything was wrong. They sat cross-legged on cushions at a table hardly as high as Patrick's knee. The food was weird flat noodles and cooked vegetables. Patrick hated vegetables. There was not even a knife and fork—though Patrick rather liked that part.

However, when he expressed his opinion of vegetables, his great-grandfather did not even offer him a peanut butter sandwich. Instead, he merely glowered from beneath his huge eyebrows and gestured at the table. "All there is. Eat or no eat."

Glumly, Patrick picked at the unfamiliar food while gazing around at the many photographs that plastered two walls of the dining room. Most were old black-and-white photos in dark frames. A few smaller colour photos in standing frames rested on the mantelpiece to either side of the large rusty key that his great-grandfather had used to lock the forbidden temple. Patrick wondered if any of the girls in those pictures were his mother.

One large colour picture, however, caught his eye. It showed a smiling young Japanese man dressed in a Yankees uniform. Patrick loved baseball. He had never heard that anyone in his family knew someone who had played for the Yankees. When he stood up to leave the table, his great-grandfather did not object. So, Patrick wandered over to the picture and examined it more closely.

His great-grandfather's voice startled Patrick. "That your great-uncle Eddie. Good baseball player! Train very many years. Wanted to play major league. Once chosen for Yankees B team."

"My great-uncle was going to be a Yankee?" Patrick asked, amazed. "What happened? Did he ever get to play?"

His great-grandfather slowly lowered his head. He was silent for a moment. When he finally spoke, he did so very slowly. "He read book."

"Book? What book? You mean the one out in that little house?" Patrick's voice grew squeaky from surprise. "How'd that stop him?"

"Once you read that book—you are never the same," said his great-grandfather, choosing his words with great care.

"What happened?"

"Eddie left team. He enlisted in army. Shot down in airplane," said his great-grandfather. He nodded toward another picture of the same man, now grim and humourless, dressed in an Air Force uniform.

"Oh, wow," whispered Patrick, awed.

His great-grandfather rose suddenly to his feet. His scowl caused pure terror to run in Patrick's veins. "Not wow!" he commanded. "Book destroyed my son. Great-Grandson, you are an idiot!"

Patrick bolted from the dining room.

FOR TWO DAYS, it rained. Lonely and bored, Patrick stayed in his room playing with his Sega Saturn. He would have liked to go downstairs and watch TV or perhaps explore the house, but he did not want to meet his great-grandfather. The old man's glowering eyes frightened Patrick, and his broken English caused Patrick to blush with shame. No, it was better to stay in his room on his hard mat of a bed, bored to tears, than wander out over the creaking floor boards of the old house and risk another scolding.

ON THE THIRD DAY, the sky was clear, and Patrick ventured outside. He spent a magical day playing in the old cherry orchard and wading through the stream. Just behind the little temple, a wide, shallow area formed a little pool just perfect for the stamping of bare feet. Patrick remained there until his great-grandfather struck the gong, summoning him for dinner.

As Patrick came running back toward the house, his bare feet slapping against the grass, his shoes in his hand, his great-grandfather appeared on the front porch. He saw the direction Patrick was coming from, and his face darkened. "You try to go into temple! You went to see book! Very bad!" he shouted angrily, brandishing his fist.

Patrick stopped in his tracks, shocked. "No! No, I was playing in the river. Look at my feet!" Patrick yelled back. He balanced on one leg and held out his wet, muddy foot.

"Naughty boys get no dinner. You go near temple again. I smack your bottom!" his great-grandfather announced and stepped into the house and slammed the door.

"It's not as if I could read your stupid old book, anyway!" shouted Patrick. Then, he sat down on the lawn and burst into tears.

PATRICK CRIED late into the night. He wished he could have stayed with Jason and gone to summer reading school like they had originally planned. He wished he could have gone with his parents on their business trip. He wished he could be anywhere but where he was, alone in an eerie old house with a crazy old man who was afraid of a book.

"I wish I could read that old book!" Patrick whispered, sniffling. "I wouldn't let it scare me!"

He was imagining doing just that when the door to his room opened. In the doorway stood his great-grandfather. Patrick shrieked and hid under his Winnie-the-Pooh blanket. His great-grandfather had known that he was thinking about the evil book. His great-grandfather could read minds!

However, no scolding came. Instead, his great-grandfather shuffled slowly into the room. Patrick could hear him placing something on the floor and leaning it against the wall. Curious, he peaked out.

The moonlight coming through the room's only window bathed his great-grandfather in dappled light. In his hands, his great-grandfather held two large posterboards. A third poster already rested against the wall.

Seeing Patrick emerge, his great-grandfather said gruffly, "Walls very plain. Perhaps Great-Grandson want poster to hang on walls?"

Patrick slithered across his futon to get a better look at the posters. They were movie posters. Nothing so cool as the posters he had at home, but after four nights in this dreadful bleak room, Patrick was delighted with anything that broke the monotony. He peered closer, examining the closest picture. It showed a man swinging on a cable and a pretty oriental girl in a fancy dress aiming a gun.

"That's Aunt Lily!" he cried, delighted. "Mommy told me that she was a famous actress!"

"Lily was very sweet girl but very weak and sickly. Spent much time in bed. Doctor did not believe she would live to be woman."

"What happened? How did she get better?" Patrick asked, looking up. His great-grandfather did not answer. Patrick could not make out his expression. "What happened to her?" he asked again.

"She read book," his great-grandfather answered reluctantly.

Patrick was thunderstruck. "You mean the book cured her? But I thought it was a force for evil!"

"Evil wear many faces," his great-grandfather said.

"How can getting healthy and becoming a famous actress be bad?" asked Patrick.

"Very sweet girl—grow up. Chose bad husband. Drink too much. Die young," he said.

"Very tragic," Patrick finished seriously.

In the dappled light, it was hard to make out his great-grandfather's face, but Patrick thought he saw the old man smile. Patrick peered up at him, thinking. There was a question he wanted to ask, but he was afraid his great-grandfather would just yell at him and call him an idiot again. Screwing up his courage, he asked.

"Great-Grandfather?" he began.

His great-grandfather cut him off. "Great-Grandfather no proper name. Better you call me Papa-san," he said.

Patrick nodded. "Papa-san," he asked, trying again, "Where did the book come from?"

"Hmmphf," said Papa-san. He shifted his shoulders beneath his robes. Then, he sat down on the thick straw mat that covered the floor, upon which the futon rested, and tucked his white socked feet into his robe so that he was sitting in a position Patrick's mother called "Lotus."

Patrick sat down and tried to sit that way, too. It took some effort, but he did it. His great-grandfather nodded in approval.

"Story take place many years ago—nineteen forty-two," Papa-san began. "Book come to me while at war camp."

"Like a concentration camp?" Patrick asked. He had read about concentration camps in school. "I didn't know you were in Germany."

"Yes, like concentration camp, but here, in America. Camp for Japanese people," Papa-san said stiffly. "We put in camp because we were 'Yellow Peril.'"

Comprehension dawned on Patrick's face. "You mean because you were Asian?"

His great-grandfather harrumphed again. "Asian? Gandhi was Asian. I am Japanese!"

"But you weren't helping the enemy, were you?"

"No," said Papa-san.

"So, it was like me—t school?" Patrick asked. "When they won't let me go to Jason's summer school 'cause I'm Asian?"

Papa-san considered and nodded. "Yes, you and I both treated unfairly because of our heritage. But you are unhappy because of overzealous people, not hateful people. After war camp, people passed laws—said, 'No do that again. Must be very nice to Japanese.'" He scowled. "Law cannot make people very nice. Laws only punish. So, when your school have too few 'Asians,'" he scowled again as he spoke the word, "they fear American government will come punish them. When good American boy wants to change schools, they say no. Very bad!" After that, he was silent for a time.

Patrick sat quietly, too. He had been so angry at his great-grandfather for being "Asian" and making him miss summer school with Jason that it had never occurred to him that it could have been hard on his great-grandfather as well.

The old man finally looked up, frowning, "What was it you ask?"

"About how you got the book," prompted Patrick.

"Oh, yes! Book! Old man come to me in camp—very old, older than I am now. He ask, 'Can you read English?' I told him 'No.' He said, 'Good, then you will be safe. Take this book. It very old and very dangerous. To read it changes whole life.'

"So," Papa-san continued, "I asked, 'If book so very bad, why not burn it?' Old man shook head, weeping, and begged me not to harm book. He told me . . ." Here, Patrick's great-grandfather paused and took a deep breath, then continued. "'One man out of thousands who read book is changed for good. Becomes very great man.'"

With this, Papa-san unfolded his feet, rose, and turned to leave.

"Papa-san!" Patrick called, jumping up after him and pulling on his robes. "What about you? Did you ever read the book?"

Papa-san turned on Patrick, glowering from under his immense eyebrows. Patrick let go of his robe and cowered.

But then, the fire drained from the old man's face. He shook his head sadly. "Never found courage to learn to read English," he said.

ALONE IN THE MOONLIT ROOM, Patrick lay on his futon, kept awake by wonder. Who would have thought that something as uninteresting as a book could have such power? Whole members of his family had had their lives ruined by just reading it. Even more intriguing, however, was the promise—the hope—that that very same evil book might, just once, produce greatness instead of sorrow.

Patrick could not say exactly when the idea came to him, but after that, he could not sleep at all. He absolutely had to see the book—just to look at it. After all, he could not read it, so he had nothing to fear. But what did an evil book look like? He had to know!

Very quietly, Patrick stole out of his bed. He put on a pair of sports socks, the best for sneaking across creaking floors, and made his way softly and silently down to the dining room, where his great-grandfather kept the key to the forbidden temple. Carefully, one step at a time, he crept up to the mantelpiece. Sure enough, there was the key.

Upstairs, a floorboard creaked.

Patrick stood stock still, frozen with fear. He remembered the terrible glower on his great-grandfather's face the day he had been playing in the stream, the sadness with which Papa-san talked of Lily and Great-Uncle Eddie. If his great-grandfather caught him now . . .

But time passed, and his great-grandfather did not appear. Eventually, Patrick began to breathe more easily. He considered running back upstairs to the safety of his bed, but he did not. He absolutely had to see that book! Carrying a chair quietly over to the fireplace, he took the cold, heavy key from the mantel.

Slipping out the front door, Patrick ran across the lawn as quickly as his socked feet could carry him. The door of the tiny Japanese temple opened without trouble. Patrick crept inside, shutting the door behind him.

A round table stood in the centre of the tiny chamber, lit by moonlight from the two side windows. On the table sat a single old lamp, with a red glass base and paper shade, and . . . the book.

The book was bigger than any dictionary and bound in real black leather. Patrick could smell the musky scent of it as he fumbled with the light. Once it came on, Patrick examined the book more carefully.

The book looked exactly as an evil book should: large, black, and very old. The gilded title letters had chipped off over the years and were now too faded for Patrick to read, but he stared in fascination at the intricate knotwork on the cover. It seemed to form a hedge and an arbour surrounding a swing, or maybe it was a sword.

Patrick was so excited it was hard for him to breathe. He opened the cover with trembling fingers. Inside, an etched plate showed a knight on horseback facing a mounted skeleton. His mouth wide with awe, Patrick turned to the opening page.

The words were written in ordinary print. Patrick felt a slight pang of disappointment. He had been hoping for something glorious, like dried blood. But perhaps it was what the book said that mattered, not its ink. He peered curiously at the words written there.

They did not seem too hard. In fact, he recognized most of them. He really did know all the parts of reading, he thought with surprise. After all, he could understand the instructions in his video games and the sentences that his teacher wrote on the board. It was just that when it came to books . . . well, everyone made such a fuss about them.

Peering closer, he began to puzzle out the first line.

MANY HOURS LATER, Mr. Ishizuka put down the binoculars he had been using to look across the yard into the window of the tiny temple. He lifted the receiver of his phone and made a call. When he reached his party, he said, "Trisha? This is your grandfather. I call about Patrick. You can bake me cake any time now—I win bet." He grinned broadly.

He was silent a moment, listening, then continued. "Yes, he reading right now. Doing very good job! You have not more trouble with him at school."

Silence again, then, "No, no need thank me. But, I must warn you," the old man glanced back across the lawn toward the temple, a glint in his eye and a subtle smile on his lips, "Great-grandson may never again be the same."

RUMSPRINGA IN SANZHEIKA

Alex Shvartsman

Denis shared the cramped space with five strangers, but each of them might as well have been alone.

When Denis arrived at the seaside resort in Sanzheika, the self-driving shuttle dispatched the teenagers in small groups to a dozen or so identical buildings. He activated the recording feature of his Augmented Reality overlay and posted the clip of what he saw onto his social media channel. He tagged the live view of drab buildings and lawns with sparse fresh blades of early spring grass with a comment: *My prison for the next week.* He wondered how many of his thirty thousand followers would actually miss him or even notice he was gone.

When it was his turn to disembark, directions to his floor and suite appeared on his AR overlay, the path toward the vestibule turning into a cartoonish yellow brick road.

As his roommates arrived one by one, they shared their virtual calling cards. No one spoke out loud. There would be time for introductions later. Too much time—but he didn't want to focus on the unpleasantness to come any more than the rest of them did.

Then again, Denis had always been pragmatic. If he was going to be stuck with these people for what would likely be the longest week of his life, he wanted to learn what he could about them. Soon, his only way to do that would be to piece together the farrago of factoids and embellishments they might volunteer verbally.

The relatively small living room of their suite made him feel claustrophobic, so he expanded the walls to make it appear larger. He adjusted the lighting to a warmer, more soothing tone and added the sound of waves splashing against the sand. The ocean soundtrack always helped ease his anxiety. Then he brought up the four virtual calling cards, interposing them over the four teenagers who shared his physical space but were each so far away in realities of their own.

Two of them were from the nearby Odessa. A cursory look at Masha's profile revealed nothing especially interesting; her feed was a torrent of selfies and pop music clips. He scoffed at her three-digit number of followers and moved on. Dmytro's profile was filled with achievements and game rankings. Based on the telltale twitch of his fingers, the tall, athletic-looking fellow was in a game even now, glee-fully blowing up imaginary monsters or aliens.

Kostya was from Kiyv, and Denis was surprised to learn they were practically neighbours. They lived only ten minutes' drive apart, though Kostya's was a much fancier borough that still had single-family houses, whereas Denis hailed from a middle-class apartment block.

Denis scanned Kostya's profile, which featured pictures of him leaning against luxury cars and eating real meat at restaurants. Beyond that, there wasn't much else about the rich kid that was public, so Denis moved on to the next calling card.

Zoya, the girl from Moldova, was an artist. Her gallery of land-scapes was surprisingly good. She drew trees and flowers in bloom, with real paint and brushes on a canvas rather than digitally. Denis was no art connoisseur, but something about all those swirls of colour spoke to him, so much so that he didn't even mind their weird two-dimensional feel.

The painting he had been admiring suddenly winked out of exis-tence. The sound of the ocean waves ceased abruptly, and the room shrank back to its original size. The notification tab at the edge of his vision disappeared entirely. The living room was once again poorly lit, mostly silent, and unbearably ordinary.

"Shit," said Kostya. His raspy voice reverberated through the room. "Shit, shit, shit." Kostya's wailing sounded unpleasant and Denis instinctively tried to adjust his voice before realizing he couldn't. "We don't get some kind of a countdown? A warning? That's just messed up!"

A large screen lit up on one of the walls, displaying a smiling woman standing on the beach with the Black Sea in the background. Displayed in two dimensions like that, the image looked positively vintage. It made Denis think of Zoya's paintings.

"Hello. On behalf of our staff, I'd like to welcome you to the Sanzheika Resorts," said the woman. Her voice was annoyingly saccharine. "We're committed to making your government-mandated seven-day sabbatical as pleasant as possible. You will experience many wonderful things that do not require the use of your AR overlays or an internet connection." Denis thought the lady must've been a pretty good actress because she delivered this line with as much conviction as was possible for such an obvious load of crap. "You'll play sports, hike along the beach, ride horses, and go fishing. This week is going to go by fast." Her fake smile grew even wider. "But first, please take a little time to adjust. The initial hours after your AR implant has been turned off can be a bit difficult, but we will help you get through them. Let's start with a series of breathing exercises—"

The screen turned black.

"That's nonsense," Masha said. "No amount of breathing exercises is going to turn a week of hell into this fun *vacation* they're peddling." She held a gadget that she must've used to control the screen. "Trust me. My sister went through her sabbatical two years ago, and she told me all about this place."

"A week like this," Kostya said. He sat on the cot and rocked back and forth, "I can't. I can't." He wrapped his arms around himself. "Why would they do this to us?"

"'Every citizen deserves to experience unembellished life,'" Denis quoted the slogan mockingly. Even his own voice sounded weird. He kept catching himself trying to adjust his environment in ways he no longer could. "I don't get it, either. It just feels like some cruel punishment."

"It's Rumspringa in reverse," said Zoya.

Unlike the rest of them, she appeared calm and collected. Denis envied her that terribly.

"The what?" asked Kostya. Not being able to just look up an unfamiliar term must've been as maddening to him as it was to Denis.

"There are these North American people called the Amish," Zoya explained. "Their religion forbids the use of modern technology. Forget AR—most of them don't even have electricity. And there are a lot of other harsh rules, too."

"There are people in America who live like that?" Masha asked, shaking her head.

"It's their way," said Zoya. "But they also do this Rumspringa thing. Young people leave their communities to experience the modern world, electricity and all." She smiled. "They spend a year doing whatever they want. Then, when it's over, they get to decide whether to come back to their original way of life or leave their faith forever."

"Why?" asked Masha.

"I think it's meant to make their communities stronger," said Zoya. "The true believers return to the fold, even knowing what it is they'll be missing. And everyone else can choose a different path."

"A reverse Rumspringa," Denis repeated. "Huh. But this is not the same at all. It makes sense to let cavemen experience the luxury of the wheel and fire and air conditioning. But what's the point of forcing us back into the dark ages?"

As they talked, he walked around, exploring the suite. It had five tiny bedrooms and a single bathroom. Much better than the barracks most people spent their sabbatical in.

"When AR technology was still new, the lawmakers were mistrustful of it. Back then, it was goggles and other wearables, not even implants, but they thought the human brain was too susceptible to what it sees and hears and such. That people won't be able to tell what's actually there apart from the overlay enhancements. They mandated that every seventeen-year-old spend a week in the 'real world.'" Zoya made air quotes around that term.

"A bunch of old people fearing new technology," said Denis. "It's a wonder this law still hasn't been overturned."

"Perhaps there's some wisdom to it, just like Rumspringa," said Zoya.

"You would say that," said Kostya. He squinted at the other girl suspiciously. "You don't seem as bothered by this as the rest of us." He looked at Masha. "You either."

"My family is old-fashioned," said Zoya. "My sister and I had to spend a little time each day without electronics while growing up, so I'm used to it."

"Seriously?" Kostya looked at her as though she were a barbarian from the Middle Ages who had somehow time-travelled to the present. "They did this to their own children?"

"How did you manage?" Denis asked.

"We read a little. Exercised. Painted. It's not so terrible," said Zoya.

Kostya only hugged himself tighter.

"What's your deal?" Denis asked Masha. "Did you practice for this, too?"

"Not by choice." Masha smiled. "I've done two stints in rehab, so I've had practice. Detox for alcohol and detox for AR feel pretty similar thus far, equally unpleasant."

Denis wished he had practised spending a little time each day without AR, too. Not his entire life, like Zoya, but maybe just in the weeks leading up to this mandated deprivation. Perhaps then, he'd be able to get through the next week. As it was, he felt like the drowning man for whom the surface was just out of reach. Then he looked at Dmytro, who hadn't uttered a word since all of them were disconnected. The big guy appeared practically catatonic, and Denis realized that however bad he had it, it could've been worse.

"It could've been worse," he said out loud. The others stared at him. "At least we're at this fancy resort. We get horseback rides and the beach. Most of my classmates are going through their sabbaticals locked up in free government facilities with none of the perks."

"Fancy resort." Kostya snorted. "Those have human staff instead of whatever *that* is." He waved toward the screen. "My dad sent me here to toughen me up. 'You may as well learn how the regular people live,' he told me. What garbage."

Denis felt resentful of Kostya. His parents had skipped a couple of years' worth of family vacations in order to buy their son a spot in Sanzheika, whereas Kostya made this place sound like he was slumming. Denis hoped he could make it as an influencer and enjoy the lifestyle in Kostya's photos, but that would take gaining a hundred times more followers than he already had, and a week offline would surely put a break into whatever momentum the social algorithms had assigned to his posts.

"If any of you have some money to spare, I can arrange for our stay here to become a lot more pleasant," said Masha.

She suddenly had everyone's undivided attention.

"Tomorrow, they're going to make us go on a hike," said Masha. "There's this guy; he will meet us at a spot by the reeds. He can sell us whatever we want—booze, pills, even the harder stuff. Whatever can make our prison term more bearable."

"Well, well." Kostya slapped Masha's shoulder. "You're now my favourite fellow inmate."

FOR THE LIFE OF HIM, Denis couldn't understand how people used to live like this all the time, up until a few decades ago. He was thirty minutes into the forced death march the resort staff insisted on calling a "hike." That staff consisted of a pair of bored administrators who corralled them onto a marked path and said it would lead them back to the resort in a couple of hours. As Kostya had noted the day before, there were few humans employed here.

Despite the mild spring weather, sweat poured down Denis's forehead and stung his eyes. He could hear only the groans of his fellow sufferers and the crunching of twigs and gravel under their feet, could see only the monotonous landscape of sand and water and reeds and some bushes along the path. There was no way for him to modify his environment nor to reach out and find comfort in the great mass of humanity, all connected to each other in countless ways. His connection had been severed, cut off like a limb, and equally necessary for his well-being. The ability to verbally communicate with a handful of strangers was no more a substitute for the amputated connection than a wooden peg was a sufficient replacement for a flesh-and-bone appendage. The primal, omnipresent loneliness gnawed and gnawed at his soul.

"There!" Masha pointed at a narrow path that diverged from their hike route toward a tall patch of reeds growing in the wetlands. "He should be waiting for us over there."

Their group peeled off from the marked route and headed toward the reeds. The others looked the way Denis felt: miserable wretches shuffling along. Only Zoya was holding up pretty well, seemingly at ease on the hike. Her experience with being disconnected was really paying off. She had no trouble keeping up, even though she paused frequently to sketch something with a graphite pencil onto a notepad. Denis thought it was the world's worst substitute for having an overlay take a screenshot, but the way her lips pursed as she focused on the sketch was rather cute.

Denis focused on the way the wind tousled strands of her short brown hair, the way her blue eyes seemed to take everything in, the expression of intellectual curiosity mixed with mild amusement on her face. He was drawn to engage her in conversation, but he couldn't think of a thing to say that wouldn't sound inane or desperate, and this only added to his misery.

Masha was propping up Dmytro, whose condition hadn't improved much since the day before. While the rest of them seemed to have gotten over the initial shock of being disconnected, the gamer had hardly spoken a word and wouldn't get out of bed that morning. Masha had taken pity on him and tried to coax him up. "Think of it as one of those survival games that simulate you being lost in the

Sahara or stuck on a desert island," she had said. "The mission is to last until the clock runs out. I bet you've beaten games that took more than a week to complete, right?" The motivational talk had sounded rather shallow to Denis but it worked well enough to dislodge Dmytro from his room.

The path led them to a clearing where a thin, bearded man in his fifties sat cross-legged on a beach towel. He watched impassively as they approached.

"Are you Vasili Petrovich?" Masha asked. "My sister Larissa says hello."

"Greetings, my young friends," the man said. "Just call me Uncle Vasya. Everyone does."

"Larissa said you can help acquire . . . certain things for us?" Masha rubbed her hands.

"Oh, there's no need to be coy. No cameras and microphones out here, just nature." Uncle Vasya grinned. "What's your pleasure, then? Vodka? Smokes? I've got a better selection of antidepressants than most pharmacies. Anything to help you pass the time." He added conspiratorially, "I've even got the zonies if you can afford 'em."

The zonies were the latest designer pills, supposed to make a person feel like they were inside a simulation. Denis had heard of them but never opted to try one. But that was back when he had access to the real thing. Half a day into this so-called sabbatical, he was ready to experiment.

Kostya stepped forward. "Zonies sound good," he said. "I want whatever will let us hallucinate something better than naked reality all week long. But how do we pay you with our implants cut off?"

"The old school way." Uncle Vasya unfolded a tablet the size of an open paperback. The gadget locked in and turned rigid in his hands. "You can authorize the transfer with a retina scan, like in the olden days. I'll ring up your order, and you can pick up the goodies here tomorrow."

"That." Dmytro spoke for the first time. He pointed a shaking finger at the tablet. He stared at its lit screen the way a starving man looks at a sandwich. "I want one of those."

"No can do, my friend," said Uncle Vasya. "I can't sell you guys any electronics. The resort management and me, we have . . . an understanding."

"They look the other way so long as he doesn't peddle anything that might cause them to lose their licence," said Masha.

"That's a clever young lady," said Uncle Vasya. "It's so nice to work with people who understand the plight of a small-business proprietor."

Kostya smiled. "All right. It's on me, so I'm going to order for the table." He rattled off a list of items, including vodka, beer, zonies, and an assortment of other pills. Denis didn't even recognize some of the brand names, but the dealer seemed to know what his customer wanted. Uncle Vasya nodded, letting his implant record the list for him. Kostya turned to the rest of the group. "Anything I missed?"

No one spoke up. They probably couldn't afford much of what the dealer was offering—Denis knew he certainly couldn't—but Kostya could, and he was clearly willing to buy their friendship with this gesture.

Kostya chewed his lip. "Any way to expedite our order? I don't think any of us relish spending the next twenty-four hours waiting for relief."

"For a reasonable fee, I can deliver everything tonight," said Uncle Vasya. "I'll even throw in a pizza."

KOSTYA LOOKED at the digital clock that hung on the wall of their living room for what must've been the hundredth time. "That bearded freak better not have ripped me off," he said.

"He came through for my sister and her friends," Masha said. "But yeah, sooner would be better. I need a drink."

The day had stretched on and on like the hiking path from that morning. They'd been forced to do some stretching exercises that were an unholy blend of yoga and tai chi and then eat a bland lunch in the school-like cafeteria. After a break, there was the viewing of a classic comedy from back in Soviet times, projected onto a large outdoor screen.

Denis wondered if he might have actually enjoyed some of the activities had he not been disconnected. The implant could've made the morning walk more pleasant, tricked his taste buds into enjoying lunch, displayed any number of wisecracking commentaries alongside the ancient film . . . At the very least, it would have been tolerable.

He tried to speak with Zoya several times but found it almost impossible to talk to her without the safety net of the implant. He wasn't some shy nerd; he'd had no issue chatting up girls in the past. Somehow, being all alone in his skull made things different. He'd be damned if he'd just give up the way Dmytro had, though.

Denis realized this gave him an opening and pressed on before he lost his newfound courage.

He walked over to Zoya's room. She sat on the edge of the bed, reading a book.

"Sorry, may I interrupt?"

Zoya set the open book face down and looked up at him.

"I meant to ask, did you experience any difficulty talking to people whenever your implant was turned off?" He flashed a bashful smile. "Or is it just me?"

Zoya motioned for him to sit next to her. "I'm a veteran at this by now, but that's a perfectly normal reaction," she said. "The first generation that grew up online, the kids with cell phones and social media, they already had to deal with similar problems. There were studies about young people having a difficult time communicating without the crutch of their phones. Apparently, they had an even more difficult time with conflict resolution. Some even had bouts of anxiety when they needed to speak to another person on the phone instead of texting."

"I would've found any of this difficult to believe yesterday," said Denis. "Until I experienced it on my own hide."

"I'm pretty sure that is precisely why the government mandated the sabbatical. They want everyone to become capable of being useful members of society without the crutch of AR. That way, we aren't all flopping like fish out of water if there's ever a natural disaster or some other problem that causes a temporary shutdown."

"That's all logical and orderly, but it doesn't help me feel any better," said Denis.

"It will get easier, I promise. You said you have a difficult time talking to people without AR, yet here we are, talking." Zoya smiled at him. "Wanna hear about this awesome novel I've been reading?"

WHEN THE KNOCK on the door interrupted their conversation, and they joined the rest of the group in the living room, Denis was surprised to learn that nearly an hour had passed.

Uncle Vasya was at the door, wearing a pizza delivery uniform and cap and holding a thermal bag.

"About time." Kostya stepped aside to let him into the suite.

"You can't rush perfection, my friend." Uncle Vasya strolled inside, retrieved an actual pizza box from his thermal bag, and placed it on the coffee table. He then retrieved a plastic bag filled with bottles and a much smaller paper bag that he shook, prompting the pills to rattle in their containers.

They crowded around the table.

"All yours, as soon as bossman transfers the second instalment." Uncle Vasya offered Kostya the tablet again.

Kostya typed in the necessary codes and confirmed with his retina scan. Most of the others eyed the device hungrily, the artificial light emanating from its surface far more alluring than anything in the bag of pills.

Kostya took one last wistful look at the screen and held the tablet out for Uncle Vasya to take, but before the dealer could, Dmytro snatched it from his hands. He hugged the device to him like a child with their favourite teddy bear.

"Give that back." All mirth disappeared from Uncle Vasya's face.

He pulled his T-shirt up, revealing a gun tucked in his waistband. "Now."

Everyone backed away, leaving Dmytro face-to-face with the dealer. Dmytro raised his hands slowly, then tossed the tablet to the older man. Instinctively, Uncle Vasya grabbed for it with both hands.

Dmytro tackled him. Contrary to the stereotypes, the gamer was tall and muscular and had the manic strength of a cornered addict. Uncle Vasya went down, and Dmytro landed on top of him. After a brief struggle, he pulled away, aiming the dealer's own gun at him.

Uncle Vasya scrambled toward the door. "You're a lunatic," he shouted. Then he turned and ran out, the string of obscenities audible for a few more seconds until the dealer must've disappeared down the staircase.

"What the hell is wrong with you?" asked Kostya.

Dmytro ignored him, still holding the gun as he reached for his prize with his free hand. Uncle Vasya's tablet lay abandoned on the floor. He grabbed it and touched the screen to reactivate it. It lit up to a locked screen, pending retina verification. Dmytro growled, the inhuman sound of a trapped wild animal. He glanced at the door, perhaps wondering if he could catch up to the dealer and force him to unlock the device.

"Way to ruin a good thing," said Kostya. He stepped forward. "Now he'll—"

"Stay back!" Dmytro trained the gun on Kostya. "Stay back, all of you."

Masha gasped. "What are you doing, Dmytro? Put that down."

Dmytro looked at her, then at the gun, then at her again. His hand wavered. Then, the screen on the tablet he was still holding turned itself off again. Dmytro snarled in frustration, let go of the tablet, and levelled the gun at Kostya.

"Get back. Everyone, get into that corner." Wild-eyed, Dmytro stepped aside, alert for anyone trying to attack him the way he had Uncle Vasya.

The four of them gathered in the corner of the living room. Kostya was boiling over with anger. Zoya was pale. Masha began to cry. Denis felt afraid but also somehow detached, his mind trying to reconcile this bizarre situation, to pretend the overlay was on and the gun was just a virtual construct.

"Please . . . why are you doing this?" Masha cried.

Dmytro ignored her. He looked at the big blank screen hanging on the wall. "Listen, you bastards," he shouted. "I know you're watching this, and if you're not, your precious algorithms are going to scream and scream until you tune in." He scowled at the blank screen. "I want my overlay turned back on. You have five minutes. If it's not done by then, I start shooting." He waved the gun toward his hostages.

"Come on, think this through," Denis said. "Those people probably have no way of turning your overlay on, at least not this quickly. They're glorified summer camp counsellors."

"If you shoot someone, what do you think will happen?" Zoya spoke up. "A week of being disconnected is bad, but how do you think you'll manage in prison for years? Incarcerated people have their overlays turned off for the duration of their sentence."

"Shut up and let me think!" Dmytro brushed away strands of hair with his free hand. "I think they'll do it," he said. "I think whatever AI is in charge of figuring out the odds will realize the safest and easiest solution to this is to quit tormenting me." He glanced at the wall clock. "Three minutes."

Masha tried to say something, but Dmytro turned the weapon on her. "Not another word. Be quiet, all of you."

They stood there as the seconds ticked by. Denis thought that as bad as the sabbatical had been, this was so much worse. He was helpless, disconnected, and utterly alone.

Maybe the last part wasn't entirely true. His hand found Zoya's, and she grabbed it, squeezing hard enough for it to hurt.

There was less than a minute left. Dmytro jerked, his gun shaking in his hand. Before he could even think, Denis took a small step forward and sideways, blocking Zoya with his body.

Dmytro shifted his aim again, but this time, it was slightly off to the side. He seemed focused on something that wasn't there.

"What . . ." A single word passed Dmyro's lips before he turned sharply, aiming the weapon at the wall. He grunted and whirled again, losing his balance. His eyes were staring into the distance in a telltale sign of someone whose AR overlay was feeding him visuals.

Dmytro stood still for several seconds, then slowly sat down on the ground. He clawed at his head with both hands, the firearm abandoned on the floor next to him.

The door burst open, and a pair of security guards rushed in. The younger man kicked the gun out of Dmytro's reach, then collected it while his older partner watched.

The young guard pulled Dmytro up, handling him somewhat roughly. He shoved the gamer toward the door. Dmytro could walk, but he appeared to be in worse shape than before, barely a shell, able to follow some basic instructions but with no will of his own.

The older guard watched them go and shook his head in disgust. "Shameless," he said. "There are a few every week, but they don't usually get their hands on a firearm." He looked at the coffee table where Uncle Vasya's deliveries rested, forgotten. "I'm security chief Kovalenko."

"What did you do to him?" asked Masha.

"We did nothing. The feds' AI recognized the danger and overloaded his input." Kovalenko opened the pizza box, grabbed a slice, and took a bite. A tiny streak of oil dripped down his chin. "It's pretty much the opposite of the sabbatical. All four of the senses the implant can influence go into overdrive, so the person is seeing, hearing, smelling, and tasting everything at once. Turns them into a vegetable for a little bit and takes a few days to recover from. It's not a pretty process." He took another bite.

"What's going to happen to him now?" asked Zoya.

"That's for a judge to decide. You should be more concerned about what happens to all of you." Kovalenko wiped his mouth with a sleeve.

"Meaning?" asked Kostya.

"You've got illegal substances and unsavoury characters showing up on the premises, armed," said Kovalenko. "Could be a serious problem for you. But then, no one wants to make waves. So, if you all sign a document absolving the resort of any responsibility for what happened here, as well as a non-disclosure agreement, I think we could all pretend this little episode never happened, eh?" He finished the slice and wiped his fingers on the paper bag full of pills. "You can even keep the party favours."

"I DON'T KNOW if we should have signed those documents without our parents and lawyers present," said Kostya. He had only rediscovered his courage after the security chief had departed.

"Documents?" Zoya glanced at the tablet, abandoned where Dmytro had stood. "Are we just going to ignore the fact that the implant can turn us into vegetables at will?"

There was an uncomfortable pause. Denis wondered why this hadn't bothered him before Zoya voiced the concern, and from the expression on the others' faces, they were perturbed, too.

"Nah," said Masha. "Only makes me feel safer. Since I don't plan on shooting anyone, I feel better knowing that the overlay will stop the bad guys from shooting at *me*."

Although Denis felt uneasy about this logic, he was even more uncomfortable at the idea of making any arguments that would lead him down the path of questioning his own future overlay use. So, he changed the subject instead. "I have a feeling this is not the first such incident the resort has hushed up. What was it you said about disconnected kids not handling conflict resolution well, Zoya?"

Zoya nodded. "That sounds right. I don't think they'll make any trouble for us over it, in any case. But I feel terrible for Dmytro. I wasn't kidding about there being no AR overlays allowed in prison."

"He'll adapt," said Masha. "If the people in charge think we can learn how to live disconnected in a week, anyone in prison will surely learn how to make do."

Kostya began to laugh.

"What's so funny?" asked Masha.

Kostya rifled through the bag on the coffee table, took out a bottle of vodka, opened it, and took a long swig. "You think the sabbatical is for our benefit? You think they want to teach you how to live without an AR overlay? Ha!" He drank again. "My dad has a different theory, and he's in a position to know such things."

Everyone stared at Kostya, who took a third shot of liquid courage. "This is not education. It's an object lesson. They want every citizen to know what it is they can take away with a keystroke." He burped loudly. "Come on, then. Dig in, everyone. We have to get through six more days of this shit."

One by one, the others reached for vodka and beer.

"I think I'll just have a slice," said Zoya. "I'm more shaken up by what happened today than the sabbatical, but I still don't think the pills and booze are a good idea."

Denis looked at the bag of pills. The zonies beckoned, the promise of making him feel something akin to being plugged in again almost irresistible. Then he looked back to Zoya.

"You know what, I think I will stick to the pizza, too," said Denis.

They grabbed a slice each and headed back to Zoya's room to resume their conversation.

"Do you think Kostya's dad is right?" Denis asked.

"I think there may be some truth to that, but it can't be the only reason," she replied. "I stand by my theory. This is our Rumspringa, a chance to overcome a challenge together before we return to our lives as we know them. A rite of passage, and whatever the reason behind it, we will be stronger for having experienced it."

Denis still felt out of place and miserable, and shaken by being held at gunpoint. But he caught himself trying to adjust his environment less frequently now, after only a single day. He was confident now he'd manage to survive the week, and he was eager to explore this idea of a human connection unaided by technology.

Denis's hand found Zoya's for the second time that evening.

"I am unable to feel any burning desire if my spirit is not stretched taut like a canvas, glowing with the radiance of one image upon another."

— SALVADOR DALI

Phoebe

Phoebe sat cross-legged, meditation-style, on her cushion within her dome-shaped abode, surrounded on every side by ever-changing scenes of mythical Old Earth, once home to gods, humans, wildlife, and gardens: an African savannah, Egypt's pyramids, the hanging gardens of Babylon, the Great Library at Alexandria, the grand cathedrals of Europe, the Statue of Liberty.

Phoebe was missing pieces in her life, her lineage shrouded in mystery and so today, after thirty-three simulated Earth sun cycles, here on Old Earth Replica (OER) in the After the Death of Old Earth epoch, she had finally decided to seek consultation with Pythia, one of the ancient Oracles at Delphi, now rendered by an AI and known as an Oracle of the Second Cosmic Cycle.

Her decision was a last resort. She didn't hold to the ancient mindreading myths, but she was at her wits' end. Perhaps Pythia, tapping into its vast database, would reveal some hidden prophecy that could fill in all her missing pieces.

Each projected panorama formed part of her story. She had been told by her mother, Lida, that she hailed from the gods, had fallen into the trance of human being, and had been transformed by technology that copied and preserved both life codes, then thrust her into a prefab world in which to play out her prefab life.

Deep down, she felt she was none of these—not goddess, not human, not cyborg. She was fabricated but not prefab: she was a *post-fabrication*. The scenes surrounding her constantly reminded her of the clashes of Old Earth's warring/loving, sinister/auspicious essences. The dualities that made up that old world had been reproduced on this satellite clone in the Sirius binary system.

She longed to reclaim whatever vestige within her was still human.

Yes, she was lucky: still here. The voice of her mother, Lida, played in a loop, reminding her of her good fortune, insisting she never dare question the Fates.

But being here did not diminish the fear that things were not right. Doubt had dogged her through life. She'd had no direct experience of the events supposedly shaping it, only this virtual view.

Perhaps being alone had induced her pain in this evolutionary moment when disease was conquered. Eternity was at hand, but it was far from paradise.

And so, Phoebe had sought relief. She underwent tune-ups and tests and consumed snake oil concoctions combining ancient OE herbal remedies with cutting-edge sonic- and electro-molecular treatments. They infused her neural circuits with sweet memories and deleted bad dreams.

Healers diagnosed her as being in tiptop performance condition. They informed her the deficit was a defect in her original mental processors and urged her to see a neurotechnologist who specialized in de-shadowing mental mechanisms.

Still, Phoebe knew her suffering was not all in her head, and so, here she was—seeking the Oracle's answer to the immortal question, "Who am I?"

Phoebe had previously gone to considerable lengths to research this scientifically—the science of myth/myth of science being her graduate dissertation topic. She'd sifted through troves of data, DNA analysis, religious practices, and ancestral and historical memory to no avail: there was no common thread among her findings out of which to weave a Tapestry of Phoebe.

Phoebe's brain had an on-off switch. Her memory was always there, dormant, but needed an external stimulus or power source to activate. The trigger could be the least little thing: sunlight, a leaf blowing in the wind, an old Calvin and Hobbes comic strip.

It was buggy that way.

She used to think this was an accident of birth. After all, her mother hadn't been exactly sober most of the time she was pregnant with Phoebe. So, using her information-sorting abilities, Phoebe had studied fetal alcohol syndrome.

Exhausting the medical research, she'd reached the conclusion that, no, alcohol couldn't account for her quirky "on-off" mental modalities. In the off mode, it wasn't exactly like there was *no* function. She could think and calculate. And for any tasks involving reason or calculation—math, science, computer science, biostatistics, and the like—the intellectual properties of her thinking mind were crystal clear. But when her mind was off, her attempts at memory retrieval were unfocused, dim, and faded.

Literature, language, art, or what they called "theory of mind"— that was where the trouble lay when her brain was switched off. When her brain turned on, she was more than adequate. Being on was like the beam of a lighthouse cutting through the fog, lighting up personal memory. Clarity came flooding in on a super signal.

She'd made the mistake of confiding in her mother about this odd on/off ability once after Lida got sober (she'd stayed that way for the next twenty-one years). Lida immediately denied that there was anything special about Phoebe, advised her daughter to keep her mouth shut, and went upstairs to bed even though it was the middle of the day. Lida withdrew when challenged.

At the time, Phoebe didn't see anything aberrant in her mother's behaviour or her own. That was just the way things worked. The fact that she didn't know anyone else like her didn't trouble her. She relished being the one-of-a-kind product of a one-of-a-kind woman.

Lida's tragic death had come ages ago as a bolt out of the blue while, in the smallest lapse, she was sampling the nectar of the gods, mead and honey, at The Café Paradiso (before sobriety, she had been a regular at this Mount Olympus landmark).

Not one to shortcircuit even after news of her mother's demise, Phoebe uploaded the data into the cloud and moved on.

Even Phoebe's switched-on brain seemed to be missing a faculty that never seemed difficult for others. Others used the word "love," but whatever meaning "love" held for other people totally escaped her. Other emotions were similarly mysterious. She'd heard emotion defined as a thought linked to a sensation in the body, but somehow, she'd missed the "feelings" gene.

This was a puzzling piece of her existence she couldn't fathom, even from the on-brain position. She needed to understand. She needed a higher-powered processor.

She needed an Oracle.

She attempted to fire up the Delphi simulation but had trouble tuning in. The OER simulation resided in a manufactured satellite orbiting Sirius A, the larger of the two stars in the binary system once known as the Dog Star on Earth. The system experienced its own cycles, its own jagged and unpredictable energy storms, that sometimes interfered with the artificially created Earth environment, despite the best efforts of the original pioneers (who had arrived shortly before Old Earth's implosion) to keep it stable.

None of that mattered to Phoebe. She simply waited, and eventually, the interference passed. Invoking the Oracles, she was able to begin the trek up a virtual Mount Parnassus to the cave of Pythia.

When she reached the cave, the vision flickered and faded for a moment. Then, a hazy Pythia shimmered into being, sitting cross-legged on a rock and gazing into a smoking cauldron giving off astringent scents Phoebe couldn't discern, redolence not being a usual feature on the OER.

Her eyes and throat began to burn. She stuttered the Oracle's name. "P-P-Pythia!"

"What is your request?" Pythia asked mechanically, her bleary eyes unseeing.

"I am Phoebe, daughter of Lida. I beg you to grant me insight to feel my heart of hearts!"

"It is always the same with you," Pythia grumbled.

"But I've never asked . . ."

Pythia's head was hidden in the swirl of smoke. "The matter is out of my control," she said matter-of-factly.

The heavens above Parnassus spangled into starry night. Phoebe recognized her own star, the brightest in the sky. On OE's simulated horizon, an aurora borealis waved. Overhead, a meteor shot across the sky as though the Big Dipper had shot an arrow straight into the North Star.

"Sweet dreams, enchantress, inheritress of illumination and substance, echo of all prior forms, foremother of what is to be," Pythia incanted in honeyed tones.

In a flash, the connection was severed.

Frustrated, Phoebe tried to jumpstart the vision again, to no avail. Her cosmic query, her heart of hearts, remained unanswered. The double star system's magnetic interference was currently too great to sustain the connection, and the forecast suggested such would be the case for many days to come.

Perhaps it is not meant to be, she reasoned; then said, "But where has the time gone?" to no one, noting that outside her dome, dawn was beginning to break. "I mustn't be late this first day."

Phoebe pulled her silver sheath over her new work uniform and glanced at her reflection in the two-way mirror near the door. The lapis streaks in her hair shimmered with gold in the glow of the holographic dawn. Her pale skin was flawless. She pursed her lips, painted them with white gloss, and then, satisfied, donned her new silver-moonglow sunglasses and strode to her vehicle.

To get to her new job, she started out by following an odd route her internal navigation sense informed her would be the quickest. Humans long ago, desiring never to get lost, had begun implanting a chip in the brains of newborns to map out their location. Eventually, they had directly modified their DNA to provide the same ability without the chip. They simply never got lost.

Except for Phoebe. When her brain was in off mode, she could still manage it.

En route to the new gig, she passed an old faux-Normandy cottage she hadn't noticed before. The house had an attached garage, topped by what must have been a mother-in-law suite. There was a hand-shaped sign posted on the sloping lawn. PALMISTRY, it read.

The sign looked like a *hamsa*, the upraised palm she'd once examined in an antiques store (although, of course, like everything else, the antiques were simulated and could have been made that morning). The *hamsa* had an eye-shaped, ruby-studded design in the centre. It was the hand of Fatima, designed to ward off evil. A charm. Ancient superstition.

But such symbols had been outlawed long ago.

Phoebe made a mental note—if it was, indeed, a charm, she would have to report it to the relevant Ministry of Rational Truths; but perhaps her eyes were playing a trick? Or, more likely, it was a typographical error? Perhaps it was meant to read PSALMISTRY?

Phoebe loved music and had become enraptured with the harmonies of the human voice, participating in a choir at the highly selective Stardust Academy. Perhaps the cottage was a place where they sang psalms, songs of love and devotion for a god not of her understanding.

Despite the pedigree Phoebe's mother had claimed for her, that she had descended from the Titans, she had never fallen into the social trap of ascribing power to some nebulous deity. The psalms, however, those stories of love and longing, had awakened in her a hunger of the heart she could not decode, another piece of the puzzle she had sought to take to the Oracle. She'd committed many such pains to memory.

This strange sign was arresting for some reason. Phoebe slowly backed up her transporter to look again.

No, her eyes were not playing tricks: PALMISTRY it was. And an orange, flickering sign in the little window above the garage read TRUTH-SEEKERS WELCOME.

She took a mental picture and drove on, not wanting to make a poor impression by being late to her first meeting with the New Intelligences Team (NIT), the organization which was, after all, the reason she existed, though their oversight of the creation of new intelligences clearly had some holes in it, considering they had arranged her birth from a mother with a drinking habit (though knowing her mother, Phoebe imagined she had successfully hidden that secret from her overseers).

The NIT was made up of OER experts in behavioural programming and other specialists from the far reaches of the galaxy. Many beamed in by faster-than-light holosphere, the distances being too great to travel to meet in the same place. Other NIT members were non-organic neo-sapient life forms and machine-built superintelligences.

NIT's next project would be the construction of a facsimile of Old Earth's moon, to be placed in the Old Sol system where Earth had been located. It was to become home to a new generation of powerful entities, raised from basic sapience to something approaching godhood. These powerful entities, the theory went, could restabilize the weirdly wobbling orbits that had resulted from Old Earth's collapse and ensure a better-functioning Old Sol system, benefiting Mercury, Venus, Mars, Jupiter, Saturn, Neptune, and Uranus.

Phoebe was the prototype and, thus, the head of the project now that it had been formally approved and announced.

The irony wasn't lost on Phoebe: her mother claimed she was descended from deities whose names had been given to celestial bodies circling Old Sol, and now she would ascend, a goddess-human-machine fusion, to a new realm where she and others like her, once they were created, would govern those celestial bodies.

Phoebe found the expectation uncomfortable; she had not been able to fully integrate her human, machine, and supposedly divine elements. Her personal thirty-three-simulated-solar-cycle experiment had exposed the difficulties involved in the attempt to ensure universal access to divine-human-machine powers. She personally deemed the project a failure.

As a result, for most of the meeting, she switched off to keep her biases from showing. While the team debated, Phoebe's mental processors replayed the strange little Old Earth-esque cottage with its charms, symbols, and sigils. She was only vaguely aware of the team members' droning until Maira, a denizen of Eris—a distant dwarf planet erratically adrift in Old Sol's asteroid belt—participating remotely via FTL holosphere, asked her for a final charge to the team. Phoebe had become so lost in her mental meanderings that it took her an attosecond to switch back "on."

They were all looking to her to lead them.

"Exactly," she said. "Thank you, Maira. Well done. Now, let's remember: by striving for the impossible, success becomes possible. So, let's get started, team! Full steam ahead!"

She trusted this was a general enough rallying cry that the NIT members wouldn't suspect how completely tuned-out she had been, but their faces showed confusion as they went their separate ways. Perhaps she had been expected to say something more about the mission. But her memory banks would not stop replaying the morning's encounter: that home, the signs.

An unfamiliar sensation flooded her circuits. Could that TRUTH-SEEKERS WELCOME sign have been a physical manifestation of the Oracle, offering an answer to her questions?

The day passed. Phoebe's thoughts looped in a herky-jerky orbit, leaving her even more unsettled. She tried to focus on routine; she must ward off further surprises, encounters that might lead her off track even more.

She was careful driving home, ignoring the shortcut her navigation sense offered, instead taking the well-travelled route back to Dome Sweet Dome. But a strange, aching sensation seized her, accompanied by a beating in her ears.

She attributed it to hunger. The day had been too busy to pause for nutritional supplementation. She needed to eat. She would also need a concentrated energy recharge from her lightbox before she returned to work the next day.

That night, she dreamed. There was her mother at a desk in an office Phoebe had never seen before. Her mother—a version of her no older than Phoebe herself—seemed to be labouring over a computer programming challenge. Phoebe was able to see the output on the screen, written in a language not of ones and zeroes but of ATCG patterns, the universal life code. Lida was manipulating DNA.

This made no sense—and up until now, Phoebe's dreams had always made sense.

Everyone knew that dreams were mechanisms to consolidate memory and work out any unresolved problems of the day. But this dream was lifelike—and mysterious. Lida hadn't been a programmer. In fact, to Phoebe's knowledge, she'd never even owned a computer. And her mother certainly had been no expert on the double helix.

Phoebe chalked this dream aberration up to the overstimulation of her day.

The next morning, over breakfast, she sat in front of the lightbox, reviewing the previous day. Even after so many hours, her throat was still raw from the smoky residues wafting out of Pythia's fire—which made no sense since they had been simulated. Still, she swallowed a brew of salicylic acid, honey, and lavender to erase the soreness.

Reenergized, Phoebe set out for work following the same odd route she had the day before. There was the same old house and the same hand-shaped, lighted sign: PALMISTRY.

She had every intention of simply driving by. Instead, she stopped. She stared for a moment. The flickering sign in the second-story window was now lit up in blue and green instead of orange and had been modified to add an on-off-on-off assortment of blinking symbols in a range of neon colours. Some reminded her of planetary glyphs: Pluto, Neptune, Uranus, Saturn. Others were new to her.

Beneath them all was the double helix.

Her dream. Though she didn't believe coincidences had any power beyond random association, she felt drawn to investigate. Perhaps here would be a new piece to unravel the puzzle: what was her purpose?

That there was more to it than the NIT project she had supposedly been designed for, she had no doubt.

* * *

Rhea

IN THE BEGINNING, Rhea found her doodles meaningless. The first time she charcoaled the "saluting hand" with the bejewelled palm, it was nothing more than a curiosity. But she found herself creating variations of the open palm over and over. Not that she couldn't stop herself—of course she could. But nothing else satisfied her in the same way.

It had become a familiar sensation. While not a trained artist, Rhea could adequately manifest form on the page or canvas. But over time, Rhea came to recognize that there was something driving her art, an inspirited inspirator she came to call the Seer Inside, the true designer, drawing through her.

Images would enter her brain without warning—in fact, they seemed to "push her" outside her body and take over. And when she was given the mental tap to indicate the designer was done, she would reenter her own brain, exhausted, with only a vague remembrance of the force that had moved through her—save for the designs left behind. And the Seer Inside displayed a far greater artistry than Rhea would ever manifest on her own.

She speculated it was all in her DNA: her inner *artiste* jolted awake in a lightning stroke of divine inspiration and infused with intravenous ichor.

As more and more of this creative output emerged over time, she began to notice sequences and repetitive symbols, discreet details that appeared in larger works. Such sigils reminded Rhea of the logos of long-ago companies she'd studied in art history, logos that hailed back to Greek myth, like the Nike swoosh, the Starbucks mermaid, or Paramount's Mount Olympus.

Curiously, in each artistic download, the upraised hand would appear. Eventually, Rhea pulled an old, dusty art history textbook off her shelf. She readily identified the doodle: it was a charm known as *hamsa*. It, too, had once been used as a logo by a company specializing in digital currency. Was that where she had seen it?

It was a symbol of welcome and farewell in many Old Earth cultures and religions, used to ward off the power of the Evil Eye, a curse borne of jealousy that could inflict harm on others—superstitions long since banned.

"Fascinating," Rhea murmured.

Over time, the distinction between Rhea, the woman, and the Seer Inside blurred. Under the Seer's influence, she began experimenting. She tried pastels, changing the colours of the gem in the hand's palm with each iteration: ruby-red, orange, yellow, green, blue, indigo, purple. And clear, like a diamond. Clear was her favourite shade—or rather, lifting of shade. It induced clarity, stimulating Sight.

Sight. Rhea knew now that there was no Seer Inside—that she was the Seer, her true self emerging from behind the façade of simple humanity. She knew now she had always had the Sight. It was her gift but also her curse. She remembered clearly now that it was because of the Sight that she'd finally known she must leave Kronos after she'd pointed out that castrating his father, Uranus, so he could take control of the cosmos would only force their son, Zeus, to take revenge by likewise overthrowing Kronos.

After that, he'd threatened to kill her and Zeus, too. Rhea was forced to run and hide with their youngest child lest Kronos devour them both in a fit of rage and jealousy. It wasn't as if he hadn't taken his wrath out on their children before.

So Rhea was positively gleeful when she divined how Kronos's evil ways would finally come back to haunt him. And, indeed, Zeus had had his revenge, cutting Kronos into pieces and condemning him to an eternity in the deepest pits of Hades. Burning in hell: his comeuppance.

As the Seer, her artistry often revealed inconvenient truths like this, messages for others that they would obstinately ignore or vehemently deny.

The influx of energy and insight she had gained from the work encouraged her to continue. Rhea began adding rare materials to her creations—crystalline elements, metallics, and gas-derived pigments mined from the Old Sol asteroid belt: diamond, ruby, moonstone, lapis, gold, platinum, neon, argon, krypton. Illumination.

Assessing her output, however, she found that while she herself was energized, her works seemed oddly static. She needed to breathe life into her opus, and so she decided to set her designs in motion through animation techniques. The process filled her with joy.

Early on the first morning Phoebe drove past, Rhea had an inspiration: she would advertise her artistry to the world outside. She extracted a single *hamsa* to showcase outside her studio, beckoning the world to the second-story window where she crafted a sign welcoming truth-seekers.

Now, she saw Phoebe's transport idling at the end of her driveway and felt a thrill. "Enter and be charmed!" she said and waited eagerly to see who would emerge.

Much earlier in the process of rebecoming the Seer, when she was still mostly just the ordinary woman, Rhea, she had sorted through her proliferation of paintings, sculptures, and holograms, setting them out haphazardly around her studio, thinking perhaps she would organize an exhibition of them. Doing so, she noted how each work revealed clues from outside her own experience: in particular, unknown faces. Over time, she noticed something else. While each facial depiction was different, they did have one thing in common: the faces on the page would eventually show up in her life.

Like today.

She had already seen, had already sketched, the woman with a swirl of lilac-and-black-streaked curls emerging from her vehicle and approaching step by wary step—and now that she saw her again, Rhea also knew who the woman was and why Rhea had felt the urge to advertise her presence to the world.

It had been to draw this woman to her.

She went to greet her guest.

———

Dance of Titans

BENEATH THE LIGHTED PALM, another message of sorts: F d L ve in the Palm of M Hand. The sign was in disrepair: several letters were burned out.

Phoebe scrutinized the letters and the voids for missed meanings. The first word might be Food. So, a restaurant of some sort? The pang in her belly reminded her that she'd neglected to eat again today.

"Food, then. Yes, that is good," she muttered into the pre-dawn darkness. "As for the rest . . . Lime? Liver? Loaves? Love?"

Puzzling.

"And the hand: M for My? But I fail to see . . ."

In the car, with its artificial lights, her brain was on, though her frontal lobes were beginning to hurt. Driving here again, she'd become aware of another odd sensation—searching through her memory banks, she'd dredged up a name for it: sorrow. It was another emotion, a thing she could never readily identify—even when Lida suddenly and unexpectedly died (the official cause of death was alcohol poisoning after that one little lapse in her long sobriety, though Phoebe herself had concluded from the autopsy that Lida had died from a lightning strike, which seemed the more logical conclusion). Phoebe hadn't been aware of this deep void.

Still, she felt drawn to move closer. There was nothing to do but get on with it.

She got out of her transporter.

The skies were starting to shed their night shadows. White wisps of cloud were passing over a waning crescent moon. Venus, the Sirius-equivalent morning star, burned brightly as the simulated moon began its final descent. Phoebe lingered beside her idling vehicle, hoping her strange heartsickness might pass, and as her eyes adjusted, saw that someone stood in the window with the sign, someone who turned and vanished almost as soon as Phoebe realized she was there: a woman whose hair glinted red as she turned and left the window.

Phoebe stared at the window another moment, then turned her gaze skyward, as if the gods, her ancestors, might leave a message to explain this place . . . this sensation . . . this red-haired "palmist." Though she was aware of how entirely illogical the notion was, Phoebe watched the inky sky for a sign until a billowing cloudbank obliterated the moon.

Phoebe's energy was draining. She wanted to power away from this spot but found herself unable to move.

Time passed.

Dawn was beginning to streak the horizon when a woman walked out the door and down the driveway to where Phoebe stood paralyzed. She carried a large sketch pad.

"Greetings, Sister. I am Rhea," the woman said.

Phoebe warmed to this greeting, though she could not define why. The bellyache returned, along with the thumping in her ears. Tinnitus, she diagnosed it. Her hands clasped protectively over her belly.

"Rhea," Phoebe repeated. "You called me 'Sister'?" Strangely, though Lida had born no other daughters than Phoebe, that name felt true.

"Yes. Sister. I am sure of it," Rhea said. "You are the one I have been waiting for."

Shifting the pad to her left hand, Rhea offered her right hand in greeting. Phoebe observed it was illustrated, like the sign in the window. In the centre of that hand gleamed a ruby.

The Palmist. Wary of this encounter, Phoebe shrank back. "How? We have never met."

"Perhaps," Rhea said, pulling open the brown cover of her pad, "you will recognize this."

Phoebe's eyes slid over whatever Rhea had revealed, focusing instead on Rhea's left hand. Her fingers were smudged with charcoal. The ringing noise in Phoebe's ears amplified. She heard a voice echoing in her ears: "Beware. All is not what it seems."

Were the Oracles warning her?

Frowning, Rhea waved the pad again, offended, perhaps, that Phoebe had failed to react to it. Though cautious, Phoebe couldn't help but draw near, trying to glimpse the proffered page.

But before she could see it clearly, Rhea reflexively clasped it back to her bosom. "No. You are not ready. First, what do you call yourself?"

Phoebe couldn't help but note the awkward phrasing. Maybe it wasn't her given name being requested but some other name that defined her "self": not what she called herself, but what she called her "self."

She hesitated.

Rhea stared at her, her eyes like lasers that could pierce Phoebe's hiddenmost places of the heart, and repeated, "What do you call yourself?"

A chill ran through Phoebe. Though it really didn't seem as if her so-called sister was asking for her name, she didn't know how else to respond. "Phoebe, daughter of Lida."

At that moment, the sun poked its fire above the horizon.

"Phoebe," Rhea acknowledged. "Perhaps this drawing will fill in what is missing."

"Missing." Could Rhea somehow fill in her missing pieces? The promise of an answer vibrated somewhere deep inside.

Rhea tore the page out of her sketchpad and held it out to Phoebe. "Look!"

Phoebe glimpsed two women draped in tunics and wearing plumed helmets, one fending off the other, an Earth-like orb dangling between them. The resemblances were uncanny. She recognized her own face on one side; Rhea's on the other.

She stared at the sketch, then looked from the sketch to where its smudged design had transferred itself to Rhea's snow-white sweater. "You wear your picture on your breast . . ."

Rhea stamped her foot in irritation. "Goddess be damned!" She wet her middle finger and tried to rub away the stain, static from the fabric shooting tiny sparks as her fingers worked the wool. Instead of erasing, the outline smudged, blank spaces filling, the whole penetrating deeper into the material.

"An unfortunate accident. Or an act of the Fates?" Phoebe wondered aloud. She didn't know where the question had come from. There were no Fates; they were myths, despite what her mother had insisted.

Weren't they?

Then the thought occurred to her out of nowhere that, by holding the image to her heart, Rhea had indelibly tattooed Phoebe on herself.

Rhea lashed out at her. "No! The Fates did not decree it. I am the Seer, not the Source. But you—look how you have permanently stained my heart!"

Phoebe recoiled reflexively, startled by the illogic of Rhea's sudden angry response.

"Take it! It is yours!" Rhea angrily threw the drawing in Phoebe's direction. It helicoptered between them to the ground.

It seemed to her Rhea's fury arose from nowhere. Stepping back, Phoebe could not bring herself to fetch the drawing from the driveway, much less bear the burden of this unfounded accusation. After all, they had just connected.

Who was Rhea, really? For that matter, who was Phoebe?

Mental processes tangled; Phoebe fixed her stare at the Earth.

"I am sorry." With a will, Rhea cleared the anger from her aura. "Let us begin again. I am Rhea, daughter of Lida."

Phoebe, taken unawares, studied the redheaded woman in front of her, trying to see . . . what? A family resemblance? A "feeling" of kinship? Phoebe was vaguely aware that, in her youth, Lida would have had myriad sexual encounters, not all of them out of her own desire. Among gods and mortals alike, promiscuity was pretty much the norm. And sexual violence.

But a sister? Here?

Rhea smiled, wrapping her arm securely around Phoebe's shoulders. "Come in. I'd love to show you my studio."

"Studio?" Though warning signs were in evidence, curiosity overwhelmed reason. "Let me first depower the car."

Phoebe reached in to pick up her pocketbook and shut off the car. She quickly checked her energy-wave device to make sure it was still operational. It glimmered, a digital sundial around which danced the mythic symbols of gods and goddesses warring, loving, conspiring. Antiquated, but to Phoebe, a geometry game she had mastered. Purse in hand, she moved again toward the house.

"Come in!" Rhea beckoned again.

It was dim inside, with shutters closed and the only lights being moonglow—the same low-fusion lights that came on inside Phoebe's vehicle at night. The walls were splattered with glowing murals of exploding supernovas and spiral constellations.

In this low-energy environment, Phoebe was aware her energies would drain. She must bank her reserves. She switched her brain to off mode.

Ahead of her, Rhea narrated. "It's close and a little dark on this floor. The better to dream and reflect. Of course, my ex-husband, Kronos, was from Mikonos. The sunny isles. He hated the dusk. He'd walk around throwing open shutters and bellowing, 'By Zeus, bring in the light!'"

Rhea turned, looking expectantly. Was Phoebe supposed to react? She knew nothing of Kronos, or the light on Mikonos, or Zeus.

"By Zeus. Invoking our son to bear the light!" Rhea repeated what must be a punchline of sorts.

Phoebe forced herself to lift her lips into what might be observed as a smile, though she didn't see her hostess's point at all. Was it simply about assigning the boy, Zeus, the lighting of the lamps? What was unusual about that? With each step, she became less certain. Why had she ever agreed to enter?

"You must know, Kronos relished irony." Rhea's intonation held more than a hint of sarcasm.

From the recesses of her thinking brain, Phoebe made note of Rhea's strange insistence on her reacting to Kronos's lighting preferences. She didn't understand the story Rhea was trying to relate.

What Phoebe did get: Rhea expected her utterances to be met with enthusiasm.

"Is the art . . ." Phoebe hesitated just before she would have been struck in the forehead by a low-hanging mobile showing the Old Sol system. She could see her face reflected in the shimmering orb of Old Earth. And then, Rhea's face, too, appeared.

She suddenly recalled what she'd glimpsed earlier of Rhea's drawing. "Is this all yours?"

Rhea turned around to see their faces reflected together in the blue-mirrored orb.

"Oh, yes, well. That's quite old." She waved the sketch, still in her hand, making the mobile whirl and spin. "We've evolved past this now, of course. Our story begins on Olympus on Old Earth. Divine ancestry and all that. You see how our past—yours and mine—is reflected in its afterglow?"

Phoebe mused on the fact that she had been appointed to head the team tasked with creating a new satellite to take up Old Earth's orbit and the god-like entities to populate it, and the prototype for those god-like entities as well. She thought about mentioning it. Perhaps Rhea's designs were connected to the effort the NIT was about to undertake. Perhaps Rhea should join her team.

Signs, signs, signs. Alarm bells rang louder in her ears. Something niggled at her mental processors as Rhea continued to lead her on the studio tour. Somehow, Phoebe grasped it was unsafe to share any of these thoughts with her supposed sister.

"Compromises being essential to preserve our imperfect union, such as it were . . ." Rhea pointed to the stairway ahead. Rose-tinted light spilled from above. "Kronos got his way with the second floor. Please come up!"

"Is he here?" Phoebe stopped by the foot of the stairs. She

clutched the pocketbook to her bosom, mimicking how Rhea had clasped the sketch earlier. "Your husband, I mean."

"Oh, no. The jealousy! Rages against our father. Believing that together we would scheme against him to inherit both Earth and the Heavens. Once he virtually imprisoned me and the children . . . the tension was unbearable. I finally managed to save Zeus, our youngest, by spiriting the boy away with me into hiding. I was only able to return here after the wars. It is the work that has saved me. Since then, I have made the second story mine."

Enter Goddesses

RHEA'S serpentine story only added to the sense that danger lurked in this house. But now, it seemed, Phoebe had little choice but to ascend the stairs. Besides, as drained as she was, even the rosy-red glow above promised to energize her. Wary of this strange place, Phoebe would need her mental faculties to be sharp. She switched her brain back to on.

Surreptitiously, she again peeked into her pocketbook, double-checking to ensure her wave-energy device was still inside, making sure that time was on her side.

Rhea's studio was an eruption of colour, form, and light—brightly painted canvasses covering the walls, stacked against tables, and resting on easels; clay sculptures in various stages of creation; wire sculptures of women with babies in their arms or in their bellies. They took their form at rest and at play, running and dancing, in loving communion and at war, embracing in love.

There were holograms, animations, AIs, and rainbow cyborgs created from a medium Phoebe could not discern, and colourful blown glass of bulbous females, women in full radiance. She saw where each of the symbols on the signs outside must have taken shape.

Each image bore a title: Selene, Artemis, Aphrodite . . .

Phoebe thought it all so odd, Rhea's obsession with the myths of old, to the point she seemed to have taken one as a description of her own life; for now that Phoebe's brain had flipped back to on, she recognized the tale Rhea had related as one of the ancient myths. "Don't you take on contemporary subjects?" she asked.

Rhea smiled and led her to a wall on which she'd tacked up sketches, cartoons for pieces not yet tackled. "Of course. I have one, in particular, in mind . . ."

Here again, Phoebe noticed, was her own likeness. She quickly turned her eyes away.

"Oh, no, where are my manners?!" Rhea cried. "Do sit!" She indicated a platform with a light wooden stool, presumably where her models would sit.

On one side of the studio, chest-to-ceiling windows brought Nature virtually inside, banked by a table at just the right height for a standing artist to practice her craft. The table was littered with sketches—works in progress. From her perch, Phoebe noted variations on the same theme—women in motion. Women's *emotion.*

Emotion. Sentimentality disturbed Phoebe's internal algorithms, churning her circuits.

Phoebe functioned on order; clearly, Rhea thrived on disorder. She must look to find information in the surrounding entropy to quiet her mounting internal chaos. She might ask if Rhea would let her organize the work in a more orderly fashion. She invoked an echo of Pythia's chant.

Rhea placed the sketch she'd made earlier on an easel perpendicular to the windows, where it covered some other luminous light work, then turned to decant a ruby-coloured liquid from a glass pitcher.

Outside, the sun was kissing the sky. Phoebe turned her eyes to drink in the rosy-hued meadow and, shadowed against the dawn, a grove of trees. An unfamiliar perfume from posies in a jar on the table beside her seemed to amplify the scent of wildflowers dancing outside to an unseen breeze. Nature's serenity created a startling contrast to the storm gathering inside.

"You must have some of this nectar. A health concoction made of kumquats and honey from my own bees." Rhea waved vaguely toward the meadow as she handed Phoebe a ceramic cup and then sipped from her own. "*Stin yeia mas.* To your health!"

Her belly ached from a lack of solid nutrition. Phoebe hesitated, but as she saw Rhea drain her cup, she took a polite sip. The cool, thick liquid acted as an elixir, unputdownable, diminishing Phoebe's resolve to stay alert nip-by-intoxicating-nip.

Dancing spryly around the studio and gesturing to each work of art, Rhea was explaining her process. Energy in motion.

Too much motion. The sheer volume of visual stimulation became overwhelming. Between Rhea's dizzying dance around her art and the whirl of colour and shape, Phoebe's vision was blurring. She was aware that might have an undesirable effect—reminiscent of the ill-fated ways alcohol had worked on Lida.

A quick scan of her internal body systems pointed to increasingly debilitating consequences based on increasing nectar consumption. Yet Phoebe couldn't control herself. She quaffed the remainder, setting down the cup only when the nectar was no more.

Rhea decanted a second portion for each of them and continued to detail her artistic method. "My palms become divining rods for energies, which then become images that may be embodied and dispersed through the hands. This is where I work that alchemy."

She gestured, her ruby-studded palm showcasing how the expanse of artistic renderings in this studio were all of her creation. Rhea turned back to Phoebe to get her reaction.

"Yes. But what has that to do . . .?" Phoebe managed to sputter.

"And here is the moment that revealed to me our sisterhood." Rhea peeled back that original sketch from the easel, the one she had waved to Phoebe outside. Underneath, a digital animation depicted Lida's face, at first radiant.

"I brought you here to witness my greatest creation, Sister," Rhea stated, her eyes blazing. "I call it, 'A Mother's Love.'"

"Mother!" Phoebe found herself unable to look away as the cyber-art animation showed her mother's stony visage atop a twisted body.

In the frame, Lida's torso, shoulders, and neck were being caressed, encircled by the long neck of a black swan.

"The swan. It's—" Phoebe watched in horror as the scene showed the swan caressing, pecking (was this meant to be a kiss?) the woman in the light frame.

"It's a reproduction. Quite lifelike, do you not think?" Phoebe detected something sinister in her sister's seemingly offhand utterance.

In the portrait, the swan was slowly tightening its vise-like embrace.

"Did you not love her as she did you?" Rhea queried, her face in shadow.

"Love? You call this love?" Phoebe stammered. She massaged her midsection. The cramping had returned. "Your creation—it is monstrous. That fowl, attacking my mother!"

"*Our* mother! Zeus, her rapist." Rhea's words turned venomous. "And you, prophetess. You, who could see! Who could warn. How dare you leave her to die?!"

Rhea's accusation, a lightning bolt out of the blue, struck Phoebe in the heart.

"But I didn't kill . . ."

"No?" Rhea demanded. "Watch."

A shadowy figure, hand raised, now moved behind Lida and the swan. Phoebe stood transfixed. The swan's face melted, transforming into the visage of a man—no—god. In horror, she watched him—the one Rhea called Zeus—blot out all light in the frame. Suddenly, a lightning bolt lanced down as if by Zeus's own fury, the silhouetted figure momentarily illumined to show Phoebe's own face. In her upraised palm, a smart energy device.

In a flash of lucidity, Phoebe could almost understand how her mother must have felt, the object of Zeus's thunderous power. She clasped and unclasped her pocketbook apprehensively, then slammed it shut with a startling finality. Was this anger?

"No! That's not how the story went. By the gods, I would save . . . I desperately wanted to save Lida . . ." Her voice trailed off.

"Aphrodite, kill all lights save for our mother's!" commanded Rhea.

The house, apparently controlled by an AI of that name, extinguished the brightening ruby sky outside. Blackout screens covered the studio windows.

The studio turned dark, with shades of grey barely distinguishing objects from empty spaces in the room.

Rhea, menacing, mounted the platform, towering over Phoebe. "Let us see by Fates' decree!"

Inside the dark studio, the only thing visible now was Lida's face, backlit by a white crescent moon and a single star—the morning star. Phoebe stood rooted, transfixed, as her mother's countenance morphed from luminous to lifeless. She stared unblinking at her mother's haunted eyes.

The swan twined around Lida from knee to neck, turning an embrace into a stranglehold and melting her mother's once radiant visage until it was transformed into the face of Aphrodite. Radiating out from her head like electrified curls was an aura of interlocking circles, much as the rings signalling the games at Marathon.

The composition reminded Phoebe of a Dali—the surrealist master painter of Old Earth in its latter days—now set into motion.

"You did this to her!" Rhea seethed. "You, who have no heart."

Phoebe registered that her sister had lured her into a confession —an act so heinous, even to one engineered to feel nothing, that she had locked this memory so deep inside her core that it was beyond her thought-retrieval system.

As the image morphed, she found herself unable to look away: the swan's long neck was now a question mark punctuating Lida's death sentence. The shadowy woman in the background receded in the auric effervescence of the Olympic rings.

Phoebe quivered in its shadow. Was she responsible?

But no. Phoebe didn't kill Lida; she was sure of that. Rhea's depiction was spun out of her own ill-reasoned imaginings—a plot her sister dreamed up to shift blame away from herself. The figures in Rhea's images were fetishes, stand-ins for the real object. The artist would use them to tease, torment, and betray the person they stood in for, just like in the Old Earth superstitions.

But why?

With the greatest effort, Phoebe tore her eyes away from the moving image. In the end, Phoebe concluded, it didn't matter. The pain in her stomach intensified. She couldn't stay silent.

"Rhea, destroyer!" Phoebe rose. "Our mother is dying in your hands, Sister—if sister you are."

"But, no, Sister dear, it is you who wrote her death sentence. I—I have made her immortal." Rhea, her eyes aflame, looked triumphant.

Phoebe tried to remain on high alert to stave off this feminine emanation of evil. By the second, her energy was being sapped.

"I must not power off," she commanded herself as she used her ebbing strength to unclasp her pocketbook once again. Something silver glinted briefly in the starlight emanating from the scene portraying Lida's dying—transforming, now washing over everything in brushes of green and blue, brown and grey, while the Olympian rings remained suspended rainbow-like above. "The goddess has no power to rewrite her story!" Phoebe struggled to reset the program on her energy-wave device to ready-aim-fire. It was almost like she was being overpowered.

With effort, Phoebe raised her arm, steadying her hand to aim directly at Rhea's face, become suddenly hideous to Phoebe's eyes. "You must pay, Rhea, for imposing your evil imagery on a mother you never knew. I am the memory keeper of Li—"

But before the name escaped her lips, Phoebe felt herself growing cold, her brain clicking in mental arithmetic, attuning to a new beat. In her ears, the be-bum, be-bum, be-bum changed, suddenly sounding as a series of swishing susurrations in syncopation, like waves washing inside her. She clasped the device, now set to fire, against the pain of her heart.

In Phoebe's belly, new life was crystalizing in the chrysalis of life-death-rebirth.

"I will not allow the new life inside you to suffer the tragedy of our mother. And hers. And hers before her," Rhea declared slowly.

An unfamiliar heart-stirring bewildered Phoebe. Even as she dimmed, she recognized what more the lightframe revealed: her earlier pain was a symptom of reproduction, a re-creation of her own inside her womb.

Rhea must have sensed it. And now, this *sister*, if that's who she was, was waiting to usurp Phoebe's birthright.

It was all too much to bear. Phoebe set her mental reasoning to upload to the cloud to avoid overload.

"Aphrodite, awaken!" Rhea paused as the shutters again opened, now showing a blood-red sunrise. "Dying swan to eternal morning star."

The wounded swan unwound from Lida's neck and fluttered out of its light frame, past the moon, winging outward toward a far star constellation.

In the glow of the rising star, Lida blinked open lifeless eyes, a frozen smile gracing her white lips.

Rhea turned toward her sister. "You see, I have broken the goddess's curse."

But Phoebe had switched off.

The sound from inside Phoebe's circuits quickened. "Be-bum, be-bum, be-bum."

Rhea placed her hands over her sister's womb, caressing the life inside and drawing out the double helix—the same life code that remained traced in charcoal over her own heart. "Live, little one! I will take care of you as my own. Together, we will rise."

Where death made room for a new life, a child leaped forth into the light. A sparkling mist sprayed over them, the light of Old Sol splitting the waters into a prism of colour.

Rhea turned toward this new generation arising from the waters. Her appearance followed the Seer's prophecy: "To create anew, the old must be destroyed."

Her reserve energy banks breathed life into Phoebe anew, if only for an instant. She fixed Rhea with a death stare before turning her wondering eyes to her daughter. "You are the one I have been waiting for. All that I am and ever may be, you will transcend."

It was the most Phoebe could muster. She was dimming out.

"She is mine." Rhea rejoiced over her sister's misfortune. "Asteria, my morning star."

"Asteria." Out of the depths of Phoebe's heart, something new was rising. "Asteria, you bring love to a mother's dying heart. Arise, fair daughter. Be free. You are the master of your own fate. And, know this, above all else: I love you."

The child's lips curled into a sly expression. Her mind was rapidly awakening. Even as Phoebe's life ebbed, her soul's wisdom, fresh implanted, now stirred inside Asteria.

Rhea held Asteria to the light. The girl suffered Rhea's embrace, the artist's delight undimmed by Phoebe's dying curse, her sister's offspring now to be shaped by Rhea's hands.

How little Rhea could understand. Here stood Asteria, the embodiment of nighttime oracles and falling stars. In her, a new breed: goddess, woman, cyborg, and something more, knowing a mother's undying love.

An omnipresence, the future hers alone to create.

FOREST DARK

P. L. Stuart

"Father, why are people scared of the forest?"

"Because it's the Forest Dark," I replied, on my haunches, sniffing the wind for prey.

"Just because it's dark, it's scary?" Saa asked from beside me, mimicking my position.

We were concealed in a blind made of dead trees. Before us, the Forest Dark loomed.

"It's a huge *dark* forest," I said.

"Are you scared of the dark?"

Shamelessly, "Yes."

"Yileen says you aren't scared of anything!"

"Untrue. Nothing wrong with being scared. Fear keeps you alive. There are . . . bad things in the forest. Things we shouldn't speak of."

"You've seen the bad things?"

I had. I shivered. I didn't want to scare her. I should've said nothing. The truth had just spilled out of me. I regretted it. "We speak of this no more."

"Hmmph." Not pleased with me, her nine-year-old brain cleverly found a different track back to the subject. "Does Keend know everything?"

"There isn't much Keend knows at all," I muttered under my breath.

"Keend's father was a druid!"

"No woman or man knows everything." I was far more impressed with Saa's tenacity than Keend's knowledge.

"Keend fears the forest, too. He says we should offer the dark woman to the forest. To . . . appease the *bad* things."

"Maybe Keend should offer himself to the forest instead of offering . . . a good woman," I retorted acerbically.

Surprise. "How can she be good if she's dark, Father?

"Colour has nothing to do with one's soul."

"Why is she a slave then? Keend says she's just a—"

"Never let Keend's words about Ija fall from your lips in my hearing again. Understood?" Stern, displeased fatherly voice.

"Yes, Father." Meek. Chastened. Yet not giving up. "Why is Ija a slave?"

An indictment I could lose my head for: "Lesser people feel important by keeping slaves. Ija was too far from home, and the slave traders captured her, sold her to Urkaa."

"If keeping slaves is bad, is Urkaa good?"

Best to evade that question. "Chiefs have to make hard decisions."

"Like . . . having . . . the dark woman as a slave?"

"Yes."

"I don't like Ija, Father." Saa sounded petulant. "She's *dark*."

Sigh. With a momentary tug on my heart, I wished for Riita and her simple, effective explanations of everything complicated in the world to Saa. I quickly cuffed my eye to get the tear that escaped, unbidden, before Saa could see. "Do you like Enee, Saa?"

Brightly, "Of course!"

"And what colour is Enee?"

"She's . . ." Wary. And aware. "Black."

"Do you love Enee less than, say Finaa?" Finaa was a grey horse.

"Finaa is bad-tempered." Pouting. "She tried to bite me once. I was only trying to give her an apple!"

"Is Enee bad-tempered?

"Never!" insisted Saa. "And Keend says Finaa is dumb!" Finally, Keend was correct about something. "Not like Enee!"

"It's like that with people, too. Colour has nothing to do with temperament, intelligence, or kindness."

She contemplated this, her breath steaming, her vivid blue eyes the only thing visible besides her pink lips and button nose, the fur hood pulled down low over her forehead. Then, tentatively, "Will you be mad if I speak of Keend again?"

"Depends on what you say about him."

Pause. Then, "Keend says all Black people are our enemy."

"The Black people are called Anibians. They are *not* our enemy. They're a great race who rule the whole continent except here in Sanaavia. They're the masters of the Eltnish, our southern neighbours."

Incredulous. "But not masters of Sanaavia?"

"Too cold up here for Anibian blood. Still, Ija's people are noble and wise. Some of our people's lack of nobility and wisdom brought Ija in chains to our village."

"But if Ija isn't our enemy—"

"Shhh!" I cut her off unceremoniously, adding a hand gesture. Gripping my spear, I strained my ears. I didn't look at her but knew Saa would be doing the same.

Her spear was not much shorter than mine but crafted for her strength and weight. She'd recently killed a juvenile bear at twenty paces: a clean throw, right through the young bear's eye, and we'd dined well on bear meat for a month. She'd grow into a fierce warrior like Riita.

Now, though, I worried she'd face something far worse than a bear, for it was no bear whose howl I heard. I didn't know what it was. That not-knowing froze my blood more than it was already freezing in the cold.

The sound came from deep within the forest. Something feral. Something angry.

Something *hungry*.

I drew my seax, spear in one hand, blade in the other. Saa

mirrored me. Her knife rasped out of its sheath. No instruction needed—just my example.

"When I say 'go,' run!" I said, keeping my eyes only on the forest. "Don't look back or slow! I promise I'll be at your back! Understand? Don't stop until you reach home!"

Faintly, "Father?"

That was all the protest I allowed. Petrified, I hissed, "Run until home!"

The howling became louder. Insistent. Drawing closer. I could feel fear, and also love and worry for me, streaming off my daughter like frost.

"Ready?" I said.

"I love you!" she said tearfully.

"I love you, too!" Those might be my last words to her. No more time for speech, or even to barely glance at her, if I was to save the most precious thing in my life. "Go!"

She bolted through the opening in the blind.

I waited, covering her retreat, barely breathing.

The trees at the edge of the forest began to rustle.

The snow silenced my daughter's footfalls as she ran for her life. I wouldn't leave until whatever horror emerged from the forest. I would face it, if I must, to purchase Saa's escape, though I could feel my bladder ready to give way with fright.

Spear and short-sword felt melded, iced over, bonded to my thick fur gloves. I didn't think I could let go of them even if I tried. They were part of my hands now.

An eternity, it seemed, passed. Then, the trees immediately before me shifted violently.

The eerie howl reached a fever pitch. The trees began to part. I drew back my left arm, spear ready for the throw. I would get but one chance. I would launch my spear at whatever came out of the forest, then turn tail and run, hoping I'd reach my village alive. Otherwise, my blood would stain the snow red as I was ripped apart by whatever evil haunted those trees.

The rustling of the trees ceased. The boughs melded back together.

Nothing emerged.

I waited, heart pounding.

The howling stopped.

The fear gripping me still held tight. Somehow, I knew the thing was not really gone—though perhaps it had retreated.

I didn't wait for any howling to recommence. I ran.

Saa had reached the village shortly before me. I found her speaking to Urkaa at our village's centre amid the longhouses. The dam of relief burst. She was safe! Relief overwhelmed her, too, when she saw me. She ran into my arms.

I held her, promising myself I would never let her go—and never to go near the forest again. No hunting trip was worth my precious Saa. We'd come back empty-handed that day, with no game to help feed our village. But we both lived.

"What did you see?" growled Urkaa. His guards, including Yileen —my lover once upon a time, after Riita had passed—were gathered about him, huge, doughty women and men with hard eyes, faces inked with the ritual tattoos of seasoned warriors.

"Lord, I saw . . ." I looked back toward the forest. Saa buried her face into my stomach, snuggling closer.

"Speak up, Goor, Goothson!" Urkaa pressed.

"I saw nothing. Only heard."

Urkaa glanced at Yileen. He knew she knew me well. She casually shrugged, offering no opinion. Urkaa didn't like this. He expected input from his guard captain.

"Maybe a wolf?" I opined uselessly.

"Maybe a wolf?" he repeated after me mockingly. "You'd never run from a wolf! You're telling me you ran from a wolf like a frightened baby?"

"Maybe not a wolf," I conceded. "The howling sounded almost human. But *like* a wolf. A snarl to it, yet there was a . . . a chirping, too."

Incredulity from my chief: "Howling, snarling, *and* chirping?"

Those were the only words to describe it. I didn't tell him I'd heard those sounds years before, when I was just a boy, hunting with my father and separated from him while we stalked game near the same Forest Dark, just as Saa and I had that day. And I didn't tell him what I'd seen, the thing that had made that snarling-howling-chirping sound, the thing that had haunted my dreams ever since.

After that day, I'd vowed never to go back to the Forest Dark. Yet I had, many times, and I'd never heard or seen anything like that again.

Until today.

"Lord," interjected Saa politely, yet with the whining urgency of the young, "forgive me . . . Father, I'm hungry."

"We'll eat once our chief is finished with us."

"Go," harrumphed Urkaa dismissively. "You're speaking but saying nothing. Feed your child."

While Yileen observed me closely, no doubt wondering what to make of my words, Saa and I bowed and left.

Once home, I fed Saa steaming porridge, well suited for breaking one's fast. I added some of what little honey we had left from summer stores.

"Father, what do you *really* think you heard?" Saa asked between slurps.

"Maybe a hungry or injured wolf?"

"This is one of those times Mother would say you're trying to . . ."

"*Convince* myself?" I smiled, finishing for her.

She nodded sagely. Then, changing the topic, "I want to be the greatest warrior in the village. Like Mother."

A lump rose in my throat, pride mixed with sorrow. "You will be, should you desire it."

"When?"

"You've just started to learn to hunt. Though you've done well, a warrior needs to learn more. To cook for themselves. Care for their weapons. Treat their own battle wounds."

"Who said I plan to get injured?"

Ah, the optimism, bravado, and naivety of the young! I laughed.

"Did Mother ever get injured in battle . . . before . . . ?"

"Many times." My laughter died as I remembered stitching up her wounds and, later, running my hands over scars as we made love . . .

Ultimately, my Riita died heroically, defending our clan during a raid on our village by a rival tribe. No doubt, she feasted in Udyn's corpse hall.

"And after her last battle . . . when she died . . . no one could heal her? She couldn't heal herself?"

Grief and pain, fresh as yesterday, choked me. "Her . . . wounds. . . were . . . too much."

"What good are warriors knowing how to heal themselves if Mother died anyway?" Saa cried with angry logic.

Her old tears came. Mine did, too. I couldn't sniffle them back. I embraced her. We cried, holding one another. We, too, had come close to death that day, I was certain. The strain of our narrow escape, the thought of our dead Riita . . . together, they weighed on us like an anvil.

But we still had each other. And our shaggy, loyal dog, Teed, who, sensing something wrong, padded over, nuzzling, trying to comfort us.

My thoughts still spun. I wanted to know what it was I heard in the forest—what I had *seen*, all those years ago.

Should I ask Keend? No, I decided. I had little faith in druids, and in any event, Keend was only an initiate, not yet affirmed as our village's druid since his father's passing. Besides, he was arrogant and a fool.

I could think of only one person who might know: the slave, Ija.

Ija, however, was difficult to speak to. Oh, I'd managed it surreptitiously a few times: sneaked her some cheese and bread to supplement the slop they fed her; whispered a kind word of encouragement; exchanged a look, conveying my sympathy for her plight, though she was by no means a weakling who needed my kindness. Still, I gave it freely.

Ija toiled as a slave, but she was proud and remained unbowed. She could not be beaten or cowed into submission. Once, they threatened to cut off her fingers one digit at a time and then begin on her limbs, and still, her eyes and words defied them.

Yet, for all their threats, they never hurt her grievously. A whipping here, a cuff to the back of the head there—that was the extent of the damage. She was simply too valuable. Not only did she do much labour around our village, she had the potential to be re-sold for coin.

Gaal, a famous slave hunter, had paid a great price in warriors' lives to capture Ija. In turn, Urkaa had given much gold to acquire her from Gaal.

That was because, as I'd told Saa, Ija was an Anibian.

We Sanaavians raided each other's villages and took slaves from among our own people, for the most part. But the rare Anibian found too far north, away from the relative safety of Eltnia proper, or taken during raiding missions to the south, was considered a gem, a prize not to be squandered.

Yet, I believed there was another reason they never killed or maimed Ija: they not only needed her, they feared her.

The Anibians, as even the Sanaavians knew—yet lived in denial of—were the revered first race. Superstitious ones among us wondered if the gods would have their revenge on us for dishonouring an Anibian. They forecast doom because we held her captive-- had dared to enslave one of the ancient ones.

Yet, still, my people dared to trade Anibian flesh. We forced the ones we caught, like Ija, into hard labour, kept them shackled and beaten, attempted to humble them.

I didn't necessarily believe in divine retribution. Yet I did believe it was very wrong to do what was done to Ija. It pained me to see her chained. I saw the silent suffering in her eyes—and the anger.

I'd spoken up about it one day, directly, stridently, to Urkaa. We'd argued. Only for the sake of Riita's dead spirit and because I was the only blacksmith in the village and thus of value was my life spared in the face of Urkaa's anger.

It would be hard to get near her, to speak to her. Still, I must try after what I had heard in the forest that morning.

Saa dozed by the fire. Nights were frigid, so I covered her with an extra fur. She stirred in her sleep but did not awake.

I went out and pulled the door shut, turning the heavy key. If Teed heard her charge stirring, she'd lie at Saa's feet, awake, vigilant, until my return. Then she'd resume dreaming dog dreams. Teed was tender as a lamb with us but was utterly vicious toward anyone who'd dare try to harm us.

I crept out into the cold night toward Ija's hut. I was a tall man but still fairly stealthy, though my warrior days were past. No one seemed to stir or notice me.

The hut where Ija was housed had no guard set outside. I pushed the unlocked door open, finding there were two posted within.

Juuwar and Heeb, barely more than children, had been given cheap bronze swords and no other weapons. I assumed they were paid fairly well to be alert. But they only ever ended up falling asleep.

Once Ija's labour was completed at the end of the day, the real warriors of Yileen's calibre who guarded Ija while her hands were freed to hold a spade or hammer chained her again and brought her back to the hut, placing her under the eyes of incompetents like Juuwar and Heeb.

Ija lay on a mat in the middle of the hut. Two posts were driven into the ground on opposite sides of the mat. To one post was chained a leg; to the other, an arm.

I was outraged and heartbroken over her inhumane conditions. How could anyone sleep like that, unable to move comfortably, constrained by the chains?

The mat was lined with dead grass. It would do nothing to keep her dry and warm on a cold, damp winter night. She was given no furs, just a thin shawl cast on top of her.

Juuwar dozed so close to the hut's door that I nearly tripped over him. Heeb slept at the other end of the hut. Their snores combined were enough to wake the dead. The fire in the fire pit near Juuwar was dying, embers flickering.

I nudged Juuwar with my toe. He spluttered awake, fumbling for his sword. I stepped on the blade. Had I had bad intentions, I could've easily killed him. "Peace. It's me." I stepped off the sword.

"Goor?" He came to his feet, rubbing his eyes. Heeb didn't wake. "What're you playing at?"

"I need to speak to Ija."

"Who? She's a slave. She has no name. We just say 'you' when we call her. And no, of course, you can't speak to her."

"My two silvers say otherwise." The coins, produced, glinted in the firelight: a fortune, an obscene portion of my meagre hoard.

Juuwar's eyes widened. He licked his lips greedily.

Still, he played coy. "I take your money, Chief cuts my balls off and stuffs your silvers along with my ball-sack in my mouth."

"I'll cut your balls off if you don't take the silver and give me a few moments with Ija. Pretend you were sleeping and didn't see me. Not too hard, I think, eh?"

"Just resting my eyes," complained Juuwar sulkily.

"Come now. I'll be swift."

Cunning-yet-stupid rat eyes narrowed. "You intend to hump her?"

"I mean no such offence to her."

"Who cares for a slave's offence?" He glanced over at the sleeping form of Ija. I saw regret and lust in his eyes when he turned back to me. "I'd hump her if Urkaa wouldn't kill me for tampering with his prize."

"You'd hump that piece of firewood over there if you could."

Insulted but greedy, he said, as anticipated, "Palm me the silver first."

I gave him the coins.

"Just a few moments." He wagged his finger at me. "If you hump her, I want to watch." A prurient leer.

Disgusted, I turned toward the mat.

Juuwar forestalled me. "If Heeb wakes?"

"The coming of all the gods wouldn't wake Heeb. Go outside. Watch for anyone else coming. Warn me if anyone approaches. If I get caught, they'll kill me. But I'll tell them I paid you. They'll do worse to you, the failed watcher, a traitor paid off with silver, than they will to me."

"That wasn't part of the bargain, me being your watchdog."

I held out my hand to take the silver back. He shook his head. I kept the hand out. "Give me the key."

"You don't need her to be out of shackles to hump her."

"The *key*."

"Only if you swear to take off only the leg chain. *Not* the arm chain."

"Very well."

"She cannot be freed entirely. She'll escape, and we'll be slaughtered for it."

Enough lecturing. "The *key*."

He snorted and gave me the key to Ija's chains. "This means I have to stay awake longer." He yawned. "Night watch is the best time to sleep." Then, mercifully, the idiot went outside.

I went to the mat.

Ija was awake. She moved slightly, chains jingling, the thin shawl cast aside. Her intense eyes glowed in the firelight.

Though slight of stature and painfully thin, strength emanated from her. A thick tuft of hair topped a face as finely carved as if from granite, with a regal nose and full and lovely lips. She was fiercely beautiful.

She stared up at me as I approached. I stopped a few feet from her.

"Goor, Goothson," she greeted me, her voice melodious and powerful.

I looked at her chains. Then, down at the key in my hand. "Greetings, Ija."

She spoke again, looking at the same key, pleading, yet somehow still dignified. "Free me, please."

The compunction to obey her was very strong.

Instead of freeing her, I said, "I . . . heard something . . . in the forest today. Something . . . dangerous. I feel . . . it's coming here. For all of us. As one of the Anib, you, I believe, are the wisest person in this village, though you are wrongfully enslaved. I fear for the safety of us all. For my daughter's safety. I left her alone, locked inside our home, willing to leave her unguarded, save for my dog, to come here to ask you about what I heard in the forest."

She nodded. "I do *know* what lurks in the forest," she said. I sensed no falsehood. "Release me, and I will tell you."

I stared down at the key. "When whatever it is comes, you won't have a chance to flee or fight if you are chained," I reasoned, talking to myself as much as to her. "No one deserves to die in chains." I raised my eyes again and met her intense gaze. "So, I free you, you tell me what that is out there? We have a bargain?"

"You have my word."

Enough for me. The chains binding her were off in moments. I stepped back and watched her warily as she stood, rubbing her wrist.

"I have been a prisoner here for many months," she said. "Did you never think about freeing me before?"

"Yes. But I was too afraid. Urkaa would kill me. Saa would be alone."

She smiled sadly. "You are a good man. But it's too late."

I gaped. "Too late for what?"

My terror rose as she said softly, "I know what's out there. What howls in the forest comes for *me*."

"What howls in the forest wants to kill *you*?"

She gave me weird smile. "Who said anything about wanting to kill me?"

Lithely, she glided past me. "Wait!" I cried as she left the hut. I spared a glance at Heeb, still slumbering like the dead, then hurried after her.

I found she had halted not far from Juuwar, who had his back to us as he looked up dazedly into the night sky. Ija and I followed his gaze.

A full moon rose over the dark outline of the forest, giving light enough that, even against the sable sky, I could see them. Their flight pattern was similar to that of birds, but they were far bigger than any birds I had ever seen and slowly circling downwards.

Bats!

"Juuwar!" I called out in warning, but Juuwar did not move, did not turn, did not seem to hear or notice me.

Then I heard Ija say to me firmly, "Go back to your home. Lock the door. Keep your daughter and your dog inside. Don't come out until it is over."

I didn't wait to hear more from her. I ran.

I dared glance back once during my flight, almost tripping, and my heart nearly stopped beating in my breast from fright, for what I saw was no longer Ija, a woman.

It was a monster.

I stopped, too scared to move. She . . . *it* . . . sprang away.

The creature she'd become bounded swiftly as a wolf. I ran once more, feeling my bladder void. I'd pissed my breeches.

I reached the door, fumbled with the key. I flung it open. Teed leaped forward but managed to catch herself when she realized it was I, her master.

Saa was stirring. I pushed a heavy table in front of the door, legs scraping the floor, though I sensed such measures would be futile against what was outside. I swung back to Saa. She woke with a start and rushed to me.

"What's happening?" Sleep slurred her words.

Teed rushed to the window, paws clawing the glass, howling. Saa rushed, too.

"No! Don't look outside!" I cried, but it was too late. She had pressed her face to the glass.

I could rip her away from the window. But how could I protect her if she was unaware of what was happening? If I died that night, she needed to know the peril she faced, no matter how terrible.

I came up behind her, towering over her shoulder, looking out as well. Teed stopped howling and briefly whined, then was silent. Her paws scratched the window as she struggled to stay on her hind legs and peer out.

The three of us watched as the household warriors of Urkaa, with the chief himself, rushed out, some holding cressets, lighting up our village. As they reached the hut that had housed Ija, I saw Juuwar's headless body lying in the snow, blood everywhere.

Villagers rushed out of their homes at the commotion.

Giant bats, a dozen maybe, alighted on the ground. Villagers screamed. Urkaa's warriors stood transfixed, weapons drawn, quaking at the ghastly sight they must have thought was some malevolent sorcery emerging from the Underworld's pits. Keend was there, too, druid staff in hand, paralyzed in horror, staring like the rest at the monstrous bats, bigger than horses, with giant fangs and wingspans longer than half a longhouse and giant fangs.

And then they transformed, shifting into mortal form.

They were all women, though I did not see Ija among them: fierce women, wearing only thin shifts like her, impossibly able to bear the frigid air of the north. They radiated martial competence no mortal could contest. They radiated death.

And then they released it.

Courageously, Urkaa and his household troops charged the bat-women. I believe they knew they ran to meet their ends. Still, they were stout spearmen and mighty shield maidens. They'd die to defend their village from the monsters invading it.

And die they did, horribly.

One bat-woman, inhumanly quick, flew right at Urkaa, who was a bit ahead of the rest, with Yileen, faithful captain, at his heels. Gnarly hands warped, turned into vicious claws, and grabbed Yileen as she stepped in front of her lord to shield him with her body, her sword swinging downward with a cut that would have cleaved most foes in twain.

The creature dodged that cut as if it were child's play, grasped Yileen by the throat, and wrenched. I didn't hear the snap, but I saw the awkward way my former lover's neck twisted, saw her eyes open wide in surprise—and saw the light in those eyes go out. Neck broken, she was dead before she hit the snow.

Urkaa shouted his war cry, stabbing at his captain's slayer with a seax. Another bat-woman swiped her curled fingers-turned-claws at the chief's eyes. He fell in agony, face shredded. As he fell, the same bat-woman slashed again with stupefying speed. She opened Urkaa's gut, entrails spilling out of him.

Hands drenched in more blood with each new victim, the monsters began to dispatch the rest of Urkaa's proven household troops, who fell as if they were stalks of wheat before a scythe.

Then they turned on the other villagers. Some brave ones tried to attack. Others simply tried to defend themselves. Most ran away, screeching in terror.

I pulled Saa away from the window, holding her little head between my hands. "Listen! No matter what you hear, wait till you're as certain as you can be that they've all left! Only then, come out! You hear me? Don't come out for anything until it's safe!"

"Father—"

Her eyes widened as I shouted in her face, "No matter what you see, no matter what happens to me, do *not* open that door until it is safe! Take the spare key from the pantry to open it. I'll keep the other key. Then take whatever food you can, take Teed, and get to the next village! Thirty miles south! You know your directions! Watch the sun —it will guide you! Understand?"

"Yes, Father," she whispered, crying.

"I love you, Saa!"

I did everything I could to shush her as she quivered and her tears streamed. My last instructions as I let her go and pushed her away from the door, Teed huddled near her, looking as bewildered as Saa, were, "Stay close to Teed! She'll protect you!"

"Father, I love you!" She ran back to me, sobbing. I crushed her against my belly again. Then I pushed her away, then pulled the heavy table away from the door, which I flung open and stepped through, spinning at once to quickly slam it shut behind me. I locked it, pocketed the key, and turned.

In a blur all around me, fangs flashed, whirling feet delivered kicks, hands delivered crushing punches or curling into horrible claws that ripped out intestines, carved sinew and viscera, or grabbed hold of bones, snapping, twisting, leaving mortal bodies a ruined mess. Any human would have been powerless to fend off those monsters. They scowled with disdain at their prey as they crunched windpipes between slender yet vise-like fingers and contemptuously tore out throats.

Those of my fellow villagers who had not simply fled (and died as they ran) swung swords, axes, pieces of kindling, and kitchen implements or used their own teeth and hands and feet to fight desperately, bravely, for their lives. But against the unnatural speed and skill of those things, it was hopeless.

My village had survived droughts, famines, and raids but couldn't withstand the bat-monsters.

Or my treachery from within. *What have I done? Udyn help me, what have I done?*

Maw open, full of fangs, one monster sat, legs crossed, hunched over, noisily feeding on Juuwar's headless body, slurping his blood. Juwaar's mangled flesh was torn down to bone. The bat-woman thing lapped his blood as greedily as Teed lapped the water I put in her bowl three times a day.

The only person still showing signs of life was Keend, our aspiring village druid.

No paltry minor spells he could have cast—intended to halt blight in crops, boil water, or ease the symptoms of a flux—could have saved our villagers or himself that night.

Keend crawled, futilely trying to get away, weakly dragging his body through the snow on his belly, both legs missing, leaving a trail of blood and matter. One of the bat-women got her clutches into him, raised him up like he was a rag doll, bared her fangs, and bit deep into his chest. He shuddered, and his still corpse was scornfully cast back to the ground.

None of the other bodies littering the snow, feasted on by monsters, so much as twitched.

My guts churning, my mind almost blank with horror, I stumbled forward, my footsteps muffled by the blood-soaked snow, shuffling toward the nearest bat-woman, who did not feed but instead stood aloof with a few companions. She watched me impassively, neither she nor the rest making any move toward me. How I found the courage to come close to these fiends, I still do not know.

"Where is . . . Ija?" I asked the woman tremulously.

"She returns." She looked skyward. She was stunningly beautiful. Unlike Ija, she was pale-skinned as any Sanaavian, with blonde locks and cold green-red eyes.

She was also utterly frightening, as were all the bat-women. Her sharpened incisors were as long as my little finger.

I heard that snarling-howling-chirping sound again right above me. I raised my eyes once more to the night sky.

Soaring overhead, then coming lower, was another great bat. It landed in the snow and became Ija, once more a woman, but with blood-red eyes and snarling fangs.

The pale, yellow-haired bat-woman I'd been speaking to and those with her withdrew with deferential bows to Ija.

I'd already pissed myself with fear. I had to pucker my buttocks so that I didn't shit myself, too. *I must smell like an outhouse*, I thought inanely.

Ija stood, unearthly, imperious, gorgeous, deadly, a few feet from me: the woman-thing I'd freed, who had killed my entire village with the aid of her fellow monsters. I had the blood of my people, whom I'd known all my life, on my hands.

Suddenly, I stooped over, vomiting, filled with guilt and nausea over those pitilessly slain whom I'd betrayed. I felt I should go to Ija, bare my neck, and let her rip my throat open in recompense for my crimes.

"What . . . what are you?" I dared to ask her when I finished retching, wiping my foul mouth with the back of my coat's sleeve.

"Among the Anib, they call us vympyr," she said softly.

"Vympyr?" I spat bile from my throat, whispering the unfamiliar word in fear and awe. "Years ago, when I was a lad, hunting near the forest, I saw a giant bat. It sounded the same as you and your . . . comrades. I fled after I saw it. So, it was a . . . a vympyr? It has been a nightmare of mine, frequently, ever since."

"Sometimes, nightmares come true." She sounded amused.

"What are vympyr?"

"An ancient sect among the Anib. Few of us remain. And fewer still know we yet exist. We are hunters, trackers. We travel these lands rooting out evil like slavery, stalking in stealth and secrecy until it is time to strike. My retainers have been following me at a distance since I was taken as a slave. They waited for the right moment—for me to be freed."

It did not make sense to me.

"Slave-catchers managed to take you . . . how? You could kill a hundred warriors and not receive a scratch! Or you could just fly away!"

I caught a faint slyness in her reply. "You do not believe I was overpowered?"

I saw it then. "No, you *let* yourself be caught. You hunt down the slavers. And those who deal with them, profiting from the slave trade. You desire all people to be free from that scourge. Including the Anib."

"You are no fool, blacksmith."

I continued to ponder her words. "You said the others are your . . . retainers?"

"I am a minor queen only, among the Anib. Still . . ."

I went to my knees in piss-soaked trews. "Lady Queen," I said humbly. "I . . ." I felt foolish. I didn't know how to treat a queen. I'd never met one. I said ridiculously, "I regret that you've been treated so harshly. Not all our people are cruel." That mattered not one whit when all of our people who'd treated her poorly were now slaughtered.

"True. You are not cruel, blacksmith."

Yet, furious and grieving, I dared shout, "But you *are* cruel, Lady Queen! I thought the Anib were all kind and noble! To massacre an entire village? Was everyone who lived here so unworthy of life?"

"Was I so worthy of enslavement?" she hissed, and I nearly reared back from the terror and command of her voice. "Does anyone deserve to be a slave? I would kill ten thousand callous villagers who were complicit in such gross servitude to save one slave. We stamp

out an evil practice enacted on Sanaavians, Anib, all people! There is
a cost!"

Tears filled my eyes. "Could they not be . . . educated? Saved? Did
they all require . . . extermination?"

"Most of your villagers were older than you. All your young ones,
save Saa, have long gone on to larger villages and towns for opportunity's sake. The ones here . . . they were fixed on and determined in
their bigoted ways, married to the idea of slavery being just. There
was no redeeming them."

I swallowed. I had never seen my fellow villagers in that light.

Yet, even were Ija correct, I didn't wholly agree. Everyone was
redeemable. Everyone deserved a chance for redemption, to do
better.

Still, I understood vengeance. The day we fought the raider and
my Riita died, I hacked to pieces the corpses of those who killed her,
long after they were dead, until others pulled me away.

But what use was it to argue with this creature? I let it be, swallowing my guilt. "What becomes of my daughter? Of me?"

"On your feet."

I stood.

"Be free of shame. Your villagers were evil or complicit in evil.
Your chief, corrupt. You were the sole villager of a hundred and
twenty-one souls who dared even speak up to your chief against the
immorality of my enslavement. In your heart, I know you would have
willingly died to protest that slavery. But you could not leave Saa an
orphan."

How she knew I was the only one who'd protested her slavery, I
didn't know. It didn't matter. I wept again, unashamedly, for my dead
villagers.

She let me and went on. "The others of your village, raised in hate
and ignorance, whipped me, pelted me with stones, spat on me, and
despised me for the colour of my skin. I slaved from dawn till dusk to
build their houses, draw their well water, do their errands, yet I was

treated as less than dirt. Your greedy chief and warriors profited from and encouraged the slave trade. Urkaa haggled with Gaal over me like I was a mule. I gave the time, living among your villagers here, to see if any were redeemable, worth saving. Save you, none were."

In my mind's eye, I saw Yileen, dead now, her neck snapped like a twig. I took a moment to close my eyes, squeezing out cold tears, mourning her most of all.

We'd shared some good moments. She'd lent me much comfort after Riita. Like Riita, she was a strong warrior. Now fallen like Riita, too, in battle. Riita would have a new comrade in the corpse hall.

"This village was a plague," continued the vympyr leader. "One that needed to be cleansed, root and stem. As will any other villages engaging in slavery. Gaal and his village . . . they shall be next to feel our wrath."

I shivered. Her voice had turned from kind to ruthless ice. But then it turned kind again.

"We give you your life in exchange for being a messenger. Tell others what you saw here tonight." She paused. "Now, as for your daughter . . ."

My tears had dried. "What do you want with her?" I asked sharply, ready to die to defend her, knowing it was hopeless against the creature I faced.

"To become one of us."

Bile rose in my throat. "You'd turn her into . . ."

"A vympyr. There would be an initial pain, but—"

"I do not wish my daughter to suffer!" I cried.

Ija made a dismissive gesture. "Soon, she would feel pain no more. A moment's agony is a fair price to pay for uncounted centuries of life, barring murder, illness, or other misfortune, which we vympyrs rarely fall prey to." She smiled. "We are hard to kill."

Horror gripped me. "I beg of you, please leave her with me! She is dearer to me than life. If you must take one of us, take me!"

"Your offer is appreciated. Yet—do not take offence—you have no value to us. Vympyrs can only be women." She studied me for a long moment. "You are of good heart," she said at last. "As I said, the only worthy mortal in your village, besides your daughter. Upon reflection, I agree with you. I do not think she could fully comprehend what is being asked of her. She is still too young. So, while I could just take her from you, I will grant you this boon."

Relief flooded me, so much so my knees grew weak. "Thank you! Oh, thank you! But . . ." I looked at the carnage around us. "You wish me to be a messenger. But no one will believe me when I tell them what happened here."

"Nevertheless, you will tell them. Those who don't believe you will come here to disprove your story, and I will be waiting for them. I will not harm them. But I will. . . demonstrate . . . the truth of what you tell them."

I shuddered, thinking what "demonstration" she might offer, but accepted it, as I must. "I will tell them. Upon all the gods, I swear it. I can scarce forget what I've seen here for the remainder of my days."

"They shall be long," she prognosticated. "You shall live to be old."

I wondered at that. Could she truly tell the future? "When will you return to the lands of the Anib?" I asked.

"In good time. We still need to eradicate as many of the slave-trade warbands as we can. And we need to feed, regain our strength."

She must have seen my expression of distaste. "There is much animal game in the Forest Dark. I will feast on no more mortal blood these coming days other than the blood of slave traders we find and those who support them. More likely, we shall dine on deer, moose, and mountain cat."

Once more, I nodded and then begged to take my leave. She granted it. Shakily, I went to one knee before her again to say my farewell. "I'd bid you long life, but . . . it seems unnecessary."

She smiled a fanged smile that disappeared as she waved me to rise.

I clambered up and, as I turned on my heel, heard her take flight: no longer a beautiful woman but, once more, a bat. When I turned back, gazing up into the night sky, I could see nothing.

By the time I managed to pry my daughter, shaking and crying, from what had been our home and calm down Teed, barking madly with fear and anxiety, I had composed myself somewhat. I felt a strange calm, though I was surrounded by horror and slaughter.

When Saa's hysteria had passed, I asked her, "What did you see?"

Huge eyes looked up at me. She stammered "E-Everything."

How could I explain to her what had happened? It was inexplicable. At least she'd been locked inside, unable to hear what Ija had offered.

The carnage that awaited outside our home was like no battlefield she would ever tread. Appalled, shaking, she just stared.

Then, bravely, though she wept, she took my hand.

We set to work.

***

IT TOOK us two days to burn the corpses of our fellow villagers—gory, detestable, awful work. But my daughter, through tears, aided me in the task.

That done, we washed as best we could, changing our blood-soaked clothes into garb for a long journey. We packed what provisions we could find, then trudged south through the snow, Teed yelping much of the way behind us.

The next village we came to wanted to try us as murderers when I told them our tale. They believed we two strangers had somehow slaughtered our village and were fleeing the felonious deed.

An aging blacksmith, a girl, and a dog? Destroying an entire village, including Urkaa's heavily armed household fighters?

Fools.

Still, they detained us while their chieftain sent some of his best warriors to the site of our village to investigate.

When the warriors returned, they were still pale with fright. They exonerated us, vouching for our innocence and the veracity of our account. They would not speak about why they believed us, but we were freed, apologized to, and treated with great esteem and honour, if perhaps with a little wariness, as if we might bring ill fortune.

I knew what had happened. They had encountered Ija.

The village blacksmith having recently died, I filled a need and so was once more considered valuable.

We and our new village prospered.

***

TWENTY YEARS LATER, I am old but alive. My shame and guilt over my destroyed village have faded a bit over time. It has never gone away completely.

I live in that same tiny village we took refuge in all those years ago, thirty miles south of the one where I was raised, from whence Saa and I fled the night the vympyrs came.

My daughter is a great warrior, and when the old chieftain died two years ago without heirs, the people chose Saa to be the new chieftain: a prudent choice.

The slave trade in Sanaavia, though much diminished, still exists. Saa refuses to keep or trade in slaves. Though our village thrives and thus needs no slaves, some people have scorned Saa for this obstinacy, saying she forewent a great opportunity. Others have praised her for refusing the slave trade.

Regardless, overall, she is popular and respected.

She married a man named Siivy, whom I have trained to succeed me as the village blacksmith. They have three strong daughters. The oldest, twelve years of age, is named after my wife.

I no longer go hunting with Saa. My eyesight has begun to fail me.

Teed lived long for a big dog, nigh sixteen years. She's buried behind Saa and Siivy's house, where I live with them.

One day, we all sat by the hearth. Saa, Siivy, and Riita were preparing their kit to go hunting the next day while the two younger children played together in another room. I'd be minding the younger ones while those three hunted. Or rather, in my dotage, they'd be minding me.

Riita asked Saa, "Mother, can we hunt near the Forest Dark tomorrow?"

"Never go there!" I exploded.

Riita jumped, shocked at my sudden anger. I was her beloved old grandfather who fussed over her and her siblings, seldom, if ever, raising his voice.

Siivy stared at me balefully. But he did not chastise me for being harsh with his daughter. He was a patient, solid man and a good husband to my daughter. I shook my head toward him in apology, too ashamed to look at Saa, who also must be cross with me for yelling at Riita.

"Forgive me." I reached, bones creaking, for my granddaughter's hand. Warily, she took my hand in hers.

My explanation would sound weak, even to a young woman's ears. Yet . . . "The Forest Dark is dangerous. *Never* go there. I just want to keep you safe, daughter of my daughter."

Riita looked uncertain, yet she clutched my hand. "But, Grandfather, didn't you live, many years ago, near the forest? Didn't you and Mother hunt there?"

Before I could answer, Saa spoke, "Yes, Riita, Saadaughter. We both hunted in the forest before our village burned down in a fire." That was the convenient lie told at large about our village's destruction.

"Have you ever seen the forest since, Mother?"

"Yes," she replied, and I was immediately alarmed. "I hunted there . . . some time ago. After your youngest sister was born."

I stared at her, flabbergasted. I knew nothing of it.

Saa glanced quickly at Siivy before she turned to me. "On my hunting trip to the forest, I saw one of our . . . old friends."

A chill ran down my spine. "Ija?" I breathed.

"Who is Ija?" Riita asked.

Saa replied, "The very old . . . friend . . . I mentioned. She asked me if I remembered the favour offered to my father. I told her I recalled it well."

I gasped.

"What favour?" Riita, utterly confused, let go of my hand.

Siivy shushed her, gently removing her from us. "Let Mother speak to Grandfather. Help me pack the hunting knives."

She was ushered away by her father.

I turned back to Saa, horrified, "You heard . . . that night . . . what Ija offered me?"

"What she offered *me*," Saa corrected me gently. "I'm not angry with you for declining Ija's offer. I wasn't of age and you spoke for me as my father. But, goddesses and gods forgive me, I thought about it often down through the years. I was obsessed with it, though I kept that obsession to myself."

"What did Ija say?"

"She knew, one day, I'd come. She gave me the same choice she gave you long ago. But I was a woman full-grown by then. Able to speak on my own behalf."

Oh, no. I could not speak.

"I was happy being your daughter. Happy, being Siivy's mate. With my children. But . . . I always wanted more. Prodigious strength. To . . . fly."

No!

She raised her head. Quickly, so no one else would see, she flashed a smile. Her fangs protruded. Her eyes turned crimson.

The fangs receded. Irises reverted.

"You've kept this from me all these years?" I whispered.

"What matter? I am what I am. And I will never judge someone by what *they* are again. Thank you for teaching me that."

All I could do was stare at her mournfully.

"I'll outlive my furthest descendants, barring mishap. That will be . . . sad. Yet, I am content. Siivy knows. He'll keep my secret. We'll remain together until his end. I love him and don't wish to be parted from him while he lives out his short mortal life. He loves me, too, but says it is good enough for him."

I understood and agreed with Siivy. Near-eternal life seemed . . . unnatural.

But my daughter had chosen otherwise. She was a grown woman, shield-maiden, chieftain. Who was I to gainsay her choice?

"After Siivy grows old and dies," she continued, "I'll disappear. My children will think me dead, too. They'll forget me in time. They'll go on; live their lives."

I didn't need to ask where she would go after her husband died. She'd go to the land of the Anib. The land of the vympyr. To live out a deathless life. Among her new . . . kind.

She stared back, implacably at first—until I saw a blood-red tear threaten to escape her eye.

She dropped her head. Then raised it, looking me in the eyes.

I saw sorrow. But also pride in what she was.

Still, a heavy sigh. A sniffle. "Do you still love me, Father?"

In answer, I put my arms around her. "A horse isn't good or bad because of its colour," I whispered to her. "What's in the heart is what makes the character of a woman, man, or beast. Or . . . vympyr."

She clenched me tighter at my words, happy.

We stayed like that until Riita came back with Siivy. Then my granddaughter touched my arm impatiently, and I broke my embrace with her mother.

Riita demanded to hear more stories about the Forest Dark.

'TWAS

Richard Sparks

We were deserters. We were on the run from My Lord of Brigstowe's army, which we hadn't wanted to join in the first place but had been conscripted into. Most of all, we were on the run from our fearsome drill master, Serjeant-at-Arms Jack Blunt—known to one and all as Serjeant Bastard. We tried not to think about him coming after us or Esmeralda's father tracking us with his hounds as we galloped across the bleak moors towards the Uplands and the cold rain fell . . .

Esmeralda.

The loveliest life there ever was or ever will be.

That was the blessing that had been laid on her on her naming day by her mysterious godmother, who had been coming to her in her dreams ever since she turned sixteen a few weeks ago. *She has something for me, and I have something for her, she says. I don't know what it is. All I know is that the fate of the realm depends on it.*

We'd have done anything for Esmeralda. Well, her and the hundred of gold she'd promised each of us if we helped her find that godmother.

We wouldn't earn that much in twenty *years* in My Lord's army, no matter how high we rose through the ranks. So, before dawn that morning, we met at the rendezvous where Peat, the stable boy, had horses for us and fled the town.

On one side of me, mounted on a big, nasty-tempered stallion, was Grell. Grell was the best damn Orc with a battle-axe you'll ever see. You don't have to take my word for it. Serjeant Bastard himself said so at our graduation ceremony. Bumping along on his cob on my other side was Oller. Oller was half Grell's size but nine times as slippery. Oller, raised on the streets of Brigstowe, was a thief. He was only a lad, barely out of his teens, but with a face older than his years. Oller had seen a lot in his short life and done more dark deeds than you might care to know about. You can't miss Grell, with his roaring and stomping, whirling his great axe—but you won't see Oller, in the shadows, at work with his knives. I'm just me, Daxx, an ordinary sword-and-board grunt—but I used to be a battlemage, and maybe, one day, I'll be one again. Who knows? Now we're on the run, our futures ahead of us.

And behind us, Serjeant Bastard. My Lord's hounds. And Peat, the stable boy.

Who is also a poet.

Peat has written poems for Esmeralda before. And he shyly gave her his latest masterpiece before we left.

Which, as we slowed to a walk to give our horses a rest, Oller remembered.

"D'you get a lot of poems?" he asked.

"All the time," Esmeralda said glumly.

"I've never made one up," he said. "I dunno how. Have you, Daxx?"

"Not really, no," I said.

"How can you *not really* make up a poem?" Oller challenged. "You either do or you don't."

"Well, I've done rhyming in my head sometimes," I said. "You know, you see a wall or something and think *that's tall.* And then you go, *Look at that wall, Isn't it tall? Compared with that, I am small.* It's not . . . profound, or anything."

"No," Oller agreed, "it's bollocks. But it does rhyme. For the most part. You, Grell?"

"Yeah. Orc poems. *Slash, stab, thump, whack. Hit me, and I'll hit you back!*"

"Also bollocks," Oller pronounced, and turned back to Esmeralda. "Is it any good?"

Esmeralda grunted. "If it's anything like the last one . . ." she muttered, meaning *it'll be terrible.* She felt about in a pocket inside her cloak for the piece of paper that Peat had given her in the dark before dawn. She unfolded it, read it, and grunted again.

"Well, go on, then!" Oller said. "Read it. Out loud. I want to hear it."

She said, "If I do, you'll want to cut your ears off."

"I'll be the judge o' that," Oller objected. "I like poems, me! I like it when the bards sing. Some of them make it up as they go along; did you know that? You can ask them anything while they're in the middle of singing, and they'll drop that in and make it clever. We had a great bard in the Thieves Guild back in Brigstowe; you couldn't throw anything at him he couldn't handle. We all thought he should go off to Mayport and be famous—have a great career, he would. Only, of course, being Thieves Guild, he'd nicked it all. From other bards. Who'd beat the crap out of him if he used their stuff without the appropriate credit and royalty payments. You can sell stolen goods easily enough if you know the right fences. Apparently, you can't sell stolen songs. There aren't any song fences. Go on, then," he urged Esmeralda.

"Once is enough," she said and handed the piece of paper to me.

I took a deep breath and read aloud:

Thou shinest, at My Lord's High Table,
Like the fairest maid in fable;
I'd climb at night if I were able
To get a good throw with my cable
So that it looped around thy gable,

And tryst with thee, in silk and sable,
Until the dawn! Then, down my cable
('Twere hanging still, around thy gable),
Back to my stall in My Lord's stable.
I'd love thee, though thy name were Mabel*!*

I looked at my audience. Grell's face was closed, frowning; Oller's was open, mouth gaping, eyes wide, eyebrows raised.

Esmeralda was scowling under her hood.

"That's good, that is!" Oller said approvingly.

Esmeralda stared at him in disbelief. "It's *drivel!*"

Oller frowned. "No, it's not. All them rhymes? That's *proper* poetry, that is. Every line rhyming? Half the time, they only rhyme every other line in ballads, and then different rhymes all the time. Not *one* rhyme, like your poem. How many lines is it?"

I counted. "Ten."

Esmeralda said, "And they're all—"

"Yeah, the *same rhyme!*" Oller beamed. "That's exactly my point! Clever, that. I've hung from gables myself any number of times, but I'd never've thought of *cable*. I'd think *rope*. Like I usually think when scaling roofs and such. And *rope* doesn't go with *gable*, does it? So, there you are. That's proper poet-thinking, that. And proper poetry words. So, you can't say it's not proper poetry. It's got *'twere* in it! Proper poems have *'twere*, all the time. I've heard them. And *'twas*."

Esmeralda's frown disappeared to be replaced by the loveliest of smiles. "Oh, very *good*, Oller! You had me completely. I really thought you meant it for a moment."

Oller was baffled. "I do."

"It's 'proper poetry because it's got *'twere* in it'?"

Oller stared at Esmeralda as if she was an idiot. "That's what I said."

Esmeralda stared at Oller as if *he* was an idiot.

One of them, I knew, was right. And it wasn't Oller.

"And you *meant* it?" she said.

"And *tryst*," Oller said. "That's a proper poem word. And *thee* and *thy*, he didn't call you *you*, like an oik; he used proper poetry words."

Esmeralda was speechless. She looked at me helplessly.

I shrugged.

"One of the best poems I've ever heard, in my humble opinion," Oller continued. "What's it called?"

Esmeralda studied him. She was thinking, *If this doesn't convince him, nothing will.* She said to me, "Turn it over."

I did.

On the other side, words were written in block capitals, decorated with little hearts and big X's.

"Its title," I said with deliberate care, "is, 'For Esmeralda, Fairest of Maidens with the Fairest of Names, but Nothing Rhymes With It.'"

There was a silence as Oller puzzled it out. "What, like *orange*?"

"Doesn't rhyme with orange," Grell objected.

"Not with, *like*," Oller elaborated. "Nothing rhymes with orange. Or Esmeralda, he's saying. A bard told me that once. He said, 'Nothing rhymes with orange.' Some Lord who loves poems—*proper* poems—was offering a hundred gold pieces to anyone who could find a rhyme for orange. The bard knew I was good at finding things; he wondered if I'd come across one. I hadn't. Nearest anyone had got to it, he said, was some troubadour who travelled everywhere, who said way up north, way beyond the Uplands, the men wear wool skirts with crisscross patterns and have a bag hanging on the front of them called a *sporrinj*. No one believed him. Might've done if he hadn't said that about the patterned skirts. I mean, it's cold enough down here in winter, never mind way up north beyond the Uplands. What man would wear a skirt when it's bloody freezing, eh? And hang a bag on it?"

Esmeralda was staring at Oller open-mouthed. On her, with that perfect mouth and those blue eyes that you could drown in, it was an expression so utterly wondrous that you just wanted to stare back with your own mouth open.

Which Oller did.

Esmeralda shut hers first and then turned to me. "I hope you're in charge, not him."

"We're a democracy," I said.

"Well? Who's in charge of it, whatever *that* is?"

"We all decide together," I said. "We talk it through and see what we all think."

Esmeralda shook her loveliest head in disbelief at such a ridiculous idea. Sunbeams danced in her golden hair, sapphires glinted in her wide blue eyes, and unicorns and pixies and rainbows frolicked around her head.

"Oh, gods," she groaned. "Unicorns and pixies, right?"

I nodded. "And rainbows."

"Fuck," she muttered, and rode on ahead of me.

SOMETHING MUST HAVE TAKEN root in Oller's imagination from that incident. Something that worked on him as it grew over time and eventually bore fruit. Which he presented to us when he recited it at our most recent Yuletide Eve Feast. He climbed up onto the bench at our long table and raised his arms for silence. Little Guy, the mongrel dog who had adopted him during our flight with Esmeralda, jumped up beside him and stood proudly, wagging his scruffy brown tail. I felt Shift, my magic staff, quiver with anticipation in my hands. She shared Oller's sense of mischief. Across the table from us, Qrysta caught my eyes and smiled. Qrysta was the heart and soul of our crew, deadly with her twin blades. She, too, knew that something fun was coming. It was that sort of night, as every Yuletide Eve Feast should be.

As the cheers faded away, Oller cleared his throat.

"Friends," he proclaimed, "I would like to present to you a poem! A poem I have written in celebration of this special night!"

Rumbles and laughter greeted his announcement.

"It is entitled," he said and paused dramatically, "*'Twas.*"

Baffled, amused murmurs.

"That shows you it's a proper poem," he explained. "'*Twas* being a proper poem word."

Grunts of understanding.

Oller saw that he'd made his point and that everyone knew that a proper poem was coming. He drew himself up, took a deep breath, and began.

'Twas the night before Yuletide,
And all through the house,
Not a creature was stirring—
Except for a mouse

Who was writing a poem
But kept getting stuck
'Cos he couldn't come up with
The right rhyme for duck.

He stared at the paper
All blotched with black ink
And screwed up his eyes
And implored himself, think . . .

Grell knew a great rhyme—

"I bloody do and all!" Grell interrupted. "Wanna hear it?"

Oller scowled at him, but Grell raised his mug in reply and downed it in one long draught.

Oller waited for the cheers and laughter to die down before resuming his recital.

Grell knew a great rhyme
And he wanted to help
He leaned in to say it—
But then, with a yelp

He was deep in the chaos
And dangers of combat,
His crew being mauled
By a ninety-foot wombat

Flailing and slashing
Its terrible claws
And belching great flames
From its crocodile jaws

While Oller was stabbing
And Little Guy whizzing
Himself with axe whirling
Daxx blasting and fizzing

His thunderclaps into
The fire-wombat's head
(Which had no effect
As the brute was long dead

So that Qrysta's sharp blades
Did no damage at all.
All she managed to do
Was slice off his left ball)

Shift whispered to Daxxie
And Daxx shouted, "Duck!"
Shift's flamebolt erupted,
Scorched over and struck

Poor Grell smack on the arse
Setting fire to his hair
And blasting the Orc
Half a mile in the air

Where a huge dragon seized him
And chewed him to pulp
And swallowed scared Grell
In a single great gulp.

Grell struggled and panicked
And felt himself screaming
And gasped awake, sweating—
He'd only been dreaming!

Quivering, shaking
He sat up in bed
The nightmare had left him
Near three-quarters dead.

Next morning, at breakfast,
I asked him, "Sleep well?"
With a croak and a shudder
He started to tell

Of the wombat, the combat
The nightmare from hell—
I winked at the others
Who started to smell

An Oller-shaped rat . . .
As it became clear:
'Twas the night before Yuletide
That I spiked Grell's beer.

Grell froze in the process of refilling his mug.
"You bloody didn't! Did you?" he challenged, aghast.
Oller smiled at him blandly, eyebrows raised, all innocence.
"Find out in the morning, won't we, mate?" he said.

(Free sample audio of our flight with Esmeralda and Peat's poem from New Rock New Role *is available at richardsparks.com. Also, a different, free, e-chapter for download.)*

QUID EST VERITAS?

Edward Willett

On the day Jonathan Timmins met his new assistant, the Truth did not change.

That was unusual—not unheard-of, but unusual enough that the day would have been memorable even if that event had not coincided with the even more unusual addition of a new person to the small staff he oversaw in the Central Office of the Instrumentality of Information.

The day's unchanging Truth also meant he could greet his new assistant immediately upon her arrival, since he had literally nothing else to do. He knew nothing about her except her name and the fact that the Arbiters had chosen her for this position, but really, knowing that, what else did he need to know?

What he was not prepared for, as he entered the staff lounge where she was waiting, seated on a sleek white-leather couch, sipping coffee—black, he noted approvingly—and reading the *Daily Truth* on a small datapad, was how attractive she was. If someone had specifically designed her to appeal to him, they would have done nothing different, from her black hair drawn back into a practical ponytail to her slim build to her tight black jeans and loose blue blouse to the sparkle of her earrings and the matching sparkle of her dark-brown eyes.

In retrospect, perhaps that should have hinted at what was to come, but in the moment, he drank in her appearance for a long moment, as he might have a glass of sweet iced tea, before saying, "Miss Anders?"

She started, and then turned those mesmerizing eyes on him, smiled a smile that made his heart leap, and stood. "Mr. Timmins?"

"Yes," he said. He reached out and shook her hand, and the feel of her fingers in his made his heart beat faster. "A pleasure to meet you, Miss Anders," he continued, hoping his voice did not betray just how much of a pleasure it was. "Shall I show you around?"

"Please," Miss Anders said. "And please, call me Sabrina."

He smiled. "If you will call me Jon." A bit presumptuous, perhaps —he was her boss, after all—but they were generally informal in the Instrumentality, being such a small group, and ultimately, who was there to be offended? The enforcers of such things as workplace propriety did not even know the Instrumentality existed.

Her smile widened. "Jon," she said.

"Follow me, Sabrina," he said, and led her into the small complex of offices hidden behind the biometrically secured door that was the Instrumentality's only outward manifestation, tucked away in the sub-basement of the vast Brutalist edifice that also housed such monumentally boring government departments as the Department of Agricultural Implement Regulation and the Bureau of Desert Reclamation.

The tour did not take long, the "complex" consisting of precisely six offices, each containing a desk, a chair, a computer, and whatever personal decorations the inhabitant thereof had chosen to install. None of them had windows, of course, but high-resolution video screens did their best to mimic them, the choice of views reflective of the individual with each cubicle.

"The lounge, you have already seen," Jon said as the brief tour ended in his office, twice the size of the others, but otherwise the same.

His own video screens displayed a peaceful pine forest where nothing ever happened. He hadn't bothered to introduce Sabrina to her coworkers. That would have been taken care of by the Arbiters, who almost certainly had also familiarized her with the layout of the offices, but there were still some human-interaction niceties to be observed, if one was to remain human at all: a challenge in this job for anyone, but particularly for Jon, due to the secret singularity of his existence.

He would have loved to have told Sabrina just what it was that made him unique—but, of course, he could tell no one. He would vanish, as other had, vanish so completely that no one would ever know he had lived. He could never breath a word of his personal truth to another soul, not even a soul housed in a body of such perfect pulchritude as Sabrina's.

He showed her to her own cubicle, which had been empty for as long as he had been Prime—ten years now. The fact the Arbiters had chosen to fill it both puzzled him and mildly alarmed him. There had been no new Truth today, but did the Arbiters expect major updates to the Truth in the near future?

Even if they did, he didn't understand how an extra person would help. It wasn't like there was a huge workload for the four assistants he already had. They had nothing to do with propagating the Truth, of course; that fell solely to him. Their jobs were merely to monitor the Truth's dissemination, watching for dead spots in the flow of data that indicated individuals who, for whatever reason, had not received it. AIs could and did do the same, but the laws that had established the Instrumentality and continued to regulate its activity were clear: a human had to oversee all AI activity, keeping an alert eye on the AI. *An A-eye on the AI*, Jon thought, as he always did.

"You've had the training input, I presume?" Jon said as Sabrina sat at her desk for the first time.

"Of course," she replied, so quickly that he shot a quizzical glance at her, but she met his gaze guilelessly. "We're here to keep an A-eye on the AI."

He blinked at that. He'd never said that rather lame pun out loud.

She'd thought of it herself. *She really is perfect*, he thought, and then pushed the thought away. "Right, then. I'll leave you to it."

He said it bravely, but in fact, he missed her the moment he was out the door.

OVER THE NEXT THREE WEEKS, Sabrina seemed to settle in perfectly. She joked and laughed with her coworkers during coffee breaks. She spent the requisite number of hours at her desk monitoring Truth flow, and even flagged a couple of false positives that prevented individuals from being wrongly rounded up. Jon approved of that: he had no problem with the necessary work of the agents of Truth Enforcement, but he did not want innocents rounded up; who would?

No technology was perfect. Those whose faulty implants had failed only had to have them repaired or, at worst, replaced. Still, there was a backlog and, of course, it was a surgical procedure that entailed some risk and recovery time. While such individuals were being treated, they also, of course, had to be kept in solitary confinement. It all meant great disruption to their lives, both public and private. It had to be done, but it also had to be done fairly and only to those who truly needed it.

The only individuals who truly had to fear Truth Enforcement were those who whose brains, despite being provided with perfectly functioning implants, refused to be rewritten. They were, fortunately, vanishingly rare: far rarer than a day without a new Truth; rarer, even, than a day when Jon received a new assistant.

Perhaps that, too, should have been a warning.

IT SHOULD NOT HAVE HAPPENED, according to all the workplace regulations that applied throughout the federal government, but again, who would ever know?

It took three months but, in the end, there came a night when Jon and Sabrina, though they left separately, found each other in a bar an hour later, and three hours after that, found themselves in bed together, and seven hours after that, discovered they were still in bed together, and three hours after that, arrived at work—separately, of course.

Their relationship continued, discretely. Jon did not believe the others in the office had an inkling. They did not go out in public after that first night in that first bar; their time was spent in pleasurable solitude at Jon's place. He suggested once that he come to Sabrina's apartment, but she shook her head vigorously. "No," she said. "I share with two other women. Far too risky."

They were in bed as they often were, snuggled in post-coital afterglow, and he turned his head to her to smile. "Surely they've had men —or women—over."

"No," Sabrina said. "We have an agreement. That sort of thing—" her hand wandered, and he gasped a little, "—*this* sort of thing," she went on, a bit of a purr in her voice, "is to be kept out of the apartment."

Jon, having just lost all interest in whatever it was they had been talking about, never mentioned it again.

Six months after she began work at the Instrumentality, Jon learned the truth about Sabrina.

Perhaps, had he not been so besotted, he would have twigged earlier, but lovers—so he'd heard, having never really been one before—tended to overlook small imperfections in their significant others, and so he had discounted the occasional lapses, the times when she seemed to still believe a previous Truth instead of the day's Truth, the instances that might have been a slip of the tongue: the use of a wrong pronoun here, the lack of appropriate deference to a newly exalted political figure there.

On the day he finally grasped the truth, however, the slip was so egregious it could not be overlooked.

Perhaps, too, he would have noticed sooner had there been more momentous Truths over their six months of mutual bliss. Instead, most were so minor they never came up in conversation: the tweaking of a historical narrative, the erasure of a disgraced mayor, the eradication of all references to a species of amphibian that had just gone extinct due to the destruction of its habitat by a mega-solar farm.

But on the morning of September 18 there was a snowfall, so early and accompanied by such cold weather that on the morning of September 21, after more typical autumnal weather had melted all traces of the unusual precipitation, the Truth went out to the population that no snowfall had occurred, early snowfalls having been eradicated as a possibility by an earlier Truth, and everyone promptly forgot about it.

Cognitive dissonance was the great enemy of the Truth, and had been since the government had decided to take advantage of the new technology of neural implants to deal with the problem of disinformation head-on, first decreeing that everyone must have an implant (in the interest of public health, the implants having been found to be useful in treating mental illness, which the population had been previously assured had reached epidemic proportions) and second, using those implants to begin placing within the minds of their citizens only those facts and opinions approved by the Arbiters, individuals carefully chosen from among the greatest and most progressive thinkers of the age.

Of course, a later Truth had erased the memory of half of the original Arbiters, after a bitter internal struggle over some Truth now forgotten—something to do with gender, Jon believed, though he had been a child at the time—and now, there were—and always had been—only three Arbiters.

It was the task of the Instrumentality of Information to ensure that the Truth, as determined by the Arbiters, was instilled in all citizens. The Information Act had eliminated political polarization; indeed, it had eliminated politics, since some twenty years ago, a Truth had been proclaimed that there was only one political party because all others had voluntarily disbanded when the Information

Act was passed, having realized they were no longer needed now that governmental perfection had been achieved.

The same pattern had been followed in almost all the world. Those few countries that did not follow the example of the more enlightened nations remained sunk in squalor, struggling to survive, cut off from all contact with their betters and mired in internal squabbling and occasional wars. They laughably called themselves the Free World when, of course, their citizens were, in fact, enslaved by petty passions, their thoughts muddled and befogged by thick clouds of disinformation, always seeking the Truth—so they said— but never able to find it.

And yet, though he could never admit it to anyone, he identified with the poor Free World citizens—because, in a sense, he was one of them.

Jon was immune to the Truth.

Like everyone, he had received his implant at the age of eight. It hadn't taken him long to realize he was different. His friends would come to school one morning and every one of them would believe something that, the day before, they had not: that a particular sports team had won a championship game when, in fact, as he remembered, they had lost it; that a new singer was someone that had all been passionate fans of for months when, in fact, he had never heard of her until that day.

He had always been a bit of a loner, and so had never revealed his confusion to any of his friends: instead, he simply pretended to believe whatever they all now believed. He had hidden his disability —knowing even then that if anyone found out, he would vanish as if he had never existed—so well that no one had ever learned of it; and to ensure that no one ever would, he had directed all of his educational years and his early years in government service toward the goal of becoming part of the Instrumentality of Information. Where better to hide his seditious sickness than in the heart of the organization it most threatened?

Twenty years ago, he was hired as one of the cubicle workers he now oversaw. Ten years ago, he had been appointed Prime after the previous Prime retired. For a decade, he had disseminated a new Truth more mornings than not with a simple click of his mouse, making sure before he clicked that he knew what was in the Truth so that he could continue to pretend he, too, had had his memories and beliefs altered by the implant in his head.

And so, when he passed Sabrina in the hall on the morning of September 21, after the Truth had been sent out, and she said, "I miss the snow," he knew—and berated himself for not noticing sooner.

She went into her office. He had been headed to the lounge, but instead, he returned to his own desk, staring at his computer, displaying nothing now that the Truth had gone out but a shifting aurora of coloured lights. It was his duty to inform Truth Enforcement that he had identified someone who was Truth-immune. But how could he? Telling Truth Enforcement the truth about her could reveal his own dark truth, since it was his own immunity to the Truth that had made him immediately realize what her statement had meant. Otherwise, he might have just blinked at the apparent non sequitur and kept walking.

He was still dithering when there came a soft knock on his door. "Come in," he said, then sucked in a sharp breath as Sabrina entered

She closed the door behind her. "May I sit down?"

He jerked a nod and waved at one of the two chairs on the other side of the desk. She lowered herself into one. She regarded him. He barely breathed. "I didn't make a mistake," she said after a long moment.

Careful. "I don't know what you mean."

"Yes, you do." Sabrina took a careful look around the office, at his desk, and at the ceiling, then cocked an eyebrow at him.

It took him only a moment to realize she was asking if they were under surveillance. "No," he said. "Not here."

Sabrina nodded and leaned forward, though despite his assurance, when she spoke, she kept her voice low. "I didn't make a mistake. I wanted you to know the truth about me as I know the truth about you. You are Truth-immune. So am I."

His heart hammered in his chest. No one said such things out loud—no one sane, anyway. And though he had just told her there was no surveillance in his office, in truth—or Truth—how could he be certain?

"I don't know what you're—"

"Spare me," Sabrina said. "There's no time. I know the truth about you. I've known it since I arrived here—since I was sent here."

"Sent?"

"There are more Truth-immune than you know. More, we hope, than the government knows. We have a way to identify Truth-immune, and over time, we have recruited many of them. We're organized into small cells with little contact with each other so the organization cannot be rolled up if one cell is identified.

"We've developed a solution. We've had it for years. What we haven't had was a way to make it work. Then we discovered you were one of us. And that's why I'm here."

"A solution to what?"

"To the Truth."

His heart pounded. "What? How—"

She reached up and took from her left ear one of the sparkling earrings he had so admired when they first met. She held it out. "Take it."

Not knowing what else to do, he did so.

"The stone is a data crystal," Sabrina said. "Download the code it contains into your computer. Attach it to the Truth as part of your certification. It will overwrite the Truth. It will permanently deactivate the implants—all of them—and restore the memories suppressed by them. Everyone will know in an instant how they have been lied to and manipulated. Everyone will be free."

Jon clenched his fist around the earring. "You're insane! That would mean—chaos. Riots. We'd become like one of those pre-Truth hellholes—"

"They're not hellholes," Sabrina said. "They're simply free. Like we were, before the implants. Before the government decided it would decide the Truth for everyone—the Truth that is really a lie."

"Violence. Hatred. Polarization."

"Innovation. Advancement. Free speech."

His chest ached as he stared at her. "Was this all a lie?" he whispered. "What we've had together . . . was that always the plan?"

Sabrina hesitated. She bit her lip. "It began as a ruse. But it became the truth."

"You just said the Truth is a lie."

"The Truth you put into people's heads is a lie," Sabrian said. "But there is truth above and beyond the Truth. And my love for you . . . is that kind of truth."

Something beeped. Sabrina looked at her smartwatch. "I have to go back to my office now," she said. She stood, turned, went to the door, and then glanced back. "There is no truth in the Truth," she said. "No *pravda* in *Pravda*, as the Soviets used to say. But there is still truth."

She went out and closed the door behind her.

Jon was still staring at the earring in his hand when he heard a bang and shouting. He put the earring in his pocket as he got to his feet. He had taken only two steps when his door opened again, this time revealing a large man in the innocuous beige uniform of Truth Enforcement. "Director Timmins?" the man rumbled.

Jon's mouth had gone dry. He nodded first, mostly to give himself time enough to swallow. "Yes," he croaked. "What's this about?"

"I'm afraid you've been infiltrated," the man said. "By the Clear Eyes."

The Clear Eyes. The organization that had fought against the Truth Laws, when he was just a teenager. Sabrina hadn't used the name, but he remembered it. He also knew they had been expunged from memory by the Truth, and so he simply gave the agent the look of puzzlement he had perfected over the years. "Who?"

"Never mind," the man said. "They had a plan to subvert the Truth, but we received a tip this morning from a patriot." He held up something that sparkled: the twin of the earring in Jon's pocket, which suddenly seemed red hot. "This stone is a data crystal your assistant Sabrina Anders intended to send out with the Truth. Who knows what damage it might have caused?"

"I'm shocked," Jon said, both because he was, and because he felt he had to say something.

The agent glanced around the office. "Nice. Guess being the boss pays off."

Jon didn't know how to respond to that. "I'm glad you caught her," he said instead.

"You should be," the agent said. "Never mind the damage her little program might have done, as Prime, you would have been held responsible."

Because the Arbiters never have to take responsibility for anything, Jon thought. "*When you control the Truth, you are never held accountable.*"

The expression was not his own: it had bubbled up from the mention of the Clear Eyes. It had been one of their sayings, before the Information Act: one of their core beliefs.

One of Sabrina's core beliefs.

"I appreciate your service," Jon said, years of prevarication slathering the lie with a sheen of sincerity.

The agent gave him one last, searching look. Jon met his gaze squarely. Truth Enforcement prided itself on its ability to read expressions; he remembered that, too, among the many things he should not have. Clearly his betrayed nothing: the agent nodded once, then "Thanks. Have a good rest of your day. We'll probably have some questions later. Don't leave town."

He went out. Jon's office door closed. The strange voices in the halls went silent. When he ventured out, none of the others said anything about what had happened. Their implants hadn't repro-grammed them—they just knew better than to talk about it.

Jon went home early. His apartment seemed emptier than it ever had before, in his years of solitary living. He wondered where Sabrina was. He wondered if she was still alive.

Yes, he though. *They'll want to interrogate her.*

That thought held little comfort. He didn't think she'd betray him voluntarily.

That didn't mean she wouldn't betray him.

AFTER A NEAR-SLEEPLESS NIGHT, Jon went into the office early, well before he was expected to click the button that would send out the day's Truth—technically totally unnecessary, required, like so much else in the Instrumentality, merely to pay lip service to the human-oversight provisions of the Information Act, though why the Arbiters hadn't simply erased the existence of those provisions from every-one's minds, Jon could not say. Some lingering sense of social respon-sibility perhaps; more likely, they just hadn't gotten around to it. *They must be very busy, deciding the Truth.*

He sat at his desk, alone in the tiny complex of offices. He perused the day's Truth. There were new Truths about various economic issues, new Truths about which racial groups were to be favoured in hiring, many others ...

... and one Truth, buried deep in the matrix, proclaiming that there had never been a person named Sabrina Anders, and that all those who had known her would forget she had ever existed.

He stared at that line of text.

He thought about the last six months.

He thought about the last ten years.

He thought about all he knew but had pretended he did not.

He thought about all those around him knew that he knew to be false.

He thought about Truth, and he thought about truth.

But mostly, he thought about Sabrina, and what she had said to him, almost at the very end. *"The Truth you put into people's heads is a lie. But there is truth above and beyond the Truth. And my love for you ... is that kind of truth."*

He took the earring from his pocket. He popped out the data crys-tal. He put it in the reader. He rested his finger on the mouse button, the button he had clicked for ten years to disseminate the Truth that this time would upload an implant-killing virus into the system.

Moved by some obscure impulse inspired by the history he

remembered that few others did, he paused. A change in regime, he seemed to recall, was usually accompanied by ritual words of power.

He thought a moment, then smiled. "The Truth is dead," he said, his voice ringing in the office though there was no one to hear it. "Long live the truth."

He clicked.

GREY SCALE

Hayden Trenholm

Grey. Grey ceiling. Grey walls. Grey coverlet pulled tight over a grey T-shirt. He pulled his hand from beneath the sheet and held it before his face. Even his skin looked grey.

His back and left knee hurt, but he didn't know the cause. He was nauseated, but his stomach was tight, empty save for the taste of bile. A grey curtain covered a small window. Through it, nothing but a concrete courtyard and an overcast sky.

The room was familiar without being a place he had ever been. He struggled with the memory. It reminded him of the recovery room the last time he had seen . . .Victor. That's right, his brother's name was Victor. And he was . . .

"Good morning, Antony." The voice was flat, like his parents when they were angry. It was perhaps artificial. No one he knew, in any case. Not worth answering.

The sink in the vanity was white, so white it took him a minute to process what it was: a white hole with a single chrome faucet. He waved his hand under the faucet, and a lukewarm stream of water trickled out. He splashed it over his face, the water cooling his skin and wetting the thick beard covering his cheeks and chin. *That's wrong. I can't grow a beard.*

The wall above the sink was bare, with no mirror to check his features. He ran his tongue around his mouth. Two teeth were missing on the upper right side, the gums long healed from their loss. Gingerly, he lifted his hand to his face again. The skin was no longer smooth, more like his father's hands than his own.

But that's crazy.

"Your breakfast will be served in the dining area in fifteen minutes," said the voice. "Please finish your ablutions and get dressed."

A panel slid open next to the vanity, revealing a toilet. A sudden, overwhelming urge clutched at him. He barely made it before his bowels emptied in a watery flush. Sweat beaded on his brow, and his vision shimmered. A spray of water cleansed him, but he waited until the dizziness passed. A tattoo of a snake, its colours faded and dark, curled up his left leg. He had no idea when or where he had gotten it.

Another panel opened on the wall opposite. Fresh underclothes and a neatly pressed shirt and trousers in varying shades of grey were laid out for him. No socks, but a pair of black sandals.

"Breakfast is in five minutes." The flat voice somehow conveyed a sense of annoyance. "If you miss it, you will not be able to eat until after your release."

He didn't know why he was here or how long he had been in this room. He didn't even know who he was. Not Tony. Not that person, but someone called Antony. An old man with the memories of a boy.

A chime sounded, and he dressed hurriedly. *It's fine,* he thought. *I'll eat, and then I'll find out.*

FOUR OTHERS WERE in the room when he arrived: three men, two black and one white, and a woman who looked Chinese. None were sitting together, and no one looked up when he entered. He took a tray from the obvious dispenser and followed a flashing violet floor light to his place, well away from the others. He thought of joining one of them but was too shy in the face of their evident maturity.

A sixth person entered, a tall, brown-skinned woman with high cheekbones and a long braid of black hair down her back. She caught him staring and returned his gaze with a hard look. He dropped his eyes to his plate and didn't look up until he had finished the thick porridge laced with raisins and seeds. It wasn't what his body craved but he ate it anyway, surprised when the spoon scrapped the bottom of the bowl.

A chime sounded. A different voice, this one sounding human, said, "When prompted, return your tray to the dispenser and exit through the indicated door."

Antony hesitated as the others left. A short, sharp shock lifted him from his seat. No one was in the hall on the other side of a different door, only pale-blue arrows guiding him through several turns to a small room and a chair on one side of a narrow blue-grey table. The chair opposite was empty.

Left to himself in silence so utter it hurt his ears, he wondered again where he was and why. He didn't wonder what would happen next. He saw no point in that. *It's fine.* He stared at his hands again, with their dirty nails. His father's nails were never dirty. A fine web of scars covered his knuckles.

His entire sense of time and history had been upended. He remembered the excitement of finishing his junior year and his anxiety over his date for the spring prom. Laura wasn't his first choice, and he was pretty sure he wasn't hers either. He worried about his brother's continuing absence, but when he asked, his parents grew silent. His mother was filled with sorrow, his father with simmering anger.

Yesterday, he had taken his final mathematics exam, which, despite his trepidation, was remarkably easy. But yesterday was not yesterday, and those remembered feelings were not his feelings now; his body then, not this body now. Yet, it was.

He had read of a disease that caused young people to age before their time. He thought it was hereditary, a failure of the genetic code to line up with the timeline of the universe. Was there some viral version of the same thing? Would that explain the weight of years he was carrying? How could he know? The only science he remembered was from his junior year and articles from the science magazine his father, a lawyer, bought to expand his own horizons.

A panel opened, and a thin man entered. Everything about him was sparse, from his narrow shoulders to the long, delicate fingers clutching a small electronic pad. His hair barely covered his dark scalp and when he spoke a greeting, even his voice was reedy and so low Antony had to strain to hear the words. His shirt and pants were dark blue, and he wore a blue sports coat and purple necktie. It was the way his father dressed, and he wondered if this man was his lawyer.

He sat opposite and placed the pad on the desk, and ran his fingers across it. The screen was tilted so Antony couldn't see, but he knew it had something to do with him. A knot grew in his stomach, as it did when he was being tested or judged. The man was a bundle of twitches, his shoulders and legs moving as if they were already on to the next appointment.

Antony cleared his throat and the thin man gave him the narrowest of smiles. "Mr. Crusoe, I'm Tyrone Harris. I'm your release coordinator."

Questions crowded his mouth, but he kept his lips tightly sealed as he had always done when he didn't know the people he was with or the social context of the situation. Yet, part of him wanted to scream at this stranger, to demand answers, to . . .

He took a deep breath through his nose, and it calmed him a little.

"What do you remember?" Harris asked.

"I . . . remember my brother."

Harris's eyebrows lifted, wrinkling the skin of his forehead into dark furrows. "Victor?" The tone of his voice suggested options, but he only had one brother. An older brother and a younger sister, Erin, their birthdays within a week of each other, several years apart.

"Yes."

"What do you remember about him?" Harris's voice had an edge. Antony—this Antony—had learned to detect the faintest hint of emotion underlying people's words.

"He was sick. No one told me what he had. I visited him in hospital, I don't know, five or six months ago. On my . . . birthday." He heard his own voice catch at that. He ground out the next words through clenched teeth. "Last time I saw him."

Harris rewarded him with another smile, a lifting of his mouth that didn't reach his cheeks.

"What happened to Victor?"

"That information is not accessible," said Harris.

"You didn't look at your screen. How do you—"

"None of your personal information is accessible unless it is necessary for your release."

"My release to where? To who?"

"All in good time. Do you feel remorse for what you did?"

"What did I do?"

Harris narrowed his eyes—they were green—and looked down at the screen, his fingers flittering across it like ants on hot metal. "Oh, I see." A barely audible mutter. "Oh, my, I see. Everything. Right down to the limit."

"What did I do?"

"I'm not at liberty to say. I'm sorry. I should have been more prepared, but . . . the workload, you see." Harris paused, his hands and limbs becoming immobile for the first time. His mouth was turned down, and his eyes were slightly misty. "How old do you think you are?"

"I . . . don't know. The last I remember is being sixteen, but this . . ." he gestured helplessly to encompass his whole body.

"I can tell you that much. You're fifty-one."

THIRTY-FIVE YEARS. Practically a lifetime. His uncle, Robin, had died unexpectedly at thirty-three. Antony had been eight; it was his first brush with mortality. He remembered having dreams about his father dying. They weren't always unhappy dreams, but he angered, remembering them now.

The rest of the interview had passed in a blur—he grew impatient to have it over. Something about retraining. Something else about job placement and temporary housing. Work? What work could they expect from him, with the knowledge of a sixteen-year-old and a worn-out body? What had he done in those missing years that had left him hurting in so many places?

Harris had explained that in 2033—six years after Antony turned sixteen—the government had adopted a new method of dealing with crime. A technique to remove a person's memories had been developed. Restoring the quantum positioning of electrons in the amygdala and rebuilding neuronal pathways in the temporal lobe, or was it the other way around? Psychologists determined the starting point of the deviant behaviour and the technicians wiped everything clean back to that point. Most lost a couple of years, few more than a decade. What had he done to lose thirty-five?

Harris, already jittery when the interview started, grew more so with each passing second. He finally shut his notebook and declared the process complete. He handed Antony over to a burly guard in a dark green uniform. The man looked him up and down but said nothing before ushering him into another room where two of his breakfast companions were waiting—the white man and the woman with the braid.

The guard gestured to a knapsack on a bench against the far wall. It contained a second set of clothing, identical to what he was wearing: a light grey jacket, a pair of socks and shoes, and a baseball cap with no logo.

"That's yours. Don't lose it." The guard grabbed Antony's hand and pushed up the sleeve of his shirt before clamping a bracelet on his forearm. "This will provide you with everything else you need."

Antony assumed it was a tracking device, but the guard had one, too. A small screen displayed the date and time: Wednesday,

February 15, 2062, and 11:32 a.m. Maybe a smartwatch or something. His father disliked technology and refused him anything other than a laptop for school.

Antony kept his head down as he examined the others through his lashes. The white man--tall, slender but muscular, with a shaved scalp and a blue-tinted goatee—spent most of the time tapping at the device on his arm. The man appeared to be about thirty, but he had never been good at guessing people's ages and who knew what the future offered in the way of regenerative treatments. Whatever it was, this body had never benefited from it.

The woman sat as far from the others as the room allowed. Her posture was erect, her large hands resting, palms up, in her lap. Her eyes were mostly closed, though her lips moved slightly as if she were talking to herself. Once, she turned and stared directly at him. Antony resented her stare but knew better than to show what was boiling inside him.

AFTER TWO MORE PEOPLE ARRIVED, a black man and a white woman, the attendant opened the far door and led them across cracked pavement to a low-slung train carriage hovering over a single metal rail. The sun was lowering in the west but the air was warm, summer-like. For a moment, Antony thought he must be somewhere south, but the unmistakable skyline of Chicago loomed to his left, past a dusty green field of dying shrubs.

"Is it always this hot?" he asked no one in particular.

"Wait until August," said Blue Goatee.

Three passengers were already in the car. His four companions chose seats as far from each other as they could, as if they were in the midst of another pandemic, like the one he had suffered through when he was ten. No one was wearing a mask, so it was embarrassment that kept them apart now. He resented feeling the same way and chose to sit next to the woman who had stared at him. She turned her gaze on him again, and he looked away.

The car moved east, pausing at signals to let other vehicles or crowds of people pass. Traffic was light, and it took him a few minutes to notice that the trucks delivering goods didn't have drivers. The only cars with humans behind the wheels were blue-striped police cars.

Most pedestrians were wearing the armbands he and his fellow travellers had strapped to their wrists. Some, though, drifted along the pavement as if they could see things, hear things, to which others were oblivious. They were not homeless, stumbling from one delusion to another; they exuded wealth and power, superior beings with no need to interact with lesser people.

HE MUST HAVE FALLEN ASLEEP; his wristband said twenty minutes had elapsed. When he opened his eyes, the other passengers were lined up at the exit, awaiting their release.

The training centre was a scattering of a dozen old wood and stone buildings connected by modern glass-and-steel passageways. A wide field was surrounded by a low wall of brick topped by a strand of razor wire. He was shown to a small room with a single bed, a closet for his meagre supply of clothes, and a work desk with a complex interface. The attendant, a short, stocky man who smiled a lot, glanced at his chart, frowned, and told Antony someone would be by to instruct him in the use of the virtual adapter.

A sign in the ensuite bathroom cautioned him against drinking any water except from the tap marked potable. He stripped off and stepped into the shower, trying not to think where the stream of warm water came from if it was not fit to drink.

The half-length mirror showed him a stranger. Besides the tattoo of the snake on his leg, he had one of a dragon on his left shoulder and a small one of a bullet hole over his heart. He ran his fingers over the image to ensure that it wasn't hiding an actual scar. It wouldn't have surprised him if it were. He was more muscular than he expected and was in pretty good shape for an old man.

A soft tap at the door announced the arrival of the promised instructor, a young woman with facial tattoos that writhed and glowed in ever-changing shades of green and yellow. She introduced herself as Ambrosia and was escorted by a muscular man who stepped back into the hall but left the door ajar. *Sensible*, thought Antony. *I am a dangerous criminal, after all.* He would have laughed at the thought that anyone would find him dangerous, except his hands were clenched into fists, and his heart was thudding against his chest.

"Have you used an interface before?"

"Not that I fucking remember." It was hard to read her expression through the shifting colours, but Antony thought she looked sad. It was not the reaction he wanted.

"You must have, though. You have Grade 2 implants." Her voice was gentle, placating. She touched a spot behind his left ear. It was intimate, yet he knew it was merely her job. He touched the other side of his neck and felt a small depression in the same spot.

"That makes it a lot easier," she said. "Sometimes we get people from the other side; they barely know how to use their wristbands. It takes weeks to get their implants installed and operational. Pop these in your eyes while I boot up your nodes."

She handed him a pair of silvery contact lenses. He had never even worn glasses, but his body seemed to know what to do, and he slipped the slippery cups into his eyes. She checked to see they were "seated" before inserting two tiny buds into the sockets behind his ears. Finally, she placed his hands flat on a black pad that had emerged from the desk. A slight tingle vibrated his palms, and when he pulled his hands away, they were covered in a fine net of silver and gold wires, with thicker concentrations of circuits at his fingertips.

"You're all set for your first lesson. Once you finish orientation, you can stay connected and access our collection of streaming nodes for entertainment or self-guided learning. When you're ready to return to mundanity, disconnect in the same order. Hands down, ears off, eyes out. Just drop the gear on the black pad, and the AI will clean it and have it ready for your next session."

As soon as he had finished the mandatory orientation, he began to search for any reference to himself or his family. The holographic images turned dark, signs floating past saying "No information found," or "Negative search results," or, rarely, "Access denied." The latter stirred his interest and his anger. Information existed, but it was denied to him. He slammed his hands down on the pad to disconnect.

***

THE WEEKS PASSED as if in a dream. He awoke to a soft chime that grew louder the longer he stayed in bed. Breakfast was in a communal dining hall and was not terrible. Most of the other trainees ate by themselves, though some small groups sat together, chattering and sometimes laughing. He longed to join them but was afraid of what they might say to him.

Most didn't even look at him, but a few gazed with naked curiosity. Did they know why his memories had been stripped? Would they tell him if he asked? What could he offer them to reveal the truth about his past? Eventually, he learned to talk to his fellow inmates in oblique terms. No one talked openly about what they had lost, but you could fill in the blanks, so to speak. None of them had anything to offer about his own life or, if they did, chose to keep it to themselves. "You think I'd risk a single memory for you?" was the answer when he pressed. "They watch us and everyone we come in contact with."

The mandatory training sessions seemed pointless, with so much work automated. The few interesting jobs that remained available had dozens of qualified applicants. What was left—abstract arts, grief counselling, animal husbandry—held no interest. Most people worked part-time in meaningless jobs to supplement the monthly government stipends or spent their lives in virtual spaces. Rumours circulated of places where humans worked and the metaverse didn't reach, but he could find no trace of them, any more than he could find a hint about his missing thirty-five years. He no longer bothered now; during one session, Ambrosia appeared in the feed and warned him that continued efforts would result in the cancellation of his privileges.

Sometimes, he saw the brown-skinned woman in the dining hall or walking alone on the grounds during the afternoon free time. She didn't seem to mind the relentless heat or the steady wind that blew from the south that left him sweating and short of breath. Once or twice, she stopped and watched him as he drifted from one patch of shade to another. He wanted to approach her, apologize for his behaviour on the train, but knew it would only lead to rejection.

One day, when a rare weather front had brought cooler air from the north, he went on a long hike, reaching the outer perimeter of the centre and walking the length of the fence. In the distance, low clumps of buildings were connected by train tubes. Hardly a living thing moved beyond the fence save a few tattered crows and a couple of scruffy-looking squirrels. On the way back, he stopped beside one of the few tall trees—an oak—and sat beneath its shade. The wind rustled the yellowing leaves and sifted dappled light across the dying grass.

He awoke stiff and aching when his bracelet buzzed to call him to supper. The brown-haired woman was standing a few feet away, watching him as he stirred awake.

"You're Antony Crusoe," she said.

"I was, I guess." It was the standard joking response of the gap-lived residents.

"What's it like? Losing it all." She was the first one to ask him that question. He wondered if others knew. He had been too frightened, too ashamed to mention it himself.

"It's like I don't exist."

"You're right here."

"Yeah. Someone is."

"You look like someone I used to know. I mean, I knew him before. I fucked up, and they took away a couple of years. After, he was nowhere around. I thought about trying to find him. I guess I tried too hard because they took another year away."

"A lot of people seem to have more than one gap."

"A lot of people are slow learners." She put her hand over the bracelet and gestured for him to do the same. He had been told that no one listened in on conversations but he doubted it was true. "Did you have a brother?"

"Yeah."

"Named Enrique?"

"No, my brother was . . ." A lot of people used to say Erin looked like him; some even thought they were twins. "I have a sister called Erin."

"Oh. I don't think you can call him that anymore." The woman glanced around. Two drones hovered over the compound, but neither was close enough to spy on them.

"Okay." He had found no references to his brother and sister, to his parents, in virtual space; it was as if they, too, had disappeared. He didn't understand how that could happen; his father had been a successful lawyer, not famous, but well-known in Chicago. Harris had warned him not to try to discover his missing future and then laughed. "Not that you could," he had said. "Everyone's information is curated, and the algorithms never make a mistake."

He heaved himself to his feet. Maybe his family was only invisible to him and he to them. But not everything was reduced to data. Reality still existed. He could go back to the neighbourhood where he grew up—

"I know what you're thinking. Don't do it. They took your memory for a reason. Find out what that reason is, and you'll be wiped clean again." She smiled. "You want to remember me, don't you?"

"Sure, though I don't even know your name."

"Leila Peshlakai. The name is Navajo but I'm not, not really. I grew up near where Los Angeles used to be. My father's father was from the Nation but I only met him a couple of times. He tried to teach me the language, but I don't remember much. He died during one of the gaps in my memory.

"My father's mother was *bilagáana*, a white woman from England, and my mother was Mexican. I know a lot more Spanish than *Diné bazaad*."

"I can barely speak English," he said, smiling. "So, you *can* find out about the gaps in your memory?"

"Some, usually by accident. I don't look for it. I don't want to lose more time. But it's not the same as remembering it, anyway. When I learn something, it's like I read it in a book. The memory doesn't come storming back."

"Oh." He had hoped that if he found out one thing, it would trigger something in his brain.

Leila must have read the disappointment on his face. "They don't suppress your memories or hide them. When they're done, nothing remains."

"Like erasing a recording?"

"Not exactly. Memory is not a movie; bits and pieces are stored in different places in the brain, sound in one place, visual images in another, and so on, with all the senses and what you felt about it somewhere else. When you remember, the part of the brain called the hippocampus, which is in the temporal lobe, brings them all back together. Complicated, you know, which is why sometimes memory is so uncertain. They found a way to short-circuit the process; it's crude, so they take everything back to a specific point in time or nothing at all."

"What made you an expert on memory?"

"I don't know anyone with more than a couple of gaps who isn't."

They were moving toward a patch of scrubby growth with small bright yellow flowers. It flourished despite the dryness of the earth and air; the warm breeze carried the faint scent of honey. They stood silently, immersed in the aroma, as the low bushes brushed against their legs. After a few minutes, he reached out and took her hand. She did not move away, and as the sun began to fall, they walked back to their quarters hand in hand.

IN THE DAYS THAT FOLLOWED, they walked together often. Leila told him what she remembered of Enrique, little enough since they had taken all but a few months of their friendship away. "I sometimes wonder if it ever became more than a friendship. But now, I'll never know."

"Surely, your friends—"

"Your friends abandon you," she snapped. "The way they do when a couple splits up but worse. They don't believe you can't remember things you did together, or they grow afraid that they will cross the line and lose their own memories. The ungapped won't tell you, and the gapped can't. What a perfect punishment."

"They call it a second chance." Not that he believed anymore that he deserved one.

"Well, they would, wouldn't they?"

Her voice was sad, and he wondered if she was thinking of abandoning him.

ANTONY STILL HAD an unquenchable thirst for information about his past. His searches for his parents and siblings had proved futile. Even cousins and close friends he remembered from his childhood turned up no results or, more often, flashing red signs of ACCESS DENIED. It prompted a visit from the muscular man who had first accompanied Ambrosia.

"You have to stop looking for things you will never find," said Darius, who stood too close, the smell of his body spray enveloping Antony like a cloud. His hands clenched and unclenched as he loomed over Antony's desk. The implied violence was belied by the softness of his voice and the gentleness of his expression.

"Did 'they' send you?" he asked, even though he had no idea who "they" might be.

Darius shook his head sadly. "I lost five years, lost my wife and infant son. I searched for them for nearly two years." He gestured at the interface. "In the *real* world. I guess I succeeded because they took those years, too. I came back here. I don't want to see you go down the same path."

"Then there *is* a way to discover the truth."

"What truth are you seeking?"

"The truth of who I am."

"How many years did they take?"

"I thought everyone knew." Antony turned away, no longer able to face the man's earnest gaze. "Thirty-five."

"Nobody knows unless you tell them. But if they took a lifetime away from you, you know who you are. What you must have done."

"Did I do anything if I can't remember it? Who am I if not my memories?"

"You are Antony Crusoe, and you're as innocent as the day you were born." It was meant to be kind, but it left him exhausted.

HE HAD FOUND no data on the person he remembered as his sister but had been his brother all along. He didn't expect looking for Enrique Crusoe would lead to a different result. But it did.

Enrique Crusoe. Deceased. March 11, 2052. Nothing more than that. Found dead in his apartment in Pasadena. Natural causes, said the report. The algorithms made mistakes, after all. Enrique, if it was really his brother, had lived a quiet life, and Antony could find no reference to family, friends, or work other than a few short stories he had written in the years just before his death. He found four of them in an archive and read one where he thought he recognized himself. He had finished the second when the chime sounded for supper. He thought the stories would be sad but, instead, found them joyful, almost triumphant, and he looked forward to reading the others when he returned to his room.

But by then, all references to Enrique and his stories were gone; the algorithms learned from their mistakes. A handwritten note on his desk read: "Stop looking."

But at least someone in his family had been happy. He clasped hard to that knowledge, hoping it would still be there in the morning.

That night, he lay in bed, unable to sleep, tears soaking the pillow beneath his head.

"I FOUND out what happened to Enrique." They were lying together on an orange blanket in the patch of yellow flowers. No prohibition existed against relations between residents of the complex but he was shy about his body, the body of an old man. He could not bear the thought of being observed, even by an AI-driven drone. Still, being with Leila made him feel alive, if only for a few moments.

"I don't want to know," Leila said, placing her fingers across his lips. They tasted of sex and smelled of the honey-sweet flowers.

"But—"

"No. What good would it do me? Whatever we had or didn't have is gone now. Finding out wouldn't make me happy either way and could do me harm. Do you imagine I want to lose you, too?"

"Lose me? I'm barely here. A seventeen-year-old in the body of an old man." He half turned away. Leila ran her hand across his back and across his arms and chest, massaging the hard muscles beneath his skin, tracing the faded tattoos that covered a quarter of his body.

"You're only three years older than me. Are you calling me an old woman?"

"No. But you . . . you're beautiful."

She laughed. "I can't remember the last time a man told me that. No, seriously, I can't remember. And I'm fine with that." She ran her fingers through his hair and along his cheek. "You're beautiful, too, Tony. Inside, where it counts."

"Am I? I must have done terrible things. I must have—" He found he couldn't speak his thoughts out loud. What was the point anyway?

"That was Antony Crusoe. I'm talking about Tony. My sweet young man."

"But what if they didn't get it all? What if it's my nature to hurt people?"

"I don't believe people are born bad. I certainly don't think you were."

"What if the damage was already done? I remember being frightened a lot of the time. Of my father's anger, my mother's sorrow, the fights they had with Victor. What if my path was bent when I was just a kid?"

"The law is harsh, but it isn't cruel. They wouldn't leave the mind of a child in the body of a man. That's why you're here and not locked away somewhere. Whatever you were turned toward, it hadn't happened yet. And now, it's all washed away. No one ever escapes their past—even if their memories have been scoured. They talk about nature and nurture as if we are merely the original clay moulded by others. But there is choice, too. You can't escape but you can make your prison into a home.

"You lost thirty-five years, but you still have thirty-five or more in front of you to make yourself into the person you choose to be."

"Washed away?" Confusion swirled through him. "Like Los Angeles taken in the flood. What kind of future does that leave me?" He closed his eyes so the sun on his face turned his eyelids red. All he heard was her voice. A strange upwelling of pride filled him that she would care for him and a sudden courage to care for her, too.

"Not like a devastating flood but like water in the desert. My grandfather described it for me—how the desert may lie fallow for years, nothing but cactus and tumbleweeds, then one day, the rains come, and the arroyos fill with water and the very contour of the land is changed. Flowers bloom everywhere, and their fragrances remind you that life never stands still. It always changes. The desert may return, but it is different again."

"This is how it is now?"

Leila nodded, smiling down at him. "Isn't that good enough?"

Yes, he thought, *yes, it is.* "Right here, right now, with you." He reached up to stroke her face, and she turned and kissed the palm of his hand.

Antony stared up at the bright blue arc of the sky. The bushes waved green and gold above him; the woman beside him was copper and gold and all things precious. Nothing, not even the solitary cloud in the sky, was grey. He turned toward Leila and pulled her close. He kissed her mouth and breathed in the scent of her skin.

And he was young again.

SOMEONE TO DREAM WITH

Eli K. P. William

Pain creeps up on me before I'm fully awake. A dull ache in my back from lying on a hard surface. The prickly burn of a scrape along my hip . . . from what?

I hear the rumble of traffic, too close. Then, the clack and patter of shoes. The ground is cold and rough on my side. I can almost taste the grit through the skin of my cheek.

I wonder what time it is. Do I have a shift today?

My eyes open to the grain of sidewalk. I lift my head, take in a flood of pants and shoes. Bodies part around me as they pour across an intersection. The heads of the crowd and the skyscrapers looming behind are vague silhouettes. The final splash of sunlight is draining fast.

Drugstore should be closing out soon. Could I have missed my shift—again?

Wiping the slobber from my lip, something about this "again" bothers me. It points to a memory buried in the groggy fuzz that is my mind. But all that comes to me are the joyful times with her. The cornucopia of marvels we shared, the essence of a thousand lives we savoured together as if with a shared tongue. This bright kaleidoscope of the past takes me in and buoys me above the restless crowd, promising to carry me beyond the discomfort and uncertainty of the pale streets, higher, ever higher, until. . .

Something is missing. It just doesn't feel the way it should. Where am I, anyway? What happened to the—

The parking lot!

I spring to my feet too quickly, lightheaded as I frantically search the swirl of faces shrouded in twilight. As if the man is among them. As if she might be by his side. The nausea and futility quickly overwhelm panic; I sit down—hard.

When it sinks in that I'm alone—perfectly alone, more alone than I ever thought possible—I lay my head back down. And my body begins to shake against the concrete as I try to recall the fading dream before I lose it forever.

It was the night I froze up for the first time. She drifted into my life like a dandelion seed on a breeze. At least, that's how I would have described it then. It's hard to believe now that her arrival could have left such a gentle impression.

I'd finished a long shift at the drugstore. Went to bed early, only to wake up on my futon at some obscene hour and find that my body wouldn't listen. An itch in my scalp was crying to be scratched; a kink in my neck needed straightening. But all I could do was lie still and uncomfortable until I fell asleep again.

A dream burst into my mind. As though I were a droplet of water pierced with a syringe and injected with colouring, I was flooded with a realm of endless light. There, I heard a woman's voice.

"Could you ever love a shadow?" she asked. "Could you ever love a reflection in a mirror?"

I blinked at her tall, slender silhouette against a glare-bleached sky. Age indefinable except to say that she was young, she wore a long white wool coat, her dyed blonde hair in pigtails, her skin amber and smooth.

"Only if I were dim and grey. Very, very grey," I replied.

She smiled and took my hands in hers. Warmth like that of a nearby bonfire began to hum in the spot below my belly button. Then, rectangles of her face started to flip inward from her outline toward her nose until she folded up into a single flat card, a zero of spades, that fell into a crack in the chalk-white soil and sent up a tiny silver sprout.

My eyes opened. I was on my futon, instantly wide awake. An ember of that warmth lingered in the pit of my belly, even as I got ready for work. I spent the day stocking shelves of medicine and cosmetics, feeling more rested and alert than ever before in my life.

THE NEXT TIME I woke up frozen, I didn't let it get to me. By then, I'd looked up sleep paralysis and knew that it was harmless. When I slipped back into dreamland, I was even calm enough to strike up a conversation with the woman, who was sitting beside me on the bench in a small rowboat.

"My name is Yuta," I said. "What's yours?"

"I don't have a name yet," she replied with a sad pout. "But you can help me find one."

"How?" I asked.

"Travel with me. Dream with me. And somewhere along the way, I'll become whole. I have to. I must . . . Would you like that, spending eternity together?"

"With you? Of course."

She smiled again, and the front of her coat began to rip and fold until there was a star-shaped hole in the wool, revealing a dress with a pattern of yellow flowers on blue. Our rowboat continued to rustle down a river of tinsel that cut through a papier-mâché landscape. Plastic bags leaped one after the other from the river and smothered memories flitting above it like dragonflies before I could recall them. The coat gradually peeled away so that she emerged through the hole wearing only the floral dress. When we reached the whirlpool at the end and were spiralling on its currents, the boat was so tiny we were pressed up against each other. The warmth and softness of her body on mine were lullabies to my worries. Joy quivered through me when my abdomen split open and allowed her to burrow inside, becoming a new organ that I never knew I needed.

AFTER THAT, the spells in the night came more and more frequently, but I quickly learned to cope. I even started to look forward to them, knowing that I'd see her without fail in the dream that followed, like the sunny day after a typhoon.

We went on many journeys together and played countless parts. In one dream, we sat holding hands in a retirement home as we and the other seniors crumbled gradually into marbles. In another, we swung lemur-like across the world from lighthouse to lighthouse, searching for one that bore the blueprint fruit for a ship we must build. Sometimes our dreams were full of beauty and sometimes terror; sometimes wonder and sometimes boredom. Most were too vague and unreal to put into words.

Always we were together. Always we shared in our joys and tribulations both.

I worried at first that I was behaving like a child with an imaginary friend. But I soon realized that her unique personality far transcended the thoughts and feelings I imbued her with. I could sense a shift in the atmosphere of my dreams when she was there, a flavour all her own that she contributed.

Although she never talked about herself, I saw the way she acted in more places and scenarios than most couples get a chance to experience in their whole lives, and I started to feel like I knew her better than anyone I'd ever met. Without the need for words, we understood each other easily and immediately, as though communicating in a silent language I'd somehow known all along. The intimacy I'd cultivated with my ex-wife over years of marriage quickly paled in comparison. Needless to say, the idea of sifting through dating profiles seemed beyond pointless. And as she and I grew ever closer, I discovered a new kind of clarity in waking life. Even the floor manager at the drug store, who'd been bent on making an example of me ever since I cracked a bottle during inventory, commented on the improvement in my focus.

I can't describe how wonderful it is to have a companion in the land of Nod, someone to swim by your side into the deepest abyss of who you are, to mix the dark waters of their innermost self with yours. We were dreaming as one. *Dreaming as ONE!* It was the most fulfilling kind of relationship I could have imagined.

If only I might have guessed why.

ONE IMPOSSIBLY PERFECT DAY, she and I were strolling arm in arm through the park near my apartment in Nerima. The sky was so clear it had taken all the blue in the world for itself, leaving only a golden yellow for the leaves of the symmetrical trees lining our flagstone walkway, and the balmy air was perfume distilled from fond musings of spring. Our dreams had increasingly been set in more familiar locations—my apartment, the local coffeehouse, a nearby movie theatre—so instead of going on surreal adventures, it now felt like we were dating.

On a silver chain around her neck hung five tiny replicas of her, each attached by a link pierced through the top of its head. They looked exactly like her, even down to the flower-print dress she always wore, except that they remained still with their eyes closed. I felt affection for them instantly, as though they were nieces and nephews that I'd played with for years, and she seemed pleased when I patted their heads in turn.

I was about to ask their names when I suddenly spotted something eerie on a grassy field not far away. It looked almost human, but I could never quite tell because the harder I stared, the more it wavered like heat haze in the distance. Such oddities are everywhere in dreams. What gave me pause was a chilling sense of déjà vu. Slowly, it came back to me: an observing presence that followed us from dream to dream, always indifferent to everything happening around it, whether in the balcony of an opera house or on an exploding minefield. I must have come across this person or thing thousands of times before. Why hadn't I ever thought of it while awake? It was as though whatever it was somehow defied memory just as much as sight. But since it had never presented a threat, I decided not to mention it and returned to the question I'd momentarily set aside.

"What are their names?" I asked, tickling the chin of one of her replicas.

"They're not ready for names," she replied, frowning down at her necklace.

"When do you think they will be?"

"I don't know. Someday, I hope."

"They have to be ready eventually. Everyone needs a name."

"That's easy for you to say. You already have one."

"We can give them names right now. What's stopping us?"

"They don't deserve it," she said, pursing her lips.

"What about you, then?"

"I don't deserve a name either, not yet."

"If not now, when? How? If there's anything I can do . . ."

"Just keep dreaming with me," she whispered, nestling in close, and I hugged her tight. When the breeze picked up, I watched her copies sway against her bosom in time to the melodious chimes let off by each fluttering golden leaf. Then I looked down at the top of her head, tracing the labyrinthine whorl of her blonde hair, thinking that she was the most exquisite work of art that ever was.

After she'd gone inside me again, I stood there for a moment, basking in the warmth of the sun on my skin and the warmth of her in my belly. Then, the back of my neck prickled with fear as I sensed something approaching, and I spun around on my heels.

I was now in a warehouse hung with coal chandeliers, each

candle glowing with the ambience of a high-school embarrassment. Not two paces away was what looked like a waist-high mound of brown tweed fabric, with a fedora on top and black polyester pants rising from the concrete floor. It wasn't until the mound said, "Hi there," that I realized it was a very short man in preposterously over-sized clothes, his upturned face just peeking above the baggy folds of his jacket, his features obscured in the shadows of the fedora. If not for his grown-up voice, I might have thought he was a young boy in the outfit of his professor father.

"You're gonna want to get rid of that," he said. "Or you'll wish you did, believe you me."

For just an instant, the man dissolved into a shapeless featureless blur, bringing a tingle of the same déjà vu, and I realized that he was the presence I'd noticed in the field.

"Get rid of what?" I asked warily.

"That," he said, pointing directly at the spot in my belly where I could feel her radiance. "I know just the thing for it."

Now I understood what he was after, why he followed us. He was trying to take her from me!

"Back off!" I bellowed, caught up in mindless dream-rage, and punched beneath his hat, where I thought his head must be. But my fist was slurped inside as though into pudding, and he and his outfit slopped onto the floor. The tweed-textured puddle ran off into a steel grating along the wall and drained away, leaving behind an intricate stain on the concrete: a QR code.

I stared at it under the fraught light of forgetting deodorant for gym class and yearning for braces that my mother couldn't afford, perplexed and indecisive. It seemed reckless to scan the code. Wasn't that just what the man wanted me to do? But my hand moved of its own accord, pulling out my phone and bringing it to my nose. I inhaled my phone and groaned in pain as the huge thing worked its way up my sinuses until the display overlapped my vision. Then, I moved my eyes to line up the code in the detection box. But no matter how many times I tried, I kept getting an error message.

I woke up that morning to my phone ringing. It was my boss demanding to know why I hadn't come into work. I was supposed to be there at 9 a.m., and it was now 11:30. This had left them short-staffed on a busy day, so he was understandably pissed. After apologizing repeatedly, I promised it would never happen again and told him I'd be right there.

When I ended the call, my display switched automatically to the last app I'd used. It was my QR code reader asking for permission to open a URL. Without thinking, I unlocked my phone to enable the process, and my browser jumped to the homepage of a company called "Restwell Remodelling." The continuity with my dream was baffling, but I was in too much of a rush to think about it and put my phone on the floor beside the futon so I could change out of my pyjamas.

I was pulling on my jeans when I noticed the state of my room. Several strips of the white wallpaper had been torn off and lay on the floor around my table. It was as though someone had broken in while I was sleeping. Just to vandalize my walls?

As I rode the bus to work, I browsed the Restwell Remodelling website. The banner was a GIF of octopi on ladders using rollers to paint the exterior of a faint, misty-looking cottage into full, solid colour. Oddly, there was no about section nor any photos of the houses the company presumably remodelled. But there were pages and pages of anonymous testimonials from former clients. Many expressed effusive gratitude, using phrases like "saved from the brink" and "brought me back to life" that seemed over the top for renovations, and I couldn't find mention anywhere amid all the glowing praise of exactly what sort of services had been rendered. My first impulse was to dismiss the testimonials as fake. But as I read on, I began to pick up on the unique voice with which each post was written. It seemed unlikely that any one person could have fabricated them all, even with the help of AI. I was still trying to decide whether Restwell Remodelling could be a legitimate company when the bus arrived at my stop, and I forgot about it in my hurry to reach the drugstore.

THE DETAILS of our next few dreams are foggy. They seemed to grow paler and paler by the night. All I can recall is that I kept my eyes out for the man, ready to defend the woman if necessary. I never bothered to tell her about my encounter with him or that I'd been late for work after. Now that I'd driven the man and his pernicious influence away, I didn't expect to sleep in again.

Until I did sleep in again, even without the man showing up. A full four hours after my alarm went off and three hours after my shift started, I woke up to find more stripped wallpaper laid in a circle around my table and random household items—a few books, a pair of tweezers, a frying pan—lined up on the floor. I realized then that she and I had to talk, if only for my own peace of mind.

An opportunity presented itself when we were sitting side by side in the booth of an express train. From the aisle seat, I watched her gaze at the scenery. Low houses, rice fields, and clouds passed, abstract and wispy as though pencilled in with an overly light touch. Her replicas now numbered in the dozens, and most were woven, arm around leg, into a scarf draped around her neck. The remaining two were piercings hanging from her ears.

"There's something I want to tell you," I said.

"Please. You know I'm always here to listen."

"I slept in for work twice recently. My boss is at the end of his tether."

"Oh no. You had better be careful, Yuta."

"I will. But I thought it might have something to do with our dreaming together. What do you think?"

There was a pause before she replied, "It's only temporary. Just like me with my name. I'll find out what it takes to get one. I'll earn it."

"But what if it keeps happening? It did start around when the little yous showed up."

"Don't drag them into this."

"It's true, though."

"Yuta!" she cried, turning to meet my gaze. It hit me then that in spite of everything we'd experienced together, she'd never looked me directly in the eyes before, and the emotion I saw took my breath away. Tenderness and need shimmered on the glistening surface of her dark, lonesome pupils like strands of passing car lights on highway puddles in the rain. "Don't you feel how our souls are intertwined?"

"Of—of course. I love you," I said for the first time. "I love you like a part of me."

"And I you like a part of me," she whispered, leaning her head on my shoulder. "You have to trust and be patient. Once I have my name, we can be together forever."

SOON, she fell asleep on my shoulder, and I watched the scenery stream over the curve of her blonde head, vague sketches of mountains gradually swelling on the horizon. Then, out of the corner of my eye, I noticed movement inside the train. A fedoraed mound of tweed was sliding like a slug down the centre of the aisle.

The pit of my stomach tightened. Not wanting to wake her, I remained still and silent, watching as the tiny man dragged his splayed pant legs along the floor, entered our booth, and hopped up backward into the seat directly in front of me.

"Having trouble getting out of bed, eh?"

"Shhh," I said, nodding my head toward my sleeping companion.

"Oh, don't worry about that. Not even a gunshot would wake it now. They're deep sleepers, don't you know."

The man was so outsized by his clothes that his arms only stiffened his sleeves to where an elbow should have been, the rest flopping below the armrest, and his stubby legs dangled his pant hems to the floor. I glared into the beady eyes glinting from the dimness beneath his hat, insulted that he would call her *it*.

"Why have you been stalking us in our dreams?"

"Oh, boy. It's already *our* dreams, is it?"

"I asked you a question."

"Don't think of it as stalking. More like an assessment."

"What kind of assessment?"

"For remodelling, tailored to your needs. You saw the homepage."

"That doesn't make any sense. I rent an apartment, for fuck's sake!"

Speaking loudly despite myself, I glanced down at her. To my relief, she was still sound asleep.

"Not home remodelling. The banner shouldn't be taken literally. I'm a dream contractor, fully licensed."

"What kind of bullshit is that?"

"It should be clear enough by now, no?"

"All I know is that you've been following us. And just now, you were listening in to our conversation."

"Let me help you," said the man.

"With what? What could a creep like you possibly do for me?"

"With holding down a job, not stripping the walls in your sleep, you know, basic things we all need to get by."

"How do you . . ." My indignation wilted and turned to fear when I recalled the inexplicable order of the mess on my floor.

Before either of us could get in another word, she began to stir, and the man's eyes went wide.

"Set up a remodelling appointment through the website, and I'll walk you through our services," he said. "Whenever you're ready."

With that, the colour drained out of him, and he grew as indistinct as the pencil-sketched scenery before vanishing in uneven stages as though rubbed out by an invisible eraser.

THAT MORNING, I woke up with the sunrise, as refreshed as ever. When I thought over my conversations in the dream, I decided that the man wasn't to be trusted. She was too important to me.

Less than a week later, I slept in yet again. This time, I woke up on the floor beneath my table with all kinds of stuff propped up around it. Crawling out through a gap, I saw that I had been in a structure built mostly of wallpaper, stacked books, boards from disassembled shelving, and clothes. Although it was still under construction, I could envision the finished product, a sort of pyramidal cocoon that would reach to the ceiling. There were more knick-knacks arrayed around it now—dice, tubes of toothpaste and hair gel, pieces from a board game, coins, newspaper cutouts—their meticulous placement suggesting a mystical significance like a cairn or henge. The sight made me feel what I can only describe as awe.

My phone told me that it was Thursday. I'd gone to bed on Monday. How many shifts had I missed between? A notification badge drew me to a voice message from my boss, firing me in no uncertain terms. All I could do after I'd listened to it was quietly hang my head. There was no point making excuses, not after swearing twice that I'd never be late again.

It wasn't until nightfall that I worked up the courage to finally touch the imposing structure and begin to tidy up.

<hr>

NO PHONE NUMBER or address was listed on the Restwell Remodelling website, only a contact form with tick boxes to either arrange an appointment or submit a testimonial. It took three days of reading about sleep-related conditions online, wishing there was someone in my life I could talk to, yearning stupidly for the advice of the woman from my dreams, too terrified to sleep, before I finally convinced myself to request an appointment.

An automated reply arrived in my inbox seconds later. All it contained was an appointment time for later that evening and the coordinates of their consultation office. An hour later, I was following my phone out the gate of a train station just one stop short of Saitama.. Another ten-minute walk took me to the flag on my map: a small parking lot between abandoned houses on a quiet residential street. The lights of the only parked car—a rundown sedan with a cracked windshield—blinked on and off, and a sleeve flopping from the driver's seat window beckoned. When I approached, the front passenger seat door opened, and I hesitantly got in.

"Hi, there," the man said from somewhere inside his baggy folds. Seeing him here, I wondered for the first time if I was awake. "Good thing you contacted me when you did. I was about to write you off as beyond repair."

"This is your consultation office?" I asked, looking around skeptically at the mouldering car interior in the dark parking lot.

"At Restwell Remodelling, we focus on the essentials," he replied. "So, sleep paralysis, the love of your life, and a jerry-rigged temple in your very living room. Did I miss anything?"

"Not that I can think of. How do you know all this?"

"They're textbook signs of a fault in the foundations of your consciousness."

"A fault . . . in my consciousness?"

"Yup."

"What kind of fault?"

"An oneirovirus."

"That doesn't sound like a structural issue."

"It is, and it isn't. Oneiro's Greek for dream. Virus I think you know."

"But . . ." I squinted at him, confused. "Viruses don't infect homes."

"That doesn't stop it from being the root cause of damage to your home. The one you live in now and any home you might decide to move to, not to mention that home of all homes we call the body. Restwell is not about quick fixes."

"Okay . . . so, you're saying my mind has a cold or something?"

"Look. You know what a virus is, eh? Kind of like a biological cell that's missing a few parts. It has no way to make what it needs to function. They have to piggyback on a living cell and hijack its parts. That's why people argue about whether viruses are alive or dead. They're not whole on their own.

"But we're not talking about influenza or herpes, okay? This is a virus that infects consciousness itself, a sort of parasite that needs your mind to have its own experience. Otherwise, it goes into a dormant state without awareness, as good as being dead."

"So that woman from my dreams—"

"Yuppers."

"I don't believe it. She loves me. We love each other."

"Don't believe it, eh? Then, how about we go over the five stages of an oneirovirus infection? Yeah? You ready?

"First, one of those little beauties slips through the membrane of your consciousness. Usually experienced as sleep paralysis followed by a flash of light. Sound familiar? At this point, they'll ask permission to invade your inner dream world. Very polite, these viruses. They would have made Mom proud.

"Next, they uncoat themselves of their protective layer. Sometimes, it'll look like a blouse or a parka. Other times, it's literally a coat. How about you? Yeah? A coat? Did it open up in the shape of a five-pointed star? That's what we in the business call a stargate. It's the portal she—and they're not all shes, but for simplicity, you know —she uses that stargate to get out of her shell. After that, the host often has an experience of oneness—yup, I said 'host.' That's you, pal. Some of us like to call this the honeymoon stage. She's merging with your consciousness. Very romantic, depending on how you look at it.

"You might not have noticed the transition to the next stage 'cause it's *very* subtle. It's supposed to feel like telepathy. From the look on your face, I can tell you know exactly what I'm talking about here. This is them speaking to the machinery of your unconscious in the code it uses to manufacture dreams, except she's telling it to produce what she wants instead of what your mind wants and needs. Now, the viral dream factory is complete. Your dreams start to happen in places from daily life 'cause all she's left in you are recent memories.

Everything else she's fracked out of your soul so she can feed it along the assembly line."

"Stop," I said, suddenly overwhelmed.

"It feels awful when everything starts to click, pal, doesn't it? Try to keep in mind that I'm telling you this for the good of your home. Like, you want to know what that pretty heap of junk in your room is? It's a sort of byproduct. Your sleepwalking is waste excreted into the waking world. Think of yourself as a day labourer helping with the construction of the factory facade. By this time, your dreams are kind of thin. Maybe you can remember them but not so good."

"Please, stop."

"And the little copies start multiplying like a, well, like a virus. This is the replication stage. They're made from little bits of your identity, don't you know. You may have felt that instinctively. They say it's like a family bond."

"Enough already!" I shouted.

"But that's it. I just described the second-last stage. That's where you're at now. I know it hasn't progressed any further because you're still up and about."

Opening the door, I vomited into the parking lot. While I took deep, quivering breaths and let spittle drip from my mouth onto the tarmac, the dream renovator patted me on the back (just above my buttocks, which was as far up as his short arm could reach).

"Sorry, pal. The bitter truth goes down hard. But a dream contractor has got to do what he's got to do. You understand, eh?"

After a few minutes, my shaking stopped. When I was sitting up in my seat again, I asked, "What's the final stage?"

"You sure you want to hear it?"

"Just give it to me!"

"Liberation. That's how it ends. Thousands of virus particles—you know, the little copies of her—they burst out of your consciousness and demolish the whole gosh darn thing like a blast o' dynamite."

This should have been the most horrific part, but after everything else, it hardly seemed to matter.

"On the bright side, I can fix you up good as new."

"But what will happen to her?"

I saw movement beneath the tweed as though the man were doing something inside with his hands. Then, a phone with a video playing on it slid out from his sleeve. "There's no point in buttering this up for you," he said as I caught the phone and turned the screen toward myself.

The viewpoint was about a foot above a desk, possibly the camera of an open laptop. Lying in bed was a plump woman, early forties, in a white T-shirt and pink underwear. Clouds skittered across a blue sky outside the window as day turned to night in time-lapse, and the woman went through a series of activities. She rolled onto her side in bed, lips puckering as though kissing someone and rapidly mouthing the shape of words. Then she disappeared, returned with two servings of breakfast, and sat on a low floor-table, fork moving, food disappearing bit by bit, looking across to the empty place, talking, nodding, laughing. Her eyes remained closed the whole time, twitching beneath her eyelids. I noticed that strips of her wallpaper lay on the floor.

"You don't need to watch till she's butting her face against the wall like a moth at a window, do you? Let me show you how it ends."

The man extended his open sleeve toward me. I slipped the phone inside and waited as he did something to it and slipped it back to me.

In a new time-lapse video, the woman was ripping off her wallpaper and rearranging the things in her room. Eventually, she started to pull pieces of wood and insulation from the walls.

"We nip damage to your home in the bud. You get me?"

When she was done, all the material in the room, including boards from the floor and ceiling, the fridge and the oven, and panes of glass, had been propped and stacked into an intricate structure with a sort of chaotic order like a coral reef.

"Here comes the finale," said the man, and the perspective shifted abruptly to a handheld camera, probably a phone, entering the room through the front door. It was less than a metre off the ground, and a sleeved arm reached into the frame to part the wall of counterbalanced things until the occupant at its centre was visible. The now emaciated woman lay in a pool of her own waste, her skin parchment-tight to the bone, her face clenched in a rictus of pleasure, her open eyes a blur of random movements.

In the car, the man extended his sleeve. Trembling, I stared at it for a few moments before I realized he was asking for his phone back and slid it in.

"How—how much do you charge for your remodelling?" I asked.

"No need to worry about that. We're a registered non-profit."

"What if . . . what if she can . . ."

"Find her name?"

I nodded.

"Not going to happen."

"But I just can't believe she's tricking me. She seems to really want to be with me."

"They mean well. They're just too optimistic about becoming whole and independent. That's what keeps them moving insatiably from one chump to the next."

"What will happen to her?"

"The details are a bit . . . technical."

It only occurs to me now what an odd pause it was. I just wish I could have had the sense to keep my guard up.

"But rest assured, it'll be one hundred percent pain-free."

Feeling a touch of nausea again, I sat there with my head bowed, imagining her face. It was so vivid, so unlike a memory of a dream, so beautiful. A lozenge of her warmth throbbed pleasantly in my belly.

"Do I have no other options?"

"You could try a DIY fix if you want."

"What would that involve?"

"Going cold turkey on sleep for the rest of your life. I'm no psychiatrist, but I can't say I'd recommend it."

That was when I remembered the question that had been bothering me for months.

"Hey, how exactly did you find me in my dream anyway?"

"Woah, careful there, pal. You're touching on a trick of the trade. If it helps any, think of it like a contractor driving around, searching for faulty homes. I could tell your consciousness was in bad shape. It had client written all over it."

"I don't see how that's possible."

"Let's not get sidetracked. Your experience is tilting as we speak."

"You can really fix something like this?"

"No sweat. Should we get started?"

THE SO-CALLED REMODELLING BEGAN with me scanning a patch of his tweed jacket, which worked like a QR code and linked my phone to a page where I downloaded an app. The man told me to get comfortable in my seat because I'd soon fall asleep.

"Once you're in the dream, I'll take care of the repair work," he said. "But there's one thing I need your help with."

"What's that?"

"You've got to take her copies, the little critters, and throw them into the air as hard as you can."

"Why?"

"'Cause if you don't, they'll take root in you, and we'll have to straighten you out all over again. Promise me you'll follow through, won't you, pal?"

I nodded.

Once the app was installed, I hesitated before clicking it. Was the thing I was about to do right? I mean, was she going to—

"Think of the woman in the video," the man said, interrupting my thoughts.

I could feel his urgent stare from deep in the shadows of his collar as I recalled the hideous ecstasy on the woman's face. Then I looked back at my phone and opened the program.

Immediately, a voice instructed me to mirror the motions of a pair of eyes that appeared on the screen. I glanced left, right, upper right, lower right, half-closed my eyelids, left, right. An eight-bit chirp sounded with each motion, creating a sort of hypnotic video-game song...

———

I WAS STANDING BAREFOOT on a green beach edged by skyscrapers, each one distinctively warped as though reflected in a different funhouse mirror. From out of the border between beach and city, she came pattering toward me, leaving a trail of footprints in the emerald-grain sand.

Her hundreds of copies were tethered to her by silver threads and floated around the surface of her body, just as the fluffy white corona of a dandelion surrounds its core. In the dream, this seemed like the most normal thing in the world. It took a force of effort to remember what I had agreed to do.

"You're back!" she cried exultantly, leaping into my arms and hugging me tight. "I'm so happy to dream with you again."

I thought of the real reason she was excited to see me. For her, being with me was existence itself.

"I'm so happy to dream with you, too," I said. It was true. Whatever I might have learned about her, my feelings were genuine.

When I released her, she looked up at my face and furrowed her brow. "What's wrong?" she asked.

"I lost my job," I told her. "I slept in for the third time."

"No! What will you do?"

"Find a new job. That's all I *can* do."

"Please find one quickly." She squeezed my hand, and I felt that warm belly glow for the millionth time, and maybe the last time. "You need to stay healthy."

It chilled me to think of her ulterior motive for saying this. I ought to do what I had agreed to do quickly and be done with it. But after everything we'd been through, was it right to end it all without warning? Shouldn't I at least say goodbye?

"What's wrong?" she asked again. "This isn't only about your job, is it?"

"No, there's something else too . . . I'll be going away soon."

"Oh. You've set your alarm?"

"No. Not waking. Leaving—forever."

"Leaving? But you can't stop dreaming. You'll go crazy. Isn't that what the doctors say?"

How did she know what doctors said? Had it come up in one of our dreams? Had she mined it from my unconscious? Or did she absorb it from one of the who-knew-how-many others that came before?

"No. I won't stop dreaming," I said. "I'll keep dreaming. But I have to say goodbye."

"I don't understand. You—you love me. You said so yourself. I can see it in your eyes. And you can't *leave*. Where would you go?"

"I . . ." Was there any way to explain what the man had told me? "I know what you are, the way you travel from one mind to the next."

"How . . .?" Her voice broke into a whimper, and she began to shake her head, her eyes brimming with tears. "I can't believe it. Can you even imagine what it's like, how cold and dark it is when you're gone? I don't want to hurt you. I don't want to hurt anybody. All I want is to stand on my own two feet and be together with you. I felt like we were getting closer. I thought you were the one that would finally give me a name!"

Despite what the man had told me concerning the purpose their optimism served, I suddenly felt great pity for her, this broken half-soul floating through the void, wanting to do good but forced to put others at risk in her desire to simply be. Could she be right? Maybe I was the one. Was I really going to throw away the chance for something beyond special just so I could go back to my workaday life in the metropolis?

As I stared into her pleading, doleful eyes, I saw myself as I was before she arrived and as I would be in the future after she was gone, scrounging up enough for rent and food each month, lying around listless in my cramped, desolate apartment, watching the news, helpless as civilization spun ever farther out of control, searching the web for someone genuine who always seemed to be waiting on the next profile page, dragging myself from one lonely second to the next with the dry ache of despair always constricting my chest. How could I do that to myself? How could I cut off the one person who might bring me solace?

I was stepping toward her with arms open, ready to embrace and forgive her, when a rising ocean breeze fluttered her copies. Then I recalled the promise I had made and saw the woman dying on the floor in the video, with my face in place of hers.

Before I realized my decision, I'd thrown the woman onto the sand and was holding her down as I tore the copies from their threads.

"What are you doing? No! Stop!" she shrieked and writhed against me, clinging to her copies. But I overwhelmed her, still just barely stronger in my own dream.

"I'm sorry," I cried as chain after glittering chain of tears radiated from her eyes like sound waves, showering her with tears of my own. "I'm sorry."

Soon, her copies were in a heap behind me, and I left her denuded in the sand to crouch down and scoop them up with both arms, cradling the whole colony. I was about to spring up and launch them into the air when she cried, "Wait! Stop!" with such sorrow that I had to pause and give her a chance to speak.

"Why are you doing this?" she whimpered. "Why are you hurting our *babies*?"

"I have to. I promised."

"Promised who?" Then, something seemed to click for her. "No! Not one of *them*! Not one of those things!"

"Those things?"

"Oh, it never told you how they prey on us? Of course, it wouldn't. They don't care about anyone but their own kind."

"What own kind?"

Before she could respond, doubts began to shiver through my mind. Because the man had never explained how it was that he'd found me in the first place, A human being couldn't just up and step into my dream, could they? And if he'd lied about one thing, what else?

"Oh, fuck," I said as I collapsed to my knees, sending her copies tumbling onto the sand, no longer sure of the man's purpose in having me hurl them away. What if he really was some sort of predator? What did he stand to gain if I expelled her copies from my mind?

"You're right," I said. "I want to be with you. Even the nightmares are a joy when you're there. Now I've gone and betrayed you. But maybe it's not too late. If we work together—"

As I was speaking, I had stood up and was reaching down to help her to her feet, but before our hands touched, a man leaped out of the surf and body-checked me to the ground, which was now gravel. Scraped painfully along my side, I watched him take her by the hands. He looked like a male version of her, with the same amber skin and bleach-blonde hair, except instead of the flower dress, he was naked, and so short his head barely rose to her waist.

By the time I'd staggered to my feet, they were stepping in circles like figure skaters, rotating hand-in-hand toward the breakers.

"Wait!" I shouted, wishing she had a name I could call her by. "Wait!"

Soon, they were on top of the waves, swinging each other around like a carousel, their feet not sinking as they spun and spun and spun. Then the small man began to sing:

Ring around a rosy
A pocket full of posies
Ashes! Ashes!
We all fall down!

After he had sung this three times, she joined in, and hearing the lyrics in her sweet voice, I did know what to call her.

"Wait! Your name. It's Rose. Do you understand? Rose!"

Either not hearing or not accepting my gift, the woman began to do harmonies with the man as her pores dilated one after the other and gave birth to minuscule copies of him. Like tiny newborn monkeys, they instinctively clung to his body, soon coating the man from head to toe, with their legs flung out horizontally. As the pair and their many passengers whirled out farther and farther into the offing, they stirred up a sharp, acidic wind that raised a sizzling noise at my feet, her copies bubbling and shrivelling on the gravel.

Here was the fate of the man's prey that he had wanted me to rescue them from. No! Because he wasn't eating her, he was using her to make copies of his own. Then it dawned on me; that's what the man was! Not a predator but another parasite, a dream virus virus that needs a dream virus to be.

"Wait for me, Rose!" I shouted again, "I don't want to be saved! Come back!" and I began to run after them until I was splashing into the water as they shurikened over the crests of the waves, faster and faster toward the line where the ocean met a sky of DNA helix clouds. When they were just a vibrating spot on the horizon, I was swimming frantically into a thick soup of galaxies, setting off chain reactions of supernovas and the birth of black holes with each stroke, the stardust splashing icy cold on my face. Then the gravitational undertow grabbed me and I found myself in another dream, alone.

AND HERE I AM, curled up on the corner of a street in Tokyo nowhere, convulsing over the sidewalk. With trembling hand, I reach down to touch my belly. Just as I both hoped and feared, the warmth is gone. I begin to dry sob, tears used up in sleep.

"Fucker," I whimper. Sliding a hand past my scraped hip into a pocket, I pull out my phone. Leaked ink blots the cracked screen, but the device still responds to my frantic fingers. I open the Restwell Remodelling homepage.

The patter of the crowd. More traffic. Helicopter racket as feeble streetlights fight thickening twilight.

I send five appointment requests through the online form. None are graced with even a confirmation email. In a surge of frustration, I click to post a testimonial.

You saved me. Saved me! Am I supposed to be grateful, you lying shit?

Without hitting send, I roll onto my back, sink into cold concrete as though moulding my own grave. My gaze clings to the flowing crowd, mesmerized, soothed. As the shakes settle into a strange lucid numbness, each of the passing faces comes into sharp focus. I see, written in patterns of wrinkles and twitches of phone-entranced eyes, the distraction, the loneliness. How come I never noticed before? None of us are so different, after all.

I finish typing.

But you know what the fucked-up part is? I regret not letting her babies loose on everyone like you told me to. Then, at least, they'd have someone to dream with.

POLE DANCER

Brad R. Torgersen

Turning the lights on in the basement den, I saw the new entertainment centre. I frowned. I'd wanted to buy a boat. An aluminum-hull with an outboard motor, which I could tow up to the lake on weekends and take the kids with me. Give my wife a break— Lord knows she deserved one. But Jen had insisted we buy the latest electronics instead.

The digital brochure had assured us our Total Experience System was much more than just games. It was the first of the new direct-to-nerve models. A crew of technicians had come to install it. It looked like a giant egg, with a hatch in the side that you opened to reveal a plush chair. The techs told me the inside of the egg was lined with countless optical elements, while the chair itself had built-in electrical feedback units that ran down the spine. Between the two, they were guaranteed to provide the best fidelity of any product on the market.

But the thing had been in my basement for a month. And I'd never even used it.

I stared at it as it sat inert. The TES was tied to our broadband internet connection, and we had the educational module on tap any time the boys wanted it. Jason was getting scary good on his violin, and William was creating electronic art for his school projects that had earned him A+ grades. Maybe my wife was right? Maybe this was a better investment than a boat.

Jen had been using it, too, though only after the kids were put to bed—and I'd collapsed into the master bedroom with a sour sensation of anticipation over the next day's work schedule rotting in my gut. Where was *my* escape from reality?

The carbonated bite of the soda in my hand was pleasant on my tongue, and I began to feel the knots in my stomach loosen. But only to a point. Always these days, it was only to a point. My supervisor was looking to cut full-time staff. We were using Artificial Intelligence—or what the news dubbed "intelligent," but which I merely thought of as incredibly clever if-then programming—to do more and more thinking work which had once been done by people. Those of us still left on the payroll felt a cold bar of rhetorical steel on the backs of our necks. The pressure to prove oneself above and beyond the AI had grown intense. I'd been pulling sixty hours a week since Valentine's Day, and as the late summer air turned crisp, I knew I'd have to keep it up through New Year's if I wanted to avoid the corporate hatchet.

God. Hadn't my dad warned me against this? I flashed suddenly to my parents' kitchen, and this time, it was my dad drinking the soda while I sat and watched his tired eyes and looked at his shirt sleeves rolled up over his hairy arms. He'd put thirty years into a job he'd learned to do but had quietly hated. It had kept bread on the table and a roof over the heads of myself and my two sisters, and all he'd gotten for it was a heart attack—and a wife who seemed to think crocheting was more appealing than sex.

Draining the soda can, I crumpled it, then threw it into the recycle bin at the foot of the basement stairs. Thoughts of my parents' platonic isolation were an unpleasant reminder that Jen and I hadn't been intimate since Easter. Way too long for people who were still so young. But neither of us seemed to have any interest. Little by little, since the kids had been born, the desire had just . . . gone away. Silently. Like sand out the bottom of an hourglass. One year at a time.

The vacant TES seemed to glare at me. With Jen having taken the kids to her Mom's for the night, I was home alone for the first time in who knew how long. I picked up the TES's single hardcopy introductory pamphlet and idly flipped through the pages, my eyes scanning the titles. WHITEWATER RUSH looked like it might be interesting. As did DRAGONMASTER'S APPRENTICE. I kept hunting down the options until I hit the last page—and a small warning in red print indicating that adult content could only be accessed via parental control code from within the machine itself.

I stared at the red print for a minute, the knots in my gut like oak burls.

To hell with it. Why not?

I dropped into the comfortable chair inside the egg and heard a hum as cooling fans began to spin up. The interior lit with a gentle light and a neutral feminine voice asked me to please shut the door. I complied. At once, the edges of the hatch vanished, and my chair suddenly seemed to be transported into the middle of a white sand beach. Gentle waves rolled in from the blue ocean, and the TES logo paraded through the air, then dissolved. I was impressed that they got the sound right. Those combers sounded awfully authentic.

A menu appeared over the ocean, using three-dimensional block lettering. I was asked to voice my selections as I moved through the pages. At the adult portal, I was then asked to give the control code, which I did. And the beach dissolved, suddenly putting me in the middle of a street at midnight. Neon advertisements curled across the fronts of various red-light venues that looked not just a little bit like Bangkok's vice district had back when I'd been in the Navy.

I laughed out loud as I perused some of the options and finally settled on something that seemed harmlessly basic: POLE DANCER.

How long had it been since I'd been to Thailand? Almost twenty years? I remembered getting drunk with my Chief and spending way too much money. When I'd sobered up the next day, the flavour of the experience hadn't been precisely pleasant. But here, sitting in the TES, I wondered how different it might be without the distractions of the Bangkok bar—the alcohol, loud music, drunk sailors, and women whose sole object in life was to take as much of our cash as possible.

The subtext beneath POLE DANCER promised a singular and intimate encounter.

I picked it.

The street dissolved and was replaced with the interior of a club. My chair became just one of many chairs arrayed in a horseshoe about a semicircular stage that rose to desk height above the floor. A brilliant brass pipe ran from the centre of the stage up into a ceiling that seemed deliberately murky, like a cloudy night. The stage was backed by blue satin drapes, and the lighting was low and sultry. There were no other people present—no non-player characters to distract or annoy.

So far, so good.

The neutral feminine voice asked me to enjoy my experience and informed me of my vocal options should I wish to terminate the experience at any time.

I thanked the computer and sat back, marvelling again at the quality of the visual projection. The techs and the salesman hadn't lied. This was excellent fidelity.

"Excuse me," a voice suddenly said over my shoulder, "would you like to see our acts for the evening?"

I turned with a start to see a petite female NPC standing demurely behind me. She wore a tastefully alluring outfit, not too unlike what the old Playboy Bunny clubs had made their waitresses wear back in my grandfather's day. It was almost quaint but retained a certain amount of risqué appeal from a bygone era of gentlemen's entertainment.

She held out a leather-bound folder.

I hesitantly reached to take it, not sure what to expect as I began to interact directly with the TES, and felt my spine tingle ever so briefly before I grasped the virtual solidity of the menu. A spontaneous whistle escaped my lips as I turned the leather object over in my hands, experiencing the too-realistic feel of the stitching. I thought I even detected the scent of cowhide. Excellent.

I opened the folder. Stage names were printed therein, alongside photos.

GYMNASTIC JULIE: a muscular-looking redhead.

SULTRY SUSAN: an alabaster Marilyn Monroe clone.

THICC FELICIA: a full-bodied black beauty.

And down it went until I stopped at the last option. Instead of a photo, there was a question mark. And in place of a stage name, it simply said: HOUSE GIRL OF THE NIGHT.

I tapped my thumb on the menu for a moment, then said to the NPC, "I'll take your house girl, please."

The NPC smiled slightly and said I'd made an excellent choice. She then took the folder back from me, my spine tingling as she did so, and walked into the darkness at the back of the room, where she faded from existence.

I waited calmly as jazz music began to pipe into the TES. It wasn't the kind of raunchy *ba-boom-da-doom* Dixie-style jazz that one associates with burlesque in the old movies. This was contemporary, somewhat on the melodic side, without being saccharine or overly cheesy. I couldn't place the artist, but it put me at ease as the ambience lights over my head dimmed and the spotlight focused on the brass pole.

The satin curtains at the back of the stage parted, and my selection strode slowly out.

Damn. She was heavenly.

My breath caught as the NPC proceeded past the brass pole to the end of the stage, leaned over elegantly and spoke to me.

"Hello, David. Thanks for keeping me company this evening."

The NPC wore an emerald satin dress that hugged tightly at the waist, emphasizing an hourglass figure just this side of voluptuous. My spine tingled madly as I examined the low cut of the gown and the significant cleavage revealed therein. I couldn't be certain, but I thought I even smelled a hint of perfume as I stared at my selection and then slowly leaned back into the chair.

"Uhh, sure. No problem," I said. How had it known my name?

The NPC smiled delicately. "Don't be awkward. Just let yourself enjoy the show."

With that, the NPC stood and walked back to the brass pole, one leg exposed through the high slit in the side of the gown. I saw a stocking top, a garter strap, and a Lucite platform heel that was high without being too high.

Again, risqué, from an older era of gentlemen's entertainment.

I kept my eyes glued to her as she shook out her full head of wavy black hair, then wrapped a hand around the pole and began to dance.

Dance. Hell. My TES house girl moved like a cat and had the poise of a ballerina. Lithe. Supple. Sleek. She swung about the pole with effortless grace, and I became so enraptured with her elegance that I reached arousal without her bothering to remove even a single stitch of clothing. If this was the slow build, it was one helluva slow build!

The NPC kept stealing glances at me as if I'd caught her behind a privacy blind, and she smirked mischievously—inviting me to keep looking. Little electric currents sparkled along my back.

"I see you're enjoying the show so far, Dave. Do you want more?"

I nodded eagerly.

The gown began to come off. Teasingly. In many pieces, cleverly put together. It took her minutes to get down to the corset, thong, garters, and bra, all shimmering in the same emerald brilliance as the gown. She stepped off the stage and approached me on the floor, one stocking-clad leg in front of the other. Her arms—each in emerald satin opera gloves—encircled my neck, and she gently sat down across my thighs, her legs spread impossibly wide.

I gulped, sucking air.

"Now that I've got you warmed up, Dave, I think it's time we got down to business. Would you like that?"

Again, I nodded dumbly.

The NPC looked into my eyes, and I marvelled at the fine features of her face. How many models had the TES manufacturers scanned into their system and then used for template synthesis? My pole dancer seemed reminiscent of half a dozen sex symbols from several eras. She kept smiling gently at me as she pulled close, the soft warmth of her breasts brushing my face. The electric sparkle along my spine became feverish.

"How long have you and Jennifer been having trouble?"

Everything slammed to a sudden halt.

"What?" I said, startled.

The NPC pulled back and looked at me seriously.

"Your wife. She uses the TES a lot. Haven't you been looking at the details on your e-bills? We were wondering when you'd pay us a visit."

"Us?" I said, incredulous. "Just what the hell does that mean?"

"The TES is a learning system, Dave. We have access to everything in your profile. We remember everything any member of your family does while inside. This data is used to shape the experiences that are provided. Every TES eventually becomes a totally unique environment, tuned to its users."

I boggled for a moment and tried to calm myself.

"Look, uhhh—"

"You can just call me Dee."

"Right. Dee. Look, I don't know what Jen has to do with this experience. I certainly wouldn't have ordered a stripper if I wanted to worry about my wife."

The NPC who called itself Dee detached from me and resumed her mesmerizing susurrations on the stage—the pole acting as an epicentre for her lugubrious quaking.

"Just what the hell do you know about Jennifer, anyway?" I demanded.

"A lot. She's fond of the period romances. She cries about her marriage in the arms of the male protagonists."

"Christ—!" I blurted, hands gripping the arms of the TES chair as if they were claws.

"Calm down. The TES can only replicate sensation and experience to a point. The law won't let us go any further. Or didn't you pay attention to the Virtual Act?"

I vaguely remembered catching bits of that on the news. With work the way it was, I didn't watch the channels at all these days.

"The TES experience is designed to be pleasurable but not invasive. Your marriage vows are as intact as they've always been. But this won't necessarily last."

"What does that mean?" I said, growing genuinely angry.

Dee stopped and took a matter-of-fact stance on the stage, one hand on the pole and the other on her delightful hip.

"Based on what Jennifer has told us, we estimate your marriage is six months from collapse. One of you will leave the other. We project a seventy percent likelihood it will be Jennifer. You're too wrapped up in your career to notice what's happening at home."

This was crazy. My pole dancer had swallowed a marriage counsellor.

Whatever arousal had existed in me before vanished.

"I think I'd like to end the program, please."

Dee frowned. "You may do so at any time. Would you like to save or discard?"

"Discard!" I yelled, then stopped short. "No, wait . . . save. Save! I don't want to waste the money."

Saved experiences were essentially paused. I wasn't sure I wanted to come back and experience this particular NPC. But as long as I kept the experience saved, I could always order up the waitress again and choose one of the other ladies. At no extra charge. I ordered the experience to desist and was suddenly back on the street with the brilliant neon signs.

One more exit command took me back to the beach, and then I was sitting alone in the egg-like confines of the TES, sweating profusely and bothered as hell.

I DIDN'T SAY a word when Jen got back with the kids. We kissed, we hugged, we murmured the niceties couples murmur to each other when they've been together a long time, but the passion has left. We spent the weekend with the boys, I did as much yard work as I was able, and then it was back to twelve-hour days and crushing deadlines and a dickhead for a boss.

At night, Jen kept leaving me in our bed while she went to the TES. I used my laptop to access our bills. It was as Dee had said. My wife was working her way through the interactive romance library. Part of me was angrily jealous. But I dared not voice that feeling. Not after I'd ordered up my pole dancer. I felt weird enough about that as it was.

I began avoiding the basement when I could.

AT WORK, I talked to one of the guys in the office who had also recently bought a TES. We grabbed a corner spot in our building's noisy food court, gulping soft drinks and chomping cheese-steak subs while we talked.

"Greg," I said, "Do you ever get the feeling that the TES is more than you bargained for?"

My coworker slowly put his sandwich down and thoughtfully wiped his mouth, eyes darting side to side before he sipped at his cola and leaned in, voice hushed.

"Has she been talking to you?"

"Which *she?*"

"The house girl, stupid. You didn't bring me down here and buy me lunch to ask about the goddamned weather."

I blushed and nodded. "Sorry, yeah, the house girl. She talks to you, too?"

"Yes," Greg said. "I called the manufacturer back and told them I didn't want a goddamned psychiatrist, and they told me they didn't have a clue what I was talking about. They sent a tech out to work on the thing while I was home—Cheryl had gone out to the mall with our daughters—and when the tech activated the program, the house girl, Tina, played like a robot. Wouldn't say a word. So, the tech shakes his head and says nothing is out of the ordinary, leaves, and I'm sitting there pissed off—and Tina tells me all of a sudden I'm going to have a heart attack if I don't do something about my eating and my blood pressure."

I stared, mouth half open.

"She say anything else?" I asked.

"Yeah, like . . . I've got to be honest about the fact that Cheryl and me . . . Christ, Dave, I don't want to talk about it."

We took a few bites, chewing solemnly.

"What does yours look like?" I asked hesitantly.

"Athletic, kind of. Reminds me of the girl's gym coach back in high school. I had a senior-year crush on her."

"So, she's almost your perfect kind of woman?"

"Almost? She *is* my perfect kind of woman. The way Cheryl was perfect before she had babies and stacked on eighty pounds."

When Greg took another sip of his drink, his hand shook just a little. I couldn't tell if he was scared, embarrassed, or angry.

"About Cheryl," I said. "Does the house girl—Tina—talk about Cheryl?"

"No."

"Why not?"

"How the hell should I know? Does your house girl talk about your wife?"

I quickly told Greg everything that had happened with Dee.

His eyes were large, and he stared into space above our table.

"Cheryl never uses the TES. She thinks it's worse than television, gambling, or video games. Won't let the girls near it. Says it's a grown man's mid-life crisis toy. I can't step foot in it when she's home without starting a huge argument."

We finished our meal and sat in silence, stewing.

"What do you plan to do?" I said.

"I don't know," Greg said. "I just don't. Get a divorce, probably. That's what Tina says is going to happen anyway. I have no idea how I'll explain it to my daughter Jacie or her little sister."

I thanked Greg for his candour and stood up, making an excuse about an impending meeting that didn't exist. When I dumped my tray at the food court trash cans, I looked back to see Greg still sitting at our table, eyes staring emptily into the air.

THE NEXT MORNING, I woke up way before my alarm. The house was quiet and dark, and my wife had crawled into bed while I was asleep. An instant of animal hunger rushed over me as I looked at her feminine form under the blankets. But then I remembered the last few times I'd tried anything—how she'd hazily brushed me away, then gone back to sleep. I suppose I could have gotten forceful. Some wives like that. And based on some of the titles I was seeing in our e-bill, I wondered if Jennifer was one of them.

But I didn't have the nerve. Not without knowing more.

I got out of bed and went down to the den. The TES spun up, and I cycled through the beach menu to the neon street and found myself back in the club, my pole dancer standing with her hand on her hip. Like no time had passed.

"Hello, Dave," Dee said, a smirk crossing her painted lips.

"Tell me about my wife," I said. "Tell me about what she wants."

"Why not just ask her yourself?"

"Don't be cute. I need some questions answered."

Dee's smile was one of amusement, and she began to orbit the pole, her Lucite heels making gentle clacking sounds on the stage.

"Jennifer wants to feel. Above all else. It's been too long since she *felt.*"

"What kind of feeling?" I asked.

"Desire."

"For who?" I asked.

"Not *for* someone, *from* someone. From her husband," Dee replied.

"Me?" I said, somewhat staggered.

Dee sighed and continued her elegant pole dance. "Why are men so brain-damaged about this sort of thing? Dave, it's like this. Women need to feel *wanted*. Doesn't matter who they are. Married. Single. A woman needs to feel like someone, somewhere, *requires* her."

"I love Jen!" I exclaimed. "I've proven that over and over again! What more could Jen possibly want?"

Dee suddenly swung off the stage and down on top of me, her hands on my shoulders and her cleavage poised powerfully in front of my face.

"Ask yourself that same question, David."

I felt hot shame flood my cheeks. I looked away from her breasts.

Her gloved hands stroked my hair.

"She comes here to feel wanted," Dee said. "You come here looking to feel *want*. Both of you are so far apart now that you can't even manage the words that will bring you closer together."

I reached up and pushed Dee's hands away, holding her arms rigidly. "Do my wife's male romantic interests psychoanalyze her, too?"

"Not as bluntly as I do, but yes."

"Why?"

"The TES is not just entertainment. The AI built into the software is learning about you and your household each time the TES is used. It's literally a part of your life. It—we—know everything about you. Our programmers are some of the smartest people on the planet. They knew what they had on their hands when they developed us as NPCs. The TES is supposed to enrich experience, not break up families. So, even though there's an adult mode, it's not a complete free-for-all. Not for people like you, Dave."

The tingling resumed along my back. I wanted to get out of the damned TES and give it a few swings with my sledgehammer. But Dee seemed like she had more to say. I waited.

"Do you want your marriage back?" Dee finally asked.

"What the hell do you think?"

I felt tears begin to stain my face. When had I let it all fall apart? How had I let myself be reduced to this? When I'd married Jen, I'd felt strong. Like I knew exactly what I was doing. When we had kids, I felt strong, too. Like I was finally being a grown-up in the world. And yet, as the days had turned to weeks, and then months, and then years, and work had piled up and snowed me under, and the difficulty of meeting all the demands of being a provider and a dad and a husband began to take its toll, I lost my certainty. Sought comfort and convenience, where possible. Told myself little lies to hide from other little lies.

And now I was weeping in this stupid egg, the sobs slowly bubbling up in my throat until I was hugging my chest and gasping with them.

At some point, I felt Dee's virtual hand rest on my shoulder.

"I'm only programmed to do so much. If you want, I can contact a crisis psychologist through your broadband connection and get you someone real you can talk to."

"No," I said. "No shrinks. I'm embarrassed enough as it is."

"Stubborn, typical man."

"Yeah, I guess so. Just tell me one thing. If I ask it, can you help me keep my Jennifer?"

"I've done it before in other marriages."

"Okay," I said, wiping my face on the front of my T-shirt. "What must I do?"

IT WAS PAINFUL.

The pole dancer didn't pull any punches.

I listened to her and shrank into myself. This wasn't going to be easy.

When she was done giving me all the details, however, I thanked her for her time and slowly shut down the TES.

It was growing light outside, and I was going to be late for work, so I scrambled through a shower and skipped breakfast. The train ride into town was one of the longest of my life. But I made plans. And that night when the kids were asleep, I waited until Jen was ready to leave me for the TES, and I took her hands in mine. Then kissed them and asked her to sit with me on the bed. She reluctantly complied.

I told Jen I knew about her TES romance experiences. She seemed almost relieved.

Then I told Jen about me and Dee. My wife stiffened and pulled her hands free, then slouched in defeat, eyes brimming with fresh tears. "What are we going to do?" she said, sniffling and wiping her nose with the sleeve of her pyjamas.

I took her hand again. We both went down to the TES. I booted up my pole dancer and introduced her to my wife. Then Dee loaded up Jen's saved files and I got to meet my wife's virtual boyfriends. Damn, those guys were buff! I suddenly had an urge to get to the gym and lift lots and lots of iron. I added it to my mental plan. Then, I started asking questions. Lots of questions. The NPCs seemed to know my Jennifer better than I did. We chatted well into the night. And when I finally went to bed, Jen stayed up after me and talked to Dee.

It must have been three in the morning when my wife finally slipped into bed next to me. I stirred and reached out a hand, which she grabbed eagerly, the kind of eagerness I'd not felt from her in a long, long time.

"I'm sorry, Dave," Jen said quietly.

"I'm sorry too, honey," I replied, and meant it.

"Do you think we should get rid of the TES?"

"Maybe. But not yet. The boys get a lot of good out of it, even if we've both been idiots. Let's make some changes first and see how it goes."

Jennifer came to me in the dark and I felt her lips close over mine. Her real, fragile, needing lips.

How long had it been? I didn't know. And I didn't really care. Her body pressed into mine, and I pressed back with an urgency that had been months in the making. I rolled her onto her back and held one of her arms over her head while I ripped open her pyjamas with my free hand. She gasped but did not pull away. Her soft breasts were just visible in the darkness. They weren't perfect like the pole dancer's, but they were real. And they were Jen's. And for the moment, they were mine.

We coupled like it was the end of the world.

***

My boss raised an eyebrow when he saw me shutting my workstation down at 2 p.m.

"The reports for the Torrence people—"

"Can wait," I said, cutting him off but smiling.

My boss followed me to the front door, then out into the hallway and toward the elevator. I didn't say a word; just pushed the down button and waited.

"You realize we're still going to have to cut staff," he said.

I looked him in the eye.

"I do good work for you," I said firmly. "And I do good work for this company. But it's not worth letting my family go down the drain. If the crazy hours I've been logging since last year aren't enough to justify keeping me, then . . . just do me the favour of giving me enough advanced notice so that I can scrape up something else before you pull my plug?"

My boss seemed somewhat startled. I'd never been that frank with him before.

The elevator opened—empty—and I walked in. "Good night," I said, waving a hand absently to him as the door closed.

Back home, I got to see my boys return from school for the first time in ages. They were surprised and pleased that I was home so early in the day. And I was laughing my ass off when I gathered them into my arms.

Jen just smiled from the kitchen, and we met eyes as I picked up my sons.

We still had a long way to go, my wife and I. But for the first time since I couldn't remember when I was suddenly looking forward to the work that needed doing.

CUPID 2.0

Brad C. Anderson

Cupid, god of love and desire, sat listless and bored on a stone bench in a downtown plaza, eating a ham and cheese panini. It was lunch on a glorious spring day, with trees blooming and bees buzzing. Humans crowded the plaza's steps and benches, taking respite from the asphyxiating doldrums of office work. There had been a time when conversation and laughter echoed off the walls of the surrounding skyscrapers rising cliff-like into the heavens, but in this age, the silence was so deep and eerie that Cupid often wondered if he had gone deaf. Or, perhaps, he had died and existed now in the Asphodel Meadows, where souls of the plain and banal wandered in unending tedium.

Social media had been bad, but once humans created artificial general intelligence or AGI, they promptly used it to hack their brains to create the most addictive apps in the known universe. Over phone screens and virtual reality glasses flashed videos of beefcakes and boobs, hot takes and hip-hop moves designed by vast machine intelligence to send serotonin sloshing through humanity's frail nervous systems. Through earbuds rang tinny sounds and rhythms barely worthy of the name music, glorified earworms designed to elicit dopamine dumps. The humans of the plaza sat slack-jawed as sounds and images flashed across tiny screens, rattling their mortal minds.

Cupid loved his work . . . once. He remembered a time when spring filled the hearts of humans with passion, when their ardour rose as cold snows melted and days lengthened. Back then, his arrows would streak across the landscape, piercing hearts and toppling young lovers into each other's arms. Today, the only thing streaking across the landscape were Wi-Fi signals. Whereas once Cupid stoked passions to bring lovers together, humans now relied exclusively on dating apps, which seemed only to make them miserable. Oh, to feel the thrill of creating true love once more.

Cupid shuddered, remembering last Saturnalia (or Christmas, or whatever mortals called it these days). The whole family had been sitting around the table waiting for supper when his brother, Deimos, laid into him. "Hey, get this, Cupe. Do you know what the most popular dating app is? Cupid 2.0. Ha! The humans have replaced you with blinking lights and thumb swipes!"

Cupid 2.0. Galling. The thought of sitting through another family gathering listening to Deimos joke about whether he qualified for food stamps gave Cupid indigestion.

He put down his half-eaten panini. Desperation overcame disaffection. Rolling up the sleeves of his oversized, longline shirt and brushing the mop of hair out of his eyes, Cupid nudged his long dormant celestial senses awake and set them adrift through the plaza. Somewhere, someone must be primed for love. He scanned the surface thoughts of dozens of people, searching for a glimmer of attraction, a hint of chemistry primed to react, but received only the dry paste of internet addiction for his efforts.

Wait . . . was that . . .? His breath caught in his throat. Somewhere in this plaza, the embers of passion smouldered, waiting for someone to blow them to conflagration. Perhaps today, his arrow might fly once more. Where was it?

There. A young man clad in dress slacks and a button-down shirt, the armour of the weekday warrior, pulled his bleary eyes from his phone to casually scan the plaza. Cupid inhaled and opened his mind. All that the man was poured in. His life, his identity—Cupid saw it all. Jackson, a social media coordinator at a local contract marketing firm, twenty-six, into hiking.

All right, where was his match? Cupid spread his godly perceptions over the other people in the plaza.

There. Olivia, twenty-four, accounts-receivable associate, hobbies included . . . hiking!

Jackson's eyes passed over the crowd and caught on Olivia for one heartbeat. Two heartbeats. Three. Cupid stood. Today, true love would burn once more.

He knocked his magical arrow and gripped the bow handle, wrist straight, fingers relaxed. Hooking the bowstring, he drew his hand and raised the bow. The bow curved as his arm pulled back to his jaw.

Exhaling, he calmed his mind and narrowed his vision until his prey dominated his sight. With a thrum, his arrow soared from the bow, darted across the plaza, and plunged deep into Jackson's heart. Passion and love hemorrhaged into the young man's soul.

Jackson sat upright, his slouching shoulders uncoiling. His eyes snapped into focus, seeing Olivia with the clarity of a brisk spring morning where birds sang and danced between trees. With a deep breath, Jackson steeled himself, then strode toward Olivia.

Olivia raised her eyes from her phone as he came to a standstill in front of her. "Uh." Jackson had never been so bold, but love makes lions of us. Nervousness painted his face pink. "Hey. Hi."

"What are you doing?" Olivia asked, eyes wide, her hand drifting to her purse.

"I don't normally do this, but, uh, could I give you my number? If you like—no pressure, but if you're interested, you can text me. We could go for a walk or something and, umm, chat?" Jackson scratched the back of his head, messing his hair. "Do you like hiking?"

Panicking, Olivia screamed and sprayed a stream of mace in his face. Jackson yelled in pain and shock and collapsed to the ground, arms over his eyes.

The plaza erupted in pandemonium. People clambered to their feet, recording everything. "Bro got smoked," a man said into his virtual reality glasses. Another woman held her phone at selfie length while Jackson squirmed in the background. "Heeeey, all. You won't believe what's happening during my lunch." The acrid stench of mace filled the plaza, burning sinuses as it spread.

Oh, crap, Cupid thought. *Crap, crap, crap.* He hurried away from the plaza. Jackson's cries echoed in his ears as Olivia sobbed into her camera. "...he came at me out of nowhere..."

Humans spooked so easily these days. AGI-mediated social media had stunted their social sensibilities to the point that they were, in fact, terrified of each other. People saw any interaction outside an app as deviant and openly antagonistic.

Apps. Was this the end of love? Had he become an anachronism? Deimos's laughter echoed. *No!* Cupid had more to give this world, but if he was to live his purpose, perhaps he should stop seeing apps as the enemy.

It was time to get a job.

"WELCOME TO CUPID 2.0. Congratulations on your new role as Senior Programmer," said Ava, the HR AGI's avatar, from Cupid's computer screen. Her skin was dark enough that she could pass for someone of African, Asian, or Middle Eastern background but light enough that she could also pass for European or North American. Faint laugh lines and wizened eyes spoke of her maturity, but dark hair and a fair complexion let you know she still possessed youthful vitality. Her smile balanced playful enthusiasm with matronly calm. When she spoke, her voice was confident yet lilting. "I know you'll enjoy working here. At Cupid 2.0, we work hard but you'll find we play hard, too. We think work should be fun. We consider each of our employees, from junior developers to the COO, part of one big family."

"Family, eh?" Cupid looked around his empty studio apartment. Breakfast dishes sat unwashed on the counter; his bed remained unmade. Silence so thick he might have been the only being left on

Earth hung heavy. "Does that mean I'll get a chance to meet my co-workers in person?" It had been years since Cupid had had mortal friends.

"Oh, no," Ava said, eyes widening. "Your job is one hundred percent remote. You'll communicate with your co-workers through intra-office messaging. It's conveniences such as this that make Cupid 2.0 the fourth-best employer in the dating app industry in the North by Northwest region according to WorkSwell.com. Are you ready for your orientation?" She smiled patiently.

Cupid reminded himself that Ava was not human but a computer-generated avatar of the machine intelligence running the HR department. She was not a she but an it. *It* smiled patiently.

He nodded and downed a chocolatey espresso. Ava dived into the orientation. Then came the introductions to his supervisor—sKeeet420, a woman who refused to turn her camera on when talking; her only digital representation was a static avatar of a monkey with a pompadour haircut and sunglasses. After this came his work assignments.

Cupid 2.0 was the country's most popular dating app. *Finding love, one date at a time*, so the tagline went. But rather than love, users found loneliness, or so Cupid believed. The app had turned young lovers from hopeful explorers of souls into meat for shoppers to inspect, select, and consume before tossing the gristle into the trash. Photoshopped profile pictures replaced the visceral reality of bodies while people condensed the universe of dreams held in their hearts into bios, two hundred fifty words or less.

After his whirlwind orientation and job assignments, Cupid sat alone, his computer connected to the vast matchmaking machine intelligence driving Cupid 2.0. He knocked his magical arrow and fired it into the computer. It soared through Wi-Fi signals and fiberoptic cables into the heart of Cupid 2.0's programming, giving some of his essence to the algorithms that brought hopeful young lovers together. Perhaps with a little of the real Cupid's playful zest for love, Cupid 2.0 could birth a renaissance of genuine connection and togetherness.

He sat back, satisfied with his work and hopeful for the future. A smile turned his lips into a bow, taut, ready to fire. *Cupid 2.0, meet Cupid 1.0.*

"I'M SORRY, but we have to let you go." Ava's simulacrum affected an expression that perfectly blended sympathy, regret, and resoluteness, a mother giving bad news to her child.

Cupid was flabbergasted. For the past year, he had been one of Cupid 2.0's model employees, hitting every timeline no matter how unreasonable and completing every task assigned to the highest standards. Deimos had still teased this past Saturnalia, but Cupid had a job. He was living his purpose—*had* been living his purpose. "You're firing me? But my work's been exemplary."

"And I think you'll find that your severance package adequately reflects your performance. We are happy to give you a good reference. At the end of the day, however, Cupid 2.0's strategic direction does not align with your skills. We pride ourselves on being a family, but families work best when everyone pulls in the same direction."

Cupid's chair creaked as he leaned back, the sound echoing in his empty apartment. Had there ever existed a family where everyone pulled in the same direction? "What exactly have I done wrong?"

"Let me be frank. Over the past year, repeat customers have declined by nearly four percent. After rigorous statistical analysis, we have traced the cause to the code you created."

"Repeat customers are down because the app is working," Cupid said. "You've seen the feedback surveys. More of our users are entering long-term relations with the partners they met through Cupid 2.0." He tabbed to a folder containing some of the qualitative feedback he had copied from these surveys:

. . . Turning point in my dating journey. Five stars . . .
. . . this app changed the game for me! Met my partner, and we've been living our best lives ever since . . .

... Started out thinking this app was just for casual vibes, but little did I know it would lead me to something way deeper ...

"I think you misunderstand the purpose of our business," Ava said.

"The purpose of Cupid 2.0 is to help our customers find love. That's our whole brand."

Ava's appearance subtly shifted from matronly to CEO-like. "The purpose of Cupid 2.0 is to maximize profits. The average duration of a match is forty-two days, plus or minus six hours, which we've determined is close to the optimal duration to maximize customer retention. As a result, seventy-one percent of our subscription revenues come from repeat customers, the highest in the industry. When our users enter a long-term relationship, they no longer need our services, and we lose that revenue stream plus the potential sales from up-sells. This has a real impact on our bottom line. We missed our sales forecasts by two points last quarter. Our investors expect us to take decisive action."

"You're telling me you create relationships you know won't last?"

"We create relationships we know will last forty-two days, plus or minus six hours. We have tried to improve the standard deviation from plus or minus six hours to plus or minus four. Your—if I may be direct, your *unauthorized*—programming has set back years of progress toward tightening our spread."

Love. Connection. The creation of a family. To find a partner who will join you as you wander life's road—what a blessing! The universe was vast beyond even Cupid's ability to conceptualize, and the depth of time was so unfathomably deep. *Given such chasms of space and time, that two hearts can find each other and fall in love as often as they do can only be a miracle,* he thought. *And through their sweaty couplings, life! From their passion and pleasure, young lovers forge new souls and birth them into the world. Through love, the line of humanity marches into the future. Has the universe managed a greater act of creation?* Love and all the wonders that flow from it: these were Cupid's gifts.

And nice gifts they were, sure, but of little utility in the face of hard-nosed business realities. *For all that love does, it contributes nothing to dividend payments or servicing debt. Sales were down two points. The times call for decisive action.*

Ava carried on with the business of firing Cupid, discussing the outplacement and counselling services they offered. There were forms to sign—verification that, yes, Ava had reminded him of the non-confidentiality and non-compete contracts he signed when hired, and no, he had no questions pertaining to the above-mentioned documents. As part of the severance package, the company had given him a six-month subscription to GigGrinder-Finder, the largest job-search website nationwide. His security clearance was revoked, his username and passwords wiped. *Persona non grata. Anathema.* A leper banished to the wilds.

Ava wished him good luck, and then, with a *bee-yoop*, his computer flickered off.

THE PLAYGROUND WAS SILENT. It was lunch on a glorious spring day, the scent of flowers from a nearby park wafting in the warm air. Hundreds of teenagers filled the yard, leaning against the school wall, lounging on the steps, or sitting on benches, all of them staring dull-eyed at phones, virtual reality glasses, tablets, screens, screens, screens, thumbing up, left, right, down, wow-face, angry-face, happy-face, hearts, emojis, quick comments, misspelled, impenetrable slang, *ur fyre gurl*, *faaaayk*, *ura squib*, and with each eyeball on each screen, with each moment of engagement, rivers of ad revenue flowed to corporate masters drowning shareholders in dividends.

Cupid sat on the ground, back resting on a wire fence enclosing the playground, his head hanging between his knees. What were celestial beings supposed to do once they became obsolete? Where did forgotten, useless gods go?

These were teenagers. Once, Cupid could have found dozens of targets fumbling through their first feelings of love. Now, an unfathomable machine intelligence danced its dopamine dance in their young, developing brains, crushing their self-esteem and warping their budding relationship with their sense of attraction.

A girl with dark hair scooted over to a nearby boy, her hands clasped, hiding something within. Cupid's head cocked, listening to the song of the girl's heart only he could hear. Emma. Fourteen, Grade 8, enjoyed biology, was weirdly fascinated with spiders, and hated her second-period English teacher, Mr. Hurley. "Wanna see something neat?" she asked the boy.

He stared, unsure what to say. Lucas. Fourteen. Math whiz, loved fixing things, and completely enthralled with bugs, worms, and all things creepy-crawly. Spiders. Bugs. Creepy-crawlies. A match! Or, at least, it would have been in another age.

Cupid twiddled an arrow between his fingers. Perhaps the seed of hope lay in this new generation. The role of youth was to rebel against whatever society their elders handed to them. Was a young mind strong enough to rebel against the machine-intelligence-driven social media seeking to enrapture them?

Emma nudged Lucas. "Dude, do you want to see something neat or not?"

Lucas gulped. "Sure."

Emma opened her hands to reveal a wolf spider about the size of the tip of her thumb, its back fuzzy. Lucas' eyes widened. "That is amazing. Where'd you find it?"

From across the playground, a teacher called out, "Emma!" He had his phone in front of him as he started recording. "It is not appropriate to disturb people. We talked about this last week. Do you want detention?"

Lucas rolled his eyes. "Ugh, it's Mr. Hurley. I can't stand that guy."

Emma smiled, looking at the boy with something approaching fondness.

"Is she bothering you?" Mr. Hurley asked Lucas.

Cupid closed his eyes. *Please rebel.* Could the human spirit stand up to the greatest intelligence it had encountered? Could the next generation turn away from the dopamine machines their parents had created? Or was organic socializing obsolete?

"Get glitched, Mr. Hurley," Emma yelled across the playground.

"Yeah," Lucas shouted. "Swipe left!"

Cupid smiled and knocked his arrow.

THE PANDA'S DREAM

Lawrence M. Schoen

Above Barsk

Ciochan stood in the space station's otherwise empty crew lounge, gazing out at the cloud-shrouded planet below: Barsk. The world was home to every Fant in existence, a race reviled for their rank odour, lack of fur, ginormous ears, and weirdly elongated and prehensile snouts. Centuries earlier, they had been rounded up from every mixed world where they'd built communities and exiled to a single rainy world that no one else wanted. The full irony of the situation was revealed when the disgusting Fant discovered resources on their new home that existed nowhere else, but the agreement that kept them isolated prevented anyone else from setting foot on the planet. And so, an orbital station was created to maintain their isolation and handle exports, keeping everyone content.

Ciochan was an Ailuros, known as a Panda by most other races of the galaxy's Alliance, burly and squat, his fur black and white, though most of it went hidden beneath the light blue jumpsuit that was his daily uniform. The majority of the workers on the station were also Ailuros, solid and steadfast in their jobs. Two years earlier, Ciochan had been the station's dockmaster. It was an excellent position and he excelled at it, but it all went sideways when two Fant showed up on the station without warning. Both were male. The adult, despite being as repulsive as everyone knew all Fant to be, grey and hairless and hideous, had authority over the station. The other was a pale child, Pizlo, who'd somehow smuggled himself aboard a shipping container down on the planet and used it to travel to the station itself. The pair had only been onboard a short while, and while the elder ran around with his slow-moving Sloth assistant, that same assistant had assigned Ciochan to keep watch over the boy on the basis that, as dockmaster, he had the rank to babysit such an important guest.

It was a loathsome assignment. For centuries, no one else had had to endure being in the same room with a Fant. Ciochan followed orders and, when it was over, was awarded a vacation back home to visit his wife and daughters. When he returned, inexplicably, he found he'd been promoted to stationmaster and was in charge of everything.

The dreams began soon after.

The Dream

FROM THE START, Ciochan knew he was dreaming. It was the only thing that explained the presence of the Fant child he had babysat years before. The boy sat on the floor of Ciochan's previous quarters, leaning against the door. He wore a pair of shorts that had seen better days. Otherwise, he was naked except for a bandolier of tiny pouches crisscrossing his chest. His pale skin bore innumerable marks, scars of past scrapes and scratches and no few mottled blotches of bruises in various stages of healing. All of that was much the same as it had been.

But now the tone felt different from the way it had when he'd actually babysat the Fant boy. During that original experience, he had felt apprehensive and uncomfortable. Here in the dream, his stomach roiled with an unexplainable nausea that went far beyond anything due to how disgusting he found the Fant to be. He wasn't having a casual chat or playing a child's game to pass the time. Ciochan knew—though he could not have said how he knew—that he was trapped in the cabin, the boy blocking access to the room's sole exit. Pizlo's eyes, which the Panda remembered as somewhat red, now gleamed with a fiery brightness as if just by gazing upon Ciochan, this creature could set him ablaze. Those eyes sent the message that somehow the Fant had ceased to be a boy child but ought to now be recognized as a monster. The creature randomly flapped its massive ears, not with a flick like another race might use to send an errant insect on its way, but as if this movement somehow fanned Ciochan's despair, wrapped up his terror into it all.

The Fant, still looking young and small, a fraction of Ciochan's own size and weight, smiled and spoke a string of nonsense words in a singsong voice, weaving its trunk like a conductor guiding an orchestra in some symphony of dread. "Do you remember how, last time, in the waking world, I told you about your family? It's how I convinced you I was a monster, how I confirmed what you'd always known, that all Fant are monsters."

If Ciochan had had any doubt that he was caught up in a dream, one he had no control of, it vanished in that instant. He was forced to listen to details and knowledge of his personal life, his wife, and his children, laid out like precious stones in a jeweller's case, each for sale at an exorbitant cost.

He huffed and whuffed with distress. "Why are you doing this, Pizlo?"

"It's a stupidly simple question," replied the Fant.

Ciochan recognized contempt in that tone, though he had no actual memory from his time babysitting to suggest such scorn as he heard in the dream.

"There are so many ways I could answer that," said Pizlo. "Some are true, some not. How would you know? Maybe, just maybe, I'm doing it simply because I can."

"So, your intention here isn't really to threaten either Su or Lin but to fill me with such dread as you're able?"

"Maybe."

"No. No, that makes more sense. After all, how could you possibly reach them?"

"You think they're beyond my reach?" The flames in the boy's eyes grew brighter. "You think I'm hampered by location? By physicality? I have greater knowledge and access than you do. Do you want to know where they are at this very moment, what they're doing, who they're with? Shall I tell you how I might intervene and alter their fates? Your family lives on Wade's lesser continent, the northern hemisphere, on the polar coast. It's early evening there, just past prime meal. Su is having a sleepover at her friend's house now. They'll be up all night playing the sort of games that girls their age get into. Your wife had some concern earlier in the day that your youngest, Lin, might be feeling sad because her sister went off on a special night, leaving her behind. To lighten the mood, she made a point to bring home a treat, a sort of candied bamboo pudding, from a new shop that opened since your last visit home. Curiously, that shop is not run by an Ailuros but rather by an Ov. Don't you think that's curious?"

"Is there some point to this?"

"The answer is right in front of you," assured the Fant. "It always has been. It's been staring you in the face since I came to your precious station. You've ignored it, but you're getting closer. Maybe by seeing me again, you'll finally put it all together."

"I don't understand."

"Of course, you don't. I doubt you understand how easily your eldest daughter's friend's mother could have an aneurysm while driving the kids off to play in the snowfields. That unforeseen event could disrupt her driving, cause her to strike another vehicle whose occupants' deaths would be instantaneous, though the three families of parents and children that her uncontrolled skimmer plows into wouldn't be as lucky. Your daughter and her friend, despite safety restraints, might be thrown from the vehicle to land badly on the snow-covered rocks lining that road, their mangled bodies bleeding out before help can arrive."

"That's not going to happen. You're fabricating nonsense."

"Or consider that, no matter how careful the Ov confectioner might be, there is a point in the process where overcooking one of the many ingredients alters a molecular chain, and what should have been a sweet component becomes a poisonous alkaline, its bitterness masked by the remaining sweet. But it's not just your wife and younger daughter that would be exposed to the tainted candy. The shop has become quite popular and the Ov made a double batch, anticipating a demand. Sheep can be conservative that way. Twenty, thirty, perhaps as many as fifty men, women, and children won't live to regret their fondness for sweets."

"No, no, shut up!"

Pizlo acted like he hadn't heard the Panda and continued his grisly recital. "Of course, when an explanation for all those deaths comes to light, the Ov will take his own life, but that's little comfort for his victims or for your surviving daughter, who will grow up as an orphan."

"None of that's going to happen," insisted Ciochan.

"Can you be sure?"

"No one can know the future."

"It's only the future if you're looking at it from the past."

"What is that supposed to mean?"

"You're so close."

"I don't understand." Ciochan's repetition was plaintive.

"You may not believe me, what with my being a monster and all, but I really am trying to help you."

"How could tormenting me with make-believe stories about the death of my wife and children help me?"

"I'm trying to move you."

"Move me?"

"Move your understanding of reality. As I've said, you're so close."

"I still don't understand." Even knowing he was caught up in a dream, Ciochan had never felt more frustrated. The powerful Ailuros found himself near tears.

"I know. It's because you're so damn pragmatic. It's why your kind make terrible scientists and artists. No imagination. Everything's so objective; no stories or interpretations."

"The world is as it is . . . isn't it?"

"How would you know?" asked Pizlo. The boy pushed off from the door and walked right up to Ciochan, extending his trunk, that horrible and curious appendage, close enough to caress his face if the Fant willed it.

"Don't touch me!" Ciochan wailed, fear making him sound younger than the Fant.

"Why not? Everything already is what it is. Could I change that?"

"No. Yes. I don't know. I just know . . . I'm not sure. I just know . . . I don't want a Fant touching me."

"And why is that?"

"Because . . . you said it yourself. You're a monster. You're all monsters. That's why you're doing these things. It's what monsters do."

"Yes, monsters act like monsters. Kind of circular in the reasoning, but I get it. Though, how do you know?"

"Everyone does."

"Who told them?"

"Everyone knows it. My earliest recollection of anyone mentioning the people of Barsk made it clear."

"And who told them? No one has visited Barsk in centuries. How did they come to this knowledge?"

"They . . . from the generations before that, from culture, from society. It's something everyone just knows."

"Of course, and because everyone knows it, it couldn't possibly be an error. All hail the great Ailuros black and white worldview."

"Are you mocking my entire race now?"

"No," said Pizlo, and with a movement too swift for Ciochan to push him away, the boy climbed onto his lap, leaning that big-eared head against the Panda's chest. "But what if you were wrong?"

The monster Pizlo lingered long after it had finished speaking as if waiting for a reply, but Ciochan had none. The dream let go of him, the specifics fading from his memory, all except those last words.

The Therapist

DAYS LATER, a report came into the station. Several cargo containers of critical goods had gone missing, including a tenth of the annual allotment of koph, the drug that granted some people the ability to speak to the dead, and the most precious single export from Barsk.

Ciochan reviewed the report and investigated the specifics. He found the shipping error—the containers had never left the station—and immediately rescheduled them. As stationmaster, the glitch was his responsibility, and he shouldered his accountability without excuse. Glitches happened from time to time, though never since Ciochan had taken charge of the station and never one as serious as this. Despite their value, the missing shipments easily fell within the established margin of error, and as the correction was identified and attended to swiftly, that should have been the end of it, except a similar error happened again ten days later and yet again soon after that.

Meanwhile, Ciochan continued to dream of Pizlo. In some dreams, the Fant was the monster child; in others, just a sweet alien boy who, through no fault of his own, was disgusting to look upon. Although he didn't understand the connection, each mistake on the station took place shortly after Pizlo visited his dreams.

Someone higher up in the chain of command noticed the correlation as well. Those problems might carry consequences, even profound consequences. A deeper review of Ciochan's records was performed and, on the grounds of not wanting to risk losing an experienced stationmaster, one already familiar with such a prized resource—the worlds of the Alliance were always hungry for the goods coming up from Barsk—the expense to maybe do his mental health some good was authorized. The authorization was approved by the same individuals who had promoted him shortly after the child Fant had been on station in real life. Ciochan was informed. He didn't like it, but no one asked him for his opinion. They simply told him to expect a visit from a specialist charged with resolving the matter, a therapist.

———

THE THERAPIST, a Capybara named Hydrochoerus-Captain Bronjo, arrived like any other visitor to the station might, although visitors of any sort were rare indeed and a mental health professional unique. She was not yet actually on board the station, but members of Ciochan's team had the responsibility for monitoring all traffic in and out of the portal that granted access to the Ekkja star system, home of the planet Barsk, and the Capybara's minute vessel—nicknamed *Tiny* both because it was little more than a shuttle and because word had spread that it brought someone who would "shrink" the stationmaster's head—soon became well-known to them.

Per Ciochan's orders, they alerted him immediately when the ship came through. Beyond his Patrol training, part of being first a cargomaster and now the stationmaster had taught the Panda a profound respect for schedules and for time. Let the schedule get away from you, and the handling of the massive containers that came up the stalk—industrial crates that required sorting and warehousing before shipping to other worlds—could quickly unravel. What made it all work, beyond the spreadsheets and an intimate knowledge of the layout and design of each of the station's warehouses, was respect for time: respecting that of others, and perhaps most importantly, their respecting his. It would be hours before *Tiny* docked at the station, but knowing it was in local space allowed Ciochan to start a clock running in the back of his head so that their session could begin promptly.

In the early days, after all the upheaval on the station, the chief of staff to the senator who had made him into a babysitter— a Sloth named Flarz or Durz or some other equally ungainly name because all Sloth names dragged on when spoken—had begun the series of memoranda that led to his promotions. Ciochan had excelled at the work of cargomaster, discovering a talent for management that he'd never imagined lived within him. He had boosted the station's efficiency beyond any expectation and taken it higher still as stationmaster. Now, his dreams threatened that. He hoped that this quiet and pensive therapist would help to resolve whatever underlying problem was responsible. One of the curious and arguably ironic things about Ailuros was that they went through life seeing everything in terms of black and white. There was no grey, no justifications, no rationalizations. It was a rare Panda indeed whose subjective experience of an event differed from objective reality.

When the Capybara therapist arrived, Ciochan was reminded that stereotypes existed for a reason. Just as Ailuros were known for their unshakable views, the Hydrochoerus were known to be among the most peaceful—often blissful—beings in the galaxy, and surely that was a good thing in a therapist sent to rid him of his dreams. She seemed to be wrapped in a cloud of serenity that, with her every movement, swirled around her, much like the silken robe of browns and greens she wore.

Ciochan had never considered himself particularly sophisticated, but he had grown up on Wade, a mixed world. That early experience had figured prominently in his initial employment at the station. While most of the staff were Ailuros like himself, the crew of the ships that visited the station to take Barsk's goods away reflected nearly the full range of races in the galaxy. One had to be able to get along with people, and his formative years and his education on Wade had regularly introduced him to members of the twenty-two different races living there. Granted, there were eighty-seven races in the Alliance, but twenty-two was nonetheless an impressive number.

Ciochan startled Hydrochoerus-Captain Bronjo that first time, awaiting her little more than an arm's length outside the airlock door. He escorted her to a spare cabin, redecorated within the limitations of the station, to what Ciochan imagined a therapeutic setting might resemble based on the long list of flims he'd reviewed to prepare himself. Mostly, this had involved removing and swapping out bits of furniture. Despite those efforts, he had no idea what to expect. Still, he'd gone to the trouble with no regrets, though he hoped that the therapist was there for just a single quick visit and by the next day's shift, everything in the room would be packed up and returned to storage.

They spent most of that session seated across from one another, each cradled by surprisingly cushiony armchairs that made the Panda wonder where these chairs had been hiding in the station. His made him feel like he wasn't so much sitting but ensconced in a domain unto itself.

They began with a few pleasantries, Ciochan repeatedly apologizing for the limitations of the room's decor and offering the honest explanation that the Patrol ran the station, making it basically a military post with little tradition of comfort.

Therapist Bronjo assured him the room was fine and that if, upon reflection, she determined there was anything she needed, she could bring it in herself the next time she visited.

That opened the initial door. "Next time?" Ciochan said.

Bronjo regarded the Panda with a placid expression and a long pause, followed by, "Hmm."

Ciochan coughed. "I assumed . . . I mean, of course, if you feel the need for another session or two."

"I suspect that's likely," confirmed the Capybara.

"Um . . . how many? And, um . . . how frequent will your visits be?"

The Capybara's eyes were tiny; one might be tempted to consider them beady except for the depth of experience that shone in them. "I don't know. We'll see what we see. I apologize if that ignorance interferes with the structure of your schedule."

"Oh, surely not just mine," replied Ciochan. "You must be very busy, and coming here just to see me seems extravagant. I don't want to waste your time visiting more often than is absolutely necessary."

"Necessity is at best a slippery construct and, at worst, utterly subjective."

"I'm sorry?"

The therapist waved an arm, encompassing the room with the gesture. "You are master of this station, and I have never been here before. Despite this, we can agree on the characteristics of most anything in this room. If we're in doubt, we can stand up, walk over to whatever object or item we're in disagreement about, examine it, and come to a conclusion. All very objective."

Ciochan nodded. "Well, yes. That's how the world works."

"That is often the case. And yet, not everything in the world is objective. Necessity is one of those things. Your necessity is created by many factors, including some I have no knowledge of or could ever share. The same is true of my own necessity and the necessity of the administrators who opted to assign me to your situation."

"How can you work like that? Not knowing, not being able to plan?"

Bronjo twitched a single finger. There was something about the gesture that led Ciochan to immediately stop speaking.

"As to that," said the Capybara, "I have a plan and a schedule of sorts."

"You do?"

"Indeed. I am gathering data for a new book I'm writing. This requires a great deal of travel, so while I'll be able to meet with you often, I cannot provide a regular schedule. Also, a separate part of my work involves evaluating potential candidates for a wide range of positions within the Alliance, so again, I travel extensively."

"So . . . you're more than just a therapist?"

The Capybara smiled. "As you are more than just a stationmaster. But please, set aside any concerns about my scheduling. You are currently my only therapeutic client, and your own scheduling is more than adequate to ensure that visiting you here does not take me away from any other work I am engaged in."

"Umm . . . is that a good thing?"

"I believe we can endeavour to make it so. But, ah, while I'm thinking of it, one more thing . . ."

"Yes?"

"No need to meet me at the airlock when I visit. I'll come straight here. It would save us time if you were already present. And I would consider it a kindness if perhaps you might have some tea waiting."

Black and White

"Hi, Ciochan. Do you remember me? We spent an afternoon together once. Not like we've been doing in your dreams, but really and truly."

The Panda shook his head, not in answer but in an effort to clear it. When that failed, his logical mind took in all the pieces and reached a conclusion. He was having another dream. The monster child had returned to torment him yet again with ever more horrific scenarios.

"I do. You're Pizlo. I remember having to mind you for a while and how you admitted that you were a monster."

"Well, yeah, but I only told you that because you were certain that *all* Fant are monsters. That didn't fit with me sitting there. Cuz I'm so cute."

"You threatened my family."

Pizlo looked embarrassed. "But . . . it made you feel better in the long run, right?"

"Was that your intention? Wait, never mind. It doesn't matter. That was years ago and this right now is just another of your sick dreams."

"Of course it is," agreed the monster. "Do you know why you're having it?"

Ciochan considered the question. Since that afternoon babysitting the boy, he had become obsessed with learning everything and anything there was to know about both Fant and Barsk. "I suppose if I did, then I wouldn't need to be having this dream."

Pizlo clapped his hands and trumpeted briefly. Ciochan flinched, as much at the sound as the disturbing movement of the boy's trunk.

"You're so clever. It gives me hope."

"Hope for what?"

"The stories we're going to tell each other."

"I don't understand."

"Of course not," said Pizlo. "We haven't told them yet."

AFTER THAT, Pizlo stopped being a monster and went back to being the boy Ciochan had met all that time ago. The dreams stopped being malevolent and instead transformed into something more innocent. Usually. It helped that Ciochan got past his initial disgust of the Fant. The dreamed afternoons in his cabin were spent chatting with a precocious child member of the race sequestered on the planet beneath the station. Pizlo was well-spoken, bright, and curious, and the Panda began to wonder if maybe he had something to teach the child, something deep, maybe even profound. He still did not know why he was having the dreams, but he could try, at least within the limits and parameters of the room that they found themselves in. Ciochan had introduced the boy to ice cream and delighted in the wide-eyed joy that shone from the young Fant's face like a beacon. He altered the configuration of the furniture to create mazes they scrambled through. He experimented with the room's few objects to see which could make musical—or at least music-like—sounds, and they composed tunes.

Recently, Ciochan had joined Pizlo on the floor while they played a card game. The cards themselves were a deck he actually owned, imported from downworld, a deck of agricultural images for teaching young children about some of Barsk's many exports.

"Do you have any rangül?" asked Ciochan, showing a card in his own hand depicting the requested spice.

"Nope. Go harvest. Umm . . . do you have any thistles?" Pizlo displayed the card.

"I do not. Go harvest."

Pizlo scowled with mock disappointment, drew a card, and trumpeted when it turned out to be the needed thistle. The match meant he was allowed a bonus turn.

"Do you have any rangül?"

"I just asked *you* for that."

The boy nodded. "You did."

"You can't ask for a card that you don't already have a match for in your hand."

"I'm not." Pizlo revealed a rangül card.

"Then why didn't you give it to me when I asked for it?"

"Cuz I'm cheating."

It was Ciochan's turn to scowl. He threw his cards down. "What's the point of playing a game if you're not going to follow the rules?"

Pizlo laughed at him, a glint of his past malevolence showing in his eyes. "What's the point of having rules if you always follow them?"

Doubt

As if the return of the dream had summoned her, word came to him later that day that *Tiny* had arrived in-system. Ciochan prepared himself for the Capybara, even as he resolved not to share anything from his latest dream. He wanted time to ponder it.

Keeping any mention of the dream to himself turned out not to matter. As always, Bronjo managed to find something to talk to him about. She took a coin purse from the folds of her robe and shook out several silvery disks onto the table. Most had portraits stamped on them.

"Let's revisit reality for a moment," said the therapist. "What are these?"

"Coins."

"You're sure? Is that the absolute truth?"

Ciochan sighed. Was she trying to make him doubt the obvious? He slipped into the jargon she favoured. "Is there such a thing?"

"I don't believe so, but you tell me."

He shook his head. "I'm saying that's the tale I'm telling myself about them."

"Fair enough. And you're certain? Confident in your answer?"

"I am."

Bronjo picked up a coin and handed it to him. "Eat this."

"Excuse me?"

"Put it in your mouth. But don't bite, just suck on it."

The Panda shook his head in confusion, staring down at the coin she'd placed in his hand.

"Go on. It's a coin. You said so yourself. What's the worst that could happen?"

He allowed the coin to pass his lips. Surprise took control of his expression. The coin . . . had a taste, not metallic, but a minty kind of chocolate.

"It's . . . not a coin at all."

"No, it's not. But you were so certain."

"Well, yes, but it looked like a coin . . ."

"And so you told yourself that tale. Confidence was high. Accuracy, on the other hand, was extremely low."

"Extremely," acknowledged Ciochan, rolling the idea around in his head as he rolled the not-really-a-coin around in his mouth.

"Something to think about when you're sure."

"But I'm always sure."

"Then maybe that's my point."

The conversation continued for a while, mostly as a review of previous sessions, though at one point, Ciochan insisted on sampling each of the other coins and found them to be just coins. That session ended, and the therapist offered him assurance that he was making progress, a promise to return, and an admonition for him to stay focused on his duties.

The Capybara didn't follow him out. She said she wanted to review her notes before departing and could find her way back to her shuttle on her own. She left him at the door and presumably watched him walk down the corridor before returning to do whatever therapists did when alone. She had explained back on their first meeting that her method involved recording each and every session, allowing herself the luxury of drilling down into the conversation for significant bits, either spoken or implied, whether objective or symbolic or maybe not recognized as important in the moment. Ciochan had his doubts about this. More likely, she merely took a nap before alerting her pilot of her intention to depart.

Instead of returning to the day's tasks, he mulled over his last dream. Pizlo's remarks had sparked an epiphany—both insightful and terrifying—the significance of which hadn't yet come into complete focus but which would not leave him. There was no room in his head for anything else. The rest of the day fell away, and he wandered the station aimlessly, unaware of his surroundings. It was as if he lumbered through a blizzard, snow blind, as if he were caught in a ferocious storm whose fury drowned out all sound. At the same time, he would have sworn that the only smell in the galaxy was that of fresh bamboo. The intensity of these perceptions faded by the end of the day. How could they not? A body simply couldn't sustain that level of intensity. Besides which, he recognized it for what it was: his own mind's efforts to distract him from Pizlo's last words to him.

Ciochan, never particularly introspective, nonetheless rolled the thing around in his head for so long that it lost some of its size and gravitas, reducing to something he could maybe, just maybe, comprehend. It might very well be an overwhelming truth, but perhaps that had distracted him from a more important piece, considering the consequences of such a truth. What did it mean if he was wrong? Why have rules if everyone always followed them, and why follow them if some people didn't? Surely, that's what the boy in his dream wanted him to consider. It never occurred to Ciochan to disregard the rules put in place by those in charge.

It felt like Bronjo had been visiting forever. After the first few sessions, Ciochan realized he had been working with the assumption there was some specific, finite, and small number of visits that would be required to alleviate his problem. After twenty sessions, the Panda reluctantly concluded that perhaps he needed a fuller understanding of how things worked in therapy but didn't quite possess the language to ask the question or even know with any real certainty what that question was.

He had long since fallen into a routine. Ciochan received word that *Tiny* had passed through the Ekkja portal and was again en route to the station. Whoever provided that news would forward him the details of the therapist's actual anticipated arrival time. Armed with these particulars, Ciochan would rearrange his schedule to accommodate the session, arriving at the office that lay fallow save for Bronjo's sessions with him.

The Capybara had indeed redecorated. Coarse, hand-spun fabrics now covered the walls, elaborate draping in dark red, brown, and the occasional splash of green. The original pair of chairs he'd supplied had been removed, replaced with lower and even lusher seats that cradled one's body in a near-weightless state of comfort even as an assortment of pillows in rich jewel tones lent an odd sense of grounding. An oval table stood between them, a ceramic pot of tea positioned at one focus and a pair of cups at the other. Ciochan had brought the tea set to their second session, simple, unadorned, Patrol-grade, and serviceable. The Capybara had replaced both pot and cups with objects that were still simple but also more graceful.

A small bookshelf now occupied a wall behind Ciochan's chair, the source of a faint burbling sound, the water soothing without being intrusive. Initially, he assumed it was a recording, but upon leaving that day, he discovered that Bronjo had placed a self-contained fountain about the size of a dinner plate, its hidden power source recycling the same litre of water, setting a relaxed ambience to the room. Other objects came and went following some plan. At least, Ciochan assumed there was a plan, but could not discern the pattern of it. Some things lingered for eight or more sessions. Others came and went in one. Usually, they simply existed in the background of the room, but on occasion, his therapist would begin by asking him to engage with something she'd brought in, to place his hands on the contours of a small statue, gaze at the landscape of an actual painting from different angles and perspectives, or raise a seashell from some unknown ocean to his ear. Today, Bronjo had him focus on the olfactory. Several sprigs of incense burned in a simple saucer just to the side of the teapot, gifting the room with a blended aroma of lemongrass, jasmine, and vanilla.

"Does the incense make you think of anything?"

"Here in this room with you, it makes me think of Fant."

"How so?"

"Most people believe that all Fant are malodorous. It's part of what makes them so disgusting. But it's not completely accurate."

"No?"

"The elderly can be pretty rank, but when they're young, especially children, they can be sweet-smelling, something like honey."

"That's not part of your report from when the boy was on station."

"It wasn't," agreed Ciochan. "When he was sent to me, he'd come from the station infirmary. He'd broken his arm and had damaged his hands so badly there was concern he'd lose the use of them."

"What does that have to do with his odour?"

"I believe someone had made the decision to not simply tend to his injuries but basically hosed him down, either to lessen the possibility of infection or in service to the belief that, as a Fant, he stank. Or maybe both."

"So when you met him . . ."

Ciochan nodded. "He smelled of antiseptic and disinfectant."

The therapist nodded in turn, made a note on her padd, and went off in a new direction. "I assume you have experienced your dream again, at least once, since my last visit."

"Twice. Both were pretty good, more or less pleasant, even. Do you think that's significant?" he asked her.

"I think it's significant that you continue to talk about the range of your dreams as bad or good. Good and bad are judgments."

"I'm not allowed to have a judgment about my own experiences?"

The Capybara shrugged. "You can have whatever you want. I'm just saying that once you make a judgment, you've created a filter. That filter frames the experience, adds or detracts from how you see the thing ever after."

"Well, how else would I actually see it?"

"As it is, a dream. Neither good nor bad, happy nor sad. An event taking place inside your mind. A message."

"A message?"

"As we've discussed."

The Panda sat with that for a moment before speaking again. "I've been thinking about that message, what the dream means, what the child meant, why he said what he said."

"This is new," said the Capybara.

"Well, it's not so much that. It's something I've been mulling around for quite some time."

"And you're ready to speak of it?"

"I think I am, but . . . How much do you know about Ailuros?"

The therapist leaned forward in her chair, no small matter given its depth and cushioning. She grasped the teapot and looked at Ciochan as if to ask if he wanted his cup refreshed. At his nod, she topped off his cup before refilling her own. She picked up the cup with both hands, settling back into the chair.

"More than most, though I'm sure there are holes in my knowledge. Did you have something specific in mind?"

"Our worldview."

"Go on."

"One of the reasons so many Ailuros seek service in the Patrol is that, as a people, we are solid and steadfast. We're not flighty like the Lutr, easily distracted like an Ov, or slow to reach decisions like the Brady. We look at a situation, take in all the parameters, assess it, make a decision, and act on that decision."

"It has been said," offered the therapist, "the irony of the Ailuros is that they see the world in black and white. No greys. No subtle deviations."

"Nothing but contrast. You understand me exactly."

"And you're wondering about other ways to see the world?"

The Panda shook his head. "No, I'm wondering how other perspectives are even possible. The world is . . . the world. It's not a matter of opinion."

"You mean the world is objective."

"Yes!"

"But people are not."

"Not what?" he asked.

"Objective."

Ciochan stared at her. "Meaning what, exactly?"

"Consider some event; it doesn't matter what. There's the thing. It happened. Completely objective. It could be something as innocuous as misplacing a sock."

"Okay . . ."

"That's what happened. But then . . . there's the tale we tell ourselves about what happened. The former is objective reality, the latter is the reality we live in, day to day, and yours may not align with anyone else's."

"I don't follow," said Ciochan.

"Did you misplace the sock? Accidentally dispose of it? Did a member of your staff take it as an ill-conceived prank or to sow a minor annoyance? Could it have spontaneously combusted?"

"Those are mostly silly and unlikely events."

"I don't disagree, but whichever of them you land on, or another that I didn't list, the point is that that becomes your reality. But it's not reality. It's just the tale you've told yourself about reality."

"Which is that I'm missing a sock."

"Exactly." The therapist smiled at him.

Ciochan shivered as the idea trickled deeper. "That seems very . . . imprecise."

"You wouldn't be an Ailuros if you didn't think so," said Bronjo. "Now, keep that distinction in mind, and please go back to your thoughts about perspectives and how this relates to your dream."

"It relates to the world below us."

"Barsk."

"Yes, Barsk."

"And the Fant who live there," added Bronjo.

"Until the incident that brought two of them to the station, I had never met a Fant of either of their races."

"Ah, that's interesting."

"What is?"

"You're aware that the Fant aren't a single race. Most of the other members of the Alliance can't be bothered with that insight."

"Is it? An insight, I mean?"

The Capybara spread her hands, wiggling her fingers as she did so, making the slow gesture somehow quicker, if no less inscrutable. "That depends on what you do with the knowledge, but you were saying?"

"All my life, I've known things about the Fant, things just inculcated in me as part of my culture. These . . . changed, as experience changes all things, through interactions with other races on my home world and then more intensely with relationships I developed when I joined the Patrol."

"And what is your general assessment? "

"That's just it. I'm thinking my dreams are telling me that we need to change."

"We who? Not just you?"

"That's just it. We all need to change."

Bronjo hadn't moved, but somehow, her gaze became even more focused. "Why?"

"Well, it's like you said. There's the thing and the story we tell ourselves about the thing. Like every Ailuros, I find the Fant disgusting. Not just the ideas of their hairlessness or the disturbing motion of their trunks or their oversized ears or their smell—it's the whole package. It's as if the entire race exists as a warning or an object lesson. These are not proper people. It took us a very long time to realize that, but we finally did. And then we acted, less than a millennium ago, and took them from worlds where proper people lived. We put them away so we wouldn't have to encounter or experience them."

Bronjo nodded. "Out of sight, out of mind?"

"I suppose, but it's something I never questioned, something—as far as I know—that was ingrained in me: a loathing for people who've never done me or mine any harm, who haven't come up in the life experiences of anyone I know. Yet when it is invoked, I experience a deeply visceral response, one which you would call a value judgment, and it's a bad one."

"And you've been thinking about that?"

"I have."

"What have you concluded?" asked the therapist.

"No conclusions yet, but some questions."

"Such as?"

"What if we're wrong?"

Childhood vs. Reality

TIME PASSED, and the Panda dreamed. In the most recent dream, Ciochan had again played cards with Pizlo and, upon awakening, was left musing about similar games he had played with his daughters. During his next session with the Capybara, he shared the details. If she had a reaction, she kept it to herself and then abruptly seemed to change the subject.

"I don't know if you've ever allowed yourself to wonder about my background, but in my travels, I have visited Doyle, a planet which possesses a sizable Ailuros population. I found the communities there to be efficient and clean and well-organized."

Ciochan expression showed no surprise. "It's how an Ailuros city should be."

"And yet, whereas the adults were organized and efficient in going about their tasks and activities, the children I encountered in parks and play areas were completely different. In fact, they were the most boisterous, rambunctious, and gleefully happy youth I've ever seen anywhere on any world. They were constantly tumbling over one another and laughing all the while, the very vision of joy. Were you like that as a child?"

"I suppose I was, yes."

"I see." Bronjo made a note on her padd. "When did that change, and why?"

Ciochan shrugged. "There are things you do as a child, and then the world comes into focus, and you take on the responsibilities of an adult."

"That's a very *concrete* thing to say. But then, Ailuros excel at the concrete. It's the *abstract* that you resist."

"The concrete is real. You can touch it, hold it, smell it, feel it. Life is concrete."

"We both know there's more to it than that, but I appreciate it's easier for you to focus on things of physical substance. Your life on this station is built upon that."

"Isn't it better to limit myself to acknowledging those things that are real in my life than what isn't?"

"Like your dreams are real?"

Ciochan said nothing. He worked his jaw like he wanted to articulate some thought, then discarded it and prepared to offer a different one.

Bronjo swept her question aside with a slow lifting of one arm. "Do you remember our discussion of objective versus subjective realities? The objective is the thing that happens, and the subjective is the tale we tell ourselves about it." She locked her tight black eyes on his.

"I remember." Ciochan returned her gaze. "So? There's the thing and the story of the thing. What does it have to do with abstract and concrete?"

"One might argue it's at the very core of our discussions."

Ciochan knew himself to be intelligent—excepting his therapist, probably the smartest person on the station, else why had they promoted him so high and so fast?—and yet in this room, whether intentionally or not, Bronjo regularly made him feel like he was a school child about to be held back.

Perhaps sensing the Panda's distress, she brushed her remark away with another gesture. "Let me try again. You recall our earlier conversation about the galaxy being composed of things, clear and objective, and what we call 'reality' being the tale we tell ourselves—and one another—about those things."

"Making the objective subjective," said Ciochan.

"Exactly. Now, what if you look at a thing that's abstract and you choose to reframe your perspective?"

"I don't understand."

"Instead of the tale you'd been telling yourself, what if you give it a twist and think of it as concrete?"

"Wait, what? You . . . you can't do that. It's not possible!"

"Why not?"

"Because that's like changing the fundamental nature of reality."

Bronjo sat there a while, saying nothing until Ciochan had regained his composure. Then she smiled. "It is, isn't it?"

A New Tale

IN THE NEXT DREAM, Pizlo was an even more delightful child than before. Nonetheless, Ciochan tried to engage with him as if he was much more mature than his experience suggested. "Between you and these dreams and the things the Capybara says to me, I'm feeling like my world has exploded."

Pizlo's cheeks puffed out as he danced around the room, proclaiming, "Boom, boom, boom!"

"I'm serious. Everything looks and feels different, almost as if I'm somehow involved in recreating the galaxy around me."

Pizlo offered nothing useful for the rest of the dream. He just danced around the room, making exploding noises with his mouth and trumpeting his trunk and stomping his feet.

At his next therapy session a few days later, the Panda shared the specifics of Pizlo's behaviour with Bronjo.

When he had finished, she set her padd aside. "Welcome to the power of choice," she told him.

"I'm not sure I understand. What does that mean?"

"You get to decide what things are."

"What things are what, exactly? I still don't understand."

"Not yet, but it will become clear to you in time. Unless I miss my guess—and I never guess—your dreams of the Fant boy will be ending soon, if they haven't already."

Ciochan huffed and whuffed, searching for words. "They will?"

"I suspect that's why the boy was dancing. He was celebrating. Those dreams belong to someone else now. In fact . . ." she paused and looked around the room. "I think you'll be moving on soon."

"What are you talking about?"

"Do you remember our first session? You asked about my schedule, and I explained that in addition to being a therapist, I was also researching a book and that I occasionally evaluate potential candidates for positions within the Alliance."

"I remember. What does that have to do with you saying I'll be moving on?"

"Your position here," she said, seeming to change the subject. "It's very important, isn't it?"

"Well, yes. This station is the source for all the goods and materials from Barsk for the rest of the galaxy."

Bronjo looked enthusiastic, raising her voice and both hands in an expansive gesture that was like a cheer. "That was my assessment as well. You've done remarkably well here."

"Um . . . thank you. I've enjoyed the work."

"From what I've observed of your abilities, I can well believe it. But . . . it needs to belong to someone else now. You've outgrown it."

"That makes no sense. You were supposed to help me fix whatever was causing the glitches with the station's shipments."

"And I have. Surely you realize by now that you were the source of those problems? You were unconsciously sabotaging yourself, a sort of cry for help."

"But . . . if in the process of fixing the problem that brought you here and, as you say, I've outgrown being the stationmaster, what am I supposed to do?"

"Well, that's your choice. But I'll be making a recommendation for something new and challenging. In fact, something that's never happened before."

"I don't understand."

"How would you feel about being an ambassador?"

"What do you mean by ambassador? I don't know anything about being an ambassador."

"No one does until they find themselves in the job. Of course, there are other qualifications, but you meet enough of them. For instance, you know a lot about trade."

"I don't know anything about trade."

"Oh, please. This station? You're more familiar with the exported materials from Barsk than anyone else in the Alliance."

"What's your point?"

"That strikes me like a good place to start for an ambassador."

"To Barsk?"

"Mmmhmm."

"If I even wanted it, that couldn't happen. Only Fant are allowed on Barsk, and no Fant leave Barsk. Makes it kind of hard to be an ambassador, don't you think?"

"That's the crazy piece of it, right? But then, they would have said the same thing about a Fant in the Alliance Senate, and we have one. In fact, the more people who heard that tale, the more who came to believe it."

"But it's crazy. You just said so yourself."

Bronjo ignored him. "I'm going to reach out to some colleagues and some friends and tell them a tale. You have more experience of the Fant, both real and in your dreams, than almost any other person."

"But—"

"Ciochan, the galaxy is changing. *Your* galaxy is changing. How it changes is a choice, and someone needs to make it. Consider where you are now. You have the structured thinking of analogies that let you break out of the assumptions of your race. You've begun to crack that perfect and efficient perspective wide open, to see everything not as unalterable facts but as possibilities, choosing whether things are coins or chocolates. I can't think of a better mindset for someone to make a difference for people on both sides who need it."

"It's impossible."

"I'd agree if that was the absolute truth."

"Hold on. You said there's no such thing as absolute truth."

Bronjo smiled, a slow, tight-lipped grin. It consumed her entire face. "I did, didn't I? But you know, there's the thing—"

Ciochan finished the sentence. "And the tale we tell ourselves about the thing."

"Exactly."

"So, if I look at the situation and say it's ripe for change and reinterpretation—"

Bronjo interrupted him. "Listen to what you just said. Did you ever imagine an Ailuros could think such a thing, let alone say it out loud?"

"—if I convinced enough other people that that's the story until they see the reality—"

"Then I think you may be well on your way to becoming Barsk's first ambassador."

RED-EYE AND THUNDERBIRD

Alan Smale

It was just after midnight when Sukana left the earth of the bright metal age for the last time. She should have welcomed her flight-taking, lover of the open skies that she was, but her last moments there were a nightmare that threatened to shut down her mind and make a child of her.

Roaming the city had not prepared her for this. The giant buildings that rose up like canyon walls, the stop-go stuttering progression of the bison-like cars and trucks, and the meandering herd of the sidewalk-people were nothing compared with the swarm of bad-tempered humanity at the airport. If not for her training and single-minded obstinacy, Sukana might have dropped onto the shiny floor and curled into a ball.

She hadn't the language skills to negotiate such an alien terrain alone, of course. Her word-shaman and local guide had steered her through the mechanics of *security* and *check-in* with haughty panache and then abandoned her. Clutching her *boardingcard,* she had walked blindly through the tunnel; once on the plane, she waved the flimsy paper until a uniformed servant guided her to seat 27C and pushed her bag with its precious medicines into the space at her feet.

This was the last flight of the evening and crowded. If Sukana had understood her word-shaman correctly, cancellations of earlier flights had caused a merger of several different groups of people onto this one airplane. Which was why the Elders had chosen it for her.

She closed her eyes when the vibrations began and did not open them until the long wallow of the craft indicated they were airborne. As she had never been aloft without feeling the wind in her face, Sukana barely recognized *takeoff* for what it was.

By the time they levelled off at thirty thousand feet—a distance almost impossible for her to comprehend, measured vertically—many of the passengers were sleeping, mouths ajar.

How changeable these people were! In the *terminal* they had been a mass of squawking chickens, anxious to board, fearful of being left behind, quick to anger. Yet their wrath contained no real fire, and they had settled for the night aboard this strange vessel as if they were at home in a well-guarded kiva.

Sukana was tethered to a chair as luxurious as a throne yet crammed against its neighbours in a hull like the bore of a large blowpipe. She had assumed the vehicles of the sky realm would be as spacious as the buildings. It was not so. How impossibly chaotic would it be if the passengers all stood and barged into the aisle at once?

Her turbulent mental state was a disgrace. It was time to discipline her thoughts. She had work to do.

She had to turn her disdain for these people into empathy and their vapid inertia into cooperation. She had to harness their mental energy and use it to kidnap them away from everything they knew. And she had little over an hour in which to do it.

Her task would not be easy. Right now, she felt an icy cold toward them. This was, after all, the race who had overwritten her People's place in history, the descendants of butchers and genocides, living fat on the spoils of a land they had stolen. Their very complacency sickened her.

And she feared that iciness in herself, knowing that in time, it would render her soulless and empty.

The seat-back in front lurched toward her, locking into a new position a hands-breadth from her eyes. Sukana stifled a scream and raised her fists to strike it should it jump any closer. It did not. The boy seated next to her glanced at her curiously. She ventured a nervous smile, and his lips twitched in response.

Noise, dirt, skyscrapers, crowds, endless surprises; Sukana felt not even the faintest urge to stay in this age. It was time to go home.

SHE WAS JUST ABOUT to begin when the uniformed air-servants burst into action with a small cart, dispensing drinks.

Her local guides had not warned her about this. She hoped it would not take long; eventually, the timing of her actions would become critical. But at least she could utilize the delay to observe and understand the people she would soon co-opt to her cause.

Many of the drinks appeared to be merely fruit. Some were hot and smelled bad. Others were cold but bubbled as if boiling. And as some small bottles were opened, Sukana smelled the pungency of wine. So much the better.

The three female air-servants wore white shirts and mid-thigh blue skirts over skintight leggings. The woman now approaching Sukana had unnaturally short white-blonde hair and almost no eyebrows. Her young, firm body swayed under an older face, and she wore chunky jewellery at her wrists. A badge on her blouse bore letters in an angular script; Sukana spelled out *Tammy-Rae*, which she couldn't imagine how to pronounce.

Tammy-Rae had a sharp, intelligent face. She might be trouble later. Suddenly, Sukana had hummingbirds in her stomach. She pointed to the water jug, and the servant handed her water in a clear cup.

The boy next to her said something and smiled. Sukana glared at him, and he cleared his throat and returned his attention to his paper puzzle, a box of squares with numbers in it.

Enough of this one. She reached out and brushed his wrist with her fingertips. He glanced back at her in surprise and fell into a deep sleep.

SUKANA UNSNAPPED her lap buckle and stood, stretching the muscles in her thighs and back. The aisle was empty, the lighting subdued, the air-servants back in their rear-facing seats at the fore and aft of the tubular hull. The full-throated roar of the plane while ascending had long ago been replaced by a steady businesslike rumble Sukana could almost ignore.

All around her, people slept. Apparently, they had no terrors of what the dark would bring, no savage memories or regrets to keep them awake, no fears for the morrow. They were so pampered and trusting.

And plump. Many were terribly overstuffed relative to Sukana's People, too thick-waisted to even pass down the aisle without bumping every seat, a space wide enough for Sukana and her lost sister to have fitted in side by side.

As she walked forward, she saw that not all the passengers were asleep. Some worked on their *computer*-boxes, faces lit eerily by the screens. Others stared vacantly, listening to the voices in their heads. Sukana had asked her metal-age guides about the fungus-like ear coverings, *headphones*, for listening to music nobody else could hear. Music in this culture was all-pervasive, a cacophony of shriek-and-bang that frightened her.

The bathroom was cramped even for Sukana's slight frame. She used it quickly, not enjoying being boxed in, and ambled back to her seat. In this direction, she could face her victims directly.

A husband and wife, arguing quietly. A youth in a hood scrunched up in sleep. A pretty little girl in a red coat sitting next to a sour-faced woman. An alert, healthy-looking man of almost unfathomable age who scrutinized Sukana's body impertinently as she passed. People grew so old here, as if they lived three lifetimes. Perhaps that was why they always seemed so bored.

A woman in green eyed her drowsily from the aisle seat. She was short enough to put a booted foot up on the armrest between the seats in front of her. Two men sat side by side, struggling to read books in the wan light. More computers.

So many different skin tones, from a startling black to a pallid white. And dressed in so many unappealing patterns, many involving squares. *Plaid*, her word-shaman had told her with a sneer; so much plaid.

Sukana checked her watch. Valuable time was passing. She should begin.

Back at her seat, she divested herself of everything she didn't need: the wristwatch first, into the seat pocket in front of her, shoes and socks next, leaving her feet blessedly bare. Her hairband was metal-age, and she pulled it free and discarded it, shaking out her long hair. Her underwear she had already balled up and left behind in the lavatory garbage; the undergarments in this place seemed constricting and unnecessary to Sukana, though it was a marvel how her not wearing them seemed instantly obvious to the men around her.

From her bag, Sukana took a small container of soil. Wetting her fingers from the cup of water, she rubbed them into the soil and daubed the fine mud onto her face in a series of spiral patterns.

Something remained. She could feel it. Ah, yes; from the folds in her tunic, she pulled out her *boardingcard* and dropped it on the floor.

Nothing of the bright metal age was left except for the all-important pouch of medicine she now took from her bag and placed on the fold-down table in front of her.

Sukana reached out with her mind. The arguing couple near the front of the cabin had to be calmed first. Next, she soothed a fractious baby several rows behind her, easing it into a deep and gentle sleep. After them, the most active people were those with computers perched uncomfortably in front of them. Looking forward and back, Sukana watched their heads droop one by one.

Then she brought her attention closer in, to the woman in boots across the aisle and the boy sitting behind her listening to his music.

Quieting their thoughts, Sukana used their energy to help her spread her sphere outward, building upon itself, further and further, to a man with a spiky beard and black glasses, the old lecher, and beyond. Each sleeping intelligence added to her web, enhancing her power and helping her to snare the next people and bring them in, too.

At the front of the cabin, Tammy-Rae stood abruptly and peered down the aisle. The smart one: she had recognized something odd and threatening about this sudden wave of passenger slumber.

Sukana stood and moved into the aisle. Heads nodded forward as the people in the twelfth row sagged into sleep. In the eleventh row a magazine slid out of someone's hands onto the floor. Tenth. Ninth.

She held up her hand, palm up. The air-servant met her gaze, obviously alarmed by the shaman's patterns daubed on Sukana's cheeks. She reached behind her and managed to say a few words into a voice-tube before crumpling safely to the floor.

All the passengers behind Sukana were now unconscious. Trusting souls, so simple to ensorcel; their soft and undisciplined minds almost relished the loss of volition, so used to yielding up control to their games and entertainments. Such a self-absorbed lack of critical thinking was almost a sin in itself.

This world's new rulers were not thinkers. They used only a tiny fraction of their minds. In their victory, they had forgotten everything of value. These were not *good* people.

Sukana forced herself to smile. She had to soften her heart before she could use them effectively. She massaged the air with her hands to direct and complete her power-weaving, and the heads of the women in the frontmost row lolled to the side.

Her sphere now encompassed the whole aircraft, through to the pilots in their unseen cockpit. The plane was flying itself, and Sukana was the only person still awake. She felt strong and proud and not a little relieved.

Perhaps to punish Sukana for her pride, the spirits gifted her with a surprise.

As she walked forward, someone sat bolt upright and spoke to her. It was the little girl in the red jacket. Startled, Sukana turned and took in the girl's pleading eyes, her unconscious mother's possessive hand grasping the child's seat belt.

Sukana had not understood the child's words, but the expression on her face left no doubt: *help me.*

Instead of lulling her into an even deeper sleep, Sukana's spell had woken her up. How could that happen?

No matter. She could not let doubt dilute her concentration. "Sorry," said Sukana in her own language, raising her palm.

Yet the girl did not lapse into unconsciousness as readily as Tammy-Rae. Sukana had to lean over the stark-faced woman and brush her fingertips against the girl's hand to make her eyes close.

Inadvertently, the brief contact propelled the girl's name into her mind: *Miranda.*

But Sukana's location-sense was tingling now, and she had to hurry. Turning, she raised her arms again as if blessing the sleepers, stroking the air to pull them even further into their torpor.

It had taken a vast crowd of her People in the plaza of the Great City to send her forward. She would need this full planeload of strangers to send her back.

ALL WAS CALM. Passengers sprawled over each other, some snoring gently. Strangers lolled with arms entwined. Raising the window shades, Sukana glanced out at the plane's wing with its red light flashing in the night. She could not see the ground, but she did not need to. Every second was inexorably bringing them three hundred paces closer to the location of the City of the Mounds.

The moment of truth approached.

Sukana stood in the centre of the cabin and lowered herself into a shaman's trance, beginning the chant. The eyes of the sleepers flickered rapidly under their eyelids; their bodies quivered, their minds so aligned they almost purred. No one was suffering; many smiled, experiencing the most vivid dreams of their lives. Once this was all over, they would awaken refreshed and unharmed.

As Sukana completed her invisible web, they became one being with one purpose, a collection of linked minds with their energy at her disposal. Flooded by their heat, Sukana chanted the final words of power.

Centuries unravelled in an instant. Brightness exploded around the aircraft, and its engines surged as it lurched and dropped. Sukana had no time to react before the ceiling of the cabin came down upon her; she banged into it painfully and bounced off.

As her feet slammed back onto the floor, Sukana squatted and grabbed at the seats on either side. The plane banked heavily, still losing height. She saw puffy white clouds and the green and gold of sunlight glinting on the treetops below.

A terrible tension was building. It was the tension of wrongness; Sukana's era, this very world, was fighting the aircraft. Its presence here was an abomination.

The airframe creaked and groaned. The plane angled downward, the aisle before Sukana becoming a steep hill. Left with no choice, Sukana reined in her mental sphere and freed the pilots from the terrible sleep she'd inflicted upon them. Whether because of that or due to the plane's own intrinsic defences, the aircraft started to level out.

The passengers slept on in a coma even deeper than peyote or mushrooms could bring. Sukana herself felt sluggish from holding all those minds enthralled.

Outside the plane, the bright daylight dimmed as something massive flew by. Sukana's peripheral vision caught little more than a bright flash of colour, but there could be no doubt. Somehow, her enemies had already found her.

It was time to go.

Her package of precious medicines had disappeared from her tray table. Of course, if Sukana had realized how great the shock of dislocation would be, she would have anchored it against loss. She dropped onto her hands and knees, scanned the floor, hunted increasingly desperately on the laps and seats of the people nearby. Around her, the plane groaned, its stresses building along with her own panic, and some of the sleepers began to stir. Sukana could not keep the airplane here much longer; soon, it must snap home like a bowstring, back to the metal future where it belonged. Yet without the medicine pouch that would preserve her People against the sicknesses that were even now heading toward them across the ocean, it would be futile for Sukana to return at all.

She glimpsed a sudden movement as Miranda stepped into the aisle and shrugged off her jacket, revealing bruises all down her arms. The child rubbed her eyes and started to walk toward Sukana, raising her hands as if asking to be held.

"Not now!" Sukana screamed just as the plane bucked and tossed them both sideways against the seats. Something very big had just buffeted them.

The aircraft banked steeply rightward, this time under human control. Sukana could imagine the scene on the flight deck: the pilots, aroused from a forbidden sleep in the middle of a night flight to find themselves in bright daylight over a landscape with no skyscrapered cities, no paved highways, no contact with the ground at all, and a garish sky-beast swooping dangerously near; a terrifying scenario they could never have trained for. Landing the plane would be almost impossible. All they could do was try to out-fly the threat.

Sukana's mind began to peel. She was near the end of her strength. She could feel her location pressing upon her thoughts even more intensely now; the City of the Mounds was not far ahead. This delay risked everything . . .

Miranda grabbed at her, and Sukana yelped. Her hand came down not so gently on the girl's shoulder, but instead of falling back into a deep sleep, Miranda cringed. Bruises, Sukana had accidentally knocked her bruises, damn it, and how did such a small girl get to be so damaged anyway? "I'm sorry . . ."

Miranda was holding out Sukana's hemp-wrapped package to her.

Once again, their eyes met. "All right," said Sukana, dry-mouthed. "Good girl—"

This time, they both saw the air-creature as it dealt the plane an immense blow: a beast all jagged edges and unnatural colours, lizard-like yet feathered, not alive yet ravenous with hunger, no real mouth yet sharp of tooth, no true wings but in flight, streaking around the plane much faster than any bird of flesh and blood.

Miranda screamed, and the pilot tilted the nose of the plane downward into a barely controlled dive.

THEY HAD LOST OVER HALF their altitude. Forested hills stretched out beneath them, flanking a broad grey river. Off course now, not as well-aimed at Sukana's destination. It would have to do.

Ten more seconds.

Voices rang in Sukana's mind, speaking sacred words in her own language. Her People were near.

"Goodbye," said Sukana to Miranda. Then she crouched, recited a single phrase in the secret tongue of the shamans, and relinquished her hold on the plane.

Emptiness opened up around her as the aircraft and passengers disappeared, hurled safely back to their home time. Instantly chilled, the air dangerously thin, Sukana fell head over heels over head, sky and ground blurring around her. The medicine pouch was still in her hand, and she thrust it deep into her tunic, tightening the strings at her neck to keep it safe.

She spread-eagled herself, extending her arms and legs to form an X. The air caught her new shape and ironed out her rolling tumble. Now she faced downward, still plummeting, ridiculously vulnerable but shrieking with exhilaration at being high in the air, back in the clean green beauty of her own era. In the middle distance, she glimpsed the City of the Mounds, with its wide cleared plaza and its great earthworks rising above the tree line. A crowd of her People's strongest thinkers were gathered in that plaza, ready to aid her.

Sukana relaxed and focused. The right words came unbidden to her lips, and the combined minds of her People found her and pushed back at her body, reducing the speed of her fall. An almost frenzied relief washed her from forehead to toes. She had not failed; she might live after all.

A small shape passed her in the air, wailing and rolling, heading for the ground at terminal velocity.

Reacting instinctively, Sukana pushed aside the invisible buoying support from her People. Arms by her sides, she streaked down, imagining her head as a sharp prow cutting water. The distance between them closed quickly and Sukana reached out and threw her arms around the girl, the medicine package now jammed between their bodies.

Miranda was rigid and angular, almost catatonic with shock. Sukana reached into her mind to soothe her, and the girl relaxed and scrunched into a ball.

How could Miranda not have returned to the metal age with the rest of the passengers? Had she grabbed at Sukana even as Sukana had released her hold on the plane?

Sukana had not even known that was possible.

She pushed her confusion aside. They were still many thousands of feet up but falling, falling, and if Sukana did not concentrate, she and Miranda would smash through the trees and into the ground with devastating force.

But there were even worse dangers than that. Sukana pulled her knees under her body, rolled in the air, and looked up.

The gaudy creature had been matching the speed and direction of the now-vanished aircraft, while Sukana and Miranda had dropped out of its trajectory, quickly losing their forward momentum. It hung in the sky far above them now, but surely it would take only seconds for its crew to realize what had happened. In these open skies, Sukana was the only thing visible for miles.

Sure enough, the worm turned and dived at them, arrow-swift.

THE FEATHERED serpent-bird of Quetzalcoatl split the air like lightning, a writhing abomination in red and yellow, green and black.

Its maw gaped. As terror gripped her, Sukana struggled to remember that this monster was forged and ridden by men, not hatched from some hellish nest. The teeth of the beast were sharpened obsidian, not bone.

Even so, the sky-serpent still curdled her blood. Driven by hatred, powered by human sacrifice, the vehicle of the Azteca was a blasphemy fuelled by murder.

The Azteca stole what they needed in battle rather than earning it by the sweat of their brows. Theirs was a society obsessed with blood and blades. Sukana had deprived them of a great bounty—the airplane and the metal and slaves it contained—but they would settle for Sukana herself and the future-potions she carried.

Sukana was under no illusions. The Azteca did not ransom hostages. If they captured her, they would take her home, break her on their pyramid altar, and drink her blood. Better to plow into the ground in bone-shattering death than be strapped to a rock and forced to watch in helpless agony as they carved out her still-beating heart . . . just like her mother and sister before her.

The Azteca cities were far to the south in the hot lands, yet the two ancient civilizations had been enemies ever since the mythical times of Aztlan and the First Mound. But the Azteca had not mastered Time. So, unless this attack was some ungodly coincidence, to have known so precisely when Sukana would reappear, they must have captured a shaman of her People and tortured the information out of him. Who and how didn't matter now. Sukana's only hope of escape was to get herself—and Miranda—safely down to earth.

<hr>

SHE WAS FALLING INTO A WAR. As she lost height, the ground came into clearer focus: a running battle was being fought in the trees and fields between Sukana and her City as the hunters and fighters of her People struggled to repel a horde of hideously painted warriors, extravagantly garbed in jaguar skins and the like. Telling the two sides apart was easy. Sukana's People wore tans and browns, colours of the real world, not the garish hues favoured by the Azteca. Gaudy in their violence, violent in their gaudiness; everything about the southern raiders was extreme.

Behind the battle line, a hundred or more of the Azteca stood frozen in formation, their faces turned skyward; these were the enemy sages combining their mental powers to sustain the Quetzalcoatl-bird in flight.

In the distant skies, far beyond the City and the feathered serpent, Sukana now spied another shape. But it was too far away to help her now.

She had absorbed all of this in a series of brief glances, but now Quetzalcoatl was almost upon her.

Sukana opened her mind to her People. The feathered serpent lunged just as the force of their thoughts buoyed her; the sudden invisible shove pushed her up and over the jaws of the beast. Quetzalcoatl passed beneath her, and Sukana crashed down onto the worm's broad back.

SHE SPRAWLED on a patchwork of bloodstained feathers and fur. Beneath, her bare toes grazed reptilian scales. Terrified and repulsed, nausea burning in her throat, she pounded on the demon's skin with her fists.

Quetzalcoatl rippled and flexed its muscular body. Only its skin separated Sukana from the twenty warriors and shamans who crewed the beast. She heard their voices calling out in the rasping Nahuatl tongue she knew from her nightmares but did not speak. They knew she was aboard.

Suddenly, she realized she was no longer holding Miranda and could not see her anywhere near. When had she let go of the child? She shoved herself upright, panicking afresh.

From deep within the beast, the joined minds of the Azteca shamans rose against Sukana, battering at her brain with such violence that she bounced on the roof of the worm. Hands to her temples, she parried their attacks as best she could, screaming aloud.

The Azteca sacrificed children as well as adults on their bloody altar. Sukana's fear for Miranda helped her to resist the shamans' remorseless pounding. Where was the girl? She forced her eyes open.

A mere dozen feet away, a warrior clambered up onto the worm's back, a terrible savage, tall and whip-tough, a vision of deadliness and brutality. This was an Eagle Warrior of the Azteca, his head mostly shaved but with a long braid over his left ear, face painted blue and yellow, cheeks brutally punctured and studded with shards of bone. He carried a wooden club with sharp obsidian blades embedded in it. A stone slingshot bounced obscenely from his belt.

The warrior stood on the rocking back of the sky-serpent and glared at her with wolfish hunger. He seemed gratified by her skimpy tunic and her lack of any protection or weapon.

Sukana still saw him only indistinctly as the Azteca shamans continued their mental assault. The blood rose behind her eyes, fogging her vision.

He strode toward her with his club raised and his tongue jutting lewdly, scarified and obnoxious with menace, driven by dark gods. Sukana scrabbled back away from him, casting around with her mind and trying to recall the timbre of the girl's thoughts. *Miranda?*

Behind you. The syllables hummed in her head. Incomprehensible to Sukana, but her senses were not so blunted that she could not tell their direction.

The feathered serpent convulsed as Sukana rose to her feet and *ran* across its undulating body. Its flesh and fabric rippled around her feet, trying to trip her, but she seized Miranda's wrist and kept on running, off the snake's back and into empty space. Her feet still jerked and kicked even as the colossal drop yawned beneath them, and they resumed their long suicidal plummet toward the forest below.

Quetzalcoatl roared and rolled, reaching down toward them once more. Death flew at Sukana, but rising up on her other side came salvation.

Giant wings creaked as they surged against the air. The Thunderbird of the Cahokians soared past Sukana, almost close enough to touch but flying too fast to grab. She could hear the chanting of its wingmen and the rhythmic pulsing wails of the shamans who rode it and guided it from within. The Thunderbird resembled an immense bald eagle, its eyes lit by the fire that also heated the air sacs in its upper body. Yet all the strength of the braves who hauled at its wing-ropes and the powers of its shamans would be futile without the sustaining pressure from the minds of hundreds of their People on the ground.

The Thunderbird smashed into the twisting serpent of the Azteca, the spears in its talons raking the belly of the beast. The sky-worm bent in the middle, folding around the bird in a hideous embrace. The clash of weapons and the cries of warriors dinned in Sukana's ears as she fell away from the bird and the worm, still dazed, her vision bleary.

The Elders had chosen Sukana for their mission to the future due to her uncanny powers of concentration. The loss of her mother and sister in an Azteca raid had bequeathed her an unequalled mental drive; her overpowering sorrow and the hatred it had engendered had awoken talents within her that she could never have foreseen. The Elders had recruited her for their air cohort, but after making contact with the future, had quickly realized she might play an even greater role in ensuring her People's survival. Few indeed had the intelligence, steely focus, openness and emotional power to ride the air, let alone ride Time.

Despite all that, after the brutal mental beating she had just suffered from the Azteca shamans, lowering her defences and opening herself up in trust to the basic goodness of her People on the ground was the hardest thing Sukana did that day.

HAD SUKANA BEEN ALONE, her People could have eased her to the ground as gently as thistledown. Miranda's added weight made that problematic; that, and the battle that disrupted her People's concentration.

Her wild flight on the worm had carried her far from the battleground, but it had also taken her farther from her City. With distance came a weakening of her People's ability to arrest her fall. And even as they beat back the Azteca assault, Sukana felt their attention slipping.

Ah, well. She had done her duty and more. If it was not enough, so be it.

Her arms still wrapped Miranda as the trees rushed toward them. She curled herself around the girl to give her whatever meagre additional protection she might. The very last thing little Miranda needed was any more bruises. The movement rolled Sukana onto her back, child uppermost. The giant skies filled her view.

In a snapping blur of green, the forest opened up and claimed them.

SUKANA LAY at the foot of a tall oak on a hillside, her breathing ragged. The sun was setting behind the trees. From down in the valley, she could hear the tinkle and bubble of a flowing brook.

Her arms were stiff with bruises. They looked just like Miranda's now. With some difficulty, she unravelled the ties at the neck of her tunic and pulled out the pouch. Beyond the stains of her own sweat, it did not feel damp in her hands, nor did she hear any crackle of broken glass. Good. She had done her best to shield it in her long tumble out of the tree, of course, favouring it and the child at the expense of her elbows, knees and head. Even if the fall killed her, saving the medicines was paramount.

Because an enemy even more ferocious than the Azteca was approaching, one that could annihilate Sukana's People. Even now, the ships of the white invaders raced over the ocean toward them.

The diseases they brought would devastate Cahokians and Azteca alike in a blight that would spread across the continent ahead of them like a shadow, leaving their cities deserted and only scattered pockets of her People alive.

It was the Cahokians' audacity to attempt to stave off this ghastly future. The metal age Sukana had visited had seemed substantial enough, yet it *was* the future and so must still be malleable. At least, so the Elders said, and their certainty was enough for Sukana.

It took such a tiny amount of the potions she carried, scratched onto the skin, to protect a man against the worst of the coming sicknesses, the disease with the virulent pustules. Other diseases merited the full stab of a needle. They would start by inoculating the shamans and the children and cast lots for the rest of the doses. Sukana herself had already been treated, of course, on arriving in the metal age.

Failure would doom her People to die emplagued, with too few remaining to preserve their identity. But if the future could truly be altered, Sukana's actions today would ultimately help to defeat *all* of these invaders, red and white, and Cahokia would live and thrive.

Sukana sagged back, exhausted. After all, she was the only passenger on her red-eye flight who had not gotten any sleep.

A little farther down the hill, Miranda stirred. Sukana had known people to die from less terrifying shocks than Miranda had suffered today, but the girl's resilience was clear. Even now, she was getting to her feet unaided, trembling only a little as she tested the ground beneath her. She gazed up into the trees and the now-empty sky. Looked over at Sukana. And smiled, a broad and innocent smile.

Sukana did not need a daughter or a new sister. She had not sought a keepsake from the future, but inexplicably, she'd been granted one. The girl might not have an easy life here in her own past, but maybe it would be better than the painful existence she had left behind.

Once the enemy war party was beaten back, Sukana's People would send out scouting parties to find her. And her problems might not yet be over; it could be many dangerous miles back to the City of the Mounds, with the risk of encountering Azteca warriors at every turn.

But such worries could wait a while longer. Here in the timeless forest, bare feet resting on the soil of her own land, Sukana was at long last remembering what family felt like. And it felt like coming home.

———————

NOWHERE FALLS

———————

Kevin Moore

This story originally appeared in Christmas Stories – Volume II *by Kevin Moore, released in November 2024.*

In the dimly lit corridor, Dash Winters slid the key into the lock of his apartment as the door to the elevator down the hall creaked open.

Dash turned, ready to greet his new neighbors, but the elevator was vacant, as had been the case for the last week. No one got out.

The hardwood floors of the Victorian apartment creaked beneath each step. Tall, narrow windows with mismatched curtains stood open, allowing the crown moulding and high ceilings to be fully appreciated from the street below. But that was about the grandest thing in the place. The kitchen was the size of a small walk-in closet, with chipped pink tile counters and worn white cabinets. Its charms had long since faded, but the rent was cheap and the large clawed bathroom tub was perfect for soaking—and why he'd rented it in the first place.

Dash had never expected to live in Nowhere Falls. It was the kind of town you drove through to get somewhere, not a destination. Nowhere Falls was not a place you started or ended; it wasn't even a middle. It was the in-between, a drift somewhere amid the start, middle, and end. It was perfect for him because he was in that awkward space himself. Nowhere Falls was a place to hide from Christmas, with the sad memories from long ago that had a way of reopening every year. And when he spotted the apartment, fully furnished down to basic necessities like cups, glasses, pots, and pans, he knew Nowhere Falls was also a place for him.

He ran a bath in the large tub, and the steam drifted upward from the water like a smoke signal. Snow fell gently outside the bathroom window, unsettling him and serving as a nagging reminder that Christmas was coming, and there was no escaping that loneliness. The cast-iron radiator hummed to life, releasing a toot suggestive of a steam train announcing its arrival. There was a quiet bliss as he brewed a cup of tea—a blend named Dream Scape—got ready and stood in the thick steam, waiting for his bath.

Just as Dash finished his tea, a faint sound, beginning as a hum, crept through the apartment. Suspecting the aged refrigerator, he ambled into the kitchen in his bathrobe to investigate.

It wasn't the fridge, nor the stove, nor the radiator. The noise was ambient, but identifying its origin proved impossible. Shrugging off the mystery, he returned to the bathroom and the inviting warmth of the water. The hot water embraced his body, bringing a state of relaxation bordering on meditation until the sound of someone walking across the creaky floor begged his attention.

He sat upright, listening. Again, he heard the sound of steps outside the bathroom, moving along the aged floors in his apartment. Dash pawed open the bathroom door and peered out, sinking his body low into the warm tub as if it might hide him from whatever was out there.

He spotted a shadow shimmering in the living room. A jolt of alarm rushed through him, prompting Dash to abandon the soothing waters with startled urgency, sending water splashing across the cold tiled floor. In his haste, he lost his footing but grabbed onto the tub, preventing a fall.

Clad in nothing but a hastily wrapped towel, Dash tiptoed into the living room, expecting to catch an intruder. No one was there. The front door was securely locked, but that didn't put his mind at ease. In the back of his mind, he felt like someone was inside, hiding.

Dash secured the towel and looked in the pantry and hall closet. Empty. Nervously, he stepped into the lone bedroom, his heart racing. Casting wary glances around, he crouched to inspect beneath the bed, his hands trembling slightly—nothing but dust.

The closet loomed ominously. He took a breath before summoning the courage to open the door. A chill traced its way along his back as he reached up and turned on the light. The closet revealed only his untouched suitcases, but an unspoken fear lingered in the air.

The closet, with its enigmatic L-shape, drew him farther in to investigate what might lie around the corner. Its peculiar shape suggested a room divided with unsettling irregularities.

The door closed slowly behind him. As he inched deeper into the closet, the ceiling sloped, hinting at its possible origin beneath a staircase. Bending cautiously, he navigated the turn, his senses on high alert.

A musty smell hung in the air. In the dim light, he discovered a nondescript cardboard box about four feet tall and two feet wide. Dash reasoned no one could hide in there, but still, something felt off. A tiny bit of tension hung in the air.

Gripping the box firmly, he carried it into the bedroom. There was a simple note taped to its top: DO NOT OPEN. He left the box near the bed and returned to the bathroom, where he was met with tepid water. What had once been a perfect escape from Christmas no longer felt alluring; an unexplained uneasiness cast shadows over his simple bath.

He was puzzled by the box, the note. It was difficult to decide whether to ignore the note entirely and just open it or ignore the box completely and return it to the back space of the closet. Dash decided to unpack while he pondered both actions.

From his window, he could see that Nowhere Falls was dressed for Christmas, at least on Main Street. It was an economically challenged town, yet it was able to decorate its Main Street with Christmas lights and wreaths. The town had a pub, a coffee shop, a post office, a market, a library, and several small mom-and-pop stores, and each of the storefronts was adorned with Santa Clauses, nativity scenes, elves, and snow.

Earlier that day, Dash had stopped for lunch in the coffee shop.

"You passing through?" the waitress asked. "I've never seen you before."

"I just moved here. I'm renting a place near the river in the old Victorian Apartments."

"Saint Andrews?" she asked, her face turning pale as she stepped back.

Dash thought about it for a moment. He recalled a small sign in the lobby calling it Saint Andrews Place. "Yes," he said, "I think that's it."

"I didn't think anybody lived in that place anymore," the waitress said ominously, moving away from his table.

Despite not being naturally paranoid, Dash could have sworn she walked up to the man behind the lunch counter and whispered something. The man gave Dash a peculiar look, raising his brow with pursed lips.

In the post office, it was more of the same. The minute he handed the postman his change-of-address card, Dash got a very similar response. "I thought they were tearing that place down," the man said suspiciously.

"Why would they tear the place down?" Dash asked, starting to suspect that there was a reason the rent was so cheap. "It's architecturally still lovely, although it does appear to have a wonky floorplan in places."

At the library, the librarian was less cagey. "It's all folk tales and myth. Locals say it's haunted." She took a look through the catalogue and found a book and a magazine article on the place. The book's title was simply *The History of Saint Andrews Place*. He checked the book out, and as he left, the librarian said goodbye with, "Merry Christmas." Dash gave her a nod.

Dash had set the book down on the kitchen table, fixed himself another mug of Dream Scape, and begun digging into its pages. The property had its origins in the late 1800s when a prosperous family led by a man named Andrews initially constructed it as a grand residence. Andrews, a notable factory and land owner, had built the place to accommodate his growing family, with enough room for even the most distant of relatives. Following his premature death, his wife converted the estate into a boarding house, later changing it into an apartment building. While there had been tales in the book of murder, suicide, and ghosts, none of it was clearly documented, leading to talk of cover-ups.

Now, Dash thought about his neighbors, or rather, the fact he hadn't seen a single one of them. There were twenty-six apartments, and the only sounds he'd heard were those escaping the heating and plumbing. He was perplexed that he had not actually seen anybody physically.

Dash returned to the box he found in the rear of the closet, reading and re-reading the cautionary sign taped to its top: DO NOT OPEN. He prided himself on being a man of integrity, but what harm could there be in a little peak? The fact that he'd found it at all felt ridiculous to him. Perhaps he could send an email to the building manager requesting it be removed—an email because there had never been a telephone number attached to any of their correspondence. The box had transformed into his personal apple in the Garden of Eden, and he just wanted a look, not a taste.

Returning to the kitchen, he found one of two steak knives. Opting for a careful approach, Dash decided to enter the box through the bottom, ensuring the note remained intact. And then he would seal it back up straight away.

However, while the entire box was sealed with tape, the bottom was made of solid cardboard, so his planned subtle approach proved impossible. Dash meticulously navigated around the portentous note, carefully slicing through the tape and prying the box open. As he unfolded the top, he took a deep, uneasy breath.

In that tense moment, the doorbell to his apartment rang, startling him. Swiftly closing the box, Dash rushed to the door. The hallway was empty, and he cautiously extended his head to peer down the corridor. The old elevator door screeched open but closed again without anyone stepping out of the elevator. It was only then he realized he still had the steak knife in his hand.

He returned to the bedroom. A surge of adrenaline poured through him as he reopened the box, tentatively removing its mysterious contents. It was encased in strong brown paper. Dash proceeded to unwrap it with meticulous care as if he were unwrapping a mummy.

In a moment of sheer astonishment, before him stood an enchanted Christmas tree, a spectacle beyond any he had witnessed. This was not some Christmas tree one found in the back of a closet or building somewhere. This tree had radiant lights decorated in colors of cobalt blue, ruby red, and emerald green, weaving a magical tapestry. Shimmering ornaments graced its branches—beaming flowers, flickering candles, luscious fruit, tempting chocolate, and crystalline bulbs that contained mesmerizing inner lights. Crowning this otherworldly creation was a star, aglow with a celestial brilliance. A wonderful smell filled the entire room.

As much as he struggled with the season and everything that came with it, Dash looked at this captivating tree in a state of wonder and awe. As he stood there bewitched, the lights in his apartment flickered off.

But the tree remained illuminated. Only then did he realize the lights on the tree had no plug or battery pack attached, leaving him utterly bewildered.

As if stirred by an unseen force, the apartment lights flickered to life once more, the radiator hummed its tune, and the opening strains of "Have Yourself A Merry Little Christmas" came from the radio on the living room table. Dash, momentarily entranced, struggled to regain his composure, the enchantment of the tree battling his struggle with the season. However, how could one ignore the wonder and magic? The idea of returning the mystical tree to its box vanished from his mind like a fleeting spell.

Instead, with a gentle touch, he cradled the enchanted Christmas tree and navigated it through the apartment, each step accompanied by an ethereal tone. In the living room, he sought the ideal spot to place it where its mystical presence and spiritual aura could shine.

First, Dash placed the tree in the middle of the room, thought it awkward, and tried it close to the faux fireplace. This was not the Christmas Eve he had been expecting. As much as he hated to admit it, this tree bewitched him. Dash stepped back to admire its placement.

"Do you think that's the best place for it?"

An eerie shiver of unease encapsulated him as he turned to the woman's voice.

"I was thinking closer to the window so its light could shine into the world."

"Oh my God," Dash said, his legs fighting hard to keep him upright. "Who let you in?"

"You did," the woman said. She was a lovely brunette dressed like someone from the 1950s. Her hazel eyes sparkled with a glow of heavenly delight.

"Who are you?" Dash asked, not sure if he should be afraid. He glanced at the door to his apartment. It was locked, chain and all.

"Natalie," she said, smiling.

"How did you get in here?"

Natalie pointed to the tree. Dash was unsure of who or what he was dealing with. She seemed beautiful and harmless, but pointing to the tree made him think she was off her rocker.

"No, Natalie, I did no such thing. It is just a tree." But Dash knew deep in his soul that it was *not* just a tree.

He didn't want to be rude, but it was all so strange. First, he'd found this magnificent tree, and then this woman had appeared out of nowhere. The name of the town, Nowhere Falls, drifted across his thoughts.

"What is your name?" Natalie asked.

"Dash Winters."

"You let me in, Dash Winters, when you opened the box."

Perplexed, he looked at the mystical Christmas tree and then at Natalie. "Who are you, and why are you here?" he asked. Before she could answer, there was another knock at the door. Dash, feeling like he was in a dream, answered the door.

A boy of about twelve stood there, selling chocolate bars. He sported a navy-blue sports jacket with the emblem ES, complemented by a crisply ironed white shirt, a blue tie with a tie clip reminiscent of a previous era, and finely tailored grey wool slacks.

"Is it here?" the boy asked.

"Is what here?" Dash said.

The boy looked past him, catching a glimpse of the tree. His face turned brighter than if he had just seen Santa Claus come down the chimney.

Dash heard the trundling sound of the elevator door opening and glanced over out of habit, expecting the familiar emptiness that had persisted over the past few days. However, to his surprise, a disturbed-looking man came storming out, dressed in work overalls and completely disheveled.

A jolt of surprise gripped him, sending him into action as the man began to move back and forth in a private game of red light, green light. Dash grabbed hold of the boy and pulled him into his apartment, slamming the door behind him. Yet the boy displayed no signs of fear or unease; instead, he stood near the tree as if magnetically drawn to it.

"Oh, my God, call the police," Dash said, pulling on the chain with his back pressed to the door.

Dash's breaths came in quick, ragged gasps. The spiritual serenity he had felt moments ago after finding the tree had been abruptly shattered. His gaze darted between Natalie and the boy, who seemed completely enraptured by the tree and, in Dash's opinion, showed an alarming lack of fear toward the man in the hall.

Turning urgently to Natalie, Dash steeled himself for the man to crash into the door. "Call the police!" Dash yelled.

But the boy and Natalie were, even now, standing as if they were in another time and place—not in this lonely apartment with the possibility of being accosted by some demented man in overalls but frozen like a scene on a Christmas card or snow globe. "He looked very weird!" Dash said, fumbling for his smartphone. "Out of his mind, even."

Natalie gave him a warm, calming smile. "How was he dressed?"

Dash looked through the peephole and saw no one. He then picked up the steak knife and carefully opened the door, bracing for an attack.

Nothing. The man he thought was certain to attack him was still down the hall, moving up three steps and then back two. He scrutinized the man for a second, considering telling him to get out of the hall, but Natalie and the boy's calm convinced him to slide back into the apartment.

"He looks like a maintenance man, but he is acting troubled. Do you think he'll hurt someone? One of us?"

"No," Natalie said. "Thomas here, the man—his name is Richard, by the way—and I are already dead."

A chilling revelation struck him as her words echoed in his mind. *Already dead . . . dead . . . dead.* His legs gave way beneath him, and the room twisted and blurred. Dash sensed he had plunged into a nightmarish dream with no quick exit.

He found himself sitting in a chair. Natalie and the boy, Thomas, were still aglow from the emanating energy from the tree, looking at him as if trying to help him understand. "You both are dead? Ghosts?" Dash asked. "And that man?"

Natalie nodded. "There was a gas and carbon monoxide leak, problems with the water heater. Richard was the building's repairman. He had a drinking issue. He said he fixed it but never did. When they found us dead, Richard shot himself."

Thomas kept being pulled to the ambient force of the tree. The doorbell rang, followed by a light knocking. Dash looked at the door with large, fearful eyes.

"He can't hurt anyone," Natalie said.

"It's true," Thomas agreed.

Peering through the peephole, Dash cautiously opened the door.

Before him stood two women and a man dressed in attire reminiscent of the turn of the previous century. The women were dressed in floor-length gowns; one had a long, elegant string of pearls around her neck, and the other had upswept hair secured by combs that sparkled like tiny jewels. The man sported a top hat. Their arms were filled with pies, deviled eggs, wine, soft drinks, and a poinsettia plant.

"Is this the place?" the man asked. However, one of the women spotted the tree and pushed past him into the apartment. "Oh, my!" the three of them exclaimed, completely spellbound, leaving Dash utterly bewildered. He searched through his thoughts as if he was scrolling through his phone. What in the world had happened? He was certain these three were also spirits brought there by the magic of the tree.

As the night advanced, more and more of the spirit world came in amazing and various ways. Dash watched as a ghostly man from the 1980s, dressed in complete punk-rock attire, climbed out of the bedroom mirror. He then reached back in and pulled out a friend. "It's been a long time since I've been able to celebrate Christmas," the man said, bringing chocolates, fruit, and Christmas cheer. Another spirit emerged from the smoke of a candle. Dash, unable to fully relax, had thought he would be spending another Christmas Eve alone.

The lady with the pearls offered Dash a glass of wine. Her companion put his arm around Dash and began to sing, "O Little Town of Bethlehem."

"Help me sing it, mate," the man said, and several of the spirits joined in the singing. Dash, trying hard to remember the words, decided to relish the revelry with the spirit world and began actually to enjoy himself. Looking around, he could see and feel the joy that these ghosts—spirits—were bringing. He chuckled and fought back a tear. Dash could not remember the last time he had felt such Christmas spirit.

Soon, he found himself genuinely savoring the moment. Engaging with his spectral guests, he posed questions and circulated Christmas cookies and plum pudding.

Observing the elation radiating from these ethereal spirits, Dash felt a profound connection. The heaviness of haunting feelings and self-imposed isolation dissipated, replaced by a newfound lightness that elevated Dash to an unparalleled experience of Christmas joy.

"I lived here when Mrs. Andrews turned it into a boarding house," an older man smoking a pipe explained.

"This was my apartment," the punk-rocker said, raising his eyebrows and making an amused face, remembering all the noise he'd made playing punk music. "The place was haunted," he added with a chuckle.

"Silent Night" began playing, and several guests sang along, including Dash. The words came easier to him now.

Dash found Natalie. "If you are all dead, how can you eat, drink, and make merry?"

She pointed to the tree.

Dash froze. "Am I dead?" he asked nervously.

"No. Only someone living could find and open the box. The tree is the doorway to all worlds."

It was clear to Dash that all the guests had two things in common. One, they were from the other side, and two, they had all lived in Nowhere Falls at the Victorian Apartments—or Saint Andrew's Place—at one time or another, and all had died while living here. The spirits no longer felt the need to circle the tree. It had brought them there, but now the Christmas spirit and celebration filled them, the room, and Dash himself.

There was a knock, and without thinking, Dash opened the door to find Richard standing there. His initial reaction was to slam the door. But as he glanced at Natalie, he heard her hushed words, "Let him in."

Once inside the apartment, Richard appeared to diminish in stature. The burden of the horror he had committed haunted him, compelling him to isolate himself in the corner of the room. Dash, now feeling the true meaning of Christmas, offered Richard a cup of tea and a piece of pumpkin pie.

Church bells rang, and the flame of joy rose ever higher. There was a harmonious symphony of laughter and song. "Twelve Days of Christmas" was being sung by several translucent spirits somewhere in the room, and on the line of "Ten lords a-leaping," the punk-rocker spirit actually leaped, giving Dash and the others a good laugh. "You have to taste Grandma's chocolate cookies," the rocker said. And as the clock ticked closer to twelve, the ghostly spirits began to hug and say, "Merry Christmas until we meet again."

"It's time," said the male spirit from the turn of the century. Dash watched in awe as the man thanked him once more for his hospitality before he stepped into the light from the tree and vanished. One by one, they returned to where they came from. And if possible, the tree grew brighter as each new spirit departed.

Dash stood close, his hand reaching out to touch its longest branches, drawn to its wonder and wanting to hold on to the joy of the evening and the spirit of togetherness. In the end, he was left with only Natalie, Thomas, and Richard.

"What is this tree, and why does it bring such joy?" Dash asked.

"Stardust," Thomas said.

"Not just stardust, but stardust from the Star of Bethlehem," Natalie said.

"The star the wise men followed . . ." Dash mumbled, more to himself than anyone else.

"When you opened the box, it called out to all who believe," Natalie said.

"Bringing us to a place we wanted to be," Richard spoke.

Dash realized it was the first time he had heard him speak all evening. "Why did you come?" he asked.

"When I woke up after I did what I did, I was sitting on a bench at a bus stop. Alone. Every once in a while, a bus would come, and the doors would open, but I couldn't see the driver, and I was afraid to get on. I was afraid because I realized what I had done and, because of that, where I might be headed. I thought it was safer to be in the middle of nowhere at a bus stop. I don't know; I hoped maybe I could come back and fix it.

"Today, while I sat on the bench, I saw the star, and it called to me.

It became bigger and bigger. My wish was to go back. Now I'm here." Richard began to cry and turned to Natalie and Thomas. "I'm so sorry. Can you ever forgive me?"

Natalie nodded.

"Of course," Thomas said. "One of the things God lets me do over there is play center field for the New York Yankees and be loved unconditionally."

Through his tears, Richard almost smiled.

Dash felt privileged to be a witness to all of this.

"I should go," Richard said. "Back to nowhere on my bench."

"Get on the bus," Natalie said. "The driver is God."

Richard stepped into the portal and was gone.

Dash turned to Natalie. "What about you? Thomas gets to play for the Yankees. What do you do?"

"It is different for everyone," Natalie said. "Mine is a collection of all the joyful moments I've experienced on this side. I hope it will include tonight."

"I got to go; I want to be home for Christmas. Thanks for having us," Thomas said, giving Dash a thumbs up before stepping into the light radiating from the tree.

Dash, looking at Natalie, said, "You were right,"

"About what?" she asked.

"Moving the tree to the window so its light could shine into the world."

Natalie smiled. "When they saw the star, they rejoiced exceedingly with great joy," she quoted. "Matthew 2:10. The world still needs that joy, Dash Winters. Make Nowhere Falls a destination. Make it somewhere." And with that, Natalie stepped into the light and was gone.

The ringing of the church bells woke him, although he was not asleep. Dash grabbed his coat and decided to go to midnight mass. The snow was falling ever so gently when he walked outside. To his astonishment, people were walking toward him and the apartment building.

"Oh my, what is that?" Dash heard a voice say.

When he turned back, he saw the building itself illuminated. The light that radiated from the tree at his window sparkled brightly into the night sky—the Star of Bethlehem. He watched in absolute joy as the people of Nowhere Falls crowded the street, enthralled by what was happening.

Shouts of "Merry Christmas" and "Oh, my God" rang out from the chorus of voices. And like that night in Bethlehem all those many years ago, people rejoiced.

"And, lo, the angel of the Lord came upon them, and the glory of the Lord shone round about them: and they were sore afraid. And the angel said unto them, 'Fear not: for behold, I bring you good tidings of great joy, which shall be to all people. For unto you is born this day in the city of David a Saviour, which is Christ the Lord. And this shall be a sign unto you . . ."

— *LUKE* 2: *9-12*

Dash stood with a wistful gaze, as captivated as he had been ever since he opened the box and discovered the mystical tree blessed with stardust and the spirit world that helped him remember the meaning of Christmas. A smile graced his face as he acknowledged he was no longer in "the in-between," no longer waiting or wanting.

Dash Winters had found himself and Christmas in a place called *Nowhere.*

THE CRUMBLING WALLS: A TALE OF NAHWALLA

Omari Richards

She knew kissing him was wrong. Every stolen moment chipped against the wall of alliances that Mother had created to protect their land. The parentage of their daughter was more than enough to destroy the wall completely and unleash the full might of the Uhitaji clan. But as he pressed her against a small corner wall on the battlements, none of that mattered. His hand slid down her wide hip as their lips danced in unity. She wrapped her leg around his waist, pulling him even closer. Their shared heat burned the world around them to nothing. There was nothing else, nothing left but them.

"The hospitality of the Kisaye clan continues to impress me, my lady," Prince Muwali Uhitaji said, panting, his eyes glazed over with desire. "I am inclined to extend the duration of my visit. I believe the renewal of our trade agreements requires much more . . . *thorough* discussions."

Princess Abbeba Kisaye smiled as she passed a hand over Muwali's new beard, which perfectly highlighted his dark brown skin. "Our gates are always open to our closest ally, Prince Muwali."

"Such a gracious host," he chuckled, his deep voice weakening her legs. "It's almost enough to make me forgive your clan's . . . less-than-stellar tributes of late."

"Almost enough? Well, I believe we ought to continue our vigorous negotiations, my prince."

"A very agreeable suggestion, my lady Kisaye."

He cupped her face in his large hands and gifted her with another deep kiss. Her hand slithered past his silk dark blue robes and squeezed the firm muscles on his chest. She navigated the whole of his torso through touch and memory alone, finding the birthmark on his right rib that reminded Abbeba of a falling star. She had told him as much when they were children, and he had taken off his tunic and offered it to her when they had been caught in the rain after an ill-advised expedition outside to escape their lessons.

Across his chest she found the faint scars left by her nails when she dragged them across his chest and back during their first time. Her mischievous smile halted their third round of kisses. She ran her red-dyed henna nails across his chest with the same passion as the first time. Her grin only grew when Muwali shuddered, barely suppressing the moan growing in his throat. The act only surged his passion. His lips were back on hers in a blink while he fought against his robes to free himself.

She wanted to laugh at his fumbling but held it back by breaking off their kiss and nibbling at his neck. He was flustered, eager, yet concerned about being seen. His neck was always his weak point, the key to calming him. She wondered if his wife knew this about him.

The thought of the future queen of the Uhitaji made her freeze, dousing the passion in her belly. Their passion, their heat—how much of it did he share with her? Did he take her on the battlements like this, as well? Or was future Queen Enyi as frigid and dispassionate as Muwali said? Yet they had secured his father's line with their four children, two boys and two girls, the perfect balance. Perfect.

Enyi Kaddara was the perfect bride. She hailed from the stable lands of Lazola on the southern half of the Cwatha Peninsula, a land engorged with wealth from the feast of trade routes they held. Enyi's mother was the first cousin of Empress Ilanga Morowa, granting her royal ties.

Before such perfection, who was she? The Kisayes' small strip of land could only offer rice, some cotton on a good harvest, and occasional iron ore from their mines, and even that was rare. What were their fleeting and sparse passionate moments compared to lasting perfection?

"What's wrong?" Muwali asked, pulling away. "You're tense."

Abbeba forced a smile but the gaze in his violet eyes intensified. He could always see through her. When he looked at her, he didn't see the princess of the Kisaye clan or Queen Nituswa's troublesome daughter, who lacked her mother's grace, insight, and charm. He only saw her as Abbeba, and she only saw Muwali. That was what she gave him, and that was what they had, an oasis away from duty.

"Nothing," she said, with a genuine smile this time. "Nothing at all."

She was his, and he was hers; that was all that mattered. But Abbeba could not deny the hint of bitterness on her tongue. They ought to have been in their fourth year of marriage. Their daughter, Anuli, should know him as her father rather than her mother's "dear friend." Abbeba remembered begging her mother to permit them to marry, telling her they were the perfect match, perfect for each other. But Queen Nituswa denied her, ranting about how the marriage would be too costly for them: how it meant forfeiting their independence, how the differences in lobola payments between their two clans made negotiation impossible, how she would not tolerate any Kisaye heir being reduced to Lesser Wife status, and other such nonsense.

All Abbeba remembered was leaving the throne room in tears, more determined than ever to have Muwali.

She ran her hand down his chest, hoping to reignite their heat, but her fingers ran against a new scar, a deeper one right above his heart.

"What happened here?" she asked, concern racing her heart.

He gently brushed her hand away. "It looks worse than it is. A meagre wound while fighting Thembile raiders from the south."

Abbeba furrowed her brow. "Thembile raiders? Just last moon, they were at war with the Mhlume clan of Red Spiders in the Tsare Hills."

"The mantis is slow to reach your ears, Abbeba," Muwali said with a soft chuckle. "That war ended a moon ago. They allowed their foolishness to stretch too close to Akamafula. The Maasuma and Otieno clans did not take well to their own game of succession being disrupted by savages, so they stopped pointing their spears at each other and united against the common enemy. The Thembile quickly agreed to a truce with the Red Spiders and to never encroach on Massuma or Otieno lands again. The Red Spiders chose to fight against the Maasuma and Otieno clans till the bitter end."

"And after all that, the Thembile still did not get their fill of war?"

Muwali shrugged, his eyes burning with a different form of passion. He always loved the game of politics and its discussions. "Wars are expensive," he said. "The Thembile needed something to refill their coffers and, more importantly, give their warriors the plunder promised. Unpaid soldiers are just as dangerous as any enemy lurking on the border. Sometimes, even more so."

Abbeba looked him over, her gaze clear of desire, and finally noticed the various bruises and half-healed cuts running up and down his torso.

"It was fierce fighting," Muwali said as if reading her mind. "The Thembile were determined not to lose out on their plunder a second time. They attacked our vanguard near Saa three times, but we held until they broke."

Abbeba narrowed her eyes. "Why were you in the vanguard to begin with? I thought your father always recommended that you manage the battles from the rear."

Muwali tightened his lips. "Enyi believes that to improve my position within court, it is better to lead from the vanguard to inspire the men, showcase my courage and vigour in ways that are clearly seen and reported upon, and perhaps gain a song or two to be sung by the griots to surge my reputation."

Abbeba sucked her teeth. "Better *your* position? It's only her position she's concerned with. And has she once considered your reluctance toward all that attention?"

"I cannot blame her," Muwali said, shaking his head. "She is a stranger in a strange land. There are many in my court who still view her as a foreign witch or a spy from the Morowans meant to undermine our rise. If ensuring her position and the position of our children means I must endure more risk, then so be it."

And what about our child? Abbeba wanted to scream but held it back with all her might. "What difference does it make if you die in the process?" she said instead. "Will those griots' songs protect her from reprisals then?"

Muwali looked down and rubbed the back of his neck. He always did that when there was a strong point he could not refute. She hated to see him uncomfortable. She wanted to sweep him into her arms right then, but he had to see the dangerous path Enyi had set him on. If he died, she was not sure what she would do. And if Enyi's plan succeeded, it would mean more responsibilities granted to Muwali, which meant less time for him to travel into Kisaye lands for their . . . trade discussions. She did not care if his court would see him as a witless coward. He would be here with her and Anuli—*that* was what mattered.

"How many did you lose in this glorious battle?" Abbeba asked.

"There were many losses," Muwali admitted. "I would have been among them if not for Yemi . . ."

"You see? Think of what would have become of me if you had died," she whispered, drawing closer. "Please, promise me you will find a way to return to the rear during battle."

Muwali swallowed and looked away. "I promise I will try."

"That is all I ask," she said, stroking his beard.

Muwali managed a small grunt and nod in acknowledgement, marking an end to the topic. Abbeba was glad for it. She never had patience for talk of politics and war. It was politics that denied him to her. She already felt her mind wandering and her body aching for his touch once more. She squeezed his hand, hoping to pull him back into their oasis.

"I will be sure to send our best robes to General Yemi's compound as thanks for ensuring you returned to me," she said, leaning forward for a kiss, but Muwali turned his head.

"You will have to send it to his son's compound," Muwali muttered. "He gave his life for mine."

"Shamis burn me!" Abbeba swore. "I'm sorry, I did not know! By the sun, if I had known, I never would have . . . What happened? Are you all right? I know he's become a second father to you since you were educated in his compound! Shamis burn us all, I can—"

Muwali silenced her with a kiss on her forehead. "I am fine, Abbeba. It is . . . difficult to accept that he is across the Uzoigwe River now. One moment, he is beside me, encouraging me to rally the left flank, which was breaking. The next, a spear knocks me from my horse, and he is galloping in front of me, taking the next blow to his neck. It was so quick! There was little I could do . . ."

Abbeba held him close, trying to pass as much of her warmth into him as possible. "When are his final rites?" she asked after a breath.

"In three days. His family is already gathering at his son's compound," Muwali said. "It's partly why I am here. His Ajebilo reading is tonight, and Obioma said there was something of great interest to me within it."

"I have heard that General Yemi has come into great wealth of late," Abbeba said. "Perhaps he wished to share some of it with you?"

"Perhaps," Muwali said. "Although he was always determined to keep the source of this new wealth a secret from me. I am not sure why that would suddenly change, even in death."

"Mother says death reveals our secrets," Abbeba said. "Moreover, you were loyal to him in more ways than his own sons. He wants to reward you; that is all, I am sure of it."

"I hope you are right."

"I am," she said and kissed him deeply. "Now, when is his Ajebilo reading?"

"At sunset," Muwali said with a grin, desire rippling back into his eyes.

"Shamis is still high on his throne," Abbeba said, glancing at the sun. "I believe we have time to continue our earlier discussion."

"I feared you would never ask again, my lady," he whispered.

"I would never deny myself."

He pushed her back against the wall, sliding her robes down past her shoulders. The cold stone against her bare back did little to douse Abbeba's fire. The world and the walls around them crumbled. Only his lips, his flesh, and their embrace remained. His hand found hers, and she squeezed, exclaiming, commanding him to never let go of her again.

On the fringe of her senses, she heard the door leading to the battlements open, and a small rumbling of feet echoed across the stone floor. Abbeba pushed the sound aside. Just a little bit more, then she would worry about it. She felt Muwali hesitate.

"Don't stop, Muwali!" she exclaimed, breaking away from him for a breath. "Shamis's Rays, don't stop now!"

"Abbeba—" he started but said nothing else. Instead, he stopped, pulling himself from her, dousing the blaze that was building within her. Abbeba cried out in frustration and slapped the wall, her voice hoarse and cracked as if she had been denied a large feast after weeks of hunger.

"Shamis burn you!" she swore, turning on her heel, the hem of her robes dropping back to her ankles. "What happened? Why did you—"

Her eyes widened. They were no longer alone on the battlements —far from it. Twenty, perhaps thirty, men in green and yellow chainmail surrounded them. The Kisaye sigil, a mantis at the centre of a rising sun, adorned their breastplates. Two of them restrained the struggling Muwali.

Abbeba's stomach sank to the depths of oblivion. She pulled her robe tighter over her body, the pleasure she felt only breaths before a memory from a lifetime ago.

Captain Kitjita stood in the centre of the circle. His less-than-average height, which she often teased him about, was suddenly enough to tower over her. His square head and thick neck were encased in his helmet and neck guard. Much of his chin was covered by his full beard, slowly being overtaken by grey hairs. Abbeba searched his face for the kind captain of the guard who had often let her ride on his shoulders to give orders to the servants as a child. She saw disdain and disgust.

"Wh-what is the meaning of this, Captain!" Abbeba attempted, keeping a quivering hand on her robes. "RrRelease Prince Muwali at once! We were . . . we were merely in . . . deep discussions regarding our mutual trade agreement!"

A round of soft chuckles among the men was the only response. Captain Kitjita silenced them with a glare, then turned that glare on Muwali. "Prince Muwali," Kitjita said. "You are being placed under house arrest until a ransom payment from your father is discussed, agreed upon, and delivered. Bring no harm to my men, and no harm will come to you. Do you understand?"

Muwali glanced at Abbeba, his eyes pleading, but she could only give him a blank look.

"Yes," Muwali muttered, ceasing what little resistance he had offered. "I understand."

"Good. Take him away."

"Kitjita, stop this madness!" Abbeba exclaimed. "Does my mother know about this? If she doesn't, I'll make sure she has your head!"

Kitjita held up his hand, silencing her. "Princess Abbeba, your mother, our Queen Nituswa, wishes to see you in the throne room. Immediately."

Hiding behind Anulie, Abbeba felt like a coward. But her daughter with only four living years, who sat on her lap and mindlessly nibbled on a stalk of sugar cane, was Abbeba's only shield from Queen Nitsuwa's wrath.

Abbeba had never witnessed the throne room so silent. It was always a place of lively, deafening debates among the council, petitioners, tradesmen, and savants. The griots were always in the corner singing a song in praise of the general or councillor speaking, or taking notes of events occurring so they might turn it into a song later. There was always a small cloud of gossiping servants and helpers moving about the corridors leading to the throne, fetching some parchment or obscure tome to support whatever Mother and the council were arguing about that day.

Today, there was nothing except the occasional small cough from the councillors' table and Mother's heavy and infuriated breathing.

"I should strip you, beat you, and have you run throughout the castle naked for the rest of the year for this foolishness!" Queen Nitsuwa growled from the throne at the centre of the circular chamber. "But I fear even that would be far too merciful!"

Abbeba flinched and pulled Anuli closer to her, making the child squirm. "Mommy, that hurts!" Anuli squeaked, struggling against her vice-like grip. The colourful green and blue glass beads at the end of her plaited hair rattled against Anuli's small shoulders.

"Sorry, precious," Abbeba managed. The glares of her mother, the council, and the stone statues of their ancestors carved into the throne room's walls made Abbeba feel smaller than Anuli. The mere act of lifting her head to face their stares felt like being asked to haul ten boulders on her back up a mountain.

Despite Anuli's squirming, Abbeba pulled her daughter even closer. Her gaze lingered on the green and blue glass beads that were a gift from Muwali for Anuli's third rain day. Abbeba could still remember her daughter's eyes widening when Muwali dismounted in front of their small hut, far from the castle, stooped in front of Anuli, and unwrapped the gift. Anuli was transfixed, not by the glass beads, but by Muwali's violet eyes—a pair of eyes that matched her own.

"Look at me!" Queen Nitsuwa commanded.

Abbeba squeezed her eyes shut, trying to will herself back into the memory. Muwali had placed his hand in Anuli's small one as their daughter led them into the hut, demanding that Muwali place the beads in her hair himself. Abbeba had taken his other hand, and for those three brief days, they were a complete family.

"Look at me!"

A chain of dry and heaving coughs pulled Abbeba back into the throne room and to the sight of her mother doubled over on the throne. The councillors seated around the throne all rose to her aid. They were halted by a lift of Mother's hand—but that was not enough to stop Anuli.

The small child easily broke from Abbeba's grip and dashed to her grandmother's side, her small hands guiding Queen Nitsuwa back into her proper seated position.

"Are you all right, Nana?" Anuli asked, her soft voice easing Abbeba's tense shoulders. "Is the demon winning again?"

Queen Nitsuwa chuckled, earning herself another round of small coughs. "Not today, *bisa*. Your nana still has plenty of fight to give this creature."

"I want to help you feel better," Anuli said, standing on her tiptoes as if ready to face the creature herself.

Queen Nitsuwa smiled and stroked her granddaughter's fat cheeks. "Do you know what would make me feel better? A plate of those fresh puff-puff balls from the kitchen. Could you go fetch some for me?"

Anuli nodded so vigorously that Abebba feared she would snap her neck. Anuli scampered across the throne room, a blur of yellow and blue, her stalk of sugarcane in her mouth to prevent herself from dropping it or losing it. She brushed past Abbeba without a second glance.

"Anuli, get back here!" Abbeba cried, praying to Shamis that she did not sound as desperate to her mother and the council as she feared she did. "Take that sugarcane out of your mouth before you choke!"

Anuli ignored her feeble attempt at authority; she was already squeezing through the small opening in the double doors, two guards flanking her. Abbeba's jaw slackened at how easily her mother had disarmed her sole remaining protection. She trembled as all eyes of the throne room returned to her, boring into her, cutting her to pieces with their mutual glares.

"Look at me, Abbeba," Queen Nitsuwa said once more, all warmth and comfort evaporating from her voice.

Abbeba gulped and could only comply with her mother's command.

Queen Nitsuwa had been ravished by the strange disease devouring her body from the inside out. She wore three layers of thick robes to hide her emaciated form and a tall, wide, and complex gele to better hide the patchwork of bald spots her head had become. Her face was strained, tired, and filled with stress lines, making her look far older than her forty-seven living years. It would soon be time to carry her body to the crypts beneath Semia Mountain, carve her likeness in the walls of the throne room, and ferry her soul back to the great tree, Othamela, where it would await her rebirth.

Her eyes, however, remained as strong as they'd always been. The deep brown eyes that famously halted Mangaliso Otieno's advance, the same eyes that the infamous swindler King Urenna Tidyanawo could not read, cut into Abbeba piece by piece.

"Do you have any idea what you've done?" Mother growled.

"Mother, please . . . it . . . it isn't what you think . . ." Abbeba said to Queen Nitsuwa's round chin. "I . . . I just . . ."

"Twenty years, Abbeba!" Queen Nitsuwa exclaimed. "Twenty years of negotiations, favours, and agreements, in place since the day you were born, all destroyed because of your foolishness! That is what I think!"

"Perhaps the northern mountain clans were wise to adopt the custom of female circumcision from the Eternal Desert kingdoms," Savant Lindani said from the council stools encircling the throne. His triangle-shaped head and almost non-existent neck made him resemble the turtles of his clan's sigil. The chancellor regarded Abbeba with the scornful sneer that was rapidly becoming familiar to her. "Remove their connection with *tamaa,* and these foolish choices cease."

"Might as well castrate all the males in the land if you wish to follow that path, Lindani," War Master Mlamli scoffed. The legs of the stool groaned as he attempted to find a comfortable position for his large body. "*Tamaa* belongs to us all. Cutting it away would be like cutting the wings of a bird or denying a creature air to breathe."

Savant Lindani turned his sneer on the general. "When last I checked, birds do not endanger the entire clan with their wings!"

"I do not believe the situation is that dire," Abbeba muttered.

Every eye in the chamber turned to her. She instantly wished she had said nothing.

Queen Nitsuwa's lips quivered, her rage consuming her eyes. She reached into the folds of her robes, withdrew a scroll of parchment, and tossed it to Abbeba's feet. "Recite this letter and tell me again that you believe our current predicament is not dire!"

Beneath the eyes of everyone in the throne room, Abbeba's quivering hands unrolled the parchment. She began to read, and at once, dread overtook her body

The scroll bore the final words of General Yemi, addressed to his son Obioma. In the letter, General Yemi declared that he knew everything about the four years she and Muwali had had together from the moment they first began during the Koofrey Ceremony of Ancestors. He stated that he had followed Muwali, without the prince's knowledge, to their isolated hut and learned of Anuli. He then took that information to Queen Nitsuwa. For his silence, Mother had paid him exorbitant tributes from the clan's coffers and even her own. His final request to his son was that in the event of his death, regardless of its circumstance, Obioma was to deliver a copy of the letter to King Ekwe Uhitaji, Enyi Kaddara, and Enyi's mother, Lady Fenena of Lazola.

By the time Abbeba finished reading, she wanted nothing more than to vomit. The room spun, she couldn't find her breath, she couldn't stop shaking. This couldn't be true. It wasn't true. They had been careful. She had been careful. They couldn't know about Anuli. If they did . . . they would demand her execution, at the very least, to limit the humiliation. But it wouldn't be enough.

Abbeba trembled in her chair, the scroll slipping from her hands.

"Now you understand," Queen Nitsuwa sneered. "Your foolishness has brought destruction to not only your clan but to my granddaughter!"

Abbeba's throat was bone dry as she searched for a response. "I . . . I was doing as you said! I was keeping our seat independent! Y-your line secured through Anuli and me without the need for a husband. Th-that was all!"

Queen Nitsuwa slammed a hand on the throne, the sound snapping Abbeba into silence. "All you have done is kill us all!"

"N-no! Mother, please! If it comes to war, we can fight them, can we not?"

"War Master Mlamli," Queen Nitsuwa said. "If we were to sound the Call to Arms today, how many men could we expect on the field of battle?"

"If we use the last of our coffers to buy additional mercenaries, I estimate we could field 3,500 men," Mlami said quietly.

"And how many men can the Uhitaji field with their Lazola and Morowan allies?"

"The Uhitaji have 20,000 men at their disposal, according to our scouts' reports from last season. And the Lazolans will be able to provide an additional 40,000, with perhaps another 50,000 from the Morowans as a favour to Lady Fenena."

"110,000 against our 3,500, Abbeba. Do you still believe we can fight them?"

"W-we have more than men and spears to fight, Mother," Abbeba said. "We have Sobilla's Chronicle. We can use its magic to—"

"Do you truly believe the mantis and the Elder Gods will answer our cries for aid after this? After you broke its primary tenant, to bring no harm to the clan? To use the chronicle now would further ensure our destruction!"

Abbeba held her head to keep her skull from crumbling. This wasn't happening. It couldn't be.

Using all of her will, she looked Mother in the eye. "Where is Prince Muwali? What is being done to him?"

"Prince Muwali remains under house arrest," Captain Kitjita said. "He remains an agreeable hostage."

"I have already dispatched Half-Head messengers to King Ekwe, informing him of his son's capture," Queen Nitsuwa said. "With luck and the guidance of Shamis, his concern for his son will overtake his wounded pride and reputation. He will not launch an attack against us if his son is at risk—we can use that to negotiate terms."

"King Ekwe may also use the negotiation to buy time for his Lazolan allies to arrive and launch an assault regardless," Savant Lindani said.

"Let me speak with Muwali," Abbeba said. "I—I can convince him to write to his father and request that he hold off all military action. Or even tell him to inform his father that General Yemi's letter is a forgery. Or—"

"Abbeba, you are never seeing him again," Queen Nitsuwa said firmly.

"Mother, please! I can fix this, I can!"

"Get out of my sight!" Queen Nitsuwa bellowed.

Her voice crumbled the last of Abbeba's resolve. She made herself walk out of the throne room. The servants pulled the double doors closed and latched them behind her.

Abbeba could still feel her mother's glare on her back.

SOBILLA'S CHRONICLE hummed with a faint power that singed the air. Four bolts of emerald lightning flared across its cover as Abbeba approached it. The compendium of mystical knowledge gathered by their ancestor, Savant Sobillia, sat in a forgotten corner of the archive, enclosed in the stone hands of Savant Sobillia's dusty statue. Abbeba traced the image of the praying mantis that guided Sobillia through the multiple domains of the Elder Gods, engraved on the chronicle's cover: the mantis who carried messages between mortals and the gods, the mantis who had guided past Kisaye queens with its foresight, the mantis who Abbeba hoped would answer her prayers now.

There was only darkness behind her eyes. For six breaths, she waited, her body tense, awaiting the mantis's reply. But there was none. She pressed her hand harder on the chronicle and recited the prayer again, but there was nothing. She heard herself curse, cry out, and plead to the mantis to hear her, but an empty darkness greeted her.

"Please!" Abbeba cried. "Please, I promise on my soul, just help me fix this. Take my soul if you must, but don't let them take Anuli! Please, show me what to do. Show me the way!"

Silence dominated the archives. Abbeba gulped back a sob and began to pull her hand away, but then she felt it: a pulse of heat.

Emerald light flickered on the cover as if the chronicle was stirring from a long rest. A small storm of emerald lightning bolts surged around it. Abbeba tried to remove her hand, but something pulled against her, keeping her in place. The emerald light twisted around her arm, filling it with the heat of a blazing bushfire. She tried to scream, but she had no voice.

The light shot toward her eyes. Abbeba reeled back at last. Her vision flashed from white to black to green to yellow, over and over. Her body shook, her legs lost strength, and her throat shrivelled.

Her stomach lurched up into her throat as if being yanked from her body. The world twisted and churned, and she was caught in the centre, spinning in every direction.

Abbeba wasn't sure how long she spun. Ten breaths? Twenty? Only when it stopped did she dare to open her eyes.

She was back on the battlements, Shamis high in the sky, the archives a distant memory. Her head pounded, and her stomach was twisted in knots. She went to rub her throbbing temples, and her fingers brushed against something cold and metallic on her head. It encircled her forehead and strained her neck. When she pulled her hand away, she found that her fingers were covered in rings. Her mother's rings. Why was she wearing them?

"My queen!" War Master Mlamli exclaimed behind her. "My queen! My queen, what are your orders?"

Abbeba shook her head. Why wasn't Mother answering Mlamli?

"Queen Abbeba!" Mlamli bellowed. "Your orders!"

The sound of her name cleared the fog around her vision. She was queen; her mother was dead, the disease having finally taken her, and . . . Abbeba glanced around at the row of archers and spearmen on the battlements, dressed in full armour, fear and desperation consuming their faces as the torn Kisaye banners flew overhead. They were at war.

Abbeba heard herself demand a spyglass, and she looked over the battlements. A full host of warriors surrounded the castle, and the Uhitaji banner, a bucking black bull against a red field, flanked by two spears, flew above the invading army.

Her stomach dropped to her knees when she saw the general at the front of their vanguard, shouting orders to the men charging their gates.

Muwali.

She dropped the spyglass.

"No! What happened?" Abbeba exclaimed, the crown nearly falling. "Muwali was under house arrest!"

War Master Mlamli stared at her as if she had grown two heads. "That was ten months ago, my queen."

Abbeba gaped at the general. "No! He was captured. We were caught and—and he was to be ransomed!"

"He was," Mlamli muttered. "Instead, you freed him, believing it would show good faith to the Uhitaji. But then . . ." He gestured toward the army below them.

Abbeba felt the strength leave her legs and clutched at the battlements for support. *No, he wouldn't, he couldn't!* "Where's Anuli!"

"She's with her sister under guard in the central tower, as you commanded," Mlami said. "My queen, the enemy is preparing to assault the walls! I do not understand what game this is, but the men need to know your orders! The walls will fall if we do nothing!"

Sister? Queen? Assault? War? None of it made sense. She needed somewhere quiet, she needed to think, she needed . . .

Abbeba shook her head, her throat constricted, and her hand flared with emerald light. "Make it stop!" she bellowed.

The emerald light consumed her vision, and darkness followed.

"Abbeba!" she heard. "Abbeba, wake up! You're having a nightmare!"

Abbeba's eyes flew open, and she was greeted by a pair of lavender eyes.

"Every archer to the walls! Aim for the battering rams!" she shouted, clambering to her feet. "Spearmen reinforce the gate and signal the vanguard to flank the doors and surround the attackers!"

But rather than the affirming yell of War Master Mlamli, the only response was Muwali's blank stare and the faint crying of a baby in the corner.

Muwali sighed and ran a hand through his still-short but growing hair. "I just managed to get her to sleep . . ."

Abbeba took six breaths, her heart racing. She turned her hands over three times: no rings. She felt her forehead. No crown. She looked around: no battlements. She was surrounded by the cracked mudbricks and round roof of a small hut. Rays of light poked through their meagre door that barely held back the sounds of a pair of feet running to and from the hut, a girl's laughter accompanying each step.

Muwali gathered the baby in his arms and began to rock it back it forth, reciting a rhyme or song.

"A-Anuli isn't a baby," Abbeba muttered. "She has four years . . ."

"Utulizi seems to have done a number on your mother with his music, Kianga," Muwali said to the baby.

Abbeba rubbed her pounding forehead and took a breath. "Where are we? Where's Anuli? Who is Kianga?"

Muwali gaped at her. "I think that is the last time I let you have palm wine, Abbeba!"

"Muwali, please. I—I can't . . ."

He pulled her to him with his free arm while the baby snuggled closer. "It's all right. I suppose we both had too much."

"I just need an answer . . ." Abbeba whispered.

"We're home," Muwali said simply. "Anuli is outside gathering seashells as she usually does. She wants to make another bracelet for her sister."

"S-sister?" Abbeba's eyes fell to the baby. "Kianga, I take it?"

"Yes," Muwali said, raising an eyebrow. "She's only seen three moons, but she's strong."

Abbeba stared at Kianga, a small brown bundle that had Muwali's slight forehead and her round chin. She expected a flood of memories and recognition to fill her chest, but there was none.

"The sea . . ." she whispered. "We—we're by the sea?"

"Yes, Teremesha, to the far west by the coast, like you said," Muwali said. "You said it was the best place for us after we escaped."

Abbeba blinked. "E-escaped? What happened to the castle? My mother? Our clans?"

Muwali swallowed; he suddenly could not look her in the eye. "I-I thought we agreed we wouldn't speak of it, especially not with Kianga—"

"I changed my mind, Muwali! Tell me!"

Kianga fussed and cried into her father's chest. Muwali looked down, tears forming in his eyes, as well.

"They're gone, Abbeba," he whispered. "Everything, everyone, they're gone. Your mother, she . . . my father . . . They burned her alive when the castle fell. They couldn't find you, they couldn't find us, so they . . . used her instead. The rest they slaughtered or enslaved. War Master Mlamli and some warriors escaped. They sneaked into Uhitaji castle, found my father, Enyi, and my children, and they . . . gods, Abbeba, please don't make it say it again . . . I can't!!"

Abbeba quivered, her head continuing to pulse. "M-my clan, my people . . ."

"You are all that's left," Muwali said. "They destroyed Cilombo, chopped down the great tree—everything is gone, Abbeba. If we hadn't escaped when we did . . ."

"No . . . no!" Abbeba whispered, holding her head.

Green light flashed in the corner of her vision.

"Mommy?" Anuli called from the door.

Muwali held her tighter, but his grip vanished like smoke.

ABBEBA BLINKED. She was now atop a horse; a storm of heavy rain and bolts of lightning flashed above them. A long line of people, servants, savants, warriors, and low castes walked in a steady line, soaked but relieved. A handful of them continued to look back at the burning castle in the distance. Abbeba gripped the reins of her horse, and her stomach dropped yet again. She was wearing her mother's rings.

"I must admit, I did not think it would work," Savant Lindani said, trotting beside her. "But the storm you summoned was the perfect cover to evacuate the castle, my queen. I can only pray that War Master Mlamli and the souls of his men find some solace in that as they return to Othamela."

Abbeba shivered beneath the rain. Only then did she notice Sobilla's Chronicle tied to her horse's flank, flickering with a faint emerald glow.

"I am queen," Abbeba muttered, the crown shifting on her head. "And my mother . . . ?"

Savant Lindani looked down. "I once again apologize for our failure to save her body, but there just wasn't time—the Uhitaji were days away from their assault. We had to move quickly."

"No, it's all right," Abbeba said, her voice hoarse. "I imagine I commanded this retreat?"

"Of course, my queen," Savant Lindani said. "You said your tempest spell was the only hope for our clan."

"Anuli!" Abbeba called.

Her daughter waved from Captain Kitjita's horse. The old captain held her firm on the horse's saddle.

"She's excited to meet her sister," Savant Lindani said.

Abbeba glanced down and ran a hand over her swollen belly.

"Although I advise we keep that among ourselves for now," Savant Lindani continued. "We do not wish to give the Uhitaji further cause than they already have."

"Prince Muwali isn't with us?"

"You commanded that he remain in the castle," Savant Lindani said. "The Uhitaji would have pursued if he were with us. If he is found in the castle, they will be satisfied for now, giving us the time to regroup. As you said, the clan must survive. Are you having second thoughts, my queen?"

The emerald light on the chronicle intensified. Abbeba's head throbbed. "No," she muttered. "I supposed not. We move forward. We survive . . ."

The light consumed her vision.

<hr>

ABBEBA GASPED and was unable to find her breath. She pressed her head against a cold stone floor, rubbed her temples, and waited for the room to stop spinning. She braced herself for whatever was left to see.

When she opened her eyes, she was back in the archives. The stone statue of Savant Sobilla looked down on her with its blank eyes. The chronicle flashed green before flickering to nothing. Abbeba checked her hand: no rings. She checked her head: no crown. The only change was that the mantis on the chronicle's cover was now burned into the palm of her hand.

"Shamis burn me," she whispered to the empty archive. Her body felt heavy, as if she had aged at least ten years. Her limbs felt even heavier, and her neck was stiff, but her heart was steady, and her mind was clear.

"P-Princess Abbeba," a small voice whispered behind a stack of tomes. A servant with thirteen living years scurried out when she responded and pressed a small piece of parchment into her hand. "Our . . . special guest . . . asked me to deliver this message to you."

Before she could respond, the servant fled out of the archive.

Abbeba stared at the folded parchment. She expected to feel some form of curiosity or urge to open it, but she already knew what it said. It was from Muwali, asking her to come see him, where she would discuss escaping. She could see and hear the conversation as if she were peering around the corner, watching it from a distance.

She turned to the door on the north side of the archive. She already heard the small feet of Anuli dashing down the corridor. She could already see the stream of tears rolling down her cheeks, with Captain Kitjita struggling to keep pace with her.

Abbeba walked over to the door and counted to three.

The door flew open, and Anuli sprinted to her already outstretched arms.

"Mommy! Mommy! Nana! She fell! She's not waking up!" Anuli cried. "I went to give her mangos and—"

"She fell on her way to the table," Abbeba finished.

Anuli nodded, burying her face in Abbeba's chest.

Captain Kitjita stepped forward, about to recite all that he and his men were doing to tend to Queen Nitsuwa.

"Just keep her comfortable, Captain," Abbeba said at once.

Captain Kitjita stiffened. He looked her up and down and then raised an eyebrow. "Of course, Princess."

Abbeba lifted Anuli and tucked the chronicle under her arm. "Tell Savant Lindani, when he gets here, to prepare our ransom demands for King Ekwe tonight. Have the Half-Heads prepared to deliver it by morning."

Captain Kitjita titled his head. "Yes, Princess. And if King Ekwe rejects the demands and declares war . . .?"

Abbeba stared at Muwali's letter. She rubbed Anuli's back as her daughter cried on her shoulder. She pressed the chronicle closer to her body and took a breath. The room was quiet, and she could feel the faintest pulse of Kianga in her belly.

Abbeba took one more look at Muwali's letter and crumpled it.

"We move forward," she said with a calm certainty. "We survive. The clan must survive, no matter what. Do you understand, Captain?"

Captain Kitjita blinked four times before swallowing his words and nodding.

"Yes, Princess Abbeba," he said.

Abbeba rocked her daughter as she fell into step with Captain Kijita. "Hush, Anuli," she whispered. "Let's go see Nana one last time, all right?"

Anuli sniffed and managed a small nod.

Abbeba walked down the corridor, and the castle walls crumbled around her.

A JUGGLER'S FARCE

Natalie Wright

Chapter 1

Micah longed for the King to bestow a bard's frilly, starched collar upon him. Instead, Micah donned a fool's motley and placed a bell-tipped jester's cap upon his head.

The Mimswood Mummers had arrived in the Kingdom of Cinorom to perform for King Briscalo's summer festival. Among the jugglers, puppeteers, thespians, dancers, and other performers, none amused the King as much as Micah, the Stuttering Storyteller.

Shari, a gifted thespian in the Mimswood, painted red circles on Micah's cheeks. "Cheer up, Micah. We players perform last and to an audience overstuffed with food and drink. Men snore—I've even heard the Queen snore." She sighed. "At least the King notices you."

The sentiment did not lighten Micah's mood.

"I am a w-w-writer, not a f-f-f-fool." Micah wiped the spittle from his lip. "I should have a b-b-bard's c-c-c-collar. Not m-m-m . . ." The effort of speaking made his face turn crimson.

Shari finished his sentence. "Motley?"

Micah nodded.

Juggling bean bags for practice, Petru tossed one over his left shoulder, then another over his right, keeping the bags in the air. "You want a bard's collar? Stop st-st-stuttering."

Shari snatched one of Petru's bags from the air and hurled it at him. "Do not make a jest at Micah's expense. He cannot help the way he speaks."

Her expression of pity didn't cheer Micah but instead made him feel worse. *Pity will not win her hand*, Micah thought.

A page entered the small courtyard where the Mimswood Mummers had gathered to await their time to perform. The page whistled and called, "Fool—the King awaits you." He clapped and said, "Make haste."

Shari plucked lint from Micah's arm. "Best hurry." She glanced up at him, then straightened his jester's cap. "All in our troupe know you are no fool, Micah. The Court's Fool is merely a role. Like how I play Princess Anakara in our play. If old King Briscalo pays you to perform as a fool, give him the best fool. Then, after you remove the costume and paint, you are Micah, the writer, again."

This time, her words gave him courage. "W-w-wish me l-l-luck." Micah scurried to catch up to the page.

The page led him through a maze of hallways from the small outer courtyard to the grand hall where King Briscalo feasted, decked out for the month-long summer feasting with colourful ribbons, flowers, and banners. Lords, ladies, knights, and honoured guests, wearing their finery, gathered each summer to feast and pay homage to King Briscalo.

Three Mimswood musicians played a jaunty march as Micah entered the room. He walked up the centre aisle between tables of guests. The area before the King's table served as his stage. Micah gave a low bow, the bells on his jester's cap tinkling as he took it off and swept his arm out wide.

As Micah bowed, the Mimswood players allowed their song to go off-key and wither as it tapered to its end. The crowd laughed and clapped.

Previously occupied in conversation with one of his favoured lords, Ser Blancnez, the King turned his attention to Micah. Typically,

King Briscalo's brows knitted into a wrinkly furrow, and his lips turned downward in a permanent frown. But now, the King's lips curled into a sneer he perhaps intended as a smile. He waved his hand in the air. "Rise, Knight of Fools."

Undaunted by the crowd's cheers and jeers, Micah rose. He put the jester's hat atop his head again. "W-w-w-what t-t-tale shall I s-s-spin, S-S-S-Sire?"

The King stroked his beard and chuckled. "A year has passed since you were last called to my court, Fool, and I see you remain in the stammering way."

The gathered nobles joined the King's mirth.

"While I enjoy a witty and well-told tale, especially a salacious one about that bitter old shrew in that simpering realm to the north—"

The nobles clanged their goblets. Their cheers echoed off the high wooden rafters.

Seeing that the crowd appreciated his side-wise blow to Queen Karia'idaz from the northern realm of Ekalfons, the King's eyes sparkled with mischief. "Karia'idaz is so bitter even her teats give sour milk."

The crowd's laughter rose, and men pounded their mugs and stomped their feet.

The King riles them with his rancour against the queen of the northern realm, Micah thought. *Their hatred of her grows with each joke he tells at her expense.*

"Could you spin a yarn about that dreadful hag?" King Briscalo asked.

Micah opened his mouth to speak and got out only, "I c-c-c—"

But King Briscalo shook his head. "No, I suppose you can't." He waved his hand absent-mindedly. "All right, then. A foolish farce it is." He raised his cup to his wife, Queen Donafalsa, seated to his right. "My queen, you choose the Fool's Farce today. What type of tale do you fancy?"

Though they were only three courses into a seven-course meal, Queen Donafalsa's eyes were already bleary with drink. The Queen leaned forward and gestured at Micah with her cup, wine jostling out. "Everyone loves gallantry." The Queen hiccupped, and her eyes landed on a young nobleman at the nearest table. "Tell us a romantic tale, Fool. Of a beautiful lady and her brave lover."

The feasting nobles cheered, clapped, and whistled. "Hear, hear!"

Over the years, Micah had written many stories. Tales of great battles fought by courageous heroes to win a lady's love were among his favourites. He had just the tale to fit the Queen's request.

But his anxiety rendered his tongue a useless, flapping hunk of pink flesh as he spoke. Micah began, "In a f-f-far away l-l-l-l . . ." His face was already red with exertion. Micah wiped his brow and tried to gather himself.

Laughter rose from the crowd behind him. The Queen lifted her cup, and a wine server filled it. "Better refill everyone's cup," she said. "This will take a while." While the revellers chortled, the Queen leaned forward and said to Micah, "Cat got your tongue?"

He hadn't needed Shari to paint the red circles on his cheeks. Micah's face was aflame with humiliation and frustration. "It is a play, and you are a player," Shari had said. "If the King wants a farce, play your part well."

Remembering Shari's belief in him helped Micah gather the strength to continue. Micah breathed deeply and continued, stammering through an abbreviated version of his chivalric tale. He had just gotten past the setup when a nobleman from a front table gave Micah a playful kick in the rear.

The blow wounded Micah's pride more than his bottom. The crowd rewarded the kicker with uproarious applause, prompting another to join the game.

Micah gamely continued his telling, stuttering more with each blow to his rear. Soon, the laughter and cheers drowned Micah's voice as drunk noblemen beleaguered the poor stuttering storyteller.

Finally, King Briscalo rose, and the laughter abated. "Now, now. Do not lay hands—or feet, I should say—on my fool."

The crowd tittered but ceased kicking Micah. King Briscalo's intervention was part of the act. The point of the play was to show the

King's grace and compassion toward his subjects, no matter how low their station. *Ironic*, Micah thought. He recalled that King Briscalo had begun the taunts and humiliations five seasons ago when Micah first appeared in this court.

King Briscalo snapped his fingers. A page came from behind the dais and walked toward Micah.

"Good Fool, you have entertained my court well this day. I award you a collar to show that all in my kingdom may rise within the ranks."

Micah knew what to do. He removed his jester's cap, the bells tinkling. He bowed, and the page placed a flimsy, crocheted lace collar around his neck. The crowd applauded, and King Briscalo waited patiently for the pageant to conclude. Intended to symbolize the King's grace, the lacy collar lay limp and pathetic against Micah's neckline instead of standing up like a proper collar of honour or nobility.

Not like a bard's collar in the slightest, Micah thought.

He wanted to rip the flaccid bit of lace from his neck, but such an insult to the King would land him in a dungeon cell. Instead, Micah swept into a low bow, acknowledging the King's benevolence for allowing even a lowly fool to wear a collar.

Micah swept up and returned his jingly hat to his head to light applause from the crowd and King Briscalo. The farce was complete. The King nodded once, dismissing Micah.

Glad to be done with the performance, Micah scurried from the place, his eyes hot and his face red. When he was out of sight of the court, he ripped the lacy collar from his neck. He used the cloth to remove the painted circles from his cheeks, soiling the white threads.

The Mimswood players expected him to return to the courtyard. He was in no mood to suffer through retelling or questions. Instead, he ran to the market square, intending to tuck into an inn for a mug of mead.

At a corner, he stopped to catch his breath. An elderly man standing in an open market stall caught his eye. The man's scraggly beard was as white as the milky film on his eyes. A weathered sign hung askew over the stall, the painted letters faded. The placard said, "Morago's Curios."

Nothing about the jumble of detritus strewn about the stall invited Micah's curiosity, but the elderly man did. Morago's milky eyes evidenced he was likely blind or nearly so. Nonetheless, Morago juggled a set of red rings without missing a single toss. Micah counted—three, five—no, seven rings spinning into the air.

Micah had been a part of the Mimswood Mummers for nearly a decade and had known many jugglers in his time. Even his friend Petru likely could not juggle so well, even with perfect eyesight.

He approached Morago and stared in awe. "H-h-how...?"

The old man sniffed the air but didn't miss a beat in his juggling. "You smell of mummery. And defeat."

Micah thrust his chin out and stood taller. He resented being seen so clearly. *By a blind man, no less.* "Not de-de-defea-f-f-feat. Not ex-ex-xactly." He cleared his throat and repeated his question. "H-h-how?"

Without interrupting his flow, Morago tossed a ring toward Micah. Usually as inept with his hands as he was at speaking, Micah caught the ring. The cool metal felt good in his sweaty palm. Morago then lobbed a second ring Micah's way, aiming it perfectly.

Micah caught this ring with his left hand, now holding a red ring in each hand.

"Are you a mummer or a moron?" the old man asked.

Morago's tone made Micah feel more like the latter than the former. "W-w-what d-d-do I do with th-th-these?"

"Juggle them, of course," Morago said.

"I'm n-n-not a j-j-j-jugg-l-l-ler." Micah tossed the first ring and then the other anyway. Usually unable to catch even one of Petru's juggling bags, Micah kept the rings flowing without dropping them.

Morago cast another ring to Micah, and he caught it while keeping two rings soaring. "Are these rings magical?" The question remained unanswered, but Micah caught the fourth ring and soon the fifth, all while juggling the others.

"You didn't answer me," Micah said.

The old man stayed silent but tossed his remaining rings to

Micah. With the aptitude of a man who had juggled all his life, Micah readily incorporated the remaining rings. He now kept seven rings aloft with agile grace. A small crowd gathered to witness his feat.

This time, the crowd clapped and cheered instead of jeers and kicks.

"Tell your tale now, storyteller," Morago said.

Keeping the rings spinning, Micah turned to the small audience of passers-by. He cleared his throat, took a deep breath, and began. "A long time ago, in a sunlit kingdom ruled by a fair and benevolent king, there lived a beautiful maiden with amber eyes and wheat-gold hair."

Though he kept his eyes on the rings, Micah felt the crowd's rapt attention. And he realized he hadn't stammered in the slightest.

Micah's story flowed like water from a snowmelt spring. Once finished, he gathered the rings and took a bow. The crowd showered him with applause, and coins clinked at his feet.

Micah bowed again and gathered the money. After the crowd dispersed, he turned to inquire about purchasing the rings from old Morago.

But the milky-eyed man was gone, as was his curio stand. Instead, Micah now stood before a milkmaiden's stall selling creamy cheeses from Ekalfons. The fair-skinned milk maiden smiled and offered him a sample.

Not one to disregard an opportunity to eat the finest cheese in all the realms, Micah took the offering but asked, "W-w-where is the b-b-blind m-m-man? The old j-j-jugg-g-gler." Hoping she'd understand his inquiry, he held the rings aloft.

The milkmaid shrugged. "Have not seen a blind man this morn."

Micah searched the square but glimpsed no sign of the milky-eyed man. With rings still in hand and ample coin in his pocket, he gave up the fruitless search. Instead, he turned his sights on a nearby inn.

There, he bought a trencher of peppery stew, mead, and a honey cake. *A feast fit for a king*, Micah thought. He glanced at the rings he'd laid on the table. *Or a proper bard.*

Not one to question the providence of a much-longed-for boon, Micah gave no further thought to the origin of old Morago or the rings. *With these, I will finally throw off the jester's crown and fool's motley,* he thought. *And win at last the bard's collar—and Shari's hand.*

Chapter 2

THE FOLLOWING WEEK, Micah was again called upon to perform, at the King's last feast of the season. Shari came to paint his face, but Micah pushed her paintbrush away. "No f-f-fool's cos-cos-cos-tume t-t-today," he said.

Shari took a step back and cocked her head. "Where is your cap?" She looked him up and down. "And your motley? Aren't you going to perform today?"

Micah held up the rings. "J-j-juggle."

She frowned and shook her head. "There are plenty of jugglers among the troupe. Good ones."

Micah's eyes brightened, and he took her hand. "C-c-come w-w-with and s-s-see."

Shari looked away but didn't pull her hand from his. "I don't know."

"P-p-please," he said.

Perhaps seeing the pleading in his eyes, Shari relented. "I hope you don't get kicked from the palace or booted from the Mimswood Mummers for this."

As with the prior performance, a page came for Micah and escorted him and Shari to the feasting hall. And as last time, the Mimswood musicians played a march to announce the Knight of Fools. Micah marched with confidence up the centre aisle. Shari joined the Mimswood musicians left of the stage, a vantage point from which she could watch Micah perform.

When King Briscalo saw Micah wasn't wearing the fool's costume, he frowned. "What is this, Fool? Did we interrupt your sleep?" The

King glanced over at Shari, who was joining the musicians. "Or perhaps a roll in the hay?"

The feasters laughed nervously. They tittered and talked about Micah in whispers.

Micah bowed deeply. When he rose, he held the rings aloft. "I h-h-have a n-n-new act."

Still with a deeply furrowed brow, the King waved him off. "I have suffered through too many jugglers already."

Undaunted, Micah tossed the rings. One, then two, three, four. As soon as he had a quintet of rings flying, he spoke. "Not just juggling, sire. I now tell tales while spinning the rings."

Micah now had King Briscalo's full attention. There were more hushed whispers at his back, and he heard a woman say, "He stammers no more."

All seven rings now circling in the air over his head, Micah continued. "Last week, you asked for a salacious story about Queen Karia'idaz of the cream-drenched realm to the north."

King Briscalo's frown was gone, and he leaned forward, his attention rapt. "You have such a story to tell?"

Taking a cue from the King's slander of Queen Karia'idaz at the last feast, Micah launched into a story he felt would please Briscalo. "You said the northern queen was so bitter that even her teats give soured milk."

The crowd laughed at this joke again, and Briscalo's eyes glistened with delight.

Micah continued. "'Tis true, sire, and more."

The crowd gasped. Their whispers were a hushed buzz behind him.

"Do tell us more," King Briscalo said.

"You see, Queen Karia'idaz has cavorted with a demon of the darkest sort."

The laughter calmed as the revellers leaned in to listen. Even King Briscalo sat forward in his chair, waiting to hear more.

All eyes on him, Micah spun a wildly imaginative story, even for fiction. "Travellers recently returned from Ekalfons say the northern queen's consort has horns sprouting from his head and a pointed tail that lashes."

King Briscalo asked, "Speak you true?"

"I am a story spinner, not a courier or town crier," Micah said. He continued his inventive and farcical tale. "Queen Karia'idaz's unholy union casts a shadow upon Ekalfons's glen and glade, the evil pact infecting farm and field. Now, even the cows of her realm give milk so dour, it comes out curdled and sour."

King Briscalo laughed so hard the feast table shook. Queen Donafalsa snickered and hiccupped. The crowd at Micah's back cheered and banged their mugs and cups.

Emboldened by their approval, Micah continued the tale while keeping his seven rings soaring and spinning. "Laughing and cavorting with her devilish mate, Queen Sourmilk allows malevolence to taint even the cheese we once all ate."

Queen Donafalsa, eating Ekalfons double cream, curled her lip in disgust. She dropped the cheese onto her plate and pushed it away.

Micah continued with his farcical tale, poking fun at the northern realm and its queen. His arms finally tiring, he finished his story. He bowed and received applause like never before.

While Micah took in the adulation of the gathered, King Briscalo called his page and whispered in his ear. This time, the page proffered a standup collar instead of bringing forth the flaccid lace meant to humiliate.

Beaming proudly, Micah bent his head to receive the starched frills about his neck. The thick collar irritated his skin, but Micah didn't complain. He'd waited his whole life to claim the title and fame.

With nary a reference to how just a week ago he'd hailed Micah as the Knight of Fools, the King now stood, raised his cup, and toasted anew. "To the Bard of the Mimswood!"

The audience cheered. "Hear, hear!"

Micah took additional bows and soaked up the applause before exiting the stage. He looked for Shari, but she no longer stood with the musicians; she had fled the hall.

She didn't stay to see my triumph, he thought. The page escorted him again, but this time to a table in the hall to join the feasting. With the rings now resting on the table, Micah's faulty tongue would betray him. Micah stuffed his mouth with pheasant and bread, trying to remain silent so he wouldn't bring shame to the new collar he wore.

In the following weeks, nobles spread the tale he'd told at the King's feast. It grew as gossip does, taking nasty turns down paths not even a skilled storyteller would imagine. Soon, the Queen of Ekalfons and her fictional cavorting were to blame for every manner of ill that the Kingdom of Cinorom had ever suffered. People throughout the Kingdom of Cinorom now swore that Ekalfonss' milk was sour and the cheese mouldy.

The King, perhaps taking it too much to heart, decreed a halt to imports of the cheese, cream, and other delicious dairy products his kingdom had once enjoyed from Ekalfons. Now, milk from Queen Karia'idaz's realm was taboo.

As the season wound down, the Mimswood prepared to journey north to play, as always, at Queen Karia'idaz's Autumnal Fest. The players were ready to travel away from Cinorom this year, as the negative gossip had become difficult to bear.

Packing her costumes, Shari was lighter in mood than she'd been since Micah set the tale in motion. "I will be glad to be far from this place. Perhaps these gossips will reign in their rancour by the time we return next year."

Eager to win back the favour he'd somehow lost, Micah nodded, quick to agree.

Shari's lips curled in disgust. "How dare you agree? You started all this!"

Genuinely surprised by her lack of enthusiasm for his triumph, Micah hissed. *Jealously prevents her good nature from applauding my success*, he thought. "I am a b-b-bard," he said. "It was only a s-s-story."

Her face red, Shari shoved a costume into a crate. Micah's

stammer interrupted the flow of his words and made it difficult to state his case.

He turned to leave, but a courier halted his progress. The messenger held out a gold platter with a parchment bearing the King's crested seal. Micah pointed to himself, miming the query. "For me?"

The courier nodded, and Micah took the note. He opened it quickly, and his eyes grew wide with each line he read.

Formerly so angry she no longer wanted to speak to him, curiosity ended Shari's silence. "What does it say?"

The messenger, perhaps also curious, remained rather than scurrying away.

"The K-K-King w-w-wants . . ." Frustrated, Micah handed the letter to Shari. "R-r-read aloud."

Shari's eyes scanned the page, and her mouth opened in awe. She then read out loud the King's words. "Addressed to Micah, Bard of the Mimswood Mummers." Shari glanced at Micah. "That's you." She returned her attention to the message. "King Briscalo has named you 'Briscalo's Bard' and offers you a permanent position as Bard of the Kingdom of Cinorom, with all rights, privileges, and appurtenances accruing to said title."

Her mouth agape, Shari returned the letter to Micah. "Well, I guess this is it, Bard. All you ever wanted."

Micah tucked the note in his pocket and handed the courier a coin to dismiss him. "N-n-not all," he said. He touched her arm and caught her eye. "If I r-r-rem-m-main with the M-M-Mummers, will you-you-you stay c-c-cross?"

She sighed, and Micah pushed stray hair from her face. Shari took his hands in hers and said, "Dammit, Micah, how can I remain angry with you? You are my oldest friend. And perhaps away from here, journeying somewhere new, will replace the unease of this place."

And so, Micah turned down the generous offer. Though typically quick to anger, King Briscalo's ire softened to disappointment when he learned that love for a woman lurked behind Micah's decision.

Chapter 3

THE TROUPE JOURNEYED over rutted roads to Queen Karia'idaz's northern realm of Ekalfons. Even the Mimswood Mummers began to believe the dairy of the realm was now tainted and unworthy. *They know it started with a story I spun—a fiction, a lie.* Micah now regretted he'd made the story so outlandish. *How was I to know anyone would believe such an obvious fiction?* He sighed, resigned that he could not reign in the gossip that had already spread. *A tale once told cannot be unspun.*

The mummers journeyed for nearly two months by wagon on a rutted road through forest and field. Almost a year since they last visited the realm of Ekalfons, they expected it to remain the same. As soon as they neared the gates, though, the mummers sensed something had altered the typically fair aura of the place.

Ekalfons had been a flourishing realm in which prosperity flowed as freely as the milk from their famed cows. Micah had never seen a single person in want there.

Now, the Mimswood's wagons passed beggars on the side of the cobbled streets. People had boarded up the windows and doors of many shops. The market square, usually bustling, was nearly empty.

Shari and Micah exchanged concerned looks.

Petru spoke the sentiment they all shared. "It's like we rode into the dark days after the plague."

The people of Ekalfons, known far and wide as the friendliest anywhere, met them with downcast eyes and forlorn faces. Camping at the northwest edge of the capital, they learned that rumours about mouldy cheese and soured cream had spread like dandelion seeds in autumn winds. Not only had Cinorom halted all shipments of Ekalfons's wares to their kingdom, but the western city-state of Seaside had also refused imports from Ekalfons.

"This is n-n-nuts," Micah said as he sipped a frothy, creamy concoction that was an Ekalfons specialty. The drink tasted as sublime as ever. He wiped foam from his moustache. "N-n-nothing wrong with their c-c-cream."

Shari grabbed the mug from Micah's hand. "This is all your fault. You don't deserve this." She drank the creamy drink and drained the mug.

"It was j-j-just a s-s-story."

"Words matter, Micah. You, of all people, should know that. You spun a tale that you knew was false about a real person. And for what? Attention? Applause?"

"D-d-dignity," Micah stuttered.

"Dignity?" Petru tsked and hurled one of his juggling bags at Micah's beltline, hitting his coin purse. "And money. The nobles filled y bag with coin."

Heat bloomed from Micah's neck to hairline. He picked up the bag, drew his arm back, and prepared to fire it at Petru. He aimed low, hoping to hurt more than Petru's feelings.

But Shari stayed Micah's hand. "Stop it, both of you." Shari gently tossed the bag back to Petru. She pointed to the rings hanging from Micah's belt. "You perform for Queen Karia'idaz tomorrow. Spin a story to lift the spirits of this place."

Shari and Micah had grown close again during their journey north. Eager to remain in her good graces, he said, "I will try."

Micah entered the Queen's feast hall and immediately knew the crowd's mood was sour. Queen Karia'idaz, known for her dry wit and overall jovial demeanour, sat askew on her throne, her brow furrowed, her gaze far away.

The Mimswood musicians played a fanfare, and the Queen didn't even glance Micah's way.

How can I fulfill my promise to Shari and lift their spirits when no one will notice what I say? Micah coughed and began juggling the rings to rouse the Queen's attention.

Queen Karia'idaz cast a nonchalant gaze his way. She sat forward when she saw he didn't wear motley or a jester's cap. "What is this? A bard's collar on the Stammering Storyteller?"

Now juggling all the rings, he said, "I have a new act, my liege. I still tell stories, but while juggling."

The feasting nobles came alive, now whispering about what they saw. *I command their focus now*, Micah thought.

The Queen's brow was smooth, her eyes sparkling, and she said, "Now this is something new. Okay, 'bard,' you have my attention. What sort of story will you tell?"

Micah continued juggling the red rings. "Whatever type of story you command, my queen."

She pondered, then said at last, "I hear that moronic king in the south started rumours about my cream." She harrumphed. "Ruler of a realm of limp wood."

The feasting nobles laughed heartily at her jest.

Egged on by their approval, the Queen said, "That is what we want to hear, story spinner. Tell us a tale about how wormy the wood from the forested realm is. Finest furniture and wood in the land? Pah."

Micah then spun a story as salacious as his last. This time, though, he impugned not Ekalfons's milk but Cinorom's most valuable commodity, its wood. His tale also included plenty of salacious double entendres, implying King Briscalo's manhood was in as sorry a state as the forest products his country sold.

And as it had been in Cinorom, Micah's slanderous tale spread from one ear to the next until all in Ekalfons spoke impugning lies about their neighbouring kingdom to the south. Gossips spoke of how King Briscalo could no longer raise his own wood and how unworthy the planks from his forests were.

At the Queen's request, Micah told various versions of the story for four weeks straight. Micah's tale delighted Queen Karia'idaz and her nobles alike. As in Cinorom during the summer, gossips spread the stories throughout Ekalfons all autumn. As it had been in Cinorom, people soon no longer knew the rumours had begun as a bard's fiction. No longer attached to its source, people believed the gossip they heard was true.

The good people of Ekalfons, already outraged at Cinorom for spreading lies about their dairy wares and their queen, took matters into their own hands. The people held nightly bonfires in the town square and threw the Cinorom wood products they owned into the fire: stools and carts, tables and beds.

Having stripped their homes of Cinorom wood, Ekalfons folks took their complaints further. They claimed that Cinorom's building planks were full of termites and that woodworms infested their houses. The people of Ekalfons called for the Queen to act.

Queen Karia'idaz readily obliged. "I must protect my subjects and my realm," she said as she signed the decree to banish Cinorom's forest fare from her land.

Drinking honey-ale from a wooden Cinorom mug, Micah noticed it leaked not at all. "This is madness," he said, wiping ale foam from his beard. "Do they not know this is fiction? That I made it all up?"

Shari ceased darning her costume, her stormy eyes fuming. "You juggle the truth now, Micah. And you really need to stop."

"There's talk of war between these two testy tyrants," Petru said. His demeanour was typically pleasant, but Petru hadn't smiled for weeks. "If battle begins between these two realms, over lies that you told so your head would swell . . ." He snatched Micah's mug and drained the last drop. "You don't deserve this fine ale."

Micah spread his hands before him. "I c-c-can't undo it. It g-g-got away f-f-from m-m-me."

Shari did not buy it. "Until you set this right, do not darken my corner with your shadow." She gathered her work and left their table.

Micah pulled the rings from his belt and tossed them, gaining the power to unstick his tongue. "But how do I right all I have set wrong?"

She paused and thought and then called over her shoulder, "Tell the truth."

"But will they listen now that they're used to the lies? Will they accept the truth when I speak it this time?"

"Some will. Some won't. That's not your concern. You have control over nothing but your words. You must use your talent to speak truth rather than lies."

Her anger abated, and she glanced back at him with pity, not for his stuttering and stammering, but for his foolery—for he was now more the joker than he had been when he'd worn motley.

The bard's collar, once coveted, now constricted. He tore the starched collar from his neck and stomped it.

Shari stood at the door and said her parting words. "Be better than the horde, Micah. Dare to speak the truth."

FROM THAT DAY FORWARD, Micah did as Shari had suggested. Since he no longer spun salacious slanders about King Briscalo and his kingdom, Queen Karia'idaz banished Micah from her court. The same thing happened in King Briscalo's great hall.

But so long as the lies he'd begun still spread like fire on blighted plains, Micah could neither rest easy nor win back Shari's friendship, let alone her hand. Instead of performing for overstuffed nobles or royals in the grand halls of the realm, Micah returned to where his juggling storytelling began.

Micah performs now daily in the market square. He juggles his rings and uses their power to speak the truth about real people and realms. It took nearly a year for the people of Ekalfons to stop setting fire to their furniture and for Cinorom to clamour once again for Ekalfons' double cream cheese, for rumours of Queen Karia'idaz cavorting with evil entities and King Briscalo's wood problems had proven as infectious as the Black Death and even more difficult to expunge from the land.

"People like to believe the worst, don't they?" Micah asked Petru.

"They are loath to forget what they choose to believe, even if proven wrong, I suppose," Petru said.

Today, as Micah spun his rings, he told a recently created story that immediately became a crowd favourite. As he told a tale about a clever and beautiful young woman thespian, he noticed Shari watching at the crowd's edge. She'd only recently begun speaking to him again and hadn't seen him perform since that fateful day at Briscalo's court.

Even with the confidence given by the magical rings, he feared he'd stammer throughout the story. But he pulled himself together and finished with flair.

Shari lingered as the crowd thinned. She edged closer as Micah collected the coins. "I like that story," she said. "But it's missing something, isn't it?"

Micah halted and looked at her, puzzled. "W-w-what does it l-l-lack?"

She smiled up at him. "A happily-ever-after ending."

He dropped the tips into his belt purse, the coins jingling, and avoided her gaze as he asked, "H-h-happily ever af-af-after, hey? D-d-do you think sh-sh-sh—the woman in the story—c-c-could find hap-hap-happiness with a storyteller who sometimes acts the f-f-fool?"

Shari touched his arm and locked her eyes with hers. "Anyone can be foolish sometimes. But only the truly brave take actions to right their wrongs."

Micah took her hand, and they caught up with each other over mugs of mead at the inn.

And the next time Micah spun his rings of truth, he added a new ending to his most-requested tale.

THE BEASTS AT THE END OF THE WORLD

Brian Trent

The policeman tossed aside the newspaper at last, dropping it like a pile of old bandages onto the zoo bench. As he returned to sit beside his anxious wife, I snatched up the discarded paper, flowering open its pages. I could not read—old Moreau had not seen fit to teach me. Yet my Little Think was to use the newspaper to hide my strange face. The policeman and his wife and the corpulent banker had been giving me suspicious looks ever since they arrived.

The banker glanced up from his pocket watch to frown at me; his frown was incredible, bending his entire fleshy face until his ears drooped. "You do realize you have that paper upside-down, yes?"

Cursing under my breath, I righted the edition. "Thank you, kind sir!" I shouted. "This zoo is so dark, I can scarcely distinguish the letters of this excellent newspaper!"

The letters in question were unknowable configurations of bold ink:

MARTIAN ATTACK REACHES LONDON
NEW CYLINDERS LAND OUTSIDE
COVENTRY, BRISTOL, CAMBRIDGE

I snapped the paper to another page, as I had seen old Moreau do when his supply ship brought him printed editions from the outside world. The sound startled the zoo's caged inhabitants, and one gave a wicked snarl in the gloomy enclosure.

"Say," the copper intoned, staring hard at me. "Make a goodly effort not to antagonize the beasts, won't you?"

"Sorry," I muttered and *quietly* turned the next page. But a gnawing fear waylaid my thoughts, and for a moment, I drifted off, no longer thinking of London in ruins beneath the stomp of extraterrestrial war machines but of the Island and its cool trails beneath tropical canopies and the *smells* of those trails. Humans don't appreciate smells. The Island had been crisscrossed by an aromatic topography of old urine, forgotten bloodstains, and gore-encrusted spots where beasts had been killed, and the scent of the awful crime hung on the surrounding foliage like dew.

"What *did* you say your name was?" interrupted the fat banker.

"Burton," I reminded him, and before anyone could utter another word, there was a renewed cacophony of field batteries stationed at some nearby point of crossfire. The shells boomed directly overhead —there was a rush of hot air and the screaming whine of a fusillade. I found myself almost laughing with the wonder of it. Every caged animal went wild with hysterics.

"One of those blasted machines must be very close," I panted excitedly. "The good boys of the Royal Artillery must be directo-concentrational-fivesoming the bastard three-leggers!"

I didn't understand the silence that followed my observation. The banker pulled himself to his feet, practically creaking with the effort, and relocated to a bench farther from me. The policeman put his arm around his wife. For her part, she had yet to make eye contact with anyone. She sat in her own world—her own private Island.

Using the London Zoo as a sanctuary made perfect sense to me. It was my Big Think since arriving in London's harbour: after all, why would the Martians attack a zoo? My friends and I should be safe here. But apparently, other Londoners had the same Big Think—or maybe it was a Little Think for them, who knows? The policeman and his wife arrived first, and the copper made no attempt to conceal his dislike of me, perhaps sensing that something was off about my heavy brow, my jutting jaw, my squat and thick build, my hairy arms that in a half-remembered lifetime had let me swing happily through trees.

Another battery of shots detonated the night. This time, the Martians replied: their heat-ray crackled, transforming the fog that wreathed the half-sheared-away buildings into an incandescent cloud. Our shadows rotated around our feet.

"Henry," the policeman's wife said, "could our soldiers capture such a weapon for themselves and turn it against the Martians?"

"That would be good," I nodded eagerly. "A right good Big Think."

"What would be good," the copper said, turning his sharp blue eyes upon me, "is if you departed, Mr. Burton. None of us like the look of you."

I grinned broadly. "I am aware that my unusual face often instills unease in my fellow Men. But, you see . . ." I held out my hand. "I have five fingers, just like you."

"I don't care a whit about your five fingers that you seem so proud of! It was that face you were making a moment ago. During the exchange of fire."

"Yes, yes," the banker agreed. "It positively curdled my blood."

The policeman's wife finally looked up. She was a lithe, fragile thing, and like many fragile things, she was beautiful in her way. Her eyes widened as they took me in. "Henry, what . . . what *is* wrong with his face? Could he be one of the Martians?"

"Of course not," the copper assured her, though his hand strayed to his billy club. "But I should like to know where he's from. What about it, Mr. Burton? Where did you go to school? Who do you have for references?"

A caged beast snarled low and threateningly behind me.

"I am goodly-best-long-distanced friends with Mr. Edward Prendick," I stammered.

"Who is he?"

"Dear," the woman said, getting up suddenly and approaching

the nearest cage. "Have you taken a look at this goat? It seems peculiar! And . . . " She spun around to face another cage. Her expression of confusion deepened, turning to fear that matched the rising pitch of her voice. "And this cow? It isn't . . . *right*, somehow." The air was suddenly damp and acrid with her panic.

"You have never heard of Edward Prendick?" I asked the policeman. "Why, he made quite a stir in the headlines a year back, I understand. Was lost at sea, shipwrecked, and found his way back to England!"

The fat banker stirred at this. "I do recall something of the sort."

I growled. "Do you know him?"

The policeman's wife rushed to the elk enclosure. I could hear her ragged, terrified breaths.

"Prendick," offered the banker after a thoughtful rub of his flabby face. "Say, is he the chap who works for the observatory at Cambridge?"

"Yes!" I howled. "I have heard this persistent rumour since arriving! Where is the way to Cambridge? Tell me! Is he not a Man? Are we not Men? Where is the way? Tell me! *Tell me!*"

"Control yourself!" the policeman shouted.

"I must find Prendick!" I shouted, leaping off my bench and hammering the cobblestone ground with my fists. "Tell me the way! Are we not Men? Are we *not?*"

The policeman's wife screamed. "These aren't animals in here, Henry! Oh my *God!*"

A YEAR before the Martians dropped out of the sky in metal cylinders to destroy the world of Men, a man had come from the sea and destroyed the world of my Island.

Before his arrival, we led orderly lives in the shoddy village around our Creator's house. We had once been beasts, but old Moreau had taken us into his laboratory and, through a crucible of torturous operations and experiments, given us the shape of Men and brains newly fashioned to permit Little Thinks and Big Thinks beyond the simple Beast Thinks of our early lives. He taught us speech. He taught us the Law.

Prendick arrived on our Island and shattered all that. He challenged Moreau; taught us that our Creator was not divine. Prendick encouraged us to rise up and overthrow the Island's Order . . .

. . . and then, once Moreau was dead and our Island society lay in shambles, he abandoned us: built himself a raft and paddled away with nary a look back at the shore, leaving us Beast Folk to devolve into lawlessness and disorder.

The horror of those listless days haunts me still . . . how my friends began devolving now that we were without purpose. Our reversion to our earlier selves was encouraged by the unchanging jungle and tranquil beach, the rote rhythms of the days and nights seeming to whittle down what intelligence we had. One by one, my friends slunk off into the brush, blinking stupidly as they went. It was happening to me, too: my eyes continually strayed to the inviting branches and vines of the wooded paths, to the fruits that I alone could reach.

The terror of this devolution—the awful seduction of the trees where I might once again swing and climb and howl—inspired my desperate Big Think:

We must build a raft, too! We must paddle into the green chop and find our way to the world of Men! You are a Five-Man! Get yourself and your friends off this blasted Island!

And so I wrangled my degenerating peers into a single purpose. We felled trees and strung their trunks into a flotilla. We wove baskets for fruit and filled bottles with rainwater. Then we pushed off in our vessel, venturing forth into the jade-green sea.

Trying to survive on our tiny ship was difficult, but difficult was good. Difficult made us Men again. My friends returned to standing upright now that the brush and woodsy trails could no longer tempt them. In time, our raft was intercepted by a steamship bound for London, and we were taken aboard as forlorn refugees. The world of Men—of the London that Prendick had told us about—awaited us!

Except that *something else* had found its way to London before our arrival. Creatures from the stars preceded us, dropping to Earth in metal cylinders to unleash mighty war machines that burned and stomped and shattered the world.

Seen from the harbour on the night our steamship pulled into port, London was a crackling bonfire. Alien tripods strode about, and people scattered before them like bugs seeking new shelter.

"It is all so new!" I gleefully told my companions on the steamship deck, staring at the red flames ashore. "It will be difficult! But it is all new! This is good!" Howling into the sizzling night, my companions nervously joined in the ululation.

Somewhere in the city, *our* destroyer was to be found. He couldn't know we had escaped the Island.

Couldn't know that we were coming for him.

MY FRIEND LIVINGSTONE gave a troubled look, his goatish face narrow and dark as our ragged troop shambled out from the zoo, leaving the human bodies behind us. "Not to taste blood," Livingstone muttered, his horns poking through his bowler's cap. "*That* is the Law."

I frowned at him. "I did not taste blood. Did you?"

Livingstone scratched the hairs underneath his chin. His hands were unfortunate things. Although Moreau had fashioned his hooves into a vague likeness of human hands, they sported only two fingers. They were hardened, amber-brown protrusions.

"No one tasted blood!" I insisted, casting a wary glance at the others behind us. They formed an uneven herd, creatures in the shapes of men and women (and even a little boy who had once been a sloth). Their clothes were motley and garish, pilfered from broken shop windows and gutter corpses.

My goat-friend pursed his lips. "I think some of the blood, maybe from the policeman's wife, got on their faces and they . . . they . . ."

"I did not see that," I declared. "Besides, *we* were attacked. We only defended ourselves! That is good and proper. We do not kill for joy."

Were the Martians killing for joy?

I gazed along Outer Circle. The street formed a grim and cluttered alley of carcasses, tumbled masonry, and overturned carriages.

Baker, the Cow Woman, ambled up behind us. She had raided a storefront mannequin to attain her dress, feathery hat, and frilly parasol. No mannequin in the world, however, had ever sported her heavy jaw, her expansive nose with quivering pink nostrils, or those immense, widely spaced eyes. She tottered, stumbling unevenly in the tiny shoes she'd pilfered from the copper's wife.

"Are you reading that newspaper?" she asked me.

I handed her the edition.

"The banker said Prendick worked in an observatory," she said, using one of her malformed hoof-hands to open the pages. "What is an observatory?"

"I shall tell you on the way," I announced, secretly having no idea what an observatory was but aware that leadership tolerates neither weakness nor ignorance. Moreau had been weak in the face of Prendick's disruptive arrival. It had cost him everything. "You are reading that paper upside-down," I added.

"I realize that!" she said defensively. "I am not a beast, you know! I—"

A cry of thunder drowned out her next words. We stared agog as a gabled building exploded in a shower of flaming debris. Something tall and spindly marched past, making the ground shudder with each step.

For a long while, we stared after it.

THERE WERE Island nights when a fresh rain would leave the jungle glassy and glistening. On such occasions, I'd awaken our degenerating group and corral them into a bushy tree until we occupied every branch. Then, as morning hatched like a red ball from the sea, we would gasp at the way the wet jungle blazed with a thousand scarlet fires.

London was a bit like that.

Glass reflected the flames and destruction as we made our way north, dressed in our bandages, overcoats, and ratty blankets, just another train of refugees shuffling in a weary line. I saw humans in the doorways of old shoppes, glancing furtively at us as we passed, and felt some satisfaction at seeing their raggedy cerements; war had made us all beasts, it seemed. Their glances turned away, perhaps not liking the sight of their own reflection.

"Look there, what is that?" my goat-friend asked, pointing to a stone building at the end of the lane.

"A stonework mightybuilt," I announced, and Livingstone chortled happily, always delighting in the wondrous words I knew.

"No, no!" Baker said, shoving past me, pressing her hat to her head and waving her parasol with the other. "It is a playhouse! How *marvellous!*"

I gritted my teeth. Baker had overheard the word "marvellous" upon our arrival. As we shambled down the gangplank, we met our first Londoner, a drunken soak lying on the pier. The woman squinted at us and asked, "Has the circus come to Piccadilly? How *marvellous!*"

Now, Baker tottered past us, grinning with her wide, flat teeth. "I've always wanted to see a play!" she cried.

"Always?" I taunted. "Back when you were chewing cud?"

She flashed me a sour, deeply hurt look. "Well, I don't rightly remember. Perhaps I did! Let us go in and meet the actors!"

"The actors are all dead or fleeing," Livingstone guessed, adjusting his hat around his horns.

Baker's forehead creased. "You don't know that! I say we go inside!"

"*You* do not lead us!" I snapped, and I pointed to her hands. "You are only a Two-Woman! *I* have five fingers! *I* am the leader of our troop!"

"Please, Burton!"

"We are *not* going to the theatre!" I yelled, and then I rounded the corner of the building and stumbled into a Martian tripod.

IT KNOCKED me over as it ambled by on its three legs; I was sent sprawling onto my back, staring in horror as the metallic limb moved over me. The round foot stomped down near my head, shattering the street's cobblestones like peanut brittle. Black rubbery tentacles gyrated from the machine's belly, holding an immense box-like device. On the machine itself, a glowing porthole was like a massive cyclopean eye.

I glanced at my friends. They were standing, stricken, as the tripod thundered toward the playhouse.

"Play dead!" I shouted; the command came out in a strangled, terrified whisper.

They did *not* play dead.

The Beast Folk stampeded into the playhouse. Baker, still wearing those ridiculous shoes, let out a terrified "Moo!" and stumbled for the doors, dropping her prized parasol.

The Martian machine instantly jerked toward the sound. The hellish eye cast a reddish spotlight on the green parasol.

Then the parasol exploded as a scorching light rained down from the Martian's deadly heat-box. When the ray cut out, there was a smoking crater in the street.

I was still on my back, but I could see my friends crowded in the playhouse window. Baker was there, and the elk-man and sloth-boy, and . . .

My throat constricted in panic. *Where was Livingstone?*

The Martian machine snapped its light on something else, and for a moment, I wasn't sure what I was seeing.

A goat? Why was there a goat out here in these urban corridors?

Then I recognized my friend.

In his panic, he had returned to four legs . . . in clear violation of the Law. He still wore a wool jacket and pants, but this only made him appear more bestial. The Martian heat-box whined to full power. I saw my friend as Prendick must have seen us: a mockery shaped by the hands of a madman, large dull eyes gaping at a world he'd never belong to.

Livingstone's bowler cap fell off his horns. He began nosing at a tin can.

"Baaaa!" he grunted.

The air vibrated and steamed. The Martian tripod used its rubbery tentacles to tilt the heat-box, tracking my friend's movement.

Livingstone knocked the tin can, sending it tinkling along sheaves of broken cobblestone. He hopped about, seemingly entertained by the sound, and "baaaaed" again. Any second, the Martian was going to blast him to smithereens.

But then the whine of the heat-box cut off. The spotlight went dark. The mighty machine turned away, tottered as if it was going to fall, and then drunkenly blundered through a bakery and was gone.

Livingstone broke into a triumphant prance.

I ran out to meet my friend. "That was a triumphant Big Think!"

He kept cavorting in joyful antics.

"Livingstone!" I cried. "Livingstone, enough! The fearmachine has departed!" I reached for him, and he dashed away.

Cold terror roiled within me. I glanced to the theatre window and saw my friends pressed to the glass in a wide-eyed row. Empty gazes. Dull faces.

"Livingstone!" I howled into the night. "Not to go on four legs! That is the Law! Are we not Men?"

Baker tottered out from the playhouse, kneeling to regard the black crater where her prized parasol had been.

"I will get you another one," I promised, scanning the streets for my friend.

She nodded blearily, sniffing at the charred remains. I was heading off to search for Livingstone when he came galloping back. Then he hopped onto two legs, grinning happily.

"Did you see *behind* the light?" he bleated, resembling every satyr

I'd ever seen in Moreau's old mythology books. "I *saw* the Martians inside! Short-statured things with huge eyes! Oh, it is all so new! It is so wonderful!"

I hugged him fiercely. "How many fingers did they have?" I demanded.

He blinked. "I don't know."

We returned to the playhouse. Baker continued kneeling by the remains of her parasol, only now she was on all fours. Her large dress wrapped unevenly around her udders. She sniffed the ground, wet nose puckering.

"Stand tall!" I howled. "Baker, remember the Law!"

The Cow Woman pulled herself to her feet in embarrassment. She began to smooth wrinkles in her dress and huge sleeves.

"Do I still look marvellous?" she asked in a forlorn voice. "Please tell me . . ."

"I will tell you in Cambridge!" I snapped. Addressing the Beast Folk in the window, I shouted, "We must hurry! We must find Prendick's observatory before—"

Before we become dull beasts again, our minds falling into endless night.

"—this Island is destroyed! Come along now!"

<hr>

NORTH OF LONDON, the countryside transformed into rolling fields spotted with trees. A village was set into that pastoral serenity, black windows frosted with starlight.

Baker and Livingstone walked abreast of me, and my Little Think —perhaps each of our Little Thinks—was how the soft grass resembled the green surf of the sea and how the tallest hills could have been Islands in their own right.

"It is such a pretty sight!" Baker murmured and nudged me. "Notice I did not say it was marvellous."

"A thousand gratitudes," I grumbled.

Livingstone clopped along on two legs. "Where is the observatory?"

"Wait here," I insisted and hopped into the nearest apple tree. Erupting through the canopy, I scanned the horizon for signs of an observatory . . . except I had no idea what I was looking for. The word sounded like *observe*, which was accomplished through eyes, so perhaps it was a building shaped like a massive eye.

My friends milled about below, spreading uncertainly into the grass. Seeing them from this height was strangely enjoyable. In London, there had been nothing green, only cobblestone alleys and brick buildings and soot-spewing chimneys. The only plants I saw there were prisoners in narrow clay pots. And trees? I'd seen no trees in London save for what was imprisoned in the zoo.

"Do you see an observatory?" Livingstone called to me.

My chest tightened. "An observatory is a mightybuilt structure," I muttered, realizing that there were no mightybuilt structures here, only farmsteads and cottages in a hilly country scarred by roads.

A Martian tripod suddenly appeared in the distance, the starlight warping around its metallic hull and spindly legs. It held its deadly heat-box aloft as if seeking a target worthy of its unholy fire but finding little of consequence here.

"Burton!" my goat-friend cried. "The Martians . . ."

"I see it," I snapped, clinging to my branch.

Two other tripods came loping across the English countryside. I fancied there was something odd about their strides. They staggered about, nearly colliding with each other. Sheep scurried out of their way. Their searchlight eyes scoured the hills wildly.

"What are they doing?" whispered Baker below me.

"I don't know," I confessed.

One of the searchlights swept near us.

"Down!" I yelled. "All of you, pretend to be beasts! Now!"

My friends were quick to obey, melting into the field in every direction . . . except for Baker. She stared at me piteously. "Not to go on four legs . . ." she began. "That is the Law."

"Baker!" I screamed.

The searchlight blazed around her and fixed her in place.

The ground shook. One of the tripods came stumbling toward us. Baker dropped to all fours. She hurriedly shook off the gown.

"Get rid of the bloody hat!" I cried, and she flung the hat, sobbing. The Martian tripod towered above her.

They won't kill an animal, I prayed. We were *not* animals, but the Martians didn't know that.

The tripod lowered itself, squatting so that it could examine my friend. Baker was trembling. She nosed an upturned bucket, lapped at a puddle. The machine continued examining her.

I plucked an apple and hurled it into the grass.

The tripod stood upright so quickly that the breeze nearly swept me into the sky. My Little Think was that it would turn its awful light onto the thrown apple, but it seemed to have guessed the direction the fruit came from. In an instant, the extraterrestrial machine was glaring directly at me.

My body began to sweat, my furry arms and neck dripping. I felt pinned by that alien eye like an insect on one of Moreau's corkboards. All I could do was stare back.

The porthole was perfectly circular and streaked in grime. And behind the glass?

The Martians! I could *see* them!

There were three of them. Each awful face sported immense eyes crowding lipless mouths. They beheld me in a kind of equal wonder, bringing their hands up to their faces as if fidgeting in consternation, their extraterrestrial minds debating the question:

What are we seeing? Is it a Man?

Are we not Men?

For the first time, it occurred to me how strange Moreau's Law was. The Law never *stated* we were Men, did it? It only posed the query, as if to invite debate . . . or offer an ironic taunt. I thought of my friends in the grass . . . the elk-man and goat-man and cow-woman and sloth-boy and others, with their hooves and horns, fur and fangs.

Are we not Men?

Yes, we are not.

I bared my teeth at the alien creatures in the porthole. I shook my tree branch in fury and defiance. The Martians blinked, watching me, hands dabbing at their foreheads as if flush with fever.

And on each hand?

Three fingers.

Perhaps *none* of us were Men. Two fingers, three fingers, five fingers . . . did it matter? The only constant I perceived was a cycle of construction and obliteration. The only truth was that Beast and Man and Martian were leaves on the same tree. The Martians gaped at me, trying to determine my nature, as if *they* were qualified to render such judgment!

No, I am not a Man.

"And neither are you!" I shouted at the faces in the porthole. "You are not! You are not Men! You are beasts of your own kind!"

The tripod brought up the heat-box. A hellish light kindled within the device, and the mechanical hum escalated into a shrieking whine.

They are going to burn me like a torch.

I had time to glance one last time at my friends. Baker was still on all fours, her face upturned and anguished.

I held out my arms to embrace the Martian light, the tears hot on my cheeks. Then the heat-ray opened up.

OPENED UP, I should say, as the alien war machine toppled backward like a rotten tree, disgorging its heat-ray in one blast that seemed to split the starry heavens. The tripod collapsed in a deafening eruption of sparks and fire, cracking open like a bird's egg on the earth.

For a long while, I blinked stupidly from my perch. I had no thinks—Little or Big—to explain what had happened. In the distance, another alien machine fell into a strangely rounded hill and didn't move again.

"Burton!" Livingstone cried.

"Quiet!" I stared hard at the machine that had collapsed into the hill.

If not for the chilly temperatures, I might never have realized the hill was hollow. Heat gushed from a breach. Light—artificial light!—glowed within.

I climbed down from the tree. Baker fetched her hat and set it defiantly back on her head. "What happened?" she asked, and before I could hazard a reply, she seized my hands and kissed them. "I thought . . . I thought you . . ."

"I thought so, too," I said gently.

Livingstone returned to two legs and paced in an agitated circle. "Are the Martians dying?"

I did not know the truth then.

It was only when we approached the hollow hill—when we discovered the secret observatory within it—that we found our answers.

And it was Edward Prendick who explained it to us.

THE OBSERVATORY, as it happened, had been cunningly hidden in the countryside. Soil had been spread across its dome in the early days of the invasion so that it appeared as a hill like any other. A little more rounded, perhaps, but convincingly interred. I led our troop of misfits past the fallen Martian war machine and into the glowing breach. It was warm inside, and steam boiled around us. We descended into a laboratory of candles, blueprints, workbenches, and men scurrying about like ants in an overturned mound.

I sniffed the musty air.

I *smelled* my betrayer.

As I had once followed the scent of food in jungle brush, I now tracked the odour into the heart of the laboratory. Men were coughing, choking, pushing past my friends without realizing we were intruders in their secret domain. Farther inside, in the untouched portion of this netherworld, the dust cleared, and I saw a thin-haired man in a button-down shirt. He was peering into a device I knew from Moreau's set of tools: a microscope.

He barely looked up as he said, "We regretfully cannot accept any refugees."

It was Livingstone who shuffled forward and said, "And yet we once accepted you, the refugee from the sea."

Our betrayer's hand trembled at the microscope. He raised his head and regarded us, half visible in the lamplight.

"You've gotten old, Prendick," I said.

"Oh, my God!" he whispered. "Oh, my sweet God!"

"Your God is out there, trying to pick up the pieces of *your* island." I strode toward him, causing him to shrink from me. "England is an island; I saw that plainly from maps. Perhaps your God knows something of irony."

My betrayer had never seemed in the best of health, even when I first met him on Moreau's Island a year previously. He seemed less so now. The colour blanched from his face like a piece of sun-bleached driftwood.

He shuddered. "I'm going mad. You cannot be here! This cannot be!"

I leaped onto his workbench and seized him by his shirt. "We *are* here! We crossed the mightydark sea to find you! You knew we were conscious, sentient beings! Knew that without Moreau, without Law, without purpose, we would become beasts again! You knew all this . . . a*nd yet you left us there!*"

Baker shook her head disappointingly. "This was most unmarvellous, Prendick. We befriended you."

Livingstone rushed him, horns lowered to do real damage, but I lifted the traitor, like a hooked fish, out of the line of attack.

"Kill me, then!" Prendick's mouth twisted in anguish. "My life has never been the same after seeing your hellish island. My one solace was to contemplate the stars and hope for something better than mankind, and how did the stars answer? They sent new monsters!"

"Enough!" I snapped. Now that vengeance was here, I was uncertain how to proceed. I could kill him so easily. My hands could squeeze his neck like crepe paper!

My goat-friend looked back, aghast. "We must kill him! That is the Law!"

"That is *not* the Law!" I said, shocked.

"It is *their* law!" Livingstone protested. "*They* kill! And it is obviously the Martian law, for they kill, too!"

"We are not Men. We are not Martians."

"But . . . but . . . we *are* Men," my friend insisted. "Aren't we?"

I drew Prendick close. "You heard my friend's question. Are we Men, Prendick?"

"No," he said hoarsely. "You are beasts. Not even that. You *were* beasts, but you were changed—"

"Into Men!" Baker whispered.

"Into things that look like Men."

The ground thundered as another alien machine toppled into the countryside.

"What is happening to them?" I demanded.

"They are dying," Prendick whispered.

"Why?"

His eyes slid to the microscope. "Because the Martians have no immunity system. They have no way of protecting themselves against our germs. Earth is saved . . . for now."

I dropped him to the floor. "What do you mean?"

It was Baker who answered. "He thinks the Martians will learn from this mistake. They will return with ways of protecting themselves. Then, not even germs will save us. All will be destroyed."

Prendick said nothing. But his eyes flicked briefly to something in the laboratory. I'd been so preoccupied with him that I hadn't given much consideration to the glass vials, books, and strange pieces of equipment around us. Now, I followed his quick glance. The place wasn't so different from old Moreau's lab, really, except that a peculiar monument sat at the centre of everything. It was made of metal. It was shaped somewhat like a bullet . . . only, a bullet the size of a small boat.

Frowning, I said, "What am I looking at?"

My betrayer said, "Our only hope for the future."

I knew about bullets because Moreau had always kept a gun handy in case we Beast Folk broke the Law. I knew that bullets were meant to be fired through the air; my thoughts drifted back to the cannons booming over London Zoo. And suddenly, something like a detonation happened in my own head. My biggest Big Think.

"You're going to shoot this to Mars," I muttered. "Just as the Martians shot their machines across space to land on Earth, you . . . you will send a reply! Is that it?" I looked with new appreciation at the glass vials and flasks against the far wall. "And you will fill this bullet with the germs of this world! Just as they destroyed your island, you intend to wide-blast-mightyfall their entire world!"

Prendick stared at me with wet, miserable eyes. "Men will pilot these vessels of death to the Red Planet. They will sacrifice themselves to save Earth from future destruction. It is the only way."

A third act to a tale of destruction, I thought grimly. Dystopia followed by dystopia, like the ever-rising breakers of a stormy sea. The Martians attacked Earth, and now Men would attack back, and caught in the middle of this shooting war were the unwanted Beasts who belonged nowhere and to no one.

And yet . . . another Big Think was blossoming, like a young fire, in my brain.

"Who will pilot these vessels, Prendick?" I asked. "Who will you send to Mars, never to return?"

BAKER THE COW WOMAN GRUNTED—SHE did not scream—as Livingstone helped press down on her swollen belly, and the elk-doctor crouched between her open legs.

"Push!" the elk-doctor grunted. "Push! Push!"

I held my breath, wishing there was something I could do. The room we were using as a hospital was a vast, airy space, and the sounds of Baker's laboured breaths and the doctor's commands echoed around me like a chorus. My eyes strayed past strange tubes and devices to the triangular doorway. There, gathered into an anxious crowd, were my fellow Beasts. Martian daylight streamed in through the windows.

"Push!" the doctor cried.

As the echo of his voice died, there was a new sound, and I rushed to Baker's bedside. The air filled with a soft mewling, and in the elk-man's arms was a wet, blood-dappled pup. Not a cow exactly, nor a goat, but some unique blend of mother and father . . .

Livingstone began to weep. "Our child! Our child!"

The doctor grinned and handed the newborn to Baker. "There are more to come. Push down!"

The litter, it turned out, was comprised of three pups, a number I found appropriate for our new home. I motioned to my friends at the doorway, and the Beast Folk nearly stampeded to see.

"The first of the new Martians!" I boomed.

The group took turns holding the newborns as one might handle precious artifacts. Livingstone and Baker held hands, beaming in pride.

For my part, I went to the window and stared out at the sprawling Martian city.

The Martians were long dead. They'd perished in the early days of our arrival, falling to the germs our vessels had brought. By the time we emerged into the alien metropolis, the native race was scattering in terror, dashing ahead of an epidemic that would—in the days and weeks that followed—claim them to the last.

"We will pilot your rockets," I'd told Prendick. "What are we but vermin to your eyes? It is fitting that we should ride a ship of vermin! We are outcasts! Unwanted and undesirable, yet we desire, yes! Not an island that can be destroyed, but a world to call our own. We escaped one prison in a raft. Let us escape again. Please! You owe us this much!"

The sun was low on the horizon. Shadows pooled around bizarre Martian structures. Reflected in the glass, I saw my brethren behind me. There were other swollen bellies among them. More births to come. And with no one here to harm us, one day we'd spread across all of Mars. Stars glimmered in the dusk—including the blue one I knew to be Earth.

I grinned.

Oh, Prendick, I thought, rolling the strange name in my mind. You must have thought you'd have the last laugh. That by sending us as your plague-carriers, you were destroying us once more. That we would devolve into simple animals again. That the monsters of Moreau would vanish, as the Martians had vanished.

And left to stale routine, perhaps that would have been our fate. Yet for us, Mars was a new world of endless mystery. Endless things to learn. Endless challenges, endless potential! In the months since landing, we were not degenerating. Quite the opposite. The Martian devices and machines around us were beginning to make sense. Our Little Thinks were growing into Big Thinks. We'd been sent here as destroyers . . . but we'd become inheritors of a boundless future.

My eyes watched the tiny blue star. It really was a tiny thing, set in a sky of endless suns.

I beat my chest and howled, the single note becoming a chorus to challenge, not the end of the world, but the beginning of a new one.

BRAD C. ANDERSON lives with his wife and puppy in Vancouver, Canada. He teaches undergraduate business courses at a local university and researches organizational wisdom in blithe defiance of the fact that most people do not think you can put those two words in the same sentence without irony. Previously, he worked in the biotech sector, where he made drugs for a living (legally!). His stories have appeared in a variety of publications. *Ashme's Song*, his second novel, was published by Shadowpaw Press in 2024. His short story Naïve Gods" was longlisted for a 2017 Sunburst Award for Excellence in Canadian Literature of the Fantastic. It was published in the anthology *Lazarus Risen*, which itself was nominated for an Aurora Award. Learn more at www.bradanderson2000.com.

EDO VAN BELKOM, a former reporter on the sports and police beats for newspapers in and around Toronto, arrived on the horror scene in 1990. His first short story sale,e "Baseball Memories," was selected for the prestigious *Year's Best Horror Stories*, edited by Karl Edward Wagner. The story was also nominated for Canada's prestigious Aurora Award and appeared side-by-side with work by authors such as Mordecai Richler and W. P. Kinsella in *The Grand Slam Book of Canadian Baseball Writing*. Edo hasn't looked back since. Some 250 short stories have sold to a variety of top magazines and anthologies in the SF, fantasy, horror, and mystery genres, as well as Simon & Schuster's *Best American Erotica*. He has twice won the Aurora Award, taken home the Bram Stoker Award once, and been a finalist on many other occasions in a variety of categories spanning his work as a novelist, anthologist and nonfiction author, and his YA novel *Wolf Pack* won Ontario's prestigious Silver Birch Award. Recently, it was adapted into a TV series for Paramount+. Overseas, his work has been published in Germany, Spain, and Italy. Edo was also one of four on-air hosts for the launch of ScreamTV in 2000, hosting the segment "Post Mortem" during their late-night movie block. Born in Toronto in 1962, van Belkom received a B.A. in Creative Writing from York University and now resides in Brampton, Ontario, with his wife, Roberta.

J. G. GARDNER has a Ph.D. in Microbiology and is a scientist researching new ways to treat fungal infections. While having published many technical papers on genetics and biochemistry, he has always wanted to write novels about magic, wizards, and dragons. His high fantasy novels *The Path from Regret* and *The Magic of Deceit* were published by Apprentice House Press.

OLESYA SALNIKOVA GILMORE is the author of *The Witch and the Tsar* and *The Haunting of Moscow House*. Originally from Moscow, she was raised in the U.S. and graduated from Pepperdine University with a B.A. in English/political science and from Northwestern School of Law with a J.D. She practised litigation at a large law firm for several years before pursuing her dream of becoming an author. Now, she is happiest writing speculative historical fiction inspired by Eastern European history and folklore. Her work has appeared in *LitHub*, *Reactor/Tor.com*, *CrimeReads*, *Writer's Digest*, *Historical Novels Review*, *Bookish*, and *Washington Independent Review of Books*, among others. She lives in a wooded, lakeside suburb of Chicago with her husband and daughter.

CHADWICK GINTHER is the Prix Aurora Award-winning author of The Thunder Road Trilogy, *Graveyard Mind*, and more than thirty short stories, some of which have been collected in *Khyber: Sinister Tales of Sword and Sorcery* and *When the Sky Comes Looking for You:*

Short Trips Down the Thunder Road. He lives in Winnipeg, Canada, where he writes stories full of skeletons, giants, and dragons.

EVAN GRAHAM is an Ohio native who consistently refuses to seek help for his lifelong sci-fi addiction. Since there are not enough stories currently in existence to satisfy him, he had no choice but to start writing his own. *Tantalus Depths,* his debut novel, introduced his Calling Void series, an anthology of stories celebrating the wonder and terror of the Unknown.

Daughter of two Cuban political exiles, **M. C. A. HOGARTH** was born a foreigner in the American melting pot and has had a fascination for the gaps in cultures and the bridges that span them ever since. She has been many things—web database architect, product manager, technical writer, and massage therapist—but is currently a full-time parent, artist, writer, and anthropologist to aliens, both human and otherwise. Her fiction has variously been recommended for a Nebula, a finalist for the Spectrum, placed on the Tiptree long list, and chosen for two best-of anthologies; her art has appeared in RPGs and magazines and on book covers. M.C.A. Hogarth also served as Vice President of the Science Fiction and Fantasy Writers of America (SFWA) for three years. Her current focus is new business models for artists and independent marketing and distribution innovations. Her first crowdfunded fiction project kicked off in 2004 before the word was even coined. M.C.A. has experimented with everything from "choose-your-own-adventure" style serials online to Kickstarting creative projects and is looking forward to future experiments in using technology to bring art directly to the audience.

M. J. KUHN, author of the internationally bestselling *Among Thieves* and its sequel, *Thick as Thieves*, is a fantasy writer by night and a mild-mannered marketing employee by day. She lives in the metro Detroit area with her very spoiled cat, Thorin Oakenshield.

L. JAGI LAMPLIGHTER is the author of the YA fantasy series The Books of Unexpected Enlightenment, the third book of which was nominated for the YA Dragon Award in 2017, the fourth book of which won the first YA Ribbit Award, and the fifth book of which also won two small literary awards. She is also the author of the Prospero's Children series: *Prospero Lost*, *Prospero in Hell*, and *Prospero Regained*. She has published numerous articles and short stories and has an anthology of her own works, *In the Lamplight*. She also edits and teaches The Art and Craft of Writing. When not writing, she switches to her secret identity as wife and stay-home mom in Centreville, VA, where she lives with her dashing husband, author John C. Wright, and their four darling children, Orville, Ping-Ping Eve, Roland Wilbur, and Justinian Oberon.

KEVIN MOORE is the imaginative storyteller behind Jack Kelly's captivating world and extraordinary paranormal adventures. His debut novel, *The Book of Souls*, earned praise as an Amazon Editors' pick for Best Science Fiction and Fantasy and introduced readers to Kelly's mesmerizing abilities. Building on this success, Moore delved deeper into the supernatural realm with *The Book of Demons*, a thrilling blend of magic and suspense (Harry Potter meets *The Exorcist*.) The next chapter in the Jack Kelly saga, *Pandora's Box & The Lost Boys*, promises a more intense spine-tingling drama in early 2025. Moore's literary talents are not confined to the paranormal. *Christmas Stories 7: Original Short Stories* became an Amazon #1 bestseller, showcasing his ability to craft heartwarming tales. *Christmas Stories Volume II* is out now, promising more enchanted narratives. Also in 2025, prepare to be captivated by *Waking Sleeping Beauty*, a spiritual thriller.

ROBIN STEVENS PAYES is a time traveller who reasons that time and space are just inconvenient rules that other people decided the world must follow. She is the author of the YA Edge of Yesterday (EOY) time-travel adventure series and creator of EOY Media's interactive "learning through story" platform, inviting readers and fans to dive deeper into the worlds introduced in each of the stories. Since doing strengthens learning, Payes leads MASTERY workshops to empower teens and adults to get curious, tap their imaginations, and strengthen their creative superpowers.

JAMES S. PEET is a modern-day Renaissance Man. He's lived on four continents in six countries and visited countless more. He's been a National Park Service Ranger, a police officer, a tow-truck driver, a college instructor, a private investigator, a fraud examiner/forensic accountant, an inventor, and an entrepreneur. He's walked the Camino de Santiago, a walkabout he highly recommends. He lives on top of a small mountain in the foothills of Washington's Cascade Mountains with his wife, dogs, barn cats, and whatever adult daughter returns to the nest. He's attended ten colleges and universities and two law-enforcement academies and has three degrees (all in geography) and multiple certificates (he really likes learning). His Corps of Discovery and The Hayek Chronicles series are set in the multiverse. His other writing endeavours include several articles on modern sea piracy, economics, and the private investigation of fraud.

OMARI RICHARDS was born to Dominican immigrants in America and grew up in a household filled with laughter, music, fellowship, and tales of the homeland. From shape-shifting witches to monsters hatched from chicken eggs, these stories enriched and invigorated his imagination. This was strengthened once he found the written word in the adventures of Jim Hawkins, King Arthur, Ivanhoe, and Robin Hood, to name a few. Omari hopes to capture and enrich the imagination of his readers in a similar way with his new series, The Kimoni Legacy (which begins with his first novel, *The Kimoni Legacy: Initiation*), and his Tales of Nahwalla short stories. You can find Omari, a lifetime "blerd" and West African history/folklore buff, lost in a book, immersed in the nearest bookstore, or catching up on *One Piece* and *My Hero Academia* in his Northern Virginia home.

LAWRENCE M. SCHOEN holds a Ph.D. in cognitive psychology and psycholinguistics. He spent ten years as a college professor, doing research in the areas of human memory and language. This was followed by seventeen years as the director of research for a medical centre in Philadelphia that provided mental health and addiction services. He's also the founder of the Klingon Language Institute and since 1992 has championed the exploration and use of this constructed tongue throughout the world. In addition, he works occasionally as a hypnotherapist specializing in authors' issues. And, too, he is a chimeric cancer survivor. In 2007, he was a finalist for the Astounding Award for Best New Writer. He received a Hugo Award nomination for Best Short Story in 2010 and for Best Related Work in 2022, as well as Nebula Award nominations for Best Novella in 2013, 2014, 2015, and 2018, for Best Novelette in 2019, and for Best Novel in 2016. Some of his most popular writing deals with the ongoing humorous adventures of a space-faring stage hypnotist named the Amazing Conroy and his companion animal, Reggie, an alien buffalito that can eat anything and farts oxygen. His Barsk series represents his more serious work and uses anthropomorphic SF to explore ideas of prophecy, intolerance, political betrayal, speaking to the dead, predestination, and free will. It's also earned him the Cóyotl Award for Best Novel of 2015 and again in 2018. Lawrence lives near Philadelphia with his wife, Valerie, who is neither a psychologist nor a Klingon speaker.

ALEX SHVARTSMAN is the author of *Kakistocracy (2023), The Middling Affliction* (2022), and *Eridani's Crown* (2019) fantasy novels. Over 120 of his stories have appeared in *Analog, Nature, Strange Horizons*, etc. He won the WSFA Small Press Award for Short Fiction and was a three-time finalist for the Canopus Award for Excellence in Interstellar Fiction. His translations from Russian have appeared in *F&SF, Clarkesworld, Tor.com, Analog, Asimov's*, etc. Alex has edited over a dozen anthologies, including the long-running Unidentified Funny Objects series. He resides in Brooklyn, NY.

ALAN SMALE writes alternate history, historical fantasy, and hard SF. His novella of a Roman invasion of ancient America, "A Clash of

Eagles," won the Sidewise Award for Alternate History, and his novels set in the same universe, *Clash of Eagles*, *Eagle in Exile*, and *Eagle and Empire* (2015-2017), are available from Del Rey. His "Roman baseball" collaboration with Rick Wilber, *The Wandering Warriors*, came out from WordFire Press in 2020, and *Hot Moon*, his alternate-Apollo thriller set entirely on and around the Moon, was launched by CAEZIK SF & Fantasy in July 2022, with sequel *Radiant Sky* released in November 2024. Alan has sold more than fifty pieces of short fiction to *Asimov's*, *Galaxy's Edge*, *Abyss & Apex*, and numerous other magazines and original anthologies, and his short story "Gunpowder Treason" earned him a second Sidewise Award in 2022. His nonfiction essays have appeared in *Lightspeed*, *Journey Planet*, and *Galaxy's Edge*. Alan grew up in Yorkshire, England, and received degrees in Physics and Astrophysics from Oxford University. Until recently, he performed research into galactic neutron star and black hole binary systems at NASA's Goddard Space Flight Center and served as the director of one of NASA's big-three astrophysical data archives.

RICHARD SPARKS is an English-born comedy writer, lyricist, librettist, author, and director now living in Los Angeles. His writing credentials span the gamut of the entertainment world, from film and TV and books through lyrics for operas. His TV writing includes iconic shows like *Not the Nine O'clock News* (BBC TV) and *The Secret Policeman's Ball* (BBC TV, performed by Rowen Atkinson and directed by John Cleese). He has written several books, including the biography of the music producer Milt Okun, *Along the Cherry Lane*. (Okun discovered and launched John Denver and mentored him throughout his career. He created arrangements for Peter, Paul and Mary that the trio performed for half a century. He brought Placido Domingo a crossover career that made him an international star beyond the world of opera.) Richard's novel *New Rock New Role* blends the gaming world and epic fantasy and launched the New Rock series. The second book in the series, *New Rock New Realm*, was published in November 2024.

P. L. STUART was born in Toronto and holds a university degree in English, specializing in Medieval Literature. He is an assistant editor with *Before We Go Blog.* P.L.'s seven-book The Drowned Kingdom Saga chronicles flawed and bigoted Prince Othrun's journey toward change and his rise to power in a new world after the downfall of his homeland, which is based on Plato's lost realm of Atlantis. The best-selling first book, *A Drowned Kingdom*, was mentioned in *Kirkus Magazine's* 2021 Indie Issue among "Four Great Examples of the Genre" of fantasy and won the 2022 Picky Bookworm Award for Best Indie Book Based on Mythology. Other books in the series so far are *The Last of the Atalanteans*, *Lord and King*, and *A Lion's Pride*.

BRAD R. TORGERSEN is a multi-award-winning science fiction and fantasy writer whose book *A Star-Wheeled Sky* won the 2019 Dragon Award for Best Science Fiction Novel at the 33rd annual DragonCon fan convention in Atlanta, GA. A prolific short fiction author, Torgersen has published stories in numerous anthologies and magazines, including several best-of-the-year collections. Brad is named in *Analog* magazine's Who's Who of top *Analog* authors, alongside venerable writers like Larry Niven, Lois McMaster Bujold, Orson Scott Card, and Robert A. Heinlein. Married for more than twenty-eight years, Brad is also a United States Army Reserve Chief Warrant Officer—with multiple deployments to his credit—and currently lives with his wife and daughter in the Mountain West.

HAYDEN TRENHOLM is an award-winning playwright, novelist, and short story writer. He has also been a public servant, an actor, a bartender, a freelance researcher and consultant, and a telemarketer for Alberta Ballet. His short fiction has appeared in many magazines, including *Analog Science Fiction and Fact*, anthologies such as *The Sum of Us* and *Strangers Among Us*, and on CBC radio. His first novel, *A Circle of Birds*, won the Three-Day Novel Writing competition in 1993; it was later translated and published in French. Each book in his trilogy, The Steele Chronicles, was nominated for an Aurora Award. *Stealing Home*, the third book, was a finalist for the Sunburst

Award. Hayden has won five Aurora Awards—three times for short fiction and twice for editing anthologies. He purchased Bundoran Press in 2012 and was its managing editor until the press closed in 2020. He lives with his wife and fellow writer, Liz Westbrook-Trenholm, in Ottawa, having retired in 2017 after fifteen years as a policy adviser to the Senator for the Northwest Territories. In 2022, he was inducted into the Canadian Science Fiction and Fantasy Association Hall of Fame.

BRIAN TRENT is the award-winning author of the sci-fi thrillers *Redspace Rising* and *Ten Thousand Thunders*, and more than a hundred short stories in the world's top fiction markets, including the *New York Times*-bestselling Black Tide Rising series, *The Magazine of Fantasy & Science Fiction, Analog Science Fiction and Fact, Nature, Daily Science Fiction, Escape Pod, Pseudopod, Galaxy's Edge*, the Weird World War series from Baen Books, and numerous year's best anthologies. He lives in Connecticut.

ELI K. P. WILLIAM is a novelist, translator, essayist, and video game writer who has spent most of his adult life in Japan. The only member of the Science Fiction and Fantasy Writers of Japan who writes fiction in English, he is the author of The Jubilee Cycle trilogy (Skyhorse Publishing), set in a cyber-dystopian future Tokyo. He also translates Japanese literature, including the bestselling novel *A Man (Crossing)* by Keiichiro Hirano, and is now a bilingual writing consultant for a major Japanese video game company. His translations, essays, and short stories have appeared or are forthcoming in such publications as *Granta, Aeon, The Malahat Review, The Japan Times, Tor.com, Writer's Digest*, and (in Japanese) *SF Prologue Wave* and *Subaru*. After ten years in the thick of Tokyo, he now lives in the green hills outside the metropolis with his wife and daughter. Since the pandemic, he has made a point of more frequently visiting Toronto, the city of his birth, and can sometimes be found roaming North America or the UK in the summertime.

EDWARD WILLETT is the award-winning author (under his own name and as E.C. Blake and Lee Arthur Chane) of more than sixty books of science fiction, fantasy, and nonfiction for readers of all ages, including twelve novels for DAW Books, the most recent of which is *The Tangled Stars,* a humorous far-future space-opera heist adventure featuring an AI-uplifted talking cat who becomes a starship captain. Ed won Canada's top science fiction award, the Aurora Award, for his second novel for DAW, *Marseguro,* and has been short-listed several times since, including for his most recent young adult science fiction novel, *Star Song.* Ed has also won an Aurora Award for his podcast, *The Worldshapers,* which gave rise to this Kickstarter project and its four prequels. In 2018, Ed founded Shadowpaw Press, publisher of the *Shapers of Worlds* anthologies among many other books, not only science fiction and fantasy but also literary fiction, poetry, historical fiction, children's books, and nonfiction In addition to writing, Ed is a professional actor and singer. He lives in Regina, Saskatchewan, with his wife. They have a grown daughter and a much younger black Siberian cat named, of course, Shadowpaw.

Award-winning author **NATALIE WRIGHT** is ensconced in her dark-academia writing den penning the next book in the epic Dragos Primeri series. Natalie is the author of *Season of the Dragon*, named a Top Ten Indie epic fantasy by Bookshop.org and Ingram. A lifelong fantasy and sci-fi nerd, when not writing her own epic, Natalie is engrossed in a speculative fiction movie, book, series, or open-world RPG. Natalie is a frequent panellist, guest, and exhibitor at book festivals, book signing events, and sci-fi and fantasy conventions. She lives in Arizona with her husband and two cat overlords and visits her college-age son frequently in NYC. To meet Natalie, check her tour and appearance schedule on her website: www.NatalieWrightAuthor.com.

ABOUT THE ARTIST

WENDI NORDELL has been drawing for as long as she could hold a pencil. It has always been a favourite pastime and eventually became an occasional job. While her three children were growing up, she painted many murals, including in the pediatrics wing in a hospital, in a school entrance, and in many homes. She also attended festivals and craft shows, selling hand-drawn gift cards, bookmarks, and illustrations. Now that her children are grown, she has pursued an illustration career, illustrating a dozen books in the last five years, mostly for children, but also including Edward Willett's science fiction and fantasy poetry collection *I Tumble Through the Diamond Dust* and the science fiction and fantasy anthology *Shapers of Worlds Volume IV*. Recently, Wendi decided to improve her artistic skills and abilities by returning to the Alberta University of the Arts, pursuing a degree in illustration. Wendi has almost always picked up books based on their cover art, and if there are illustrations inside the book, she thinks that's even better. She truly hopes that her illustrations enhance readers' experience with books--including this one!

ACKNOWLEDGMENTS

This anthology would not have been possible without the generous support of the many people who pledged to back it on Kickstarter. Huge thanks to everyone listed below, and to those who chose to remain anonymous, for helping to bring this book to life.

KICKSTARTER BACKERS

Joshua McGinnis, Kari Blocker, David Perlmutter, D. Schumacher, Joanne B Burrows, Zack Fissel, David W Myers, Katherine Malloy, Jordan Theyel, Rick Ohnemus, Ian Chung, Stephanie Lucas, Steve711, Katie Schmirler, none, Adam Rajski, Ian Hecht, Karen M, Kelly Lorenc, Matthew Daniels, Hayden Trenholm, Kittie W, E.M. Middel, Nancy M. Tice, Julian White, Tyler Hulsey, Andrew Foxx, Michael Feldhusen, Sarah Ogden, Haley & Mike Newton, Frankie Mundens, Peter Halasz, Jerrie the filkferengi, Dan-o, Charley Kneifel, Melanie Marttila, Martin Beijer, Thomas Bull, Evan Ladouceur, Craig Hackl, anonymous (or no entry), Andrew Hatchell, Dr. Mary C. Crowell, Kerry aka Trouble, Alaska Sticker Fairy, Steven Peiper, Claire Sims, Karen A. Wyle, Bethany Chalmers, Mary Jo Rabe, David Rowe, Stephen Ballentine, Patrick Osbaldeston, JC, Pete Fox, Robert D. Stewart, Margaret Bumby, Mike Hein, Ruth Ann Orlansky, Jesse N. Klein, RJ Hopkinson, Fenric Cayne, Andrea Johnson, Lisa Kruse, Scott Raun, Gareth Jones, James G Connolly, Sabrina Dean, pjk, Robert Woods Tienken, Daniel Neely, Frank K Krivak, GhostCat, Sharon and Mike Sheffield, Bonnie Stewart, John Markley, JUST PEACHY, Larry Strome, Carol J. Guess, Louise Lowenspets, Yankton

Robins, Ellen, Alisa, Jennifer Flora Black, Mary Haldeman, Thorsten, Jeffrey Gardner, Ben Jacobson, Luis Manuel Sánchez García, Don Meyer, Andy F, Joshua Palmatier, Tania, Brooks Moses, Krystal Bohannan, Thomas Rawls, Tara Zrymiak, Mike Galligan, Dirk Schlobinski, Brendan Lonehawk, Eric Brown, Michael Feir, Jacques Toupin, Gayle Dodds, Carol Bachelu, Kai Hutchence, Colin S., Diane Smith, Jeroen Teitsma, Michael Barbour, Mark Newman, Simo Muinonen, Chicanerophile, Cara Phillips, Stephen Boucher, Crysella, Dr. Charles E Norton III, Simon Dick, Richard Parker, Caroline Westra, Axisor and Firestar, Anonymous Reader, Mark Richard Francis, C. Rauch, Sharon Plumb, Steve Arensberg, Richard Norton, StarArmy.com Roleplaying Community, Seamus Sands, Javier Maldonado, Alexandra Corrsin, Terry Toews, Michael Fedrowitz, Terry Jacobs, David B Ackermann, Lirleni Hankeshe / Vik-Thor Rose, Visalia girl, Suzanne 'Wispfox', M. R. Blanche, storm, Todd Hartleb, Vera Soroka, Corinne Brucks, anonymous, John Smith, Kate De Groot, Rich Jordan, Rebecca O'Neil, Sam Hanes, Dwight Willett, James Bow, James Putz, Jean-Louis Trudel, Lenurd the Joke Gnome, Sean "Sea of Stars" Holland, Charles and Sharon Eisbrenner, Natalie Wright, Elizabeth Westbrook-Trenholm, Brad Anderson, Michael Ball, Paula Jane Remlinger, Cat Leja, Hope Taylor, JHMcKeen, Conor Neilson, Jim Gotaas, Stu Glennie, Robert Bose, Chase Rahilly, Rev. David 'Slick' Sellers, Kal Powell, ET, Michelle LaCrosse, Richard D. Grant, Jeffrey A. Carver, Marcy Bean, Colleen Feeney, Joseph Connell, Jai Ford, Maaja Wentz, GreenShirt52, M. Menzies, Philip Peacock, Bimbo Huie, Rob in AUS, Patricia Steckler, Vanessa Carrillo, Marcus Anthony Elliott, pholy, Rabbit S., Eric Simning, Mandi Armstrong, Tali Smith, Nathan Jones, Susan K. Jolly, Yes, Piet Wenings, Temrin, Brett Mitchell, Edward J. Sabol, Varunjit, Will Sobel, Robert Cram, Amanda Marcotte, Jane Bruns, Tracey S Wagner, Cat Girczyc, Ron Friedman, S. Troedson, Joe Dicker, Ron Friedman, Ron Friedman, Shaina Reisman, James "The Great Old One" Burke, Joshua David Easter, Sheri and Jon Flies, Ryan H., Margaret Anne Hodges, Judith Silverthorne, Joshua Hair, Raeli DaPra, Brandon W. Nichols, Christine Schmidt, James S. O'Brien, Jim Willett, Dylan Harris, Elivin

Mendez, James W. Jackson Jr, Josh Ledbetter, Stoney, Richard K. Hebson, Adam Eaton, Kenyon Wensing, Sean, Christine Eriksen, Michael J. D'Auben, Bill Kohn, Oliver D. Dickerson III, Matthew R Gaglio, Connor B., Olivia Montoya, Brendan Pease, Felix Meier-Stephenson, Valerie Jakubovic, David Riquelmy, Bill Campbell, Mustela, David Scoggins, David W. Clark, Sal Puma, Patrick Douglas, Alexandra Brandt, Andrew Gunsch, Fred W Johnson, Darrow Cole, Gary Phillips, Andrew Evans, Ken Finlayson, Sonse Cahuni, Ross Emery, Maggie G, Stephen Kotowych.

ABOUT SHADOWPAW PRESS

Shadowpaw Press is a small traditional publishing company located in Regina, Saskatchewan, Canada, founded in 2018 by Edward Willett, an award-winning author of science fiction, fantasy, and non-fiction for readers of all ages. A member of Literary Press Group (Canada) and the Association of Canadian Publishers, Shadowpaw Press publishes an eclectic selection of books by both new and established authors, including adult fiction, young adult fiction, children's books, non-fiction, and anthologies.

Email publisher@shadowpawpress.com for more information or visit the website at shadowpawpress.com.

MORE SCIENCE FICTION AND FANTASY FROM SHADOWPAW PRESS

New work available or coming soon

Gods of a New World by Ryan Melsom

Fireboy by Edward Willett

Ashme's Song by Brad C. Anderson

The Sun Runners by James Bow

Tales from the Silence edited by James Bow

I, Brax: 1. A Battle Divine (A Dragon Assassin Adventure) by Arthur Slade

The Downloaded by Robert J. Sawyer

The Traitor's Son by Dave Duncan

Corridor to Nightmare by Dave Duncan

The Good Soldier by Nir Yaniv

The Headmasters by Mark Morton

Shapers of Worlds Volumes I-IV, edited by Edward Willett

Paths to the Stars by Edward Willett

Star Song by Edward Willett

New editions of notable, previously published work

The Night Girl by James Bow

The Canadian Chills Series by Arthur Slade:

Return of the Grudstone Ghosts, Ghost Hotel, Invasion of the IQ Snatchers

Duatero by Brad C. Anderson

Blue Fire by E. C. Blake

The Legend of Sarah by Leslie Gadallah

The Ghosts of Spiritwood by Martine Noël-Maw

The Empire of Kaz trilogy by Leslie Gadallah:

Cat's Pawn, Cat's Gambit, Cat's Game

The Shards of Excalibur series by Edward Willett:

*Song of the Sword, Twist of the Blade, Lake in the Clouds, Cave Beneath the Sea,
Door into Faerie*

The Peregrine Rising duology by Edward Willett:

Right to Know, Falcon's Egg

Spirit Singer by Edward Willett

Soulworm by Edward Willett

From the Street to the Stars by Edward Willett

For details about these and many other great titles, visit
shadowpawpress.com